THE SOUL
MURDERER

A Psychological Mystery
BY BILL LENDERKING

ISBN: 0988902109
ISBN 13: 9780988902107

"Our whole being is nothing but a fight against the dark forces within ourselves."

Henrik Ibsen

For Those Who Serve

CHAPTER ONE

July 15, 1971. Yaounde, capital of Cameroon, West Africa.

"Ade, I'm getting tired of going to all these diplomatic receptions." Nadherny took his eyes off the road for a moment to glance at Ginger, checking her mood. She was out of sorts for sure, but even pouting there was some kind of magic about her, almost a mystical force that he sometimes could sense even if she was talking about something mundane like grocery shopping. Tonight, she'd coiffed her usual auburn ponytail into something more formal, put it together in less than ten minutes and it was stunning.

Despite the effect, Ginger wasn't the same person he'd come to rely on, almost unconsciously, as lover, wife, mother, and general support engine. Her expansive cheerfulness was less on display, replaced all too often by unsmiling querulousness.

Ade frowned. One of the bedrock certainties of his life, Ginger's enthusiastic support of his career as a diplomat, seemed to be slipping into quicksand. He said, "You know how important these things are – it's never what's on the surface, and you're good at it. You used to really enjoy them."

"Used to, is right. Part of that glittering Foreign Service life. But enough is enough. It's your career, not mine."

Ade brushed away a clump of sandy hair that had fallen over his forehead, using his fingers as a comb. "OK, OK. I think you're being bitchy, but please keep all options open. We're still new enough here that I don't have a handle on things yet and I think there's a lot going on we don't know about."

Ginger didn't answer, but her face was tight.

Ade said, "God, Ginger, I know it's always toughest on wives and kids in the Foreign Service, especially when you go to a new post. But that goes with the territory. We have to deal with life as it is."

"Who disagrees with that? Of course I know that. But at some point the downsides pile up, and this life begins to pall. It may be exciting for you, but for us much of our day seems superficial. Life is passing us by. I'm not an adjunct of you, Ade, I'm my own person. And some days, comparing what we have overseas, pleasant as it is, just doesn't compensate for lost opportunities, stunted careers, constant upheaval for children. Greg's only twelve, and already he's been to five schools."

This wasn't the time for a counter-argument, so Ginger's words left a silent gulf between them until they reached the French Ambassador's residence, the largest in Yaounde. Tonight's affair was in honor of the Minister of Petroleum, visiting from Paris. Ade wondered why he was here. Cameroon wasn't a player in the African oil game.

As they walked into the large entrance hall toward the receiving line, Ade squeezed Ginger's hand, but it was mush. Inside, they went separate ways, working the room purposefully. Ginger's lustrous smile quickly came into play, as though she couldn't imagine being anywhere more fascinating than right here this very minute. Ade inched over to where the Nigerian Ambassador was holding forth amid a clot of African diplomats and Cameroon officials. The Ambassador deftly handed the conversation to the Cameroon Deputy Foreign Minister, and when all eyes had shifted, he disengaged and took Nadherny aside.

"Your charming wife just told me you're going to Tanako tomorrow." Nadherny and the Ambassador had established good rapport, and often exchanged political notes over a quick hour of tennis at the International Club, in lieu of lunch.

"Just for a day. It'll be my first trip, and our two officers there, Jack Kohler and George Ellerbee, arrived only a few months ago. Washington was going to close the embassy there last year. Not cost effective, they said. Well, somehow a lot seems to be going on there."

"Starting with the disappearance of Barreras's Ambassador to Cameroon."

"So you've noticed that too. The government over there doesn't share information with us on what it's done with people who've fallen out of favor."

The Ambassador looked at Ade as though there was no doubt about what had happened. "It's a safe bet that he's either dead or imprisoned in the Black Bitch. The second would be worse than the first. He's not the only one. Five cabinet ministers last week. Maybe they're still alive, but I wouldn't give much for their chances."

Ade's mind was racing. Kohler had been trying to cultivate Barreras's Ambassador, certainly a useful contact. But suddenly he was a blank space on the diplomatic list, maybe even killed by his own government on suspicion of spying for the Americans. Never mind that it wasn't true. Sure, the CIA had placed two low key informants in Barreras's entourage, but their reporting was sporadic. Kohler didn't even know about them, since they were controlled from the Embassy in Cameroon and, in security parlance, he had no "need to know."

But they hadn't been heard from since the latest crackdown and the Station Chief assumed they'd been rolled up. Marginal as they were, it would take time to replace them in Tanako's tiny culture of suspicion. On the island, everyone seemed to be regarded as a potential plotter except for Barreras's inner circle and his personal guard force, about a hundred men. Mercenaries from Spanish Morocco. A tough bunch.

"You really believe there was a plot against Barreras?" Ade asked the Nigerian. "He's already killed off all his enemies or sent them into exile."

"Over there anything's possible. The rules are different – they're all made by Barreras. Be careful Ade, and don't take anything for granted."

"Thanks. It looks like there's a lot more to that little hellhole than a paranoid dictator and an isolated American listening post."

Later, at home, Ade said to Ginger, "The evening was useful. The circuit can wear you down, but I'm never tired of the dealing. And you're still great at it." He reached out and patted her affectionately on the shoulder.

"I used to think it was fascinating, but I have no stake in it anymore," she said without turning to face him.

"Only your country's interests, Ginger."

"Don't be pompous, Ade. You sound like such a Boy Scout. Why not try to understand what I'm saying? I know these endless receptions are important, but I'm not a player. If I do something helpful, I don't get paid. I don't get a promotion. Maybe I'm just tired of being known only as the DCM's wife. Maybe I want to be Ginger again."

Unmistakably, something vital had gone out of Ginger. Where before she'd surged with vitality, now she sagged with grumpy ennui. Ade had never seen this in fifteen years of marriage, and he didn't know how to cope with it except to throw himself into his work and hope that somehow she'd be carried along. But it wasn't happening.

"You can still be Ginger, and do this too. But I couldn't do the job nearly as well without you."

"Let's hope you won't have to," said Ginger.

CHAPTER TWO

Ade glanced up and looked out the window of the two-engine Fokker Friendship. He'd ridden in so many airplanes in the past five years, especially in Vietnam where he'd been a political reporting officer in the provinces. Airplane travel no longer gave him a rush, even to exotic places like Tanako, surely a malignant paradise, but did anyone know, or care?

The plane had just passed over Douala, Cameroon's steamy commercial hub, and was heading due west out over the Atlantic, on the final twenty-mile hop to the island. The pilot eased the plane down, and through a break in the clouds Nadherny spotted Tanako's twin volcanic peaks in the distance. They protruded through the thick gray equatorial clouds that enveloped the slopes of the mountains and gave the island a rugged and brooding look, unlike the lush and voluptuous tropical isle he'd imagined. The taller of the two volcanoes rose to about 10,000 feet, ruling over the island like a crowned king on a rocky and far-flung throne.

He wondered how many of his friends back home, most of whom were now well launched in corporate or legal careers, would have traded places with him. Very, very few, he concluded, acknowledging that for most of them visiting a remote pest-ridden island to find out how two mid-level bureaucrats were coping couldn't compare to the daily joust for status and wealth in corporate America. But for Nadherny, at this moment this was where he wanted to be, more than any other place. A new country, a new set of problems, more than a hint of menace. There was simply no choice at all.

He'd often asked himself if there was something innate that made him different from most of his contemporaries, and reluctantly concluded that he was nothing out of the ordinary. At least he had an unusual name, Nadherny, but he didn't know much about his antecedents, except that they'd come from somewhere in Czechoslovakia. He'd once asked his father, who'd fled from Hitler before Ade was born, about them, but his father only laughed. "Knowing about the old country won't help you in America. What people care about here is what you can do, now. If you want to be somebody here, never look back."

From the airplane window Ade could see a large chunk of Tanako, with some typical tropical island adornments: palm trees and coconuts, and black sand beaches washed by the clear blue Atlantic. Roads of volcanic black dirt honeycombed the coast, leading to isolated coves where rolling surf surged over the reefs, exploding into billows of heavy dark water and white froth. A surfer looking for the perfect wave and the perfect setting might find them here, on Tanako's pristine beaches.

But there were no surfers. There were no tourists. The only hotel that would accept foreigners in the capital, Arania, lacked everything except bugs, heat, and dirt, but now it was closed. Its owner was in prison, its manager nimble enough to have escaped into exile, Ade had heard.

As the plane nosed down, the thick green foliage of the jungle took on definition. It covered the island, except where thin strands of dirt road snaked through the thick and tangled growth. On the upland slopes of the volcanoes Nadherny could make out frequent large, flat, open spaces that he guessed had been cultivated cocoa plantations before Barreras had closed them and sent the Nigerian workers back to the mainland in rusting tramp steamers. The land looked to be fertile volcanic soil, but none of it was under cultivation. There were no people about, no farm trucks or machinery. In the distance, he could pick out a cluster of perhaps fifty huts with tin roofs, obviously a small village, but it looked abandoned.

The plane coasted to a smooth landing on the airport's single runway, built by the Chinese in rough exchange for Barreras's UN votes and consistent anti-imperialist rhetoric. The foliage around the airport was a dense green wall of vines and trees. The Fokker taxied to a stop in front of the main building, a squat cinderblock rectangle with only a single chain link exit and entry gate. Nadherny spotted Kohler and Ellerbee standing placidly on the edge of the tarmac, squinting into the mid-morning haze through their Ray-bans. Kohler towered over his colleague, but Ellerbee didn't look intimidated. Nadherny was glad to see them: he'd chosen both men for their jobs here.

When the plane's door was opened, the air outside felt like a clammy weight on Nadherny's skin. The day's first trickle of sweat, the consistency of warm syrup, started down his back and stained through his white short sleeve shirt. There were puddles of water on the tarmac from a brief morning shower that had just passed, leaving tiny puffs of steam rising from the runway.

Kohler stubbed out a cigarette on the tarmac and the two men advanced to planeside as Nadherny rattled down the shaky stairway. "Welcome to Tanako," Kohler said, shaking hands. "Good to see you again, Ade." Nadherny and Kohler had entered the Foreign Service together and now Nadherny was his boss, two grades ahead of him. Nadherny sometimes wondered why Jack's career hadn't kept up with his promise, and assumed that it bothered him. But Kohler was considered a professional, steady and competent. If he carried any resentment it didn't show.

"Hi Ade," said Ellerbee, smiling. Nadherny had met him only a few times, and one of those was the day he hired him. His bilious green short sleeve shirt and loosely knotted garish tie seemed vaguely familiar; Ade recalled that Ellerbee had on something similar the day he'd met him. The contrast with the conservative and buttoned-down Kohler couldn't have been greater. Ade was sure that Ellerbee was aware that a mainstream Foreign Service officer would never dress like that, and did so deliberately.

"You've come at a good time," Ellerbee said. "It's really peaceful here now. It's been raining so hard they've had to scale back the public executions in the soccer stadium. Keeps the crowds down."

The three men started into town in the embassy's large Plymouth sedan, aging before its time after too many encounters with Arania's rutted streets. Right away they had to slow before a coil of concertina wire stretched across the road, attached to two oil drums on either side. Two men brandishing vintage Soviet rifles were operating the government checkpoint, and motioned with their gun barrels for the car to stop, ignoring the car's diplomatic license plates.

"This is the *Juventud,* Barreras's youth militia," Kohler explained in a low voice. "They're everywhere and answer only to Barreras or the Interior Minister, who just happens to be Barreras's nephew. They can make arrests, but what they do best is terrorize the villages and shake down people at checkpoints like this. It's disgusting!"

Nadherny glanced at Kohler, startled by his vehemence. Petty harassment existed in many countries, and most people found a way to get around it. The driver handed over the Embassy's *laissez passer,* but the guards, who closer up appeared to be no more than surly teenagers, made no move to let them pass. Ellerbee wrapped a few dollars in local currency in a visa application form and passed it to the driver, who wordlessly handed it through the window. This had an immediate effect, and the guards waved the car through. Ellerbee permitted himself a slight smile, and Kohler fumed. "It's not right," he said, looking sour. "We should take this up with the Foreign Office."

As the car started up again towards town, Kohler recited, his voice almost trembling with outrage, that after Barreras's Ambassador to Cameroon had suddenly disappeared, Barreras had forbidden any Tanakians to meet with him or George without written permission. Adding to Kohler's sense of indignation was the fact that the secret police came around regularly to snoop through his garbage and question his household staff. "These little men think they can do anything," he said, tightening his lips, "and we let them get away with it."

Ade furrowed his brow. Kohler was understandably irritated by this harassment, but it wasn't unusual in police states. And Kohler, as the senior official American, was an obvious target for a regime that had aligned itself with America's adversaries. It wasn't a case of personal persecution, as Jack seemed to be interpreting it. More important was the need to find out what, if anything, Barreras was up to, now that their activities were limited and their diplomatic and intelligence sources largely cut off.

"Jack, you're a pro and work well under pressure. But if you let the frustrations get to you, you won't be able to deal with the important things, and they're real enough." Jack wasn't happy, but Ade's remark that his skills were recognized seemed to please him. He lit a cigarette, cupping the match with his stained fingers. "I can deal with it," he said. "But it galls me that a killer like Barreras controls everything, and we just put up with it. If I protested would the Department back me up?"

"No, they'd tell you to handle it. That's why you're here."

Kohler's mouth opened in surprise, dismayed that Ade had so baldly confirmed his suspicions of having to go it alone in this sordid place. But he caught himself and said nothing.

The car hardly slowed as it entered Arania's small commercial zone. The few traffic lights were not working, but there was no traffic anyway, just an eerie stillness on this mid-morning weekday. Only a few people were on the streets, moving about warily as though afraid of revealing their destinations. The few stores that weren't boarded up offered no goods for sale in the windows.

They entered Arania's central square, which fronted on a crescent-shaped harbor formed by an extinct volcano. The centerpiece of the port was a graceful Spanish cathedral with twin bell towers. Moorish arches and colonial buildings extended a few hundred yards on either side of it before giving way to the mud streets and shanty huts of the rest of the city. The old buildings were now shabby and boarded up, with paint peeling from the columns and chips of cement flaking from large unpatched holes.

"Where're the people?" asked Nadherny. "The stores and markets should be bustling this time of day."

"The economy's not just in the doldrums," said Ellerbee. "It's busted. The street markets are dead. Barreras seized the fishing canoes so nobody could escape, so on an island twenty miles in the Atlantic there're no fish for sale. The men used to hang out here, playing checkers on cardboard sheets and using bottle caps for pieces, but now they'd be picked up for loitering. There's no commerce, just barter. It's a risk just to be out on the street. And when Barreras seized the plantations – "

"Barreras doesn't give a shit about the economy," Kohler interrupted. "He's obsessed with coup plots, settling old tribal scores, enriching himself and his cronies, playing Big Man. Nothing else."

"Maybe he should worry about the Nigerians. They're mad as hornets because Barreras threw out their workers on the cocoa plantations," Ade said.

"Do you think they'd really take action against Tanako?" Kohler asked, as though he hoped it would happen.

"Nah. The Nigerians have their hands full with internal problems right now. They'll fulminate, but not retaliate."

"Sounds like what we do," Ellerbee said.

Suddenly, a smartly-uniformed motorcycle policeman blowing a loud whistle swept down the main street. The embassy driver shot a fearful glance in the rear view mirror, and quickly pulled over to the curb.

"Barreras is coming," Kohler said in a hushed, tense voice. "Vehicles have to pull over and the people have to stand at attention."

"If they don't, it's a free night in the Black Bitch," added Ellerbee. As he spoke, an open military jeep with two police-men manning a mounted machine gun in the back rumbled down the street. Next, Barreras's presidential limousine, a large Mercedes with shaded windows, sped by, trailed by a follow car manned by several bodyguards. In a few seconds, the motorcade was gone, the spasm it caused already spent. The town settled back into its midday torpor.

They rounded the corner and came upon a small knot of *Juventud* militia, in their trademark dirty white shirts and neckerchiefs. They'd seized a man who apparently had been trying to sell something on the street, because there were some small copper pots scattered about. One of the young thugs savagely kicked him in the shin, and down he went like a rag doll, writhing on the pavement and rubbing the shooting pain in his leg. The men prodded him to his knees, but another white shirt clubbed him with a karate chop to the neck. He fell heavily, groaning but now lying in a fetal position.

"Get up!" commanded the first white shirt, aiming another kick that caught the man just below his ribs. The militiaman's boot landed with a thud, hard enough to pro-pel his victim half a foot along the pavement, as though he'd kicked a medicine ball. The man gasped, straining to breathe, but couldn't pull in any air. He started to retch, but his stomach was empty and he gasped for breath, making high-pitched squealing sounds as he tried to fill his lungs. A few specks of white spittle foamed on his lips as the shirts yanked him to his feet, gaunt and trembling. A trickle of blood ran down his scalp where his head had struck the pavement, staining his shirt as it dripped onto the ground. A purple knot on the side of his head was rising fast.

"Show respect for the President!" the second man shouted. "Next time, it'll be Blabich. You'll learn fast there!" The two white shirts shoved the man hard and he staggered off bent over, clutching his stomach in terror and pain.

Nadherny glanced over at Kohler, who'd gone pale. "You OK Jack?" Kohler nodded, but he was shaken. "That guy's so hungry, no way he could stand at attention," he said. His voice trembled, but Ade couldn't tell if it was from rage or shock. "This is the only place in the world where being hungry earns you a beating."

"What you just saw happens everyday here," said Ellerbee. "There's much worse. Tortures at Black Bitch. Public executions. Sometimes they cut the victims' heads off and carry them around on pikes to intimidate the people."

"There used to be an opposition," Nadherny said. "Nobody left?"

Ellerbee started to answer, but Kohler cut him off. "Barreras wields absolute power here, and he's obsessed with keeping it. He's from a mainland tribe – different from most of the locals – and that makes them fair game. Here, you don't best your rivals in some political arena. You kill them, chop off their arms, rape their women, burn their houses, bulldoze their crops. Make them into non-people. It guarantees blood-letting for generations. It's genocide."

Ade looked dubious. "Wait a minute, Jack. It's awful enough, but you say genocide, I think of Hitler. Barreras isn't Hitler."

"The comparison with Hitler would appeal to Barreras," said Ellerbee, looking over at Kohler to see if he'd be able to finish his sentence.

"Yeah," Kohler said, picking up Ellerbee's thought, "Barreras has said that Hitler was Africa's savior because the imperialists wore themselves out fighting him and couldn't hold onto their colonies after the war. If Hitler's his role model, don't expect him to worry about killing people." He looked out the window and frowned. "It looks like the street entertainment is over for now. We can move on."

Nadherny realized the unreal scene he'd just witnessed was absolutely real and would become indelible in his memory, no longer just something he might read about in an unknown faraway country. The blood in the street was red and sticky, and he'd watched helplessly as it flecked onto the pavement, dripping from a man beaten up for no reason. Tanako wasn't about life at a diplomatic hardship post: it was about killing and suffering on a massive scale. Maybe Nadherny and his two colleagues on Tanako, despite whatever was going on between them, could make the Department realize that the wholesale brutalization of innocent people was a worthy issue, and try to do something about it.

But he also recalled what his boss, Ambassador Richard Hellyer, had told him before he left on home leave. "Antonio Barreras is hardly *sui generis*," he pontificated. Hellyer liked using Latin phrases. His favorite was *mutatis mutandis,* but Ade looked it up and was amused to discover that he usually misused the term. "The point is," Hellyer continued, "we can't change the world. We have to deal with it as it is. And there's a limit to what Washington can pay attention to at any given time. Tanako's never going to make that list."

"Maybe not," Ade had responded, "but sometimes it's the little places where trouble starts, especially if nobody's paying attention." Hellyer had looked at him blankly, and turned away.

As they neared the embassy, a guard standing outside unclasped the two large iron gates and the Plymouth swung into the driveway as the gate closed behind it. The embassy building was no monument to American grandeur. A squat, one-story structure surrounded by a brick wall, it provided office space for two Americans and five Tanakians. They performed the daily tasks involved in protecting America's interests in a remote island country, far away from the major battlegrounds of the cold war.

Despite its unremarkable aspect, the embassy still projected a tiny sense of the colossus it represented, even with the Stars and Stripes stirring listlessly in the heavy tropical air, and the American seal on the gate overshadowed by the glass shards and barbed wire embedded in the cement on the top of the wall. Inside, one could imagine, there was order and structure, and a sense that a visitor, whether just seeking a visa or an unemployed Tanakian looking for work, would be treated fairly and according to established rules. There would be a sense of procedure and calm inside.

For all its lack of pretension, the building was one of the few places in the country where Barreras and his goons did not rule, the others being the few diplomatic establishments scattered about Arania.

Ade and Kohler went into Jack's office and closed the door. Kohler lit a cigarette and leaned forward over his big desk. "We've got serious problems here, and I hope your visit means that I'll get better support. Your predecessor didn't bother with Tanako. He only came here once during his entire tour."

Ade decided this was not the time to tell Kohler the Department was again thinking of closing the embassy in yet another wave of budget cutting, and had asked for a preliminary assessment.

"Jack, update me on your troubles here. Start with the travel restrictions on you and George after the Tanakian Ambassador to Cameroon disappeared. The Nigerians say the man might even be dead. Do you know what really happened to him?"

"No one knows for sure, but both the Spanish Consul and the Cameroon Ambassador think he's been tortured in the Black Bitch. The rumor is that they made him sign a prepared statement saying he'd been recruited to spy by the Americans and his point of contact was me. If that's true, the travel restrictions make sense. Barreras wants me to be totally isolated."

"Well, let's at least raise your profile in Washington. Start a daily SITREP cable to the Department, focusing on the stepped-up repression. Copy our Mission to the UN.

Tanako has no ambassador in Washington, so the guy at the UN handles everything."

Jack seemed pleased that Ade was taking his plight seriously, but he was still grumpy. "OK, but it won't do any good. No one in Washington gives a crap about this place, and sure as hell, no one will do anything about it."

He looked even unhappier when Ade told him about the two informants. "Why wasn't I told?" he asked. "Another reason for Barreras to think I'm nothing but a spy."

"There was no need, Jack. You know how the system works. I'm telling you now because the disappearance of the Ambassador and your possibly being implicated changes the situation. If Barreras really believed you were involved in some plot, he'd have declared you *persona non grata* by now. But I think he'd rather have you stay here, neutralized, where he can keep an eye on you."

"In other words, I'm a pawn, played with by both sides. And as usual, the Department will do nothing."

"The Department's not just a pile of concrete, rigid and immovable. Think of it as a giant centipede, undulating in a lot of directions all at once. With the right tactics, it can be prodded into action. In a crisis, all its parts can even move together."

Kohler looked dismissive. "Who's going to prod it? There's no stick around here big enough."

"You and George and I," said Ade. "We're going to do it."

CHAPTER THREE

Ade made a special point to seek out Nguema, the embassy's political advisor, a wise and dignified African who'd explained Tanakian behavior to successive American diplomats and helped them navigate their way through local customs and taboos. Barreras's goons had picked him up the previous week and subjected him to hours of harsh questioning. They seemed convinced he was spying, and in their eyes that could mean intelligence gathering, arms smuggling, or simple contact with unnamed "enemies." He told Ade he felt lucky to be released with only a warning and a few hard blows to the stomach. "They do much worse, Mr. Nadherny," he said with a self-deprecating smile. "They do anything they want. Nobody here to stop them."

Of course, Kohler had protested to the Foreign Ministry, but they merely shrugged. The might of the US was a long way away, and it was not part of anything that was of any real concern to them.

As Nguema described how the police pummeled him, Ade thought this might explain Kohler's agitation at the checkpoint and the beating of the street vendor. When Nguema finished Nadherny said, "Working for us puts you in danger, even though you haven't done anything wrong.

We can't protect you outside the embassy, but we could give you a good job in Yaounde. You could bring your family too."

Nguema laughed out loud. "On no, Mr. Nadherny. This is Africa. My family, maybe fifty people. They all depend on me. I couldn't leave them."

Nadherny nodded. But he was sure that if Nguema's life was at risk, he'd be willing to flee with only his wife and children. "Well, keep that in mind, Nguema. It's a promise. Now, I also want to ask you about President Barreras. What's he really like?"

"Mr. Kohler, he ask me just about every day. For Americans, it's hard to understand," he said, "but an African from the tribes grows up with many taboos – you call them 'superstitions.' But if he doesn't respect them, they destroy him."

"I realize it's so different from our experience," Ade said. "But how does this affect Barreras? What motivates him? Or is he just like all the other dictators in Africa – another 'African Big Man'?"

"Tanako is a tiny country, mostly on this island, so it's easier to be Big Boss here and control everything. Barreras has all the power. But to stay safe, he has to kill his enemies and keep killing anyone who might turn against him, otherwise someone get him. So even though he's boss of everything, he worry all the time. He change his mood quick, and sometimes he lose his mind. That's why he very dangerous man. The people call him *medio loco,*" and say he smokes *bhang.*" Nguema explained that bhang, like hashish, produces hallucinations and is believed to improve sexual performance.

"Does it?" Ade asked.

Nguema's brief look of embarrassment gave way to a smile. "Not for Barreras. People say he can't. He had two mistresses, mulatto women, but no children. He married one of the mistresses. Before, she have many lovers. He killed them, and then he sent her away. I don't know who stay with him now."

Ade wondered how Nguema had picked up information like this in such a suspicious place, where even failing to stand at attention as the president passed could earn you a beating. When he said "the people say," was this common knowledge, and based on rumor or fact? Was the jungle gravevine reliable? Ade, who'd learned a lot in Vietnam about when to value local information and when to be wary, was inclined to trust Nguema's judgment, even if much of it was intuitive.

Later, Kohler pulled Ade aside and surprised him with a litany of complaints about Ellerbee. George was pleasant, Kohler said, and well-liked, but he was sloppy and Kohler frequently had to double check or even redo his work. That detracted from the time he could devote to the 'mission,' a phrasing that struck Ade as way out of proportion to the agenda of a listening post. Kohler presented his case as though he were delivering a diplomatic *demarche*.

"We can give him a few days' admin training in Cameroon," Ade said. "If this is a problem, it's easily fixed."

"I'm afraid it's more than that. He's incompetent and should be replaced."

"Jack, that's absurd. From what you said, you've got a minor admin problem. The Department won't let you sack a subordinate for that. Think of the expense, the trouble finding a replacement, what it would do to George and Maria." George was married to a friendly and vivacious Ecuadoran who loved to dance, and they had no children. They were popular in Arania's Spanish-speaking diplomatic community.

Jack looked displeased. "It won't make any difference to her," he said. She can do the *meringue* anywhere." He seemed unaware of the meanness of his remark. "I'll let it go for now," he said, as though it were solely up to him. "But I'll bring it up again if there's no improvement."

"You seem dissatisfied, to put it mildly. I realize that it wasn't your choice to come here, but it's only for two years and something good might come of it."

Kohler frowned. "Look, Ade, I'm one of the better economists at my level in the Department. I should be in Paris, Brussels or Geneva dealing with finance ministers and international bankers. Instead I'm in a dismal country and I can't even go out of my house without being spied on. I've got an assistant who hasn't a clue and I'm supposed to be dealing with a government that won't let me talk to anyone and who won't talk to me. Other than that, I'm doing just fine, busy and happy to be safeguarding my country's interests in Tanako."

"What can I say – you know the answer already."

"Yeah, I do, and I know it's not your fault even though you're the one who sent us here. But it helps to blow off steam sometimes."

Afterwards Ade spoke briefly with George, wanting to hear his view of whether keeping an embassy in Tanako was justified. He said, "This place is the pits, but we should stay. Right now it's just a low cost listening post, and we wouldn't save much by closing it. But down the road it could become really important. Guess why."

"You tell me."

"Oil."

"What?" This was startling news. What little oil Tanako used, it had to import, and there had been no exploration as far as he knew. This could explain why the French Minister of Petroleum was visiting Cameroon. The French Ambassador's remark that the Minister's visit was merely part of his "annual swing" was highly unconvincing.

Ellerbee continued. "I met a visiting geologist from Spain at their consulate last week. He told me the Gulf of Guinea is one of the last undeveloped areas for large-scale oil production on earth. Geologically, it's a huge oil barrel. No one knows how large the reserves are, but they're enormous. All the big oil companies are smacking their lips. They'd love to come in here and pin down deep water drilling rights, but Barreras is so suspicious of foreign capitalists he won't let them."

Ade wondered if anyone in Washington was tracking this. The oil companies operated like sovereign nations and didn't share their information with the Department unless they wanted help. Suddenly, Tanako didn't seem like such a backwater.

"Does Jack know about this?" Ade asked.

"I doubt it. It's not common knowledge, and I didn't want to mention it until I have more information. Jack would pick up the ball and run with it to make himself seem more important, and we really don't know much yet."

While they were talking, Ade noticed a number of papers on George's desk with random pencil calculations, relating to ships calling in Tanako's port of Arania.

"What you're peeking at," George said with an amused smile, are some lists from the old weekly newspaper here, which used to publish names of all the ships calling at Arania. Nguema would tabulate the figures, and from that we could make some pretty educated guesses about Tanako's imports and exports, communist shipping activity, all kinds of things. But then Barreras seized the plantations. Then he closed the port to almost everything but Soviet fishing trawlers. And then he turned the newspaper into a total propaganda rag, and out went the port information. Now he's shut down our contacts and we're not supposed to go outside the city, and I have to admit it's had an effect on what we can do. What I was working on here was some ballpark estimates of what Barreras has actually done to the economy."

"It's worth trying to get whatever you can. There's other kinds of things we should be curious about too. I read in the Douala newspaper that a senior Libyan official was here last week. The North Koreans and even the Cubans come and go. The Chinese are already a presence. What're they all up to?"

"I wish I knew, Ade. They don't come because they like the climate."

"Well, we have to try to find out. I agree that we'd be foolish to close up just now." George nodded assent, but said nothing. To fill the silence, Ade asked how he was getting along with Jack. "Jack's OK," George said with a shrug. "He's a nit-picker and self-important, but he snaps out of it. I heard that when he was DCM in Gabon, he demanded that inside the embassy everyone rise when he entered the room. Maybe in the old Foreign Service, for a really big ambassador, but in 1971 in Gabon for a DCM? Too much! People laughed at him and he had the sense to back off. You know, basically he's a decent guy trying to do his best, but sometimes his personality gets in the way. Just like most people. But he really cares about his family, especially the little boy. The other day, one of Barreras's street bullies came on the residence and snatched a rubber toy bow and arrow out of the kid's hands. Said it was a security threat! The kid was terrified. And when Nguema got picked up, he really took it hard. This kind of stuff eats away at him. I can't blame him for that."

Ade asked him about any administrative problems, and George laughed. "I'm no bean counter," he said, gesturing with his small hands. "I figure out a way to get something done, get the people together, and do it. Sometimes I'm a little short on the details. Last month I misplaced some petty cash. Looked all over for it. I repaid it from my own pocket, but Jack was upset. Said it reflected on the effectiveness of the mission." Ade noticed that word again.

Jack's problem with George lacked merit, he decided, probably just caused by the stress of operating a post in a place like Tanako. He'd begun to appreciate George's lack of pretense and keen interest in the world beyond his in box, but realized he knew almost nothing of the man. "How'd you happen to come into the Foreign Service, George? Where'd you grow up?"

George smiled. "All over, and nowhere. We moved a lot, and my father never settled into anything permanent. The last place we lived before I joined the Army was Oklahoma City. But all the family's long gone from there."

"So where do you call home?"

"Home is where I am, just like a turtle. I went back a few years ago to see if I could find our old row house. I found the neighborhood all right, but the house had been bulldozed and the whole block turned into a mall parking lot. So I don't even have a street address in the States."

"C'mon George, everyone has a residence somewhere."

"Not me," George said. "I guess I just slipped between the cracks."

As Ade got up to go, George asked if he'd like to get a better sense of the real Tanako beyond the colonial port area and the diplomatic enclave. "We'll go in the flatbed. I've taken the dip plates off so we'll attract less attention. They'll probably think we're Third World development guys. Maybe we can slip into the back country outside of town and see a part of the island that travelers on the airport road never come near. Want to try? We'll have to be careful at the checkpoints. There's always a risk."

"Let's go," said Ade.

With George at the wheel, the old flatbed lurched through Arania's rutted streets and away from the port and downtown, toward the outskirts of the city.

"The poorest people live in this area," George explained. "Not like the airport road. Fewer checkpoints, because there's nothing out this way but dirt and poverty."

The untidy shop houses gave way to blocks of mud hovels, with people in rags sleeping or squatting on straw mats even at the edges of the muddy streets. Cooking fires, stray dogs, piles of fetid garbage, and small children in tatters or no clothes at all.

George maneuvered the truck through the packed streets, arousing little curiosity from the sullen people. The appearance of foreigners held no interest for them. Soon, the shanties thinned out and the road narrowed as they approached a checkpoint.

"I've never been out here before," George said. "From the map, the road heads into the bush, but it ends before you get very far. We'll just go far enough to get a feel and then turn back. We should have only this one checkpoint."

George explained in unaccented Spanish to the *Juventud* guard, at the same time offering him a handful of cigarettes, that they were with the *Banco Mundial* and checking a possible development project. The guard waved them through.

"Jack gets outraged by the surveillance and petty harassment," George said. "But in Moscow it was much worse."

"If I remember, you were there about five years ago."

"Yeah. The security guys here are a pain in the ass, and they can be vicious bullies, but the Soviets were something else. They put major resources into spying and they're really good at it. They have the best technology, and never stop coming at you. We were constantly finding bugs, and realized that there must've been undiscovered ones in just about every office. So we had to cope with that, plus entrapment, surveillance, and just about every nasty trick you can think of."

Steering around the rocks, bumps, and mudholes in the road began to consume more and more of George's attention. Out here, there were no more houses or people. But Tanako's sharp mountain peaks loomed large through every clearing, high enough to serve as a snag for the billowing rain clouds that boiled up during the rainy season. The rainfall on the other side was a good twenty inches more per year than in Arania.

The flatbed lurched and slid as the dirt road gave way to mud wallows, and it took all George's skill, pulling on the wheel with his thin wiry arms, to hold the truck steady. After five miles, they entered a clearing that apparently marked the end of the road. At the far end was a simple shed, maybe used for tools or as a bunkhouse. The sun was low in the sky and there was a sudden chill in the heavy tropical air.

"Maybe I'm missing something," Ade said, "but what I see is a shack in a clearing at the end of a winding muddy road. Why would anyone build a shack here?"

George laughed. "It's funny how you notice things when you're in a strange place. Back home, you'd never notice a little shed sitting by the side of a dirt road. But here you want to know why it's there, even if it doesn't mean anything. But we should head back. It's getting late."

George maneuvered the truck around and started back. Just past the first bend Ade noticed a large treadmark veering off to the right into the thick undergrowth. There was no road and no clearing, but the fresh track was unmistakable.

"This looks like a heavy tractor tread. Pull over a second, and let's see if this goes anywhere. I wonder what's been through here."

They left the flatbed and eased their way through the undergrowth. Soon the path opened out onto a large valley. About two hundred yards in were three long buildings painted dark green, some large heavy canvas tents, and perhaps ten people in view. "Those buildings are like what you see on a military post, but the Tanakian army guys don't live in buildings like that."

"That's right, George. And those people aren't Africans."

CHAPTER FOUR

Ade and George watched for a few minutes. The people around the tents were all men, and at this moment they weren't doing much of anything. Ade said, "Let's get out of here. We can try to puzzle out what they're up to on our way back."

With the flatbed once again sliding through the muck, George said, "I know what you're thinking. The possibility of terrorists using this place as a training site suddenly looks plausible. It's an ideal location and if that's what it is, maybe we blundered into something important. But how could we ever verify it?"

"We can't risk any more on-sites. But there are other ways. Yes, sure we have satellite imagery, but raising what we're thinking with Washington is asking to have your head examined. They'd think we'd gone round the bend. But we can't just let it slide. It'll be tricky, but we've got to do what we can."

"It'll be tough, Ade. Barreras has us pretty well pinned down. And Tanako's nothing like most countries, where there are many major players and multiple sources of information. Here, it's only Barreras, and maybe one or two of his inner circle."

"We have to find a way. If Barreras is training terrorists, we have to find out. That's why we're here – to learn about anything that could affect American interests."

The bumpy ride yielded no action plan, but they were able to get back into town unchallenged just as it was getting dark. George dropped Ade off at the Kohlers' residence, before proceeding home to pick up Maria and return for dinner.

Before heading for the shower, Ade managed a quick call home to Cameroon via the embassy's single sideband radio. Ginger was home, and Greg had just returned from school. It was a relief to have an electronic escape from the threatening and secretive world of Tanako. It made him feel less vulnerable when he connected, even for a few minutes, to a world that was not far away but where order and certainty were relatively normal, and not distant abstractions.

But there were fissures in that normalcy. Greg was in some kind of trouble at school. Ginger's dissatisfaction with life in Yaounde was still on her mind, and the now-familiar litany seemed to stream out of the radio handset like a lava flow. She was busy but unfulfilled. She missed her career as a budding forensic psychologist. She'd been "thinking things over," and they'd have to talk when he got back. He felt guilty being irritated with Ginger for mentioning her unhappiness when he was in another world and could do nothing about it, but he wished she'd saved it until they were face to face, instead of straining to hear each other on a crackly radio. Anyway, that was Ginger. What was on her mind always seemed to surface spontaneously, at incongruous times. Ade had no solutions, and the conversation ended.

Ade replaced the handset, feeling empty and resentful. His boss, Hellyer, thought this trip was a waste and Tanako didn't count, but Ade had been on the island only a few hours and already he'd encountered a murderous and hostile regime that might be helping to train terrorists, a moody and uptight principal officer who wanted to fire his only subordinate, a loyal African employee who might be in real danger, and the startling news that this place held the key to developing the largest unexploited oil reserves on earth. So why couldn't his wife be a little patient and understanding, and handle family problems herself and save the recriminations at least until he got home?

Thinking these thoughts must have put a scowl on his face, because Cynthia Kohler, emerging from the kitchen, spotted him and asked him to join her for an *aperitif.* "Jack is just finishing up at the embassy and will be here shortly, so there's no reason why we can't catch our breath at the end of the day." She poured them each a Dubonnet and soda, and sat down facing Ade in one of the matching easy chairs in the living room. Ade had heard that diplomatic wives tended to let themselves go on Tanako, done in by the heat, disease, and isolation, plus Tanako's special debilitations of menace. But Cynthia wasn't one of those. She managed to look fresh and casual in a cotton print dress, hair cut short and in place, her body trim.

"We've settled in well," she began, fixing Ade with a steely smile. "I think we'll be just fine." She made it sound like it was only slightly less enjoyable than mingling with the gentry in her home town of Fayetteville, Arkansas. Whatever she felt about Tanako she wouldn't readily admit to her husband's boss, the person who sent them there.

"There's nothing easy about this place. I can see that."

Cynthia's voice softened, but she was looking straight into his eyes so directly that he felt slightly uncomfortable. Her gaze wasn't hostile, and Ade found the intensity attractive. "I'm glad you understand. You know, Foreign Service wives are like the hind legs of an elephant – their job is to follow and support." Ade couldn't help contrasting Cynthia's sardonic observation with Ginger's flat-out expressions of dissatisfaction. Compared to Cynthia's daily challenges on Tanako, Ginger's complaints, no matter how deeply felt, seemed like self-indulgence.

Cynthia quickly cut into his train of thought. "Maybe I shouldn't be saying this to you, but I think that Jack got a royal screwing when the Department sent him here. Do you have any idea how smart he is? Do you know how much he cares, how hard he works? Do you know that he's the first one in his family to even go to college? What obstacles he had to overcome before he even got there? No, of course you don't – it's not your fault. But because nobody cares about Tanako, nobody will ever know about the good work he does here, or what he has to put up with. You wait, the next promotion list will have the guys in Paris and London who just rewrite political and economic stuff they crib from the press and the foreign office and feed it back to the Department gussied up as analysis. And Jack Kohler, who toils away in one of the worst places in the world because he loves the Service, does his duty, and never, ever complains will be forgotten again. God, it burns me!"

"Maybe the next post will be better. You'll have earned it." He realized that nothing he could say would assuage her.

"Ade, you know that's simply bullshit," said Cynthia, smiling now and lightening her tone to imply that Ade couldn't be so naïve as to actually believe that. "Anyway, I'm not attacking you, it's just the system that doesn't recognize a brilliant and dedicated man if he doesn't have the right pedigree. I'm raising it because I'm steamed. But you can do something about it. You picked Jack for this job and you write his efficiency report. Ambassador Hellyer reviews it. It's up to the two of you to see that Jack gets recognized and that he gets a fair shot. That's all I'm asking. Is that too much?"

"Of course not. We've got to pay more attention to Tanako anyway – I can see that. But I promise you that Jack will get due credit." Ade wanted to find out the rest of what Cynthia was alluding to in her diatribe, but maybe even more to nudge Cynthia out of attack mode. "You just said that Jack had to overcome many obstacles from his childhood. What was that about?"

Cynthia paused, and then leaned forward. "If you knew all of it, you'd think it was a miracle that Jack's gotten to where he is. The most amazing part is that he had to do it by himself. He had no one to help him. His family situation was more than stressful, it was disabling. Jack had to cope with – "

There were voices at the door, and Cynthia looked up. "Oh, here are the Ellerbees," she said, rising to greet them. "I'll have to tell you later." Ade's list of things to look into was growing rapidly.

He'd not met Maria Ellerbee before, and after Kohler's putdown he'd been expecting some saucy bit of Latina froth. Instead, he was impressed by her common sense friendliness and her natural ability to relate to everyone in the room. Maria and George seemed unusually close, exchanging glances and smiles, as though they shared each other's thoughts without the need to speak.

The contrast with Cynthia Kohler couldn't have been greater, yet the two women seemed to be at least friendly and at ease with one another. Where Maria was informal and outgoing, Cynthia was sophisticated, controlled, and attractive but remote. She was from an old Southern family and her father was a federal judge. She'd been a legal secretary at one of Washington's A-list law firms, and married Jack only a few years ago. Their only child, two-year old Robin, cavorted about during cocktails, chattering to everyone and involving the adults in his play. Jack's look brightened while Robin was onstage, and from time to time he'd pick him up and give him a nuzzle while Robin giggled happily. He looked the very image of a Gerber's poster baby, all blue eyes and blond curls.

At dinner, seated in the Kohlers' simple but tasteful dining room, with 'Peer Gynt' playing softly in the background on the Japanese stereo, the conversation quickly came around to Barreras.

"Even in Latin America, we've never had a ruler as cruel as this one," Maria said.

"My own thinking is that without some kind of civilizing influence, either from the indigenous culture or from outside, people are all too ready to behave like animals," Jack intoned, as though delivering a lecture. "It's jugular politics and you find it anywhere. What makes us behave relatively well in America is not a higher degree of civilization but the system of checks and balances." When he'd finished, he rose and generously filled his guests' wine glasses, not neglecting his own, which was empty.

Cynthia said, "In most places, we read about terrible things in the newspaper, happening somewhere else to other people. Here, it's as immediate as our front gate." Turning to Ade, she said, "I'm thinking about Nguema, of course, and what happened to him. We'll never forget that."

"That must've been horrible," Ade said, "but he seems to have weathered it well. From what I've been hearing, it could've been much worse."

Jack frowned. "The real hurt is inside," he said. "He may look OK but his life will never be the same. He'll always be fearful of what the goons can do to him. He'll always have to live with the knowledge that he's totally vulnerable. Of course, that's what Barreras wants. He's declared war on his own people."

George added, "That's true. Nguema was actually lucky. They just gave him a beating and didn't take him to the Black Bitch. Very few come out alive from that place."

Ade thought for a moment. "Despite the obstacles, I think we should try to document what Barreras is doing, and what goes on at the Black Bitch. Maybe the Department can do something; maybe the UN; maybe the human rights groups."

Kohler and Ellerbee nodded, but Cynthia and Maria looked apprehensive. Would this bring more risk for their husbands, even for little Robin?

"The Department won't do anything unless it's linked to the cold war," said Kohler, voicing another negative. "It's not enough just trying to get more information," Kohler added, looking sharply at Ade. "Again, you have to understand that Barreras controls everything – who works, who gets rich, who lives, who dies, everything. Maybe it's a way of compensating for his impotence, but he's obsessed with total control. He'll soon find out what we're up to and throw something else at us. But you can't understand what we're up against unless you live here."

Ade ignored the putdown. Jack had good insights, even if it was Nguema who supplied the raw material, but he was surely obsessed with Barreras.

"If you were staying tomorrow, you might have a chance to flavor the rich experience of living here," George said. "There'll be a public trial in the soccer stadium. Since Barreras himself brought the charges, that means summary executions for sure. Three of the ministers accused of plotting to overthrow the government last week. Of course, we won't be able to take that one in. It's too risky, and if we were seen there Barreras would find a way to use it against us."

Ade quickly pondered his options. If they were to do anything about repression in Tanako, they had to come up with some solid evidence, believable to people who couldn't imagine what Tanako was like. Just reporting tidbits picked up on Arania's ingrown diplomatic circuit wouldn't do. He couldn't ask either Jack or George to go – they were known to the security police, and they already seemed intimidated. "I'm going," Ade said. "We'll call Yaounde in the morning and say I missed the plane." He knew that if Hellyer were not in the U.S., he'd be ordered not to go, so this was a one-time opportunity.

If he expected encouragement from the others, he didn't get it. Jack spoke first.

"Ade, you can't go. You have no idea what those spectacles are like. The crowd is whipped into a frenzy. It's like blood lust. It's reckless to even think of it!"

"Have you or George ever been to one?"

"They only started recently, and the Department has ordered us to avoid political rallies and crowds of any kind. No, we've not gone."

"That's why I'm going," Ade said. "We've got to have an eyewitness report."

"You can't exactly blend into your surroundings, Ade," said George. "I'd reconsider if I were you."

Ade wondered. They'd just made a risky trip outside the city, at George's suggestion. Now he was urging caution. Was one risk worse than the other? Were all ideas bad except those that originated with Jack and George?

"What's the worst that can happen to me?"

"The *Juventud* or the security police could arrest you and believe me, your diplomatic immunity would count for zilch. Imagine, an American government official caught in the act of spying! They'd go to town on that."

Maria had been sitting quietly, just following the conversation. Now she spoke: "You don't have to be an eyewitness, Ade. Listen to what they're telling you. Nguema can pick up things on the street from people who went. We sometimes learn things too, from other diplomats, and from the wives."

"Maybe so, Maria, but something pieced together secondhand – 'Mr. So-and-so said...' just won't cut it. And sending Nguema puts him at risk. He already got a beating for doing nothing. What d'you think they'll do to him next time? Anyway, George said this is a public trial. Don't foreigners ever go?"

"I know of a Nigerian embassy contractor who went once," George said. "He was careful to have a cutout so he couldn't be identified as a direct employee."

"That's how we know what goes on," Jack said. "People tell us."

"The Chinese go, but hell, they're among the very few foreigners regarded as friends, always whispering in Barreras' ear," George said. "They're Maoists, Ade, revolutionaries. They execute people too!"

Ade could see that daily life on Tanako and the Barreras regime had taken a big toll on his colleagues. Barreras had already won, but they didn't realize that they'd given up. "Obviously, there's a risk," Ade said. "But I'm willing to take it."

"If anything happens, we won't be able to help you, and it'll make our situation worse," Kohler said. "You won't accomplish anything, and you'll be jeopardizing us as well. It's naïve to think you can solve every problem by yourself."

Ade said, "Right now, I can't solve anything," thinking of his fraying marriage. "But unless we try, nothing will happen. Nothing. I can't live with that." Ade looked around the table at four anxious faces. He said to Cynthia, "I didn't mean for us to argue. But we're all family, and what's happening on this island affects us all. I can see that you're worried, but I've got to go."

During this exchange, a slight humming sound began to be audible. It was too faint to pinpoint the origin, but sufficiently persistent that everyone was aware of it as it slowly leached through the background music and into the conversation. It sounded like a low chant, endlessly repeated, sometimes punctuated with what might have been hand-clapping. It suddenly became louder, and then there was a sharp, high-pitched howl that startled everyone. Ade thought it must be a dog or other animal in some distress, but the sound was different, coming from some creature in agony.

"Good God, what's that?" Nadherny asked.

"That's our Friday night concert from the Black Bitch," said Kohler. He rose and turned up the stereo. Dvorak's "New World Symphony" was playing. "This piece is one of my favorites," Jack said, sitting down again and lighting a cigarette, feigning nonchalance as thin beads of sweat glistened on his hairline.

Cynthia leaned forward and touched Ade's wrist. "Sorry Ade," she said. "It kind of puts a damper on the conversation."

"You have this often?"

"Variations on the theme," Jack said. "Fridays are worst, and often it goes on most of the night. You know those poor devils are dying in the most hideous ways imaginable, and we're here, almost across the street, helpless."

Inside the Black Bitch, flares had been lit to illuminate an interior courtyard, and their shadows played on the heavy cement walls of the prison. Prison guards lined the periphery, clapping their hands slowly to an endless chant.

The dinner table guests could not have known it, but among this night's victims was the Tanakian Ambassador to Cameroon, now stripped of all dignity and fading in and out of consciousness. He had somehow survived several days' of systematic interrogation, gruesome tortures, and prolonged beatings with an *abaca,* a strong and flexible root that grows in abundance on Tanako and makes an ideal whip.

The ambassador's shirt was torn and bloody, and the dark stripes across his back were oozing pus as two prison guards dragged him to a wooden pole in the center of the courtyard. A third guard strapped his arms to the pole with leather wrist cuffs. The ambassador's head drooped against the pole.

A grizzled and burly man holding a long *abaca* stick stepped forward. Without uttering a word, he delivered a single blow across the ambassador's back, opening a fresh crease in the dirt-streaked and swollen flesh. The victim uttered a strangled cry from deep in his stomach, as his frame shuddered from the force of the blow. The *abaca* man lowered his stick and nodded to the three guards, who stepped forward and positioned themselves behind and to the sides of the ambassador. Each man had a heavy metal rod in his hands. At another nod, they raised their arms and began to hit their quarry with massive blows all over his body. Flesh parted and bones splintered, and still the men continued. The Ambassador sagged against his cuffs with the first blow to the head, mercifully losing consciousness. The second hit surely must have killed him, but the blows continued for another thirty seconds, until there was no possibility of life in his body or shape to his face. The guards cut him down, dragged him off by the shoulders face down and threw him in the back of a pickup, already nearly full with others killed earlier. They would be taken to the bush and dumped in a shallow hole, where ants and vultures would quickly consume them.

Around the Kohlers' dinner table, the howls from the Black Bitch put an uneasy end to the evening. Even though none of them could have known that the Ambassador was among the night's victims, to be sitting there debating the merits of attending more executions made them feel even more awkward.

Finally Maria said stolidly, "We've got to go," and everyone got up, relieved. Even Cynthia, still cool and gracious, looked embarrassed as though they'd been talking loudly at a funeral. Jack was fuming, both from awareness of the tortures and the howling that had invaded his home, his only sanctuary. Ade's determination to witness the trials against his advice hadn't helped. After the Ellerbees had hastily departed, Jack quickly excused himself and he and Cynthia went to their bedroom.

As Ade went to sleep, he wondered whether his show of dining table bravado would yield any good result, or whether it was just a foolhardy decision that could jeopardize his colleagues, his career, or even his life.

CHAPTER FIVE

The next morning, Ade radioed Yaounde and told the embassy duty officer that he was staying over and, since there was no plane on Sunday, would be back on the first plane on Monday. He asked him to inform Ginger. Larry Saviano from the political section would fill in for him if there was anything urgent.

Jack was still adamant that Ade shouldn't go. "I've heard all the arguments against, and they haven't persuaded me," Ade said. "The problem before us now is how to do it best."

"I still say that it's an unacceptable risk, and it gets us nothing, except maybe some political voyeurism."

Ade ignored the slight. "Jack, you and I are colleagues. We came into the Service together. Chance has made me your supervisor. I chose you for this job, and maybe now you're thinking that wasn't such a great favor. But you've had your say and I've made a decision. I'll accept the consequences, if any. But I'd like your help."

Jack shifted his feet and grumbled but didn't say anything.

Ade wanted to end the exchange more positively. "Before I came here, I knew that Barreras was brutal but I had no idea what he'd really done. You said yourself that I couldn't understand unless I lived here. Well, I've been here one day and I understand plenty, even with limited information. Jack, we *must* follow up on what we know. We can't just stand by while it goes on."

"How do you propose to stop it? Send in the Marines?"

Ignoring Jack's taunt, Ade said, "Just as I said last night – we document what we can for the Department and the international community. We try to raise awareness, shine a light. Maybe we'll fail, but at least we can try. You and George will have to follow up, find out what you can. Maybe we can make something happen. Don't you see the opportunity – or only the risk?"

Jack's severe look softened, and he looked straight into Ade's eyes. "I'm not a coward. I agree that we should do something. But I don't want to put anyone at risk, and there's danger just being here."

"Of course there is. That's why I promised Nguema an out. And if any of you are in any personal danger, we'll pull you out in a minute."

Ade then outlined his plan: he'd enter the stadium unobtrusively but naturally, as though it was perfectly reasonable for him to be there. He'd carry identification and try to talk his way out of trouble if accosted or threatened. As a safety valve, he'd drive the pickup to within two blocks of the stadium in case he had to make a run for it. It was a pretty weak plan, he had to admit, but it was better than trying to outrun a mob through the streets of Arania if they were after him.

Just before four o'clock, Ade positioned the truck and walked towards the rundown stadium, in the center of the city, a shantytown area about ten blocks from the harbor. The government had placed banners across several streets announcing that enemies of the people would receive justice.

As he mingled with the flow of people heading towards the stadium, Ade heard a sound truck a block away exhorting the people to turn out. For many of them, this would be a festive occasion, a public spectacle. Barreras had disbanded the local soccer clubs and there was no other public entertainment in Arania.

Ade spotted numerous security police and *Juventud* members watching the crowds file in, but his impression was that security was not especially tight. After all, this was a regime that had no rivals and had decimated all potential opposition. Relaxed security was also a clue that Barreras himself would not be attending. Ade was disappointed that he wouldn't be seeing the man in person. He positioned himself amid a knot of spectators who stood in the infield, about halfway between the gallows and the stands. They were tightly packed in and couldn't move.

The humid air was sodden with moisture, and Ade's light cotton shirt was quickly soaked through. The equatorial sun was starting to set, but it was still scorching and his entire body felt like a raised blister. He was grateful that Cynthia had pressed a plastic water bottle on him filled with shaved ice, although already it had melted. But the water was still cool, and Ade took a quick drink. He didn't want to do anything to call attention to himself, but he decided to offer his bottle to the man packed tightly against him. The man accepted, swigged a mouthful, and handed it back with a nod.

The arena wasn't large, probably holding about 15,000 for the discontinued sporting events. Maybe five thousand more could be expected today, filling in the infield around a cordoned area surrounding an unpainted gallows. The unweathered wood was almost shiny against the dull brown backdrop of the ramshackle stadium.

At four fifty-five, nearly an hour late, several important-looking officials took their places on a stand in front of the gallows. Five minutes later, the first of the five accused was brought in, his hands lashed tightly behind his back.

The proceedings opened with one of the officials offering a string of flowery descriptions of Barreras, and the glories Tanako was enjoying under his benevolent leadership. The crowd clapped and applauded. He then turned to the need for constant vigilance against enemies and plotters, and here he started working the crowd with rhetorical questions and answers. "We must crush our enemies!" he shouted, followed by a roar of approval. "We must fight for the motherland!" came next, with an even louder roar. The crowd knew its cue lines, and was enjoying delivering them.

After about twenty minutes, with Ade feeling increasingly uneasy, a man in a white shirt open at the neck stepped to the microphone. The festive mood faded quickly, and the crowd stood watching attentively. The man at the microphone looked young, perhaps in his mid-30's, but the others on the platform deferred to him. "The proceedings will begin," he said in Spanish. "The people will hear the charges against Saturnino Bicomo, former Minister of Finance.

Ade whispered to the man next to him, "*Quien Es?*"

"Alejandro Sudopo, Minister of Interior."

Ah, he's the guy who runs the security police, the *Juventud,* the whole apparatus, Ade thought. Next to Barreras himself, he might be the most powerful person on the island. No wonder the other guys give him room.

"Read the charges," Sudopo said.

As twelve formal charges were read, the accused stood still, his head down as far as it would go, a portrait of abject hopelessness.

The most serious of the twelve charges covered plotting to overthrow the government, stealing public money, and trying to flee the country. They'd been brought by Barreras himself, guaranteeing a guilty verdict. At each mention of Barreras's name, followed by a flowery reference to his greatness, the crowd cheered.

There was no evidence offered and no defense counsel. Sudopo announced, "You have heard the charges. How say the people?"

The stadium rocked to the loudest roar yet. "Death to all enemies!"

"The people have spoken!" shouted Sudopo.

The desolate prisoner was hustled up the steps to the gallows, and a hood placed over his head. There was a pause, and a scratchy sound came over the loud speaker system, as a recording started playing.

It was the British pop singer Mary Hopkin and her lilting rendition of "Those Were the Days." The first verse and chorus played through, and when Hopkin had finished the second verse and was launching into

"Those were the days my friend,
    We thought they'd never end,"

the trap was sprung. The crowd roared as the body heaved and lurched, then twitched, and after a very few minutes, became still.

This ritual was followed for the next two prisoners, and then it was over.

Ade felt exhausted, but not from the heat. It was the drum-head proceedings, the callousness – what bizarre mind had thought of Mary Hopkin? – that left him feeling bleak and numb. Despite military service and being in Vietnam he'd never seen a person killed before. Watching helplessly while three innocent men were hanged as an act of celebration brought home the true face of repression and unchecked power. No newspaper account, however realistic, could deliver anything like it.

As Ade shuffled out with the crowd, a security policeman carrying a rifle motioned him aside. The man was unshaven and his uniform was rumpled. As Ade approached him, he was hit by a strong odor of cheap whiskey mixed with sweat.

"Who are you, and what are you doing here?" he asked. His speech was slightly slurred, but he was standing straight.

"I came to Tanako on business, and this is a public event."

"Papers," the policeman demanded.

Ade handed him his picture ID from embassy Yaounde. It wasn't glaringly official, because "American Embassy" was written in small letters on the bottom, overridden by Ade's signature. The embossed American eagle that gave the card an official cachet was subtly displayed in the background.

The policeman was probably illiterate, because he made only a show of perusing the ID. That'll teach Barreras for closing the schools, Ade thought.

"You American?" he asked

"Yes."

The policeman glared at Ade, as if he'd been insulted. "America is the enemy of the people," he said. "The whole world is against America."

Ade squelched his urge to respond, and said nothing.

The policeman continued to glare and made no move to return the ID. Finally, he said, "I'm taking you in for questioning."

This was to be avoided at all costs, but Ade realized that if he resisted, the policeman might shoot him on the spot. No one would challenge him for killing an innocent man or dispute what he said. Ade would be just one dead foreigner, lying in the dirt until they hauled him away. His only choice was to try to bribe his way out. He pulled out a small wad of greenbacks folded in half, ten ones covered with a five, and carefully put it in the policeman's right hand, trying to make it look as though he were reaching out to shake hands. The policeman took the wad, glanced at it briefly, and thrust it into his pocket. Crude, but effective. The unstated transaction completed, Ade took back his ID and kept moving.

On Sunday morning George dropped by, and Ade briefed both Jack and George about the trials. Jack was unimpressed by Ade's close call, but George said, "The guy who presided, Alejandro Sudopo, bears watching. He's a cut above the others, smart and ruthless, no ordinary thug. He also happens to be Barreras's nephew."

Jack had ordered a British croquet set from Harrod's and set it up in the large backyard with great exactitude, keeping the grass immaculately trimmed and looking for invading weeds himself. Keenly-contested croquet matches on Jack's pristine greensward had become a Sunday staple for entertainment-starved foreigners in Arania, a tiny distraction from the misery that existed just outside the residence walls. This Sunday Jack had invited Rogelio Camejo, the Spanish consul, to play, and he was teamed with Ade to take on Jack and George.

Kohler proved very adept, clearly the best player. He threw himself into the competition, exhorting George, who was casually inept, to better efforts. "Steady, George," he'd say if Ellerbee was approaching a wicket, and "your duty is clear!" if George was within striking range of an opponent's ball. Kohler's feigned British manner was good humored, but there was an edge to it. He and Ellerbee, riding Jack's skill and enthusiasm, won the first game easily. But Ade and Camejo, getting the feel, narrowly won the second, setting the stage for a dramatic playoff.

Jack got his side off to a fast start, but Ade and Camejo gradually caught up. At a crucial moment, Ellerbee muffed an easy shot and the visitors went on to win, raising their arms in triumph. Ellerbee said with a broad grin, "Sorry Jack, I saw my duty but my nerves got to me. The crowd, the tension, the enormous stakes – "

It was refreshing to see Kohler laugh heartily. He'd really enjoyed being the best player and controlling the pace of the game. He was a good sport but he was also disappointed. "That's all right, George. A little seasoning in the Arania suburban competition and we'll get you up to scratch. Now would you all care for some ice tea?"

Sitting on the lawn drinking ice tea on a Sunday morning after a spirited game of croquet made an incongruous contrast to the realities of Tanako, less than fifty yards away. As if to keep that other world at bay for a few minutes more, their conversation avoided any mention of Tanako and turned to European politics. Ellerbee spoke only sporadically, and Ade noticed that every time he made a comment, Jack either interrupted him or ignored what he'd said, almost as though he wasn't there.

The next morning, on the way to the airport with Jack, Ade said, "I hope this was the beginning of something important. I appreciate your support and Cynthia's hospitality. Maybe we can do some good here, if we follow up."

"Yes, it was a useful visit." Jack's terse response was jarring, after the intensity of what they'd seen, heard, and talked about. He seemed even less impressed by Ade's account of the foray into the bush. "That was a reckless caper," he said. I can't trust George to use good judgment, but you should've known better."

"It was a calculated risk. And what if we really stumbled onto something?"

"You risked retaliation if Barreras's men had found you out. He's within his rights to place limits on our travel, whether justified or not. Anyway, what you saw was probably nothing. The Chinese have a barracks and storehouses for their construction workers somewhere out there. That's likely what it was."

Ade was thinking that if Jack really thought he'd been passed over unfairly for promotions, stonewalling his boss's every suggestion was not a promising comeback strategy. But this time Jack's explanation was at least plausible. All the more reason to find the truth. Jack and George had to figure out how to stretch the constraints imposed on them and learn more about what was happening on Tanako.

Trying to end his visit on an upbeat note, Ade said, "I'm glad I got to know George better. He's much more able than you give him credit for. Play to his strengths, Jack, and he can be a big help." Ade was wondering how George, a man with a keen eye and the ability to function in a restricted society like Tanako, could be only an administrative assistant after fifteen years in the Foreign Service.

Jack looked dubious. "I think he can help," he said. "But he has limited skills, and I wouldn't look to him for substance. He'd be over his head."

"You've got to work together," Ade said. "There's no other choice."

CHAPTER SIX

In Yaounde Ade went straight from the airport to the Embassy, noting with relief the contrast between the routine but unthreatening disorder of Cameroon and the brutal and sordid world of Tanako. He'd have no chance to talk with Ginger until the end of the day, and Greg might already be in bed. He wondered what the problem with Greg was that Ginger had told him about over the crackly radio while he was in Tanako. He worried about the boy – he didn't have the same enthusiasm he'd had back home, and since they'd arrived in Yaounde Ade had hardly seen him for more than a few minutes at a time except on weekends. He depended on Ginger to spot any problems and deal with them. She had even started a counseling service at the Embassy to help new arrivals adjust. It was a practical way to keep her training in psychology from eroding into atrophy, and now it appeared that they might need some counseling themselves.

When Ade got home, Greg was still up and was fretting about nothing at all, it seemed to Ade He tried to talk to Greg about the incident at school, but Greg was embarrassed and Ade couldn't break through. "I just don't want to talk about it, Dad," was all he would say.

Later, when he relayed his failure to Ginger, she stared down at the ground for a moment. "He punched out a kid at school, and now they want to suspend him," she said. She was still fresh-faced pretty, with just a few crinkles in the corners of her eyes revealing that she was no longer in her twenties. Men often turned around to sneak a second look at her, even though she seldom used makeup and usually wore just a plain unpleated skirt and blouse. She seemed oblivious of her impact on others, having vowed long ago when she was an aspiring dancer to make her way on her ability and not the looks that had been handed to her. Regardless of her intent, Ade often felt the effect of her presence, even at moments like this when her brow was furrowed and she was remonstrating.

"It's just not working here, Ade," she said. "Greg hasn't settled in well. He's thirteen, an age where his friends back home are really important to him. He misses them, and a lot of other things too. He'd never tell you, but one of the things he misses most is his father."

"Ouch. God I feel bad enough – I hardly see the kid. But do I just tell the Ambassador that I won't go to Tanako to help our new guys settle in? That I can't go to the Foreign Ministry reception tonight and I don't have time to run the Embassy properly? I don't know anyone in the entire Foreign Service who's ever resolved all these demands totally successfully. It goes with the territory, and you've known all about that for years. I'm trying to do the best I can, and when there's a shortfall we have to make up for it somehow."

"That means me. That's always the way, and I'm saying that's no solution. I have nothing against Cameroon, but Greg hasn't made the transition here at all. I think maybe I should take him back to the States, to Lexington, not Washington. The public schools are great there, I'd finish my course work and restart my career, and I could look in on mother and dad. They're both slowing down, and if I wait two years for home leave I'm not sure I'll see them again."

What Ade was seeing was that his superwoman wife wasn't capable of starting anew in a foreign place, and her daily zest had disappeared. Even so, Ade couldn't imagine her taking off for almost two years. They had to stay together and confront their problems, but he was afraid that his opposition to Ginger's escapism would cause a confrontation.

"I'm bushed," he said, squelching a yawn, and unable to carry the conversation farther. "There're some pretty wild things happening on Tanako that we need to learn more about, but I haven't had time to tell you." He was also hoping to describe Cynthia's good soldier support for her husband in a way that would help Ginger to soften her dissatisfaction without irritating her. "We can work this out," was all he could muster. "But let's rule out splitting up the family. It'd be a disaster for everyone, and I really need you."

Ginger softened. "Ade, I truly love you, but there're a lot of needs involved. What about Greg's? What about mine?"

"I don't have any answers, especially now. Must we decide this minute?"

Ginger's mood shifted again. "We don't really discuss anything. Things just happen. I'm sick of it."

That effectively ended the evening, leaving them both feeling fretful and dissatisfied.

The next day, Ade started his writeup of the executions after the morning country team meeting, and despite interruptions, had a first draft within two hours. It was written in the Department's favored unemotional prose, almost devoid of adjectives. He added a comment paragraph calling on the

Department to urge key African countries to protest the brutality, and to alert the UN and human rights organizations like Amnesty International. He gave it to his secretary to type on cable forms, and sent it in to Ambassador Hellyer, who had returned from leave in the States the previous afternoon. Ade regarded his return as fortuitous, because if Hellyer, a cautious but savvy pro, liked Ade's initiative it had a much better chance of getting support within the Department. Hellyer buzzed him within an hour. "C'mon in, Ade, and let's discuss your cable."

"So this is what kept you in Tanako. Very interesting," he said.

"The situation there is horrendous," Ade said. "You have to see it to believe it." Ade was surprised to hear himself echoing Jack Kohler.

"I like your cable, but that doesn't mean that we should send it." Ade felt that he'd been decked by a sledge hammer. "Why the hell not?" he said, and then quickly extinguished his flareup. "Dick, no one's ever come up with this kind of hard information before. Doesn't that count?"

"Sure," Hellyer said, bestowing an avuncular smile on his deputy, "but let me share with you something I learned long ago. No matter how passionately we feel about an issue, Washington won't listen unless we can relate the situation directly to their interests or the essence of our mission here. Our presentation of horror stories won't be effective unless we can put them in the language of end-users in Washington. Nobody in Washington wants to worry about Tanako as much as we do."

Ade had expected everyone to be absorbed by his revelations and what he'd done, but the reality was that he couldn't even get the cable cleared by his boss. "But this IS special," Ade said. "People are being murdered. Nigeria and Ghana are worried about the instability Barreras has caused. That's enough right there."

"Ade, I'm on your side. But you have to understand what it takes to get Washington's attention. They're not moral ciphers back there, but they've got more on their plates than they can handle. Now, if this were China, or North Vietnam, or North Korea, or somewhere we're focused on, that of course would be different."

"We can't get into any of those places, so your point is hypothetical."

"I'm not arguing philosophy," said Hellyer, contemplating his outraged deputy. He took a deep breath. "All right, let's do this: put something up front about Tanako's potential for destabilization on the continent. Add a comment that the Department could use Tanako as a test case for raising awareness on human rights problems in the Soviet Union, China, and other Iron Curtain countries. Who knows, maybe you'll get some attention." Ade felt the tension ease. "Thanks. I'll do it."

Hellyer looked at him carefully, softening his usual aspect of hard-headed pragmatism. "Ade you're an excellent officer. You have the talent to reach the highest levels. But tilting at windmills won't get you there. You have to learn to pick battles you can win. I'm sorry, but I don't think this is one of them."

CHAPTER SEVEN

By Wednesday morning, there'd been no response to Ade's cable from Washington, so he called Sally Rogers, desk officer for Cameroon, Tanako and seven other West African countries. In 1971, women Foreign Service officers were like coyotes in the desert – you knew they were there, but you didn't see many of them. Sally kept track of all the issues concerning her countries, drafted the briefing papers and policy options for the decision makers, read all the cables, and represented the African Bureau on all the daily problems concerning her countries. She did her job well, and if the Department had been an equal opportunity employer in 1971 she probably would have been a few rungs farther up the ladder, maybe even a deputy assistant secretary.

"Sally, would it be news to you to know that the Gulf of Guinea is one big oil barrel?" Ade asked.

"It sure would. Is it?"

"Apparently. Who in the Department might know more about this?"

"Try INR." That was the Department's Bureau of Intelligence and Research. "There's an oil guy there who's very good." Sally dug out his name and phone number.

Ade's instinct was not to mention his cable and wait to see what, if anything, Sally would say about it. But he couldn't hold back. "Any reaction to our cable on the executions? Did anyone read it?"

"Every gruesome detail. It's a fine report, but we're wondering what kind of risks you took to get it. Not good judgment, Ade. We wouldn't want you held for ransom."

"The Department wouldn't pay a penny for any of us, so what's the worry? Anyway, what did Harlan think?" Harlan Hastings was the head of the Bureau of African Affairs, the Assistant Secretary.

"He liked it. He also wondered why you took the risk, and if these executions are so important, why hasn't Jack Kohler gone? Isn't he there to track what's going on?"

"Kohler's coping well," Ade said, not wanting to go into all the conflicting nuances of his weekend, "but I think Barreras and his restrictions have our guys a little spooked. That's why I stepped in."

"We're going to follow up on your suggestion and have our Mission at the UN raise it with the Africans. They won't do anything, even pass a resolution, that criticizes one of their own, especially if it comes from us. But we'll add it to the agenda items for the General Assembly session next month."

"Next month! People are being killed every day!"

"Whoa, Ade. You can't expect everyone to drop what they're doing because you made a weekend trip to Tanako."

"I don't expect that. But we don't have to wait for the General Assembly to get something going."

"I think I detect some of the Nadherny impatience here. Don't saddle up and ride off all by yourself, Ade. It's pretty lonely out there without the Department behind you."

* * *

The man from INR told Ade that the Gulf contained potentially huge oil reserves, and the most promising areas were in Tanako's territorial waters. "The oil companies would love to get in there, but the government won't let them, much less give them drilling rights," he said. "Not even for big money."

"That won't last forever," Ade said. "Money always talks. I was there last week and the Embassy told me that Chevron already has a rep there, a local guy."

"That's the point. They're not letting foreigners in and for sure he's just dealing with gasoline purchases. He'd be just a sales agent."

"What's the Department's role in all this?"

"Pretty limited. What can we do? It's pretty much up to the oil companies."

This was much too complacent, Ade thought. Given the huge dependence on Middle East oil, Washington should be much more involved. But it was clear that nothing would happen without more stoking, and the key to that was to encourage Kohler and Ellerbee to develop more information, however difficult that was.

The next day, Ade called Kohler on the radio, wanting to keep the momentum going and making sure that Kohler and Ellerbee worked together. Anyone monitoring the frequency could eavesdrop on their conversations, so they'd developed an elliptical speaking style that might at least puzzle anyone listening in from Tanako.

Kohler pre-empted Ade's message. "Our friend the Ambassador has checked out," he said, his voice tense. "For good. I've passed on an account of his farewell party. You should have it by now."

Ade checked his in box and found a SECRET cable from Tanako near the top. Ellerbee had to encode Jack's messages letter by letter, using a laborious process known as a one-time pad because the Embassy was too small to merit an encoding machine. One-time pads took time, but the message was secure, unlike radio.

Nguema and Ellerbee had picked up more solid rumors that the Ambassador had been killed inside the Black Bitch. The gist was that after several days of torture he finally admitted to spying. The final sentence of Kohler's terse cable said: "After sustained and excruciating torture, he reportedly signed a statement that he was spying for the Americans and that his point of contact was the American chargé."

Ade was alarmed and radioed back immediately. Jack answered the call signal, his voice more normal this time.

"Not good news," Ade said. "Maybe we should pull you out for a while."

"It's OK. Nothing's changed on the outside. But Barreras must be planning something against me. Otherwise, why go to the trouble?"

"All right. But you and George should put together a daily SITREP to the Department on new developments, even if you can't document everything 100%."

"I'll take care of it."

CHAPTER EIGHT

Wednesday, August 13, 1971.

Early the next morning Kohler was in his office reading from a two week old Washington Post. They arrived in bunches about once a week via the unclassified pouch and provided one of Jack's few lifelines to the outside world. George knocked on the door lightly and burst into the room. He wasn't smiling and dispensed with his usual quip. "Barreras has taken Nguema again. I just talked to his wife. She says some people from their village saw him being hustled into an unmarked white sedan on his way to work. No idea of where he was taken, or why."

Kohler blanched. "Oh God, here we go," he said. "For sure, they've taken him to the Black Bitch – no surprises there. I'll call for an appointment with the Foreign Ministry, for all the good that'll do. At least let's get word to Nguema's wife and tell her we're doing all we can to find out how he is and try to get him released."

Kohler felt bitterly detached as he had his secretary call the Foreign Ministry. It was a relief to be taking some action, but he silently mocked himself as he thought of the certain futility of it. Kicking Nguema around won't faze these guys in the slightest, he thought. And sticking it to the United

States while we file an ineffectual protest will really make their day! He could feel his heart beating faster and just caught the low gurgling sound of something moving around in his stomach.

Jack was mildly surprised when his counterpart at the Ministry was not only in his office but agreed to see him that afternoon. But the meeting went poorly. The man who saw him had no real authority and was reluctant to supply any information, confirming only that Nguema had been "invited" to respond to routine questioning.

Jack summoned his best officialese: "You have no cause to hold him. He's an Embassy employee and we'll hold you responsible if he comes to any harm."

Jack knew what the officious answer would be: "We have the right to take measures to protect our security. If your employee is innocent, he has nothing to fear. But he's a Tanakian citizen, and subject to our laws."

The official's smug bureaucratic demeanor was insufferable, but Jack still hoped to learn something from the encounter. "Security seems to have increased around the city and you're carrying out more public executions. What's this in response to?"

The official frowned. "There are plots, and enemies. Some of them come from abroad. Maybe your special concern for your employee indicates that he's more important than you say." Jack realized that his efforts to help Nguema were only bringing him under greater suspicion, and left the Ministry in frustration.

Jack's first SITREP dealt with Nguema's plight, and urged Embassy Yaounde to ask the Cameroon Government to raise the matter with Tanako. "We'll see if Nadherny can deliver as well as he talks," Jack said to George as he finished dictating.

On Thursday, Kohler reported that the Tanakian representative of Chevron, for no apparent reason, had assaulted the American head of a small assistance project supervised by the U. S. Center for Disease Control while the American was walking with his wife near their home in the residential section. The two men had barely known each other and were passing on the street when the Tanakian swung his fist. The American's lip bled freely but he'd managed to hold his temper. The Chevron rep apologized immediately, and seemed to be acutely embarrassed at what was a thoroughly inexplicable act. But the American's wife became hysterical and screamed on the street for a full ten minutes.

When Kohler learned of the incident, he visited the American to learn the details. His cable reported, "I expected my expression of concern to be welcomed, but instead I was treated to a bitter diatribe against the US for not supporting the project sufficiently and only wanting it for political show. His wife was still upset and almost incoherent. They've notified their home office that they are leaving next week and will under no circumstances return. Their departure will mean that there will be no one to run the only US assistance project in the country and it will be forced to shut down."

Later that day, Jack received a call from Nadherny telling him the Cameroonians had responded to his request and would inquire into Nguema's reported disappearance. That would at least take the matter out of the unfruitful channel of US – Tanakian relations. "That's good, if they haven't killed him already," Jack said.

On Saturday afternoon, Jack and Cynthia were home. It was Robin's nap time and Cynthia was reading, but Jack was restless and lighting one cigarette from the stub of the last. The cook, Mba, rushed into the living room. "Come quick," she said. "Nguema's here. He come down street from Black Bitch."

Cynthia and Jack raced to the kitchen. Nguema was leaning against a cabinet. "Oh God," said Kohler. "Grab him, he's about to fall."

They moved to brace Nguema and led him to the guest bedroom. Cynthia said to Mba, "Quick, get the Spanish doctor, and bring some warm water and sponges."

Nguema, embarrassed to be in the Kohlers's home and in need, tried to resist, but he was too weak. "Maybe you ask your driver to take me to my village, and I'll be all right," he said, gasping with pain. His mouth was swollen and there was a large bloody slit where something had opened up his lower lip, leaving a blackened scab.

"You're not going anywhere, Nguema," Jack said. "At least until we clean you up and get a doctor."

"They let me go," Nguema said with a wan smile, his voice straining to sound above a whisper. "Lord God, it hurt so bad," he said, his eyes watering.

He had indeed paid a heavy price for working for the United States. His jailers had beaten him severely. One eye was swollen shut. His easygoing gait had deteriorated to a stiff and laborious limp, and his side was so sore that he yelped when Jack and Mba tried to remove his shirt, a good indication of broken ribs. Nguema's smooth black skin, glistening with sweat mixed with dirt and blood, was covered with sores from insect bites. Worse, large bloody welts covered his back. Strips of his outer skin were laid bare, and the open sores oozed bloody pus.

When the doctor arrived, he determined that Nguema had no permanent injuries, although he was in shock and would need time to recover. He decorously cut away Nguema's torn and filthy trousers, and discovered that he had also been given electric shocks through a wire attached to his genitals.

Jack blanched at the sight of Nguema's injuries, and suddenly felt dizzy when the doctor unbuttoned Nguema's trousers and declared that he'd received electric shocks. Cynthia came into the room after the doctor's examination and provided some soothing care, making Nguema feel comfortable and less embarrassed while gently washing the dirt and blood from his face.

The doctor confirmed that some of Nguema's ribs were surely broken, but he couldn't offer an X-ray because the only machine in the entire country was at the Arania hospital and hadn't worked for months.

When the doctor had done all he could and Nguema was able to go home, Jack had his driver take him to his village, about five miles from Arania. On Monday morning, Nguema was at the Embassy at the regular time, moving slowly but ready to work.

During the next few days, Jack talked gently to Nguema about his ordeal. At first reluctant, Nguema gradually opened up and described his experiences in detail. It was the first direct account of what went on inside the Black Bitch that the Embassy had ever heard, so Jack wrote it up in a long cable and sent it on August 20. It was too long to dictate, so he drafted it on his office typewriter, chain-smoking with the door closed.

Kohler recounted how the security police had seized Nguema just blocks from the Embassy without any explanation, taken him to the Black Bitch and thrown him into a cell too small for him to lie down, where he could just barely sit with his hands hunched around his knees:

"His cell had no window, and the only light and ventilation came from some small holes in the ceiling. The guards made him stand all day. Although the heat was stifling, Nguema received no food or water until sundown, after his initial interrogation. His cell had no toilet, so he was forced to lie in his own urine and feces. During the first day, Nguema was immersed in silence, a tactic to make prisoners feel totally isolated and break their will.

"Just before sundown, a guard told Nguema that he was going to participate in 'lowering the flag,' a term that signaled that interrogation would now begin. Nguema was dragged to an open courtyard and made to run a gauntlet of prison guards wielding truncheons. As he tried to run, they beat him on the legs, but he was able to reach the end without falling.

"At the end, the guards fastened his hands behind his back and threw him on the ground, face down. One of the guards bent his legs back and tied them tightly to his elbows. The guards called this position 'the Ethiopian,' after the people who first set up Barreras's internal security system. Barreras's bodyguards are always foreigners, supposedly immune to the tribal rivalries and betrayals that have unsettled other African despots. He changes them completely every two years.

"With Nguema now tightly trussed and lying in the dirt, interrogation began, mostly routine questions, which

Nguema answered truthfully. The interrogator was assisted by two guards, one serving as a kind of clerk who wrote down Nguema's pained answers. The other carried an *abaca* stick. Each blow with the *abaca* raises a large welt, and the pain lasts for several days.

"As the interrogator asked his questions, his assistant, a powerful old man with grizzled white whiskers, beat Nguema with full force. There was no pattern to the blows, so he could never anticipate when they were coming or what kind of answers might save him another stroke. This randomness is clearly designed to increase the prisoner's sense of total helplessness. The interrogation time seems governed by two factors: how much a prisoner can endure without losing consciousness, and the need to interrogate many prisoners. Nguema estimates that his first session lasted twenty minutes.

"After the interrogation, the guards dragged Nguema to his cell and untied his ropes. Although exhausted, he was unable to sleep in his cramped mosquito-ridden cell. Bugs crawled over his body and feasted on his wounds. Nguema explained that he was filled with a despair so massive that he began to weep uncontrollably. He thought he might go mad, even if he survived the torture.

"The next day's session included accusations of spying. His interrogators demanded to know how the Embassy smuggled arms into Tanako. A question was often punctuated with a lacerating blow from the *Abaca*. Nguema was ordered to describe contacts with the Tanakian Ambassador to Cameroon, referred to as a 'traitor.' We believe he was murdered at *Blabich* last week.

"The interrogators told Nguema that he had been uncooperative, and that he would soon be introduced to "*las tablillas"* – the planks. That afternoon, they took him to another room and placed planks of wood with notches in them on both sides of his calves, ankles, and under his feet. They threaded thin ropes through the notches and slowly tightened the pressure on the bones until Nguema, crying out in pain, finally fainted."

Kohler had been writing with total intensity, hunched over his typewriter and pounding hard on the keys. A noise from outside his office broke his concentration, and as he rose from his desk to see what it was, he stumbled and had to steady himself with his hand against the wall. He mumbled to himself, *"Hold on and get through this. I'm almost at the end."*

He opened the door to his office briefly and saw that everything was quiet. There had been no disturbance. *"Steady now, it's OK."* He went back to the typewriter and lit a cigarette.

"On Friday evening around sunset, Nguema and twenty other prisoners were brought outside to dance around a hot fire, the beginning of a weekly ritual known as *'El Baile de los Malditos'* – the Dance of the Damned. The men were naked except for banana leaves tied around their waists. They were forced to dance to a simple song, chanted endlessly to rhythmic hand-clapping. As they circled around the fire, prodded by the guards to keep moving, the men began to tire and stumble. If anyone fell, a guard would pull a white hot iron from the embers and throw it at the exhausted dancer. A hit would evoke cheering and applause; no matter how exhausted, the unfortunate victim would stagger to his feet once more, screaming in pain and terror.

"After several hours, with the dancers reeling and nearly unconscious, the jailers waded in with the *abaca* and herded the prisoners back to their cells. So ends a Saturday night's entertainment in Arania."

Jack finished his account with a comment: "Nguema's experience reveals a dysfunctional society whose only concerns are internal security and terror. His arrest and torture are part of a new wave of repression that may no longer be confined to Tanakians. Barreras is giving special attention to this Embassy, and we may all be facing new measures and personal danger."

Kohler got up to give Ellerbee the report for encoding. *"This should get the attention of those smug bastards who refuse to understand what's going on here and what we're up against."* He wasn't sure whether he felt that Ade Nadherny should be included as one of the bastards or not. *"Tanako may be the armpit of Africa, but I bet no one's giving them eyewitness reporting like this from anywhere."*

CHAPTER NINE

Jack's cable impressed Ade as an extraordinary piece of reporting. His ambivalent feelings softened as he imagined Kohler's rising anger, frustration, worry for Nguema and concern for his own family and the few other Americans still left on Tanako. He thought that if foreigners were now being targeted as well as Tanakians, maybe he should at least get the families out, maybe the husbands as well. Just a few days ago Jack himself had said that foreigners were in no danger, and now the Nguema incident seemed to have changed his feelings 180 degrees. But evacuating the Americans might be playing into Barreras's hands, when they weren't really in danger. He needed more information before he could make a decision.

Frustrated at not being on the scene in Tanako, Ade called Ron Zimmerman, the American Consul in Douala. Ron knew most of the friendly diplomats in Tanako and could do some discrete checking on how they saw the situation, without appearing to undermine Kohler.

Ron's quick survey was soothing in some ways, but disturbing in another. Most of the embassies were interested only in preserving their shrinking commercial interests, and tended to ignore political developments unless economic factors were affected. The German Embassy had not heard of any arrests; the French dismissed the reports as "possible government attempts to deal with clan conspiracies," and the Spanish, generally the most knowledgeable of the Westerners, knew of the arrests but insisted there was no special danger for any foreigners. Their *chargé*, Rogelio Camejo, and his wife were friendly with the Kohlers, so his views were especially reassuring.

The representative of the Holy See told Ron that it was more important for the Church to be a source of spiritual comfort to the sorely oppressed than to get involved in political and temporal issues. Only the Cameroon Ambassador seemed to have a full picture of what was happening. There was indeed heightened repression, he said, and he was pleased that his quiet *demarche* to the Foreign and Interior Ministries had hastened Nguema's release from prison. But he concluded that although it might be unpleasant for Westerners for a while, they were in no special danger.

Ade was relieved, but decided to give the Kohlers a short break from Tanako, to be followed by George and Maria.

When he called Washington two days later, he was hoping that Jack's account of the Black Bitch, added to his own report of the public executions, would force the Department to take the situation on Tanako more seriously.

Sally Rogers, their desk officer, told him, "Some of us read it, and thought it was great reporting. I shopped it around to some of the other bureaus, but none of them saw any connection to their own concerns. You know, sort of a fire across the river."

"What about the sixth floor?" That was where Harlan Hastings had his office. If anything important on Africa happened within the building, he had to be the spearhead. "Harlan read the summary, and urged all of us to read it, but that was it."

Ade frowned. If Hastings didn't pick up the ball, nothing would happen.

"Sally, terrible things are going on, and Jack came up with hard facts and the first ever eyewitness account. It should be dynamite, but I guess all the fuses are wet."

"Hold on, Ade," Sally said. "There's dynamite all over the place, and human rights abuses in Tanako don't make the cut right now. We're working some top priority issues I can't talk about on the phone. They're getting all our attention."

"The torture of a US Government employee isn't worth anyone's attention?"

"Ade, stop it. Of course it is, but that's why we have you and Jack there. You should deal with it at your level."

Ade liked Sally, who was junior to him but like many Washington officers sometimes talked down to people in the field, but he felt himself getting angry. He realized that she was just reflecting how Washington priorities worked, not expressing her own opinion, but even so he could feel his mouth getting dry as his temper rose. "Wholesale tortures and executions shouldn't be left to second-level bureaucratic exchanges," he said, hoping his irritation hadn't cost him an ally in Washington.

"Ade, if it's Tanako, it's not even third level."

He paused, not knowing what to say. But one thing he'd learned was not to beat his head against immovable obstacles, but to try another tack.

"OK Sally, let me try something else. What if we do a sanitized version of Jack's cable, with all official references taken out, and pass it to Amnesty International and the others? They could use it any way they wanted, release it to the press, whatever, as long as we aren't identified as the source. That way, there'd be no need for clearances and endless debates. It might even do some good."

Sally was thinking it over. "I don't think a man like Barreras cares much about world opinion," she said.

"He doesn't care what he does to his own people, but a guy like that hates to be criticized or ridiculed. He wants people to see him as powerful, a real Big Man."

"OK, Ade, but this has nothing to do with Washington, and I don't know about it."

The next day, sanitized copies of Jack's report went by international air mail to Amnesty International, Human Rights Watch and others. Ade attached a cover letter explaining that the document wasn't official, but could be used with the attribution that it had been compiled by people familiar with Tanako and that it appeared reliable.

Ade had launched some initiatives in the face of numbing bureaucratic disinterest, but waiting to see what might happen next was unthinkable. He yearned to be in Washington, where decisions were made, or Tanako, where terrible things were happening. But with Hellyer just back from home leave, he couldn't leave Yaounde again. Besides, Hellyer had a pile of new work for him and emphasized that his first priority was Cameroon and then Tanako, not the other way around.

Restless, he called Ellerbee on the radio. "I was just about to call," George said. "You remember where we got the mud on the tires?" he said, straining to sound elliptical. Before Ade could answer, George said, "I know that place better now. Just for fun, let's play twenty questions. First question: what country is known as the Middle Kingdom?" Ade answered "China," not having a clue where this was leading.

"OK, now think of an island country near there, and their word for 'good-bye.'

"Sayonara," said Ade.

"Very good. Now, I'm going to say 'sayonara' to you right away, but the people we saw are the same people as the people who say 'sayonara.' Got it?"

Ade got it. The people they'd seen in the bush encampment were Japanese.

CHAPTER TEN

Kohler's SITREP for August 25 reported that George had been able to slip out of town in a battered taxi and document that several villages had been sacked and the inhabitants dispersed. There was no reaction from the Department. That must have been the same day that George returned to the bush encampment and found out that the people there were Japanese, a fact he relayed to Ade but not to Kohler.

Ade thought that George's discovery was worth passing on to the Department, for whatever they could make of it. Maybe the fact that there were Japanese on Tanako whose presence couldn't otherwise be easily explained might turn out to be important. Readily acknowledging that he could only speculate, Ade asked the Department to check for any possible terrorist connection. There was one he could think of, although it did seem farfetched: the Japanese Red Army, a small group of radicals whom he first read about in 1970. He vaguely remembered seeing an intelligence report that said they were believed to have established ties with European terrorist groups and set up operations in Lebanon. He told the Department he would try to find out more about the encampment in the bush. The first step was to ask the CIA station chief to obtain past passenger manifests for plane flights to Tanako to see if they showed any Japanese passengers. The next was to ask the Japanese Embassy in Yaounde if there was any Japanese presence on Tanako, such as construction engineers. The answer to that was a quick "no" – the political counselor said bluntly that Japan had no interests on Tanako and therefore no need for an embassy. He added that no Japanese would have any reason to go there, not for business and certainly not for pleasure.

On August 26, Jack's SITREP reported that the infant son of the *chargé* from Ghana had gone into convulsions at home and died shortly after being taken to Arania's only hospital. The doctor on duty had misdiagnosed the case, and the baby could've been saved. Jack's terse comment was that medical facilities on Tanako were appalling and any families with children were in a permanent state of apprehension.

Jack's SITREP for Friday was confusing, an expression of concern for Jane Simmons, an American employee of the UN whom Kohler hadn't mentioned previously. She'd told Jack that she'd been followed by the Security Police twice in the past month and was now leaving for three weeks' vacation in Europe. Kohler was concerned for her safety, and saw her off at the airport. End of item.

Clumsy surveillance was such a part of life in Arania that it wasn't noteworthy. Ade made a note to remind Kohler to keep trivia out of his reporting. Then he called Ron Zimmerman and mentioned Kohler's latest SITREP. "Yeah," said Ron, who regarded Kohler as pompous and demanding, "Jack asked me to make sure the woman was OK when she transited Douala. Naturally, I had nothing else to do so I was overjoyed to drop everything and rush to the airport to make him happy."

"So was there anything to it?"

"No, she was fine. She's heading to Europe on vacation, right? But I asked her about Kohler. She told me that two nights ago at a dinner party Jack acted a bit strangely. She said, 'He's serious, but usually lightens up with a bit of wine. He kept asking, 'Do you feel safe?' and drank more than usual.' I think he's taken the whole Nguema affair heavily."

"She say anything about Cynthia?"

"She said 'Cynthia's a brick. Nothing fazes her.' But Cynthia told her that the other night Jack suddenly sat up in bed, sweating and shaking, and said, 'You know, I'm starting to see things from a new angle.' When she asked what it was, he retched, sort of a dry heave, took a tranquillizer, then fell into a sound sleep. Cynthia was worried, but said the next morning he seemed OK and probably just needed a change of scene."

"Any idea why Jack was so concerned about the UN woman? There wasn't anything between them, was there?"

"No way," said Ron. "But she was the last American on Tanako other than the Kohlers and the Ellerbees. Coming right after the disease control guy and his hysterical wife bailed out, maybe he felt the American presence unraveling."

"At the least."

"Well, whatever it was, Kohler's supposed to be a professional and handle daily frustrations. That's why you hired him, isn't it?"

"Yes, but life on Tanako's pretty rough."

"Sure it is, but everyone else seems to be handling it. I haven't heard any complaints from any of the others. Pull them out for a few days. They'll be OK."

"That's set up for next week. Let's hope nothing else happens before then."

CHAPTER ELEVEN

Monday, August 30, 1971

Over the weekend, Ade had a respite from the Embassy and Jack's SITREPS. Instead there were diplomatic community sports activities in which Greg participated with more enthusiasm than he and Ginger had seen in months. Saturday night there was only a relaxed and informal dinner with friends, and the tension with Ginger had lightened perceptibly by the time they got home. Ade hoped that the excellent French wine they'd had at dinner had put Ginger in a flexible mood and even fired up her senses. He opened up a bottle of *Montrachet* he'd been saving and they sat on the three-seater in their living room.

"I'm trying to understand how you feel, with Greg unhappy and us trying to break into a new situation here," he said. "But if you left now with Greg it would be awful. That's giving up! We're not quitters. Our tour is only three years, and we're still young. When we go back to Washington, it'll be your turn, and we can stay in the States until Greg finishes high school."

Ginger was noncommittal. "You can always build a logical case, Ade. That's one of your strengths. But what I'm hoping you can understand is that I'm dissatisfied – with everything.

With this life overseas where I'm just an adjunct to you. With you – you're never here – and mostly with myself. I don't want to sound spoiled, but I need some kind of change, something to rev me up again. I need to control something on my own, something I haven't done since I was dancing. Finishing up my degree and going to work in my field might do it. And it's not only me I'm worried about. I'm afraid that Greg's just drifting. That trouble at school is just a symptom."

"I'd even put in for a transfer if that would keep us together."

"On what grounds? The Department would never approve it. We just got here. And that would wreck your career for sure. You'd never do that. You'd regret it for the rest of your life, and you'd blame me for it."

"Well, isn't there something to be said for us staying together?"

"Oh, Ade, of course. I still love you, you know that. That's not it."

"I guess that's supposed to make me feel better. OK, I realize that you're unhappy and that makes me sad. But could you just put off a final decision for a few more weeks? Give me some time to deal with Tanako, and then I can show you I might even be able to help you and Greg discover that this place might be good for you."

Ginger looked at him without responding. Finally she said, "OK, we can't resolve this tonight. So tell me more about Tanako, so I can understand what's taken over your life this time."

To Ade's surprise, she listened intently while he provided an update of the situation facing the Kohlers and Ellerbees, and his budding initiatives.

"Kohler sounds difficult," Ginger said. "Pompous, moody, self-centered."

"Yes, he can be all of those," Ade said. "But he's also dedicated and competent. I also think he's become a bit obsessed with Barreras."

"A bit? Jesus, Ade, who wouldn't be? And that prison right across the street! You Foreign Service officers are too much! All that 'stiff upper lip' stuff. It's crap!"

Ade smiled. "You're right. But you know that underneath our stoic façades we're all seething with hidden desires." He was not at all certain about Ginger, but the wine had done its job on his senses. He looked right at her and suddenly saw her not as his restless wife of fifteen years and the mother of his teenage son, but as the most desirable woman he'd ever met. He reached over and gave her a sip of wine from his glass, which she took gently, her lips slightly protruding, and he kissed her softly, savoring the drops that lingered on her lips.

Although Ginger never used sexy talk or conversational come-ons, she seemed to glide into another gear when she was in the mood for lovemaking. Ade never knew until the first kiss whether she would respond.

He put his arms around her, and gave her a deep, smoldering kiss, noting with relief that the lights were out in the kitchen and their cook had retired to her room.

As they lowered themselves into the soft cushions Ginger slowly pressed her sleek dancer's body against Ade's so that the feel of her suffused him from head to toe. She put her leg between his and raised her knee slightly into his groin, the gentle pressure as precise and erotic as a tango dancer's. Ade's desire was escalating rapidly and he could feel her every movement and reaction. Ginger's eyes were half-closed, and Ade felt that she was enjoying the impact she was having on him as much as her own sensations.

"I love you so much," he murmured. The words sounded so banal, like some soap opera *cliché*, that he was afraid they would jar the mood.

"It's still so good, Ade," she said.

They undressed each other quickly right on the couch. Ade felt ready and almost desperate with longing, but Ginger held back. The room light was dimmed, but the vision of being enveloped in Ginger's long and powerful legs propelled him beyond his ability to prolong the sensation. They kissed and caressed, and when Ade thought she was ready, he started to go in, but she held him off.

"Not yet." Her voice was sensual but slightly anxious, as though she were saying, *You brought me this far, now make it perfect.*

They edged down a step, but the road back was steeper this time. After a moment, Ginger impulsively pulled Ade into her. Although he tried to wait, he almost exploded, helpless and thunderously. Ginger had a smaller orgasm on the aftershock, and they lay there, holding onto each other, not ready to talk.

"I love feeling your power," Ade said finally.

Ginger smiled, and kissed him gently on the cheek. What they'd just accomplished was spontaneous and powerful as an ocean breaker, but they'd just missed reaching the moment's full potential. Ginger seemed content, but Ade saw in her reticence a shadow of disappointment, although she'd never say anything. *Does this reflect our problem? Do I get Ginger involved, so that her passion and commitment propel us both, only for me to let her down in the end?*

The next morning was breezy and sunny, and their mellow mood lingered through their usually quick and businesslike breakfast. But Ade was wise enough not to read too much into Ginger's evident serenity. There'd been no real breakthrough.

On Monday, Ade wanted to get to the Embassy early, to read the cable traffic and get to any urgent problems before the country team meeting of section chiefs at nine o'clock.

He showered and dressed quickly, telling Ginger that he'd call her later. Greg was just emerging drowsily from his room. "I'm off early today," he told his son, giving him a hug. "Do your best, and remember, one step at a time." He felt awkward uttering superficial exhortations, but there wasn't time to be profound even if he'd been inspired.

By seven, he was ready. He gave Ginger a squeeze and opened the door.

"I'm glad we've talked through all our problems and come up with a rational decision," she said, half-pouting.

"Remember General Kutuzov in *War and Peace*, who beat Napoleon by doing nothing," Ade said.

"You're no General Kutuzov, and we have serious family decisions to make," Ginger responded. Despite her earnestness, her uncontrived early morning look was drop dead stunning.

He paused a second to take her in. "You still manage to look great despite your advanced age and the cares of being married to me," he said, moving away.

"I'd like it better if you loved me for my brains."

"Men are afraid of smart women, so be happy that you can still turn heads." He thought he'd paid her a compliment, but she showed no pleasure. "Bye Ade," she said.

He hopped into the Ambassador's limousine, which was backed into the driveway with the motor running.

By nine o'clock, Ade had read the inch-thick pile of overnight cables from Washington and elsewhere, skimmed the newspapers, and checked with the duty officer to see if anything was urgent. Plenty of action items, but no crises. With luck, he'd cover a lot of ground during the day.

After an hour, he called Ron to check on Tanako. Ron had spoken to both Kohler and Ellerbee yesterday on the daily radio call. Ellerbee, as usual, had ignored correct radio procedure and started the conversation with banter.

"What did the Chinese commissar say when he saw rat droppings on the floor?" Ellerbee had asked. The answer? "Mousey Dung." At the end of their routine conversation, Ron asked George how everyone was doing. "Fine, as far as I'm concerned, but next time you talk to Jack ask him why he's started flying his official flags on his car everywhere he goes now. No one else does it, and it just makes us look silly. When that American girl left last week, Jack said he was afraid she might be kidnapped, so he raced around town with his flags flying until he could find her, and then escorted her to the airport. He hasn't taken them off since. Would you say he might be overreacting, just a wee bit?"

When Ron recounted George's comment, Ade said, "After what happened to Nguema, you could make a case for Kohler's flying the flags. I won't second guess him on that."

"Maybe not, Ade, but it's not a stable situation. Jack's not coping well, he picks on Ellerbee, and you can almost smell the unhappiness. If there's anything positive going for the Americans over there, it's Ellerbee and Maria. They're at least trying to make the best of an awful situation."

"OK, thanks Ron. At least they seem to have gotten through the weekend without any new disaster. Let's hope it stays that way for a bit, while we figure out what we can do, if anything."

CHAPTER TWELVE

A few hours later, at the Embassy in Arania, Jack Kohler was standing behind his desk, fuming and biting his lip until it went white from the pressure of his teeth. "Goddamit, where's George?" he muttered. "Whenever you need the little shit, he's not here. The place is a madhouse and I have to face it all by myself." He rapped his big knuckles on the desk in frustration, and flexed his yellowstained fingers as he grabbed another cigarette from a half-smoked pack of Chesterfields.

"*Steady now*," he thought, blowing a huge breath of smoke through his nose and watching it billow into a cloud just beyond his face. "*Think it through and it'll become clear.*" Kohler had supreme confidence in his ability to deal rationally with every situation, but this was something new and uniquely threatening.

George Ellerbee stuck his head through the door into Kohler's office. "Hey Jack," he said with a smile, loosening his tie, another garish number with a huge flowered print, and unbuttoning the top button on his lavender shirt, "I missed you when you came in. I was checking out the vehicles and the flatbed had a clogged fuel line. Anyway, I've already talked to Ade Nadherry in Cameroon and everything's quiet. Did you have a good weekend? It's such a gas here in Arania we never run out of fun things to do."

"Where the fuck have you been, George? Christ, all hell's about to break loose and you haven't a clue. As usual." Kohler did not swear often, at least out loud, and the vehemence of his tone caught his assistant by surprise, erasing his breezy smile.

"OK," said George. "What's up?"

"There've been a lot of strange things the past few days. Maybe you didn't notice. They started about the time Nguema got out of the Black Bitch and the Chevron guy got belted in the street and his wife became hysterical. Remember? That's when we began sending the daily SITREPS on the repression."

"And?" George just wasn't getting it.

"It puzzled the hell out of me, until a few days ago, when I woke up suddenly and realized that all this stuff – the murder of Barreras's ambassador to Cameroon, the departure of the UN girl – was part of a pattern. I suddenly began to see things clearly."

"How about explaining it to me?" George replied, skepticism punctuating his face.

"There's no time. We've got to do a FLASH cable to warn Washington. I'll dictate it to you on a one-time pad and you'll have to encode it faster than you've done anything before. Come into the vault, and it'll become clear as I dictate."

Kohler led the way into the vault, a secure plexiglass structure of the kind built into all American embassies to ensure bugproof conversations. He looked grim as he quickly checked the room, looking under the white plastic table covered with green baize and examining the plexiglass walls. Ellerbee followed his movements closely, saying nothing. Noticing that his colleague was watching him, Kohler said, "Our offices are bugged." He secured the heavy door, and began dictating. A bead of sweat had broken out along his hairline, even though the room was air conditioned:

"A series of seemingly unrelated events has convinced me that the Government of Tanako, the Soviet Union and Chinese Communists are launching a coordinated campaign to accuse the United States of organizing a series of coups worldwide to overthrow Third World countries. Their plan will be unveiled within days at the UN Security Council in New York, with the Tanakian Ambassador accusing the United States of trying to overthrow his government. I will be named and false documents will be released as proof, part of a massive disinformation campaign initiated from the UN. The final elements of the plot are being put in place; all US diplomatic and intelligence personnel should be alerted and appropriate resources be assigned immediately to deal with this national security emergency. In the process of uncovering the outlines of this plot, I have come under suspicion and am now in great danger. The forces arrayed against us are ruthless and will stop at nothing to gain their ends."

He glanced at Ellerbee to make sure that his slow-witted deputy was keeping pace with his dictation. George had put down his pen and was looking at him open-mouthed.

"I thought I made myself clear, George. This is for real, and there's no time to waste. We and our families are in terrible danger. Not tomorrow. RIGHT NOW!"

"Jack, this is off the wall. Where's it coming from?"

"There's no time to explain. Just do as I say."

Ellerbee looked away, saying nothing, but as he did so he opened his mouth and rolled his eyes. Kohler glanced up and caught the eye-roll.

"What's that? You don't believe me? You think I'm making this up?"

"I don't know what to believe."

Kohler studied Ellerbee for a full thirty seconds, his temples pulsing, as though he was trying to look straight into his soul. "You worked in the Embassy in Moscow a few years back, didn't you?"

"Sure, so what?"

"It fits."

"Fits what? For Chrissake, Jack, what's going on here?"

"Don't tell me you don't know. Don't expect me to believe that!"

"Believe what?" George's voice rose, and his eyes were open wide.

Kohler looked triumphant. "You're part of it," he said. "You're working with them."

"Oh shit," George said, flinging his pen onto the green baize in disgust. "Jack, I know you well enough to know that you don't play jokes like this. So let's just cut the crap and go back to work."

"Don't try to be clever, George. It's all coming into focus. Just stay there a second and let me get something from my desk." Kohler kept his gaze fastened on Ellerbee and edged toward the door of the vault and wrenched it open, throwing all his weight behind his arm movements. "It's OK, George," Kohler said, dropping some of the menace from his manner. "I'll explain it in a minute. Just wait here." With a last worried look at Ellerbee, he closed the heavy vault door behind him and strode rapidly to his office.

Ellerbee rapidly tried to assess the situation and sort through his options. He had no explanation for his colleague's weird behavior, totally out of character, but what he'd just experienced convinced him that something terrible was happening and the situation was dangerous. He briefly considered trying to make a run for it, but the corridor to the vault was narrow, and the much bigger and stronger Kohler could easily block his escape. And ever since he was a kid who'd survived playground confrontations by outwitting the bullies, he'd relied on quick thinking and improvisation to propel himself through life's crises. So he kept himself calm and alert, and waited for Jack to return.

Kohler quickly reappeared, holding a length of telephone cable, and closed the door behind him. Safely back in the vault, his voice seemed less tense as he explained, "George, I'm doing this to keep you from escaping. I can't risk your screwing things up while I'm informing Washington. So just sit there quietly and don't struggle, and it'll be OK."

"Jack, let's just sit down and go over this. We're colleagues, remember? Tell me what's happened and we'll work together on it."

"I've already told you what's happening. There's a plot and I've found out about it. I'm the only one who can stop it. Almost everyone here is part of it. And now I realize that you are too. So do exactly as I say."

Ellerbee put out his hand and started to rise, but Kohler pinioned him to the chair with his body and wound the cable quickly around the back so that the smaller man was immobilized.

"Jack, what the fuck are you doing?" Ellerbee yelled, but Kohler's strength and sheer body mass weighing on him muffled his words and kept him from moving. Kohler wrapped the cord around Ellerbee's upper body and legs, and finished with a loose knot, cutting the cable with a pair of heavy shears.

The sudden effort left Kohler gasping for breath, but he'd surmounted his first challenge and was still in control. Now with Ellerbee immoblized he'd find out how much his deputy knew. "Every one of our 'loyal' staff has taken off! Even Nguema! That's gratitude, after what Cynthia and I did for him. So he's involved in this too!" He picked up the heavy scissors again, pointing them at Ellerbee with each new revelation.

"Goddamit Jack, they've just gone to lunch."

"Hush. Don't try to fool me. Just answer my questions."

"It looks like you've got your mind made up about some kind of conspiracy, but I'm telling you there's nothing wrong. You and I have worked together here since the day we arrived, and today's no different from any other."

Kohler shook his head quickly, as though shucking off a feeble attempt at distracting him. "You must've sent them home to clear the way, and you probably left the gate and front door open when you came in! That means the Embassy's wide open. The only safe place is right here, in the vault!"

"Untie me, and I'll show you that we're in no danger at all. If you want, keep the cord around my waist so I can't go anywhere."

Kohler's mouth curled into a tight smile. "That won't work, George. Don't even try."

But the dilemma of how to warn Washington was again edging him toward panic. *There isn't time to write out and encode my warning, so I'll have to risk broadcasting in the clear over the single sideband radio in the vault. But anyone on the same frequency can hear it, so the plotters will know I'm on to them. They'll accelerate their timetable and it will be even more dangerous for me. And what about Cynthia and little Robin, waiting for me to come home from work? Oh, God, someone help me! If I leave the vault I'll be killed instantly. I have no choice but to sound the warning.*

Kohler, his white shirt and tie still only slightly rumpled but now soaked with sweat, switched on the radio and started talking into the microphone, a stream of consciousness recital of what he'd pieced together. "This is Embassy Tanako calling Embassy Cameroon. I've uncovered a plot and am in great danger. There's not much time. I know this sounds wild, but it's true. I'm not crazy. My administrative officer is a communist. I'm locked in the Embassy vault with him and fear for my life. Everything's been compromised, all the crypto systems, everything. My wife and son are at home and we need to get them out. Get me help, and quick!" He paced back and forth waiting for some response, listening intently. The only sound was static. He waited a long minute and repeated his message more slowly, emphasizing each word for clarity. He paced, turned up the volume, rechecked the frequency, and transmitted a third time. No response.

Ellerbee, watching intently, said, "the frequency's OK and the radio's fine. Don't worry, someone'll hear you."

Kohler looked at him sharply, still suspicious, and didn't answer. *George is clearly pulling out all the stops to get me to lower my guard, but as long as he doesn't try anything, I'll be safe in the vault a little while longer. But why isn't anyone picking up my messages?* He looked at his watch.

At the American Embassy in Yaounde, Ade was eating a sandwich at his desk, hoping to clear a pile of reporting cables by closing time. He remembered later that the clock on his desk showed exactly two-thirty, when the phone rang. It was the Embassy communications assistant.

"Sir," he said, his voice rising, "I'm picking up a very strange radio transmission from the Embassy in Tanako. You'd better come right away."

Nadherny hung up and headed at a jog-trot down the corridor. When he reached the communications room, the assistant had set up a tape recorder and was taping the transmission. It was certainly Jack Kohler's voice, but the usual calm and confident tone was agitated, speaking to no one in particular.

Astonished, Nadherny grabbed the transmitter and broke in. "Jack, this is Ade Nadherny. Can you hear me? Tell me what's happened."

"I'll talk only to the Ambassador. There's no time!"

The only thing Nadherny could tell for sure through the static was the desperation in Kohler's usually steady voice. He answered, "Hellyer's back, but he's away from the office right now. Tell me what's happened so we can help you."

"I'm OK now but if I leave the vault I'll be killed. I have no food or water."

Nadherny strained to distill some sense from the scant details Kohler was giving him. Jack's account was confusing, but after the events of the past weeks he couldn't rule out anything. But if the Embassy was being besieged, who were the attackers? Demonstrators trying to enter the building? Nothing on Tanako happened without the approval or instigation of Barreras. Was he trying to intimidate Kohler, embarrass the US?

"Where's Ellerbee?"

"Ellerbee and his wife are communist agents. I've taken him as my prisoner. He's tied to the chair. Everyone's been fed false information and the Embassy's bugged."

Just then Nadherny heard a faint, muffled cry in the background that sounded like "Help!" but he couldn't tell if it was Ellerbee.

"Was that Ellerbee?" he asked sharply. "Let me speak to him."

"Ellerbee's a communist agent," Kohler repeated in a stern voice. "There are many others. So's the UN girl who left yesterday, but I found her out. The Interior Minister's in it too. Warn Ambassador Hellyer, because there's a plot to kill me and implicate him."

Nadherny grabbed the telephone to call Ron Zimmerman. Cameroon's sprawling port city was only twenty minutes flying time from Tanako.

"Ron, turn on your radio," he said when Zimmerman answered. "Jack Kohler's broadcasting in the clear. Something's gone terribly wrong in Tanako. Kohler says he's uncovered a communist plot and Ellerbee's part of it. He's tied George to a chair and they're in the vault. Get over there and take charge, and radio me as soon as you arrive."

Zimmerman, a huge, ponderous man with the frame of a defensive end, could accelerate quickly if there was a need. He grabbed an overnight bag he kept ready in his office and was out the door headed for the airport in ten minutes. With luck, he might make it to the airport, catch a plane and get to the Embassy in Tanako in a couple of hours. It was already after three o'clock.

Kohler's focus on his radio transmission had given Ellerbee a few moments to evaluate his situation. The telephone cord that bound him to the chair was not uniformly tight; whenever Jack looked away or changed direction, George squirmed a little more slack into his bonds by flexing his small frame. After about twenty minutes of this, he had loosened the cable considerably, but kept his arms flexed and back arched so that it would appear taut. When Kohler turned his back for an instant, he saw his moment and slipped quickly from the rest of the cords. He got to the door and wrestled it open. Kohler wheeled and saw George disappearing through the door. With a shout, he sprang to head him off. Ellerbee barely eluded Kohler's first charge and rushed to accelerate down the corridor. Kohler recovered quickly and with four quick strides he pounced and threw Ellerbee hard against the wall. Grabbing the smaller man under his arms, he manhandled him back into the vault and slammed him back into the chair. This time he tied him more securely.

"Trying to escape, eh?" said Kohler, breathing heavily. "I should've known. But your helpers haven't arrived to save you. I'm not finished yet, George. You're my prisoner, and this time you're under my control."

Ellerbee, fearing any talk would worsen his situation, said nothing. His lip was bleeding from hitting the wall, but he was fully conscious and watching Kohler carefully.

After rechecking Ellerbee's bonds, Kohler left the vault, walked to the front door and checked the lock. The locking mechanism was jammed, but Kohler tapped it with a hammer until it clicked and he was satisfied that it was firmly locked. He then checked all the offices and storerooms, and they were empty. Satisfied that no one else was inside the building, his panic began to lift. *At least I'm probably safe for a few hours. Time to work out my next move and deal with Ellerbee.* He returned to the vault and was pleased that George hadn't moved.

"You're very cunning, George," he said, his confidence growing. "You're trying to commit soul-murder on me but I won't let you. I'm going to make sure that you'll not escape again. That would ruin everything. I was careless with you before. So this time I'll try something a little different." Kohler picked up the shears from the table again, weighing the heavy black handle and sharp chromium blades in his right hand. The fingers of his left hand tightened around his belt buckle. "Don't worry, George. This won't hurt a bit. You're going to tell me everything, including what you did in Moscow."

CHAPTER THIRTEEN

At the airport, Ron Zimmerman found a German pilot who ran a local charter service and hired his plane on the spot. By four-thirty they'd landed at Arania. But since he'd arrived on an unscheduled flight, there was no one on duty in the stifling customs shed. Ron paced back and forth in vexation.

After fifteen minutes, a sour-looking customs official, large semi-circles of perspiration staining the armpits of his gray customs shirt, entered the plexiglass booth and motioned for Ron to come forward. He examined Ron's passport, shook his head, and shoved the passport back. "*Señor, usted no tiene visa.*"

Ron looked at his passport in disbelief. The date was unmistakable. His visa had expired. Standing impassively at the window while quickly doing a mental scan of available contingencies, he hit on one possibility. On previous visits, he'd always taken the time to banter with the airport people, and they seemed to have taken a liking to this hulking American who spoke muffled Spanish through a bushy mustache. Only recently, stranded at the airport by a long flight delay, he'd passed the time by chatting with the customs officials and had bought a round of beers during the long wait. Ron thought, *Blustering these guys won't get me anywhere, but maybe if I explain my predicament and buy a round, they'll let me through.*

Ron sent an airport porter to buy some beer and told the customs man that there was an urgent problem at the Embassy, maybe life or death, and he'd had no time to check his visa. The official paused, then methodically wrote out a *laissez passer* good for three days, and Ron strode rapidly past the customs line. But with no scheduled arrival or departure flights, there were no taxis either. Twenty minutes passed, the late afternoon sun still unpitying on all it touched. Ron paced nervously outside the terminal until a battered taxi finally rounded the corner. As he settled his bulk into the car, it sagged under his weight. *"Vamanos a la embajada americana,"* he ordered in his heavily-accented Spanish. *"Y lo mas rapido posible!"*

Meanwhile, Ade had recruited two colleagues to monitor the radio and try to keep Kohler talking, because he'd sometimes put down the microphone and long anxious minutes of silence would pass, with only muffled background noises to confirm that contact was still open, before he'd come on again.

Ade's secretary arrived and he dictated a FLASH cable, used only in the direst of emergencies, to the Department. As she was typing the heading, Kohler's voice came through again, pleading his case.

Ade quickly signed off on his message, which in view of Kohler's frantic call struck him as restrained: "Embassy Tanako Principal Officer John Kohler, extremely agitated, reported by radio at 1345 hours local time that he had locked himself and administrative officer George Ellerbee in the Embassy vault and was concerned for the safety of his family.

He alleges a communist plot involving his administrative officer, our African employees, and officials of Tanako and the United Nations. I have sent Consul Ronald Zimmerman to Arania to investigate and instructed him to take charge if necessary. He departed Douala by chartered Cessna at 1500 hours local time and should have arrived by 1645. Nadherny."

The message reached the Department at eight-eleven a. m. Washington time. Ade thought, "Even the old hands in the Operations Center who think they've seen it all will go bug-eyed over this one."

He then asked his secretary to get Rogelio Camejo, the Spanish Consul in Arania, and a friend of the Kohlers, on the telephone. The Consulate was near the Embassy and maybe Rogelio could find out what was going on while Ron was hurrying to the scene. The telephone connection to Arania was faint and crackly but Ade could just make out Rogelio's voice.

As bizarre as Ade's request seemed, Rogelio only asked how he could help. "I'll go there now and call you back within thirty minutes," he said.

The efforts to keep Jack on the radio were now having less success. He'd put down the microphone, only to resume after ten minutes or longer. During one of those breaks, Rogelio must have arrived at the Embassy, but Jack made no mention of it.

Rogelio called back. He'd gone to the Embassy and called to Jack through the door. Jack wouldn't let him in, and refused to talk to him.

Rogelio was disappointed that he hadn't found out more. He was also concerned about Jack, who was both his diplomatic colleague and a friend.

"Adrian," he said in his accented English, "I'm sorry I couldn't discover anything. I'll keep trying. But for sure, something's gone terribly wrong with the American *chargé*!"

Rogelio headed back to the Embassy. Jack had apparently put down the microphone again, and it was momentarily quiet. With any luck, Ron would soon arrive and then they'd find out what was happening.

Ade heaved a heavy sigh, part frustration, part relief at having a brief respite. His secretary looked at him with a rueful smile. She was a Foreign Service veteran, and knew where all the bones were buried. "I thought I'd heard everything until today," she said. "What do you make of it?"

"Kohler's around the bend," Ade said. "But why, and whether there's any kind of a plot, and what's happened to George Ellerbee, I haven't a clue."

Ade's remark unlocked her storehouse of recollections. "I don't know Kohler well, but he was always decent to the secretaries," she said. "His wife kept her distance, but she never had her nose in the air. A friend of mine served with Jack in La Paz about ten years ago, when he was still a bachelor. She and Jack got pretty close, but then he edged away." She sighed. "It's a long road from there to here."

"It sure is," Ade said. "I still remember when I met him, and how I recruited him. He was the best of the lot for a tough job. Who could've thought that a year later we'd be frantically trying to find out if he was in real danger, had flipped out, or done something awful to George Ellerbee. Or maybe all three."

CHAPTER FOURTEEN

Inside the vault, Kohler was sizing up his colleague, trussed in a chair with telephone chord, looking subdued and mournful. Kohler was feeling slightly better. He'd sounded the alarm, called for help, and thwarted Ellerbee's escape attempt. He still had a chance. Now it was time to find out what George had been up to.

"OK George. There's a communist plot beginning to unfold – falsified evidence, a worldwide disinformation campaign, sensational charges at the UN – they're going all out this time. I'm sure that you're part of it. They must've recruited you when you were assigned to Moscow. You better tell me about it."

George looked at Kohler, astonished. "This is madness."

"Don't tell me I'm crazy!" Kohler snarled, gritting his teeth. *He's trying to make a monkey of me, get me confused. He's a soul-robber, that's what he is. But I know too much.* "Look, I have evidence. A friend in the Embassy in Moscow wrote me a few weeks ago. I remember exactly what it said. One sentence reads, 'Ask your little colleague about the visa scam in Moscow, and the charge that he snared the ringleader in a homosexual act.'"

George looked relieved. "So that's it! My involvement wasn't much, but there was a huge visa fraud ring there and I helped to catch the guy who was behind it."

Kohler looked dubious. "But you were an admin assistant, same as here. You had nothing to do with visas."

Ellerbee perked up a notch. If he could keep talking, or get Jack distracted, he might increase his chances of survival. "That's right, but listen to this. The ringleader was a Russian who worked in the visa section. He came under suspicion because he had a showy life style that was way out of proportion to his income and status. One night in a nightclub he made a pass at me and I discovered he was homosexual. It turned out he was being blackmailed by the KGB not only to get the visas but to spy on us. It was pretty interesting for a while, and it was my chance encounter that led to the discovery. And that's all there was to it."

"So you were involved with homosexuals!"

"Not at all, except in this one instance."

"But you *were* dealing with espionage. Maybe you were CIA with an undercover embassy job, but were really working for the Soviets. It all fits." He looked triumphant.

Ellerbee sighed. "You're not listening, Jack."

There was a loud knock at the front door, and a voice shouting, "Jack!"

Kohler looked up and frowned. "I'm going to see who it is. Don't move."

He opened the door to the vault and went to the front door. The moment he turned the corner, Ellerbee surged frantically against the telephone cable, trying to work a little slack into his bonds. The cable had been too thick to knot, so Kohler had only tightened it by wrapping a coil around the arm of the chair. With his teeth, Ellerbee was able to grab the top strand that Kohler had wrapped around his shoulders and tied to the chair, and pull it free. Now, with only unknotted cable wrapped around him, Ellerbee was able to maneuver the swivel chair to make the cable unravel.

At the front door, Kohler recognized the voice of Rogelio Camejo. Normally he was a good friend, but certainly couldn't be trusted now. *Don't open the door and he'll go away.* So Kohler stood silently at the door, feeling his heart beat hard in his chest, until Camejo gave up and walked away.

Re-entering the vault, Kohler was astonished to see that Ellerbee had again nearly slipped his bonds and was bending over to clear the last of the cable from his feet. With a cry of rage Kohler hurled himself at Ellerbee and knocked him over, sprawling on top of him, and then manhandled him back into the chair. *I've got to stop him. He's still dangerous, and he'll never stop trying to escape.* Kohler spied the heavy shears, still lying on the table and grabbed them. *Go ahead, you've got to stab him! No, don't do it! Don't stab him.*

Kohler pierced Ellerbee's skin with the tip of the shears, gingerly at first, in the tricep of his upper arm. *Human skin is much tougher than I thought. To get the job done, I have to push harder. It takes a lot of force to pierce human skin.*

Kohler stabbed Ellerbee again, harder this time. Ellerbee struggled and Kohler stabbed him three, four, five, many times, his hand rising and descending more rapidly. Ellerbee was bleeding but somehow he got loose, pushed a chair at Kohler and tripped toward the door. He twisted open the big handle and got out into the Embassy reception room. It was happening very fast now. He lurched from a desk to a cabinet, holding on each time. He grasped at the wall for support as he tried to move faster.

I can't let him escape, I've got to stop him now. Kohler caught George in a couple of strides and hit him again just as he was making a final lunge forward. *Dear God, please don't let him make it because I just haven't the strength to do it again.*

George staggered a few more steps and slid down, clutching at a chair, and slowly collapsed on the floor and lay still. Kohler bent down, his face close to George's, who was staring up, glassy-eyed. "Is this how it was supposed to end, George?"

Kohler wasn't sure, but he thought he heard George whisper very softly, "No, not like this." He studied George's face for a moment. There was no movement. *I think he must be dead. Thank God. Thank God it's over, and I've won.*

There was blood and debris all over the two rooms, but Kohler ignored it. He was staring at George's body, soaked in crimson. He dragged George to an adjoining room, leaving a bloody smear, and covered his face with a newspaper.

CHAPTER FIFTEEN

Ron Zimmerman felt vastly relieved when his battered taxi finally passed through the airport gate and headed towards the Embassy, but the frustrating delay had taken a toll on his composure. Although it was only twenty minutes to get from the airport to the Embassy, to Ron it seemed like all eternity. He unfolded his sweat-covered frame from the old taxi and rushed through the open gate up to the Embassy door. It was locked. No employee was in sight. Kohler may have felt besieged but there was no one visible. Zimmerman banged on the heavy door and called Kohler's name. Finally, Kohler came to the door but didn't open it.

"Jack, this is Ron Zimmerman. Nadherny sent me over to see if you're OK and need help. Can you let me in?"

Kohler shouted through the door, "What's the matter with you guys? Haven't you been listening? Are you all stupid? I won't let you in! Why hasn't anything been done to help me?"

"That's what we're trying to do, so let me in."

"I want my wife and son," Kohler said. "They're in danger. If you want to help, find them and bring them here." Ron decided that Kohler was in no immediate peril and that it was best to humor him until he knew more. His concern now focused on Ellerbee.

"Is George inside?" Zimmerman asked. "If he is, let me speak to him."

"Ellerbee is unavailable," Jack said.

Zimmerman, whose fondness for Kohler quickly wore thin in the best of times, was losing his patience. "Jack, on Nadherny's authority I'm now in charge here, and I'm asking you as a professional and a colleague to cooperate."

"Very well," replied Kohler coolly. "Of course, I must see your written orders. As far as I know, I'm still the American *chargé* here."

This was ridiculous, and it was getting Zimmerman nowhere.

"OK Jack, I'll try to find your wife and son. Are they at home?"

"If they're not there, try the Cameroon Ambassador's residence. They sometimes go there in the afternoon."

This was at least something. The *chargé's* wife, infant son in tow, calling on a friend for afternoon tea. Maybe things weren't so crazy after all. Ron decided to look for Cynthia, and headed for their residence, a ten minute walk away. Kohler remained listening at the door until Zimmerman's heavy footsteps receded on the concrete walk.

Kohler returned to the vault. Ade had continued to call on the radio about every three minutes, and this time he responded. "This is Kohler," he said in a hostile voice.

Ade spoke as soothingly as he could. "Jack, this is Ade Nadherny. We're sending help. Ron Zimmerman's on the way and I've given him authority to take charge and do whatever's necessary to help you and your family. You're going to be all right. Please tell us what's happened so we can help you."

"Zimmerman's arrived," Jack said. It was the first bit of factual information he'd provided. "My wife and son are in danger and I sent him to look for them."

Ade said again, "We need to know what's happened. Where's Ellerbee?"

"Listen to me!" Jack ordered. "I've explained to you what the situation is! Do you think I'm making this up? We're in great peril!" After a pause, he added, "You don't believe me, do you? This is the truth, I tell you!"

Meanwhile, Ron had reached Jack's residence and learned from the household staff that Cynthia and Robin weren't there. The servants were quietly preparing dinner. The house was in order, everything was in place. There was no sign of any upset. In the comfortable study, lined with bookcases, Kohler's library on international politics and economics bestowed a sense of order and calm. The tranquility eased his alarm only a little, but he allowed himself to think that surely, in such a normal-looking place, with dinner cooking, there was a simple explanation for whatever had occurred.

Ron called the residence of the Cameroon Ambassador, as Kohler had suggested. Cynthia and the Ambassador's wife often exchanged late afternoon visits, having tea and talking while their children played together. She was there.

"Cynthia, this is Ron Zimmerman, calling from your house. I've come over on short notice and Jack would like to talk to you in person. Could you go to the Embassy and I'll meet you there in about fifteen minutes?"

"Of course," she answered calmly. "I have the baby with me, but that's all right. Is anything the matter? Did you talk to Jack?"

Ron wanted to avoid alarming Cynthia, but wondered if she had any idea what was going on. "Just through the Embassy door, but he didn't want me to come in until he'd talked to you. When was the last time you talked to him?"

"When he left for work this morning. He usually comes home for lunch, but today he had a lot to do and was planning to work through." Cynthia paused. "Is there something wrong? Why have you come here?"

"I'll explain at the Embassy. See you there in a few minutes."

Next, Ron called Maria Ellerbee. She was home. "Maria, this is Ron Zimmerman. I'm here from Douala. Is George there by any chance?"

"No, and I can't imagine what's keeping him." Her voice was edgy. "He said he'd be home for lunch, but he never arrived. I didn't think anything of it, because sometimes that happens, but he would've let me know by now."

"Did you try to reach him at the Embassy?"

"I called many times, but there was no answer on his line, and no answer from the receptionist. I called Jack, but no answer there, either. I thought maybe they were working late and Jack would give George a ride home. I also called Cynthia, but she's not at the residence. Ron, I'm worried."

"I'm going back to the Embassy, Maria. I'll call you when I learn anything."

"I'm going there this minute," Maria answered. "I want to find George!"

Ron moved rapidly back to the Embassy, his long legs making big strides on the concrete road. He arrived first, and Cynthia Kohler a few minutes later, with Robin in her arms.

He pounded on the heavy door again, so hard that he could hear the sound of his big fists echoing in the lobby inside, and shouted Kohler's name. After a few moments, Kohler said in a normal voice through the door, "I'm here."

Zimmerman shouted through the door, "Cynthia and Robin are here. They're safe. There's no danger. Now let us in."

"Let me speak to Cynthia," Jack demanded, and opened the door a crack.

Cynthia turned her back to Ron and put her mouth up to the crack in the door as she spoke, so that he could only hear scattered words of their conversation. As they were talking, Maria arrived, her usually finely-combed hair in strands, with deep furrows in her brow, and her eyes wide with worry.

Ron said, "We're talking to Jack now. Just wait here and I'll find George." As he looked at her, he noticed that several Tanakians had gathered in front of the Embassy, watching. It was now about six-thirty, and almost dark. Someone had found the switch to the flood lights and turned it on, so there was light around the outside of the building.

Kohler suddenly opened the door just enough to admit Cynthia and Robin. Ron also stepped forward, but Kohler's large shape loomed up quickly and he heaved it shut, stopping Ron's forward motion and propelling him backward. Ron again started for the door but he was too late. Just as he reached it a second time, he heard the lock on the heavy door click in its housing.

"Why won't he let us in?" cried Maria.

"Let's see if Cynthia can reason with him," Ron responded. "Meanwhile, stay calm, Maria. So far we don't know anything."

Ron went back to the door and put his ear to the crack. He could just make out Kohler's voice in an agitated whisper: "You've got to believe me! They'll think I'm crazy!" At that point, Kohler must have turned away because Zimmerman couldn't catch any more words, only the sounds of muffled but emotional conversation.

After about fifteen minutes, Zimmerman went to a small cafe next door to the Embassy, and called Kohler's number. Jack answered, his voice flat.

"Jack, this is Ron again. You've seen that it's safe. I have authority to take charge and I'm appealing to you as a colleague. You and your family will be all right. But you must let us in."

Kohler said, "I'm not ready to let you in. I must have assurances."

"What assurances do you need, for God's sake?" Zimmerman yelled. "If you think there's some danger, just ask Cynthia! Jack, I'm ordering you to come out."

After a pause, Jack said, "OK, I'll cooperate. Just give me some time."

"OK, you've got five minutes. "I'll be waiting by the door."

Ron wondered why Jack hadn't mentioned his fears of a communist plot or being killed. Was he making his story up as he went along?

Now the crowd was larger, including some foreign diplomats and the Minister of Interior. It was Alejandro Sudopo, the man who'd presided over the executions that Ade had witnessed a few weeks before. His arrival brought a dramatic change in the situation, because he'd surely insist on sticking his nose into what was happening. Now there really was a danger for Jack, because the Minister wouldn't hesitate to break down the door and pull Jack out himself. Diplomatic rules wouldn't restrain him.

Ron wondered how the Tanakian government, inept in everything except matters of security and brutality, was able to react so swiftly. Were the Embassy phones tapped, or did they overhear Jack's radio transmission? Or was it simply that word spread fast when anything happened in this repressive police state?

Ron recognized most of the diplomats from the circle of friends the Kohlers moved in. Chief among them was Chris Kanu, the Nigerian Ambassador and dean of Arania's diplomatic corps. A smooth, British-educated career diplomat, Kanu had a tough assignment. When Barreras destroyed the plantations, the Nigerian workers were shipped home in terror on rusty tramp steamers. Although Nigeria hadn't acted on its threats to throw Barreras out, he and his cronies were fearful. It was Kanu's job to normalize relations, secure better treatment for the two thousand Nigerians remaining, and make Barreras understand that future incidents would be punished.

Ambassador Kanu stepped forward confidently. He was dressed in navy blue tropical worsted slacks, which had a Savile Road tailor-made look, and a conservative light blue cotton sport shirt with long sleeves, open at the collar. Ron had gotten to know him during previous visits.

"Mr. Zimmerman," said Kanu in a clipped British accent, "I understand that Mr. Kohler may be having some difficulty. Please allow me to talk to him. We are quite good friends, you know."

Ron was glad to have additional diplomatic support, especially since the crowd had continued to grow and now several Tanakian security men had joined in, their tell-tale dark sunglasses and swaggering demeanor distinguishing them from the merely curious. "Give it a go, Mr. Ambassador. Jack thinks some vast plot's about to unfold, and he and his family are in danger. Cynthia and the baby are inside, and I'm trying to calm him down, get him out safely, and get inside so I can find out what happened."

Kanu stepped to the door and called out Kohler's name, and in a moment Jack was there. They conversed briefly for a few minutes, and then Kanu stepped back and said to Zimmerman, "I believe Jack's ready to come out. When he opens the door, I'll escort him and Cynthia and the baby quickly through the crowd to my car and we'll go directly to my residence where he'll be safe. When he comes out, he may or may not want to talk to you, but the way will be clear for you to get into the Embassy."

A few more minutes passed, and an expectant hush had fallen over the crowd. Everyone had seen Ambassador Kanu conversing with someone through the door, and had watched him closely in his brief huddle with Zimmerman.

The Embassy door opened and Kohler slowly emerged, followed by Cynthia, still holding the baby. Jack's appearance was a far cry from his usual correct and buttoned-down look. His rumpled blue oxford shirt was pulled out at the waist and open at the neck. His sleeves were rolled up at the wrist, exposing his powerful forearms. He was calm but disheveled, his usual neatly-combed hair hanging down lankly over his ears and forehead. His horn-rim glasses helped him retain the merest hint of the dignity that was normally a part of his persona. He and Cynthia were almost expressionless, their looks frozen in shock. As Kanu started to lead them through the crowd, Kohler spotted Zimmerman standing by the opened door and pulled him aside. The two large men together formed a massive silhouette in the lingering shadows.

"I blew my cool," Kohler said, *sotto voce.* "I killed George Ellerbee."

CHAPTER SIXTEEN

Ron gasped in shock, temporarily frozen. Several Tanakian guards surged forward, as if to take Jack into custody. Sudopo was right behind them. Ambassador Kanu held up his hand. "I'm taking this chap," he said coolly, and continued to pick his way purposefully through the crowd, the Kohlers close behind. His air of calm authority caught the Minister and his guards by surprise. Kanu led the Kohlers to his limousine, closed the doors behind them, climbed in and instructed his driver to move out.

Zimmerman hurried through the Embassy door and headed for the vault. Maria, her face drained of color and distorted with worry, rushed forward and pushed in behind him, but Zimmerman, striding ahead, didn't notice her petite frame. As he entered the building, he gave the lobby a cursory inspection in the half-light, noting an overturned waste basket, a desk chair lying on its side, and Embassy stationery and classified documents scattered on the floor and on the receptionist's desk. Zimmerman hurried on, past the utility room and Kohler's office, and into the vault.

The neat and spare vault had been transformed. The plastic chairs that normally surrounded the green baize-covered conference table were upended and lying haphazardly.

A long strand of telephone cord snaked along the floor, and there were large, dried, brownish smears on the carpet, desk, and green cloth on the table. Ron held his index finger to one of them, and it was warm and sticky. "Oh, God," he exclaimed, feeling queasy, his last slim hopes evaporating. But he still clung to the possibility that Ellerbee had somehow managed to escape.

A long dark stain led from the vault to an outside room. Three bloody hand prints were etched into the white paint of the vault door, with splashes of blood on the wall, and a large pool of dried blood on the floor. The size of the prints was small, almost dainty, and Ron realized that they couldn't be Kohler's. Ellerbee was only about five feet six, with small, almost feminine hands.

Suddenly, a succession of piercing, anguished screams near the lobby shattered the humid silence. The sound was almost inhuman, but it could only be Maria Ellerbee. Guided by her shrieks, Zimmerman headed for the utility room. As he rushed into the room, he noted massive blood spatters on the wall just below eye level. Then he saw the body. Crumpled on the floor, covered by the sobbing Maria, was George Ellerbee, lying on his side, crammed into a corner of the room. Dried blood covered his lavender short-sleeved shirt, making it a brownish red. He was still wearing a necktie, a garish print, but it was pulled down at the neck and his three top shirt buttons were open. He had massive slashes on his arms, chest, and throat, as if he had been opened up by a voracious animal. Ron pulled out a handkerchief and carefully lifted the blood-streaked copy of the Washington Post that covered George's face. There were a few small cuts, but his face had not been mutilated.

"Maria!" he called. She didn't respond. "Maria!" he shouted, dismayed that it was she who'd discovered her husband's body. "Is he still alive?"

She was too hysterical to answer. *"Mi amor, mi amor!"* she moaned, her body quivering with wrenching sobs. Ron saw that George was almost certainly dead, if not directly from the wounds, then from loss of blood, which was splashed in rivulets around his body, along with small pieces of gore.

He reached down awkwardly and tugged lightly on Maria's shoulder. "Maria, you must get up." Then, thinking to preserve any evidence, he said, "We must leave here right away. Don't touch anything. I'm here to help but please do exactly as I say."

Maria still didn't answer, but continued sobbing, more softly now, as she lay sprawled across her husband's torn body.

Ron reached down again, and with his huge arms caressingly pried Maria from her husband's corpse. She held to him fast, but gradually Ron was able to lift her gently into his arms. George looked even smaller than when he was alive, but his face in death betrayed none of the terror he must have felt in his final minutes. Maria didn't resist, but kept on sobbing and gulping uncontrollably, her body heaving.

Ron carried her to the Embassy lobby and slowly lowered her to her feet. She was wobbly but able to stand. Looking out at the crowd, he spotted Carmen Camejo, the wife of the Spanish consul. Rogelio was standing by her side, both of them looking horrified and bewildered. Ron whispered to Carmen, "George is dead, and Maria's in shock. Can you take her with you? She can't be left alone."

Carmen's expression opened wide in astonishment, but she had the sense not to say anything in earshot of the curious onlookers, now surging closer to the Embassy. "Of course," she said. "I'll take her to my house and she'll be as with her own family."

Ron said, "Reassure Maria that I'll get word to her as soon as I can, and that I'll keep George's body safe."

With Maria in the care of Carmen and Rogelio, Ron turned back to the Embassy to call Ade. Stepping back through the door, he discovered that the lock mechanism was broken and that it could only be locked from the inside. Since he had no key, he would now have to stay in the Embassy overnight in order to prevent tampering. Just as he was about to close the door from the inside, Sudopo, who'd been standing nearby with growing impatience, strode up and demanded to enter the building. Ron identified himself and said that he was investigating an emergency situation inside.

The Minister shook his head. He said in unaccented English, "You may be a diplomat in Cameroon but you are not accredited here. Since there is no qualified American official in charge, I will enter and investigate myself."

Ron was surprised by Sudopo's fluent English, something he didn't expect from the head of the dreaded security forces. He hadn't met the man before, but knew of his ruthlessness as head of the police and *Juventud*. It was off-putting that the Minister's sophisticated English was clearly better than his own correct but stilted Spanish. He assumed that he'd learned it in the Soviet Union, which offered superb training of all kinds to favored acolytes.

"Mr. Minister, an American diplomat is dead. Our *chargé*, Mr. Kohler, has gone with the Nigerian Ambassador, and I'm here to protect the Embassy and report to my government. We'll give you full cooperation, but first we need to verify the death. If you'll find a doctor, I'll ask you to be a witness. But please excuse me now while I enter the Embassy and report this tragedy to my government."

It was a good idea to try and give Sudopo a constructive role to play. But Sudopo was facing down a hated foreigner in front of an audience, and he was angry.

"This is very bad," he said, frowning and shaking his head. "You must respect our laws. Leave this building and depart Tanako at once!"

Seeing that further argument was fruitless, Zimmerman said, "Please wait here," and then darted through the door and quickly bolted it from inside, leaving the startled Sudopo locked out. As Zimmerman hurried towards Kohler's office, he noticed for the first time a large pair of shears on the desk in the reception area, scarlet-smeared. Zimmerman noted the exact location firmly in his mind, and proceeded to Kohler's office to call Nadherny. He got through right away but the connection was poor and most of what he said was garbled. What Ade could make of it was that Zimmerman said Ellerbee was dead, and the Minister of Interior was challenging his diplomatic status.

Ade told Zimmerman to avoid a confrontation, but to use every means to protect the integrity of the Embassy. He said he'd proceed to Tanako as soon as possible, but probably couldn't get there before noon the next day, Tuesday.

After hanging up, Ade dictated another FLASH cable to Washington, using mostly Zimmerman's actual words:

"I have news by garbled telephone from Consul Ron Zimmerman in Arania that is shocking beyond words. He told me, 'I walked into a real mess here. Kohler apparently really fell apart. It took over an hour to get him out of the Embassy and into the hands of the Nigerian Ambassador. I then found George Ellerbee dead. The Minister of Interior is here insisting that I leave the Embassy and depart the island tomorrow.'"

"Will proceed ASAP to Arania with Embassy medical and administrative officers and will report on arrival. Urge Department contact Tanakian government at highest level, apprise them that I am senior American in charge, and promise full cooperation in investigating and resolving any questions. Nadherny."

While Ade was sending this cable, Zimmerman's problems were mushrooming. Sudopo had begun pounding on the door, and if Zimmerman hadn't broken off his conversation with Nadherny, he surely would've ordered his thugs to break it down. Before opening the door, Zimmerman used his handkerchief to pick up all the scattered classified embassy cables and documents he could see, careful not to get any fingerprints on them, and stashed them in the big safe in the vault.

He then rushed to the door and opened it, and found Sudopo almost in his face. "OK, this is the situation as I know it," he said gravely, trying to seize the initiative and convey to the Minister that he was about to hear very sensitive information. "Let's enter the Embassy and I'll brief you."

Sudopo looked suspicious, and summoned a uniformed guard to accompany him. A man he identified as a doctor also stepped forward, looking fearful.

Zimmerman led Sudopo and the guard directly to the utility room where George's body lay, hoping that he would find this absorbing enough not to demand a search of the entire Embassy or interfere with the death scene.

"Please don't touch or move anything," Zimmerman cautioned.

Sudopo approached the corpse and leaned over tentatively. Anyone who was a high government official on Tanako had to be familiar with violence and death, but nevertheless he appeared to be shocked by the carnage.

"Ugh," he said, turning away with a look of revulsion.

The doctor knelt down and confirmed Ellerbee's death.

"How do you explain this crime?" Sudopo asked.

"I can't explain it. We'll need to do a full investigation." Ron described what had happened, and added, "We know of no plot and there's nothing about your government being involved. I have to assume that something went terribly wrong within the Embassy, and that Mr. Kohler killed his colleague."

Sudopo nodded soberly. Ron noted that it was the first time that he'd said anything that Sudopo hadn't directly challenged.

"This is very suspicious," Sudopo said. He seemed to be looking for some way to turn the situation to personal advantage, and being surly and negative might keep the edge on his side. But Ron was relieved that, having seen the body, he had no interest in further inspecting the Embassy. It was now after nine o'clock and the edges of fatigue brought on by tension and lack of food were beginning to suffuse Ron's frame. He turned to Sudopo. "You may have noticed as we came in that the front door can't be locked from the outside. I'll have to remain here overnight to safeguard the embassy."

"That's out of the question," Sudopo replied. "You don't give the orders here. You will go to the American residence and stay there until I authorize you to leave. I will post guards to ensure that you do this."

"I can't agree to that," Ron said, knowing that he lacked the power to do anything about it. "You know that I'm an American official, even though I'm not accredited here. And I know you understand why I must safeguard the body and the Embassy. We both have an interest in making sure that an investigation can be carried out."

"Quite so," acknowledged the Minister. "I shall post four of my men right outside the door, and they'll not let anyone in. We'll spread white flour on the ground around the door so that if anyone tries to enter, he will leave footprints. If I order this building to be secured, I will be obeyed."

Ron photographed in his mind how the Embassy looked and where items were placed. He was then escorted to a government car and driven to the Kohlers' residence, with an armed guard riding in the front seat.

When he arrived, Ron called Chris Kanu. "First, thanks for saving the situation this afternoon," Ron said. "Without you, it could've gotten very ugly, and I've no doubt that Jack could've been taken into custody or even killed."

"It was the least I could do," Kanu replied, "and I'm glad I was able to help."

"How're your guests holding up?"

"Jack is calm, not offering conversation. He smokes incessantly, and is consuming a fair bit of scotch. He and Cynthia have been sitting quietly in the study, not saying much. Just sitting. The baby has gone to sleep and seems fine. I leave them alone except to check on them every hour or so. I expect they'll soon go to bed."

"We are beholden to you, Mr. Ambassador. Our deputy chief of mission in Yaounde, Adrian Nadherny, should arrive tomorrow morning to head the investigation. He'll undoubtedly want to talk to you first thing."

"Yes, I know Mr. Nadherny. That's fine. I'm completely at your disposal. And rest assured that the Kohlers are safe here until the next step is decided."

Ron then called Ade and brought him up to date. This time the connection was better, and Ron described the horror of what had just unfolded. Ade's questions betrayed astonishment, but he told Ron that he'd done a fine job and to get some rest, and that he'd come to the residence directly the next morning.

Satisfied that he could do nothing more that night, Ron sat down, stretched out his massive legs, and poured himself a very tall glass of Jack Kohler's best scotch.

CHAPTER SEVENTEEN

The Department of State, Washington, D. C.

Nadherny's first FLASH cable reached the Operations Center at the Department at exactly eight-eleven a. m. Monday morning, August 30. The senior watch officer scanned it quickly and called Sally Rogers, the desk officer for Cameroon and Tanako, at home. There was no answer: she must be on her way to work. He called her office on the fifth floor. She had just walked in. He told her, "Sally, I've got a flash cable from Yaounde. Jack Kohler in Tanako is claiming that he's uncovered a huge communist plot and that George Ellerbee is part of it. He's tied up Ellerbee in the vault and is pleading for help. Got that?"

"What?" Sally shrieked. Then more deliberately, "OK. Read it again, more slowly this time." She listened intently to every word.

"Oh God," Sally said, her mind now fully engaged and leaping ahead to what she would do next.

Sally's first step was to call the Assistant Secretary for African Affairs, Harlan Hastings. As Assistant Secretary, he outranked Ambassador Dick Hellyer and all the other ambassadors in Africa, except when he was visiting their countries.

Hastings had not yet arrived in his office, but he would have a copy of the flash cable in his morning take. Sally asked his secretary to make sure he saw it first thing when he walked into the office, and to call her the second he came in.

Ten minutes later Sally's phone rang. It was Hastings, and he'd read the cable. He instructed her to establish contact with Nadherny and to keep the line open, because getting through to remote places was often difficult. He added, "Tell Nadherny to get someone to Arania as soon as possible. He's probably already done that. I'll brief the Secretary. If you get any outside queries, don't say a word. Keep me informed."

Sally called the Op Center to tell them she was the contact point for anything from Arania or Yaounde. The watch officer told her he'd tried repeatedly to get through to Arania, but there was no answer from the operator or anyone at Kohler's residence.

Next, Sally sent an *immediate* cable to Ade in Yaounde with Harlan Hastings's instructions. As she worked, she scanned her memory for clues in Kohler's most recent cables; his Black Bitch report was an eye-opener and was beginning to attract more attention as word of it filtered through the corridors. But the SITREPS were very uneven – some good, some merely personal comments. She'd wondered if the steady Jack Kohler she knew was losing his detachment. Still, as someone who'd served in hardship posts, Sally was inclined to be sympathetic when reports reflected more than the Department's bloodless recitation of facts.

It was just before ten a. m. when Ade's second cable arrived. Sally called Hastings and read him the contents. He told her, "Draft a personal cable for Secretary Markham to President Barreras requesting that he facilitate our investigation. Don't say anything about a plot – if the Tanakians monitored Kohler's broadcast it'll surely trigger their suspicions. Tell the President we're sending Nadherny to head the investigation and that Hellyer, the senior U.S. diplomat dealing with Tanako, is in Yaounde. Put in that we'll return the Kohlers and Mrs. Ellerbee to American soil right away, and all legal proceedings will be done in the U.S. That's important. If all this happened inside the Embassy, that's U.S. territory, and we don't want anyone messing with our jurisdiction. Refer to Kohler as a career Foreign Service officer, so that his diplomatic immunity is up front. Tell him that we'll brief the press that this is entirely an American problem, and that Tanako is not involved. Did you get through to Yaounde?"

"Not yet," responded Sally. "We're still trying."

"Keep at it. It'll be crucial to have an open line as this thing develops."

Hastings quickly convened an emergency meeting and formed the Tanako working group: Sally Rogers; Charlie Stubblefield, a savvy African-American from Economic Affairs who'd served with Ade in South Africa, and who also knew Kohler and had backed his selection for Tanako; and Lyle Jameson, a lawyer from the Legal Affairs Bureau. As Hastings briefed them, curiosity turned to disbelief, but subsided as professional cool asserted itself. Hastings said, "At this point we don't know much, but we have to assume the worst. That would be that George Ellerbee is dead, probably by Kohler's hand, and there may be complications with the local government. Kohler's conspiracy theory doesn't make sense, but it's still possible that he may have stumbled onto something. He's a good officer, so we shouldn't dismiss his broadcast entirely.

"Charlie's in charge. He'll deal with officials outside the building, the press, the families, and the public. Sally, you coordinate all cable traffic, handle the admin details, and be liaison to me. You have first priority on the Bureau's conference room, unless we have an even bigger crisis, God forbid. Lyle, get on top of the legal aspects and coordinate with Justice. Make sure we have a clean investigation. We'll meet briefly every morning at nine and again at six, to review where we are and where we're going.

"Our immediate task is to find out what happened. If Ellerbee is dead, we have to secure the body, preserve the evidence, and get Kohler out of Tanako and into protective custody. And don't forget the families. One man is probably dead; they'll want to know what the hell happened and what we're doing about it.

"Finally, Sally, work up a bare-bones statement with Frank Maxwell in the press office. We're probably OK for today, but this story won't stay quiet for long. The only people authorized to speak to the press are Charlie, and in his absence, Sally. For now what you can say, Charlie, is that we monitored Kohler's broadcast, that an American official is on the scene in Arania to investigate and others are on the way. Now I've got to go upstairs and brief the Secretary. Did I leave anything out?" Hastings rose to leave for the seventh floor without waiting for a response, and the members of the Department's newest task force hurried out to get things moving.

CHAPTER EIGHTEEN

American Embassy, Yaounde, Cameroon.
August 30, 1971. Ten P. M.

It was after ten o'clock, and Ade hadn't been able to reach the Department by telephone. He was dictating another cable wrapping up everything Ron had told him from Kohler's residence when Sally Rogers got through from Washington. He told her he hoped to be in Arania by mid-morning the next day, Tuesday.

Sally briefed him on the activities of the working group. Lyle Jameson and the Department's Medical Division quickly decided against an autopsy in either Arania or Douala, because crucial evidence could be contaminated and medical services there were suspect, especially in Arania. For the same reasons, the Department didn't want the body to be embalmed. Sally left it to Ade to figure out how to get a decaying and unembalmed corpse back to Washington while making sure that no one had a chance to sully whatever evidence it might reveal. Of course, Ade would also have to gather up all potential evidence from the Embassy, and keep it free from taint.

He told Sally that Kohler must have suffered some kind of mental breakdown, but he had no idea what might have caused it. She said Hastings had checked with the Medical Division and there was "no evidence of significant problems" in the records of either Kohler or Ellerbee. This was some relief, because Ade knew he'd be on the spot about selecting them for Tanako, even if there were no further problems.

After the conversation ended, Ade set up a four-hour watch in the communications office to monitor the telephone and any incoming cable traffic. Finally, there was nothing more he could do, so he went home.

Earlier, he'd called Ginger to tell her he was working on something urgent and wouldn't be home until late. After everything that had happened, he needed someone to talk to. Ginger quickly noticed Ade's face, half-numb with fatigue and horror, and said, "My God, Ade, what's happened?"

"Jack Kohler's apparently killed George Ellerbee," he blurted, "and I'm leaving tomorrow first thing to head the investigation and get the Americans out. The Department's already formed a task force and they're worried as hell. I'll have to stay at least a few days, until everybody's out."

Ginger's mouth dropped open in astonishment. Back in Washington, she'd been a counselor for victims of rape and family violence, so extremes of behavior weren't new to her. But as Ade repeated how Ron described discovering the carnage and then finding the multiple stab wounds on George's body, she shuddered and blanched.

She listened closely as Ade related the details, interrupting only to clarify a detail or two. When she finally spoke, her reaction surprised him. "Jack Kohler did that?" she asked. "I can't believe it. He's one of us!"

Ginger held no illusions that Foreign Service officers were superior to others, but the service was an elite. Unseemly behavior wasn't supposed to happen, at least in public. Acts like murder were unthinkable.

"I'm as stunned as you are – and Jack of all people! Sure, he'd been tense, but who wouldn't be? We're not bloodless! But no one guessed something could really be wrong, even George, and now he's dead. Ginger, somehow I should've known."

"You can't blame yourself because you chose them for Tanako. Cause and effect don't go back that far."

"But I've heard some things about how Kohler behaved in previous posts that make me wonder if he was as unflappable and fair-minded as everyone thought. Maybe if we'd checked more carefully..."

"What, and the Department will put everyone on the couch before sending them overseas? Sure." But the idea triggered something else in her mind, and she paused to chew on the notion. "You know, I remember from my forensic work that repeated stab wounds from a knife or other sharp instrument often suggest homosexual violence. You don't suppose there was a relationship between those two, do you?"

The notion exploded in Ade's brain like a landmine. "God, that'd be all we'd need. The Department sniffs out suspected homosexuals like they were deadly poison. Thinks they're vulnerable to communist blackmail." He thought for a bit more, coming up with counter arguments. "Wait a minute. The notion's absurd. No way. Number one, they're both married, supposedly happily. Number two, there was absolutely nothing in their files, or that anyone has ever suggested along those lines. Number three, Kohler tried to have Ellerbee transferred just two months ago – which he wouldn't do if they were lovers. Number four, it's a practical impossibility, or damn near it. Tanako's a small place, and everyone knows what everyone else is doing, all the time. No, Ginger, I think we can discard that hypothesis."

"It may seem far-fetched, but nothing that you said absolutely rules out a relationship. It *might* have been difficult, but it *could* have happened. And if there *is* something to it, watch out."

"It's too far out for me," Ade replied. "They were normal guys. Hell, I chose them, and I can tell you that they were the best of the lot."

Ginger looked at Ade as though he didn't quite get it. "I think you better think back and get straight in your own mind how you happened to pick those two. As I recall, it wasn't just the normal State Department assignment process."

"That's right," Ade admitted. "Tanako is such a weird place and a graveyard for careers, no one wanted to go. We had to find guys who could handle it."

"It certainly proved a graveyard for George Ellerbee," Ginger said. Ade looked at her sharply. She reached out with her hand. "I'm sorry, Ade. I didn't mean it the way it sounded. All I'm saying is that the Department will be burrowing into this, and you better be prepared to take some heat. The Department takes care of its own, but only up to a point, and if they decide they need a scapegoat, guess who it'll be."

Ginger's comment was ominous, but Ade had more immediate problems to face, like preventing more violence, preserving the evidence, and getting the Americans away from Tanako fast. If they got through that unscathed, he thought he'd be able to handle anything else. He threw some clothes into an overnight bag for an early getaway the next morning and fell into bed, hoping that weariness would bring sleep quickly.

Ginger said, "You know, whatever happened there today, either there was a relationship between the two and something went wrong, or Jack's steadiness was only a facade. Or maybe just being on that island made him crazy."

Could be, Ade thought, but his immediate tasks pushed any psychological aspects far to the side. "Maybe they just had an argument that flared out of control."

"No. From your description, Jack didn't just kill Ellerbee, he destroyed him. Why? There's something much deeper here."

Ade didn't have any answers to deep questions, but what concerned him was that Kohler might still be dangerous. Ade's picture of him as a rational, intelligent, in-control diplomat didn't mesh with the new snapshot of Jack unleashing the spasm of savage violence that had apparently taken the life of George Ellerbee. He wondered if they would ever reconcile the two powerful and contradictory images, as he drifted into fitful sleep.

CHAPTER NINETEEN

Ade was already up at six when the phone rang. The duty officer had obtained flight clearances, and they could take off in thirty minutes for the 400 mile flight to Tanako. He looked in on Greg, still asleep, and gave him a gentle pat on the shoulder, which made him stir only slightly. The boy looked innocent and untroubled, and Ade wondered how you could love your children so much and still find it so difficult to get through to them or understand what was really on their minds. Wives too, he thought.

He left Ginger with a hug and a mumbled apology about leaving with the family situation still unresolved. If he was expecting absolution he didn't get it. Instead, she nibbled on her lower lip, giving him a weak smile as she put her hand on his shoulder.

"Be careful," she said. "The woods are full of wolves."

"I know about the ones on Tanako. Maybe it's the ones in Washington that I should worry about."

The Ambassador's driver had the limousine backed up in the driveway with the engine running, and the outside guards were standing at the open gate as Ade hopped in and they headed for the airport. He'd asked Harry Sundel, the administrative officer, and Joe Kemper, the Embassy doctor, to accompany him.

They reached the airport in fifteen minutes, took off immediately, and settled in for the two-hour flight. The noise of the Cessna precluded conversation, so Ade passed the time going over what had happened, and trying to square this with his recollections of Jack Kohler and George Ellerbee.

When the Department had decided to keep the Embassy in Tanako open, over the objections of the budget cutters and global thinkers who saw no need for it, the main justifications were that it didn't cost much and a Senator who'd bagged a lion on a safari had the President's ear, and believed there should be an American Embassy in every African country, no matter what. As a result, Ade had to find two officers who would actually agree to go there and get the work done. Of course, they had to be steady and reliable. No chronic drinkers, womanizers, burn-outs, or office martinets for this place. There were always a few of those around, functional enough to avoid "selection out" but not competitive for the higher positions. Sally Rogers helped him screen the files of potential candidates. Kohler and Ellerbee were the two best.

Kohler, 43, had six years of African experience, the most recent being a two-year assignment as deputy chief of mission in Gabon. Earlier, he'd done well in an economic assignment with the OECD in Brussels, served in Cairo, and had picked up passable Spanish during a Latin American tour in the mid-Sixties. For the past four years he'd worked in Washington on various trade issues in the Bureau of Economic Affairs.

Ade remembered checking with Charlie Stubblefield, his old friend from a mutual tour in South Africa, and now head of the Tanako working group. Charlie, Jack, and Ade had entered the Foreign Service in the same class, and later Charlie and Jack had worked together on several economic issues. Strikingly, Charlie and Ade were both two promotions ahead of Jack.

Ade and Charlie had become close during their two years in South Africa. An African-American with unflappable charm, Charlie became one of the unsung heroes of American diplomacy when the State Department chose him to be the first black officer to challenge South Africa's apartheid policy. He was given a senior and highly visible embassy job and the embassy demanded that he receive all the access and status to which his diplomatic position entitled him.

Charlie handled the pressures beautifully. One of the ways he did so was by taking out his inner rage on Ade on the tennis court. Ade was no slouch as a player, but on Charlie's better days he could run down Ade's best shots and return many of them for winners. At least, Ade thought, apartheid produced two good things: his friendship with Charlie, and some epic tennis matches.

Charlie's low-key demeanor masked an intensity that came from being a successful black in a society where racial indignities are still part of daily life. Bright and irreverent, Charlie judged human character shrewdly, and like many minority employees in the State Department, quickly noticed any signs of phoniness or racial patronizing.

Ade had lost track of Kohler in the years following their junior officer orientation course, so he asked Charlie for insights. "Jack's a good officer," Charlie said. "He's strong on trade issues, and understands the political flak that always goes with them. He's done well at international meetings – works hard, keeps his cool, establishes good contacts, knows the issues and argues them well."

Kohler sounded good, and Ade trusted Charlie's judgment. "What's he like as a person?" he asked.

"He's a decent guy, very even-tempered. He sometimes comes across as stiff, but warms up when he gets to know you. He has a sense of humor – understated, and a bit cynical, I suppose. On economics, he's one of the best informed. I think he really enjoys being a Foreign Service officer. Not just the work, but the prestige, being an authority on important issues, the travel, the access to good food and wine."

"Wow, another water walker! The Department's full of them. Any negatives?"

"Nothing really, as far as I know. But I'm puzzled about this guy. With his intelligence and ability, you'd think he'd have come along faster. He's done OK, but not as well as he might have. He's in the lower ranks of our class."

"Hmm," Ade mumbled, curious. "Any idea why?"

"What I've heard is that he has big ideas about what he's going to do, but somehow it never turns out. It's not that he isn't capable, but he misses deadlines, or doesn't tie up the loose ends, so someone else has to step in. There seems to be a sense that you just wouldn't assign him a really big job and expect him to pull it off."

There'd been nothing of this in Kohler's file. This wasn't unusual: official files were full of extravagant praise, because a single derogatory remark could torpedo an officer's promotion chances and derail his career. Corridor reputations were unofficial and accordingly much more accurate.

"What's his wife like?"

"Cynthia? I've only met her once or twice. She was a legal secretary at one of the K Street law firms, and when she married Jack she took a job in the Department's legal division. For a non-lawyer, she knows plenty about the law. Comes across as no-nonsense and focused. Personable enough, but not the kind you'd get to know easily."

"How would they do at an isolated hardship post, like Tanako?"

"That's where you're going to send them? What did they do wrong? I have to say, you guys are all heart! But seriously, they should do as well as any. They're both tough and intelligent. The kid's young enough so there wouldn't be any school worries."

"Charlie, you're a great help. You should be head of personnel."

"Are you kidding?" Charlie laughed. "Do you know what I'd do to this white boys' club? Anyway, glad to help. Kohler'll do a good job for you."

Ade's one remaining check was with Dick Hellyer, the Ambassador in Cameroon, who would be Jack's supervisor.

Hellyer not only knew Jack, but thought he was a fine officer.

"We were at the OECD together," he told Ade over the telephone, "and Jack also worked for me in Washington. Not flashy, but strong in economics, and solid as a rock. He'd be good for the job. I'd be pleased to have him."

That cinched it. Of course, nobody had talked to Kohler yet, but Ade was confident that he wouldn't object if he presented it right.

Ade was also lucky in finding a match for the administrative position. George Ellerbee was an experienced administrative staff employee who'd never make it to the senior ranks, but was seemingly content with the unexciting routine of keeping a small embassy going. He'd served in several hardship posts, and apparently liked the extra pay and greater informality. Although at forty-five he was slightly older than Kohler, there wasn't much in his file. Apparently, George showed up for work, did his job, and went home. But several supervisors had noted that he was a pleasure to work with, sunny and outgoing, and commented on his ability to empathize with others.

He'd had mostly Latin American assignments, except for a tour in Moscow. The tiny international community in Arania was the only social outlet for foreigners there, and as a former Spanish colony Tanako had several Spanish-speaking diplomats. George and Maria would get along fine in this environment. They had no children.

Early the following week Ade called Kohler and asked him to drop by the office. He arrived at exactly the appointed time, a tall and serious man with horn-rim glasses. His handshake was firm, and he looked Ade straight in the eye. A suggestion of a smile curved his lips, moderating the impression of severity he first gave. He wasn't handsome, but he had a presence. When he talked, his eyes fastened on Ade's face as though he expected him to listen carefully to his every word. His smile was pleasant, but not broad, and in their initial conversation, used sparingly. Yet, behind the austere facade Ade sensed an intelligent man, not easily fooled, and sensitive to nuance.

He grimaced painfully as he sat down.

"Something the matter?" Ade asked.

"I have a chronic back problem, and sometimes it's painful."

"Nothing that could prevent you from going overseas, I hope."

"No, the doctors always clear me," he said with a slight smile, putting his hand to his brow. Ade noticed the heavy dark tobacco stains on his fingers. "You have to be on death's door to get out of an assignment in this place."

Kohler had surely guessed why Ade wanted to see him, so Ade came right to the point. "How would you like to go to Tanako as principal officer?"

"Well, at least I know where it is," he replied, his half-smile pulling at the corners of his mouth. "That's more than most people, even in this building. What do you see as the top priorities there?"

Ade was impressed that Jack's first reaction was not to whine, or complain about living conditions, but to ask about American interests. That struck him as professional.

He briefed Kohler on Tanako and the job requirements, stressing aspects that made the job seem inviting, and downplaying the negatives. He thought he'd picqued Kohler's interest. "This isn't an easy assignment, Jack, I'll be frank. But it's a challenge, and we're asking you because people say you're smart, steady, and competent."

Kohler was pleased, but didn't respond. He was holding onto his options, wrestling with thwarted dreams of Foreign Service glory and the notion that maybe there were aspects of this assignment that were appealing, especially if he was in charge. Kohler's body language told Ade that he was still on the line.

"The other concern is Barreras," Ade said. "We don't want him stirring up trouble on the mainland. You'll have to figure out where he's going."

"What about the Embassy?"

"Your predecessor," Ade said, as though Kohler had already taken the job, "was med-evacked with malaria two months ago. And Tanakian officials won't welcome contacts with you. Barreras has made that very clear to them."

"Sounds lovely," Kohler said with a grimace. "Maybe there's a reason to keep the Embassy staffed, but why me? My expertise is world trade."

"You also have political reporting experience, and people say you work well under pressure. 'Solid as a rock' is how Dick Hellyer described you."

"He said that? Well, I did good work for him a few years back. I'm glad he remembers." He paused. "I can do the job, no worry about that," Kohler said. "But it'll mean good-bye to my shot at a senior job afterwards."

"Maybe not," Ade hedged. "You never know with promotion panels. They might see Tanako as so tough that you deserve a reward just for being there."

"That doesn't happen, in my experience," Kohler said disdainfully. "But what's the latest news from there?" he asked. "What's Barreras up to?"

"Last week there was a failed coup attempt. The *Financial Times* reported that the plotters were executed in the city stadium. The Foreign Minister was the ringleader, but supposedly felt such remorse that he jumped out a window, right in Barreras's office. But the story said it was Barreras himself who threw him out. His own foreign minister! The paper concludes that Barreras '*defenestrated*' his foreign minister."

"Seized a window of opportunity, no doubt." observed Jack.

Ade smiled. "Well, what do you say, Jack? Will you take the job?"

"I'll check with Cynthia and call you. The answer is probably 'yes.'"

"It's to your credit that you're ready to take this on without bitterness."

"I'm not bitter, but I didn't get any of the senior jobs I was pushing for. Not even a nibble. I'm a good officer, Ade. People have told you that, but I don't spend time kissing ass, and maybe that's hurt me. I'd like to think that promotions and assignments are based on merit."

"No system's perfect, but you'll have a shot." Kohler looked skeptical and Ade changed the subject. "Last question. Do you know George Ellerbee?"

"Hmm. Yeah, he was in La Paz, but I didn't know him well. Admin type, but nice enough. Little guy, married to an Ecuadoran. Liked to dance the *merengue*. Why?"

"He's the best candidate to be your admin staffer. Would that be OK?"

"I suppose so," Kohler said. "As long as he gets the job done."

And that's how Kohler and Ellerbee got to go to Tanako. Ade thought they'd be good, and everyone agreed. Now one of them was dead. And what Ade couldn't know while he was musing in that Cessna is that the simple act of choosing Jack Kohler for Tanako would govern his life for years to come.

CHAPTER TWENTY

Arania, Tanako, Tuesday, August 31, Nine A. M.

The little Cessna coasted to a smooth landing. When the plane's door was opened, the air outside pressed in on the three men with a clammy heaviness that felt like a hot compress. They didn't know what they were moving into, and for a moment were hesitant to exchange the security of the airplane cabin for this inhospitable island, where so much violence had taken place. Ade, Dr. Kemper, and Sundel glanced at one another without speaking, reluctant to express their apprehension.

The shed was empty except for a uniformed guard with an old M-1 rifle, and officials at the visa and customs desks. They glared as the Americans approached, and then another official came up and asked, "Mr. Nadherny?"

He was from the Foreign Ministry, which had received the Secretary's cable and had sent this fellow to meet them, probably more from a desire to keep an eye on them than as a courtesy.

Ade was happy to accept his help in hurrying them through customs. He also had an official car, a battered Opel, and the three Americans squeezed into the back seat. Ade told him that they had to go to the American residence to rendezvous with a colleague, and then to the Embassy to begin the investigation.

He frowned, and said, "That is acceptable," as though they had to ask his permission. Establishing cordiality wasn't part of his assignment.

When they arrived at the residence, Ron was pacing about nervously, chafing at his confinement, and fearful that Ellerbee's body or the contents of the Embassy had been tampered with.

"I might as well be under house arrest here!" he thundered with indignation. "They have no authority to do that!"

"Well, they do and they don't, Ron," Ade said with a tight smile. "Of course it's outrageous, but we can't prevent them if they're determined to enforce it. So let's keep cool and see if we can talk our way through it."

When they arrived at the Embassy, two security guards were standing at the entrance, along with Sudopo and three Tanakian aides. Ade greeted him politely, thanking him for the cooperation they had yet to receive. Sudopo remained unsmiling. "You are Mr. Nadherny, and you are the senior American official here?"

"Yes, and these are my colleagues," he said, introducing them. Sudopo introduced only one of his aides, a doctor.

"We will enter the Embassy shortly," Sudopo said. "But first I will tell you our concerns over what has happened here." He looked grave.

Ade chose to ignore the fact that it was up to them and not Sudopo to determine who would enter and who wouldn't.

"We have been the target of sinister plots, some of them directed from abroad," Sudopo said. "Your government is clearly involved. As the Embassy *Chargé,* Mr. Kohler was coordinating support for the plotters. Mr. Ellerbee discovered the plan, refused to go along with it, and had to be killed."

"What?" Ade said. "I don't know of any basis for that. We have no reason to plot against Tanako, but you've been harassing our diplomats here."

"We know that America opposes the fraternal ties between us and the Soviet Union, Cuba, and the People's Republic of China. America intervenes all over the world to resist the struggle of the progressive forces."

Ade stared hard at Sudopo, not knowing whether he believed this or had concocted it to keep him on the defensive. He decided that he really believed it.

"Just how do you think we were doing all this plotting?" Ade asked. It was the wrong question. Conspiracy theorists have an answer for everything, and they *know* they are right.

"Recently, we've learned of arms shipments from Europe to anti-popular elements here on Tanako. Your country is clearly involved. The Embassy would be a most useful place to conceal illegal arms shipments."

Sudopo was deadly serious, and Ade had to turn him around fast. An idea popped into his head. If it turned out badly, a real possibility, it might get him sacked.

"I can show you that your charges are baseless," Ade said. "We'll do something we've never done before, anywhere. You and I and the doctors will enter the Embassy together. They'll safeguard the body while you and I inspect inside. You can go anywhere you want, and see for yourself that there's nothing to your accusation."

Sudopo seemed to be thrown off-balance by Ade's bold offer. But after a moment's reflection, he assented. Ade motioned for Harry Sundel to join the group, and all six men entered the embassy.

Dr. Kemper and the Tanakian doctor went quickly through the lobby to the room where Ellerbee's body was lying, put on surgical gloves and knelt down. Ade instructed them not to make any further examinations or move the body in any way. Harry Sundel began taking pictures, starting with photos of George's body, still crammed into a corner of the utility room. Ron whispered that it appeared that the body had not been moved.

Ade, trying not to react to the stench that filled the room, asked Sudopo for help in removing the body to cold storage. Holding his handkerchief to his nose, Sudopo left to summon a work crew. Ade asked Ron to keep the body in sight until he could verify that it had been sealed in a secure casket and placed in the morgue.

Seeing George lying dead with bloody stab wounds filled Ade with revulsion and horror at what his final, terror-filled minutes must have been like. George was a loving husband and a man who'd never harmed anyone, and to have his life ended so brutally seemed the height of unfairness. Was there any other explanation than that Jack Kohler went berserk for some mysterious reason? Was there some hostility between the two men going back to their tour overlap in Bolivia, or maybe something like what Ginger had suggested last night?

Ade said to Sudopo, "Let's start our tour now," and they proceeded. Fortunately, the Embassy was small and architecturally simple, and they covered the entire building in twenty minutes, including the vault, now so smeared with blood and disorder that its original purpose was effectively camouflaged.

They finished in Jack's office, a small room just off the main lobby.

As Ade was ending his explanation, the Minister casually opened the third drawer of Jack's desk, and immediately froze, his eyes opening wide.

"Aha!" he exclaimed triumphantly. "What's this?"

Ade leaned over to see, and his heart sank. In plain view in Jack's drawer were three hand grenades. Not souvenirs, but operational.

"What's your explanation for these?" the Minister said.

Ade cursed Jack for leaving the grenades in his desk. But the truth was that all embassies, especially ones without marine guards and only local hires for security, have a few items like grenades to be used as a last resort in dire situations, such as mobs bursting through the gates.

"All our embassies have these things," Ade said in his most confidential manner. "Especially ones without any means of self-defense. They're only for emergencies, and only to protect lives, not property. You can see this is true, because we've just checked the entire building and found nothing."

Sudopo looked skeptical. "Kohler could have gotten rid of the other arms. That's when Ellerbee discovered him and had to be killed," he said.

As they were walking outside, Ade realized that he'd never admit he was wrong. Being able to charge that he'd discovered grenades in the American Embassy might be useful to him at some point.

"My men will confiscate these weapons," he said.

"Whether you believe me or not," Ade said firmly, "this is still the American Embassy and the grenades are Embassy property. They stay here." Sudopo didn't respond, letting Ade's remark pass without conceding anything.

Ade said, "You've seen that no arms were inside. Besides, you control the checkpoints and the countryside. No one could transfer arms without you knowing it."

"We'll deal with that later. There is more immediate business. I'm going to take Mr. Kohler into custody and charge him with murder."

Of course the correct response was to point out that Kohler had diplomatic immunity, and the inviolability of the Embassy was established by the Geneva Convention, to which Tanako was a signatory. Accordingly, the host country's sovereignty stopped at the Embassy gates, and what happened inside the Embassy was strictly the business of the United States.

The problem was that Geneva was a long way from Tanako. The cultural distance was even farther than the geographical. Citing the Geneva Convention with the man who ran the security forces of one of the nastiest regimes in the world, with Ade's backup limited to debating points, didn't seem like a level playing field. Certainly not here, where one of the world's weakest countries, with not even a tank to its name or the ammunition to fire from one, held sway over the mightiest nation in history.

But Ade was thinking that Sudopo knew very well that bad publicity could ridicule Barreras. And that would not be healthy for his minions.

"Before you give any orders, let's review the situation," Ade began. "First, we have an American citizen, an Embassy official, dead. We don't know for sure who killed him, but it's likely that it was Mr. Kohler, the *Chargé* and a professional diplomat. There were no citizens of your country involved, or, as far as we know, even present. So this is entirely our business. That is international law, and your country recognizes it."

The Minister was becoming irritable. "This is Tanakian territory, and I say go to hell with your international law." He spat into the dirt. "The fact is that your man has committed a grievous crime on Tanakian soil. He must be punished. In this country, we punish murderers by public execution."

"You can't pronounce Kohler guilty without due process. Besides, he has diplomatic immunity. You may get away with executing your own people without trial, but you can't do that to an American diplomat. We'll try Kohler in the United States."

Sudopo glared. "The criminal has fled to the Nigerian Ambassador's. I'll go there and arrest him. You'll see how we handle criminals here."

Ade said, "Don't forget that the Ambassador also has diplomatic immunity. If you break into his residence, Nigeria would surely break off diplomatic relations. Nigeria's already unhappy with your government. Geneva may be far away, but the Nigerians aren't. Do you really want to cause a break with them?"

Even the arrogant Sudopo didn't want to unleash something that could end badly for Barreras, or especially himself. Ade seized on his hesitation. "Mr. Minister, let me get the Kohlers off the island as soon as possible. That way, you'll be rid of the problem for good, and we'll thank you publicly for your help. That should please the President."

The Minister had no response, but he wasn't happy. He probably already had visions of parading through the muddy streets of Arania with Kohler's head on a pike, as a warning to plotters. If he could get away with doing this to an American diplomat who'd murdered someone in his country, that would be a real achievement.

"Before we go after this criminal I must consult the President," he said. Tanakian justice was not a matter of courts and evidence, but of eliminating one's enemies and settling scores, by whatever means. By Sudopo's thinking, Kohler had to be punished immediately to demonstrate the absolute power of the regime. To now be thwarted added to his surliness, and he turned away and drove off without uttering another word.

Ade watched his car disappear down the road. He'd clearly won this encounter, but the victory was shallow. Sudopo was a key man, who not only controlled the present situation but also undoubtedly would be involved if Tanako were hosting terrorists out in the bush. Ade needed him to be something less than implacably hostile in order to find out what was going on. Yet the initial encounter with Sudopo had gone badly. Realizing he'd been bested, Sudopo would be looking to get even.

Ade had tried to co-opt him by making every cranny of the Embassy accessible. But far from being assuaged, Sudopo had hit on the only item that he might be able to exploit, the grenades. Clearly, he had no interest in rapport – he was comfortable treating Americans as the enemy. But was this because of his ideology, or his power position in the government and his relationship to Barreras, his own uncle? If Ade didn't get the psychology right, the situation could fall apart quickly.

Before Ade and Sudopo held their harangue, Ade had sent Harry Sundel to find a casket for Ellerbee. This being

Tanako, the task was not difficult, and he was back in an hour with a zinc-lined metal casket and a flatbed truck.

Ron took a final look at the body for signs of tampering. He noted the matted hair, smeared clothing, clotted wounds, and George's frail body, and realized that he'd been the last person other than Kohler to talk to him, during the previous day's radio call. There'd been no hint that George felt in danger, or that Jack was cracking up, or that the day would be different from any other.

As far as Ron could tell, the body was unchanged. He and Dr. Kemper lifted it carefully and placed it in the casket, loaded it on the flatbed and drove to the city morgue. Fortunately the morgue, a modest rectangular building of cement blocks, had its own generator, financed by the World Bank in a project to upgrade municipal services in Third World countries. This meant that it had full air conditioning, a luxury available to no living Tanakians other than those in the presidential palace. At least George's body would suffer no further deterioration, even if the city suffered one of its frequent power outages.

Ron and Joe soldered the casket closed, nailed on the top, and secured it with steel bands. Ron slipped some greenbacks to the morgue director, asking him to make sure that no one touched the coffin, and explained that they would come for it as soon as they could arrange transportation.

When Ron and Joe returned, they joined Harry Sundel and Ade and they again donned surgical gloves and reentered the vault. All appeared as before, but this time they noted things more purposefully. Several lengths of electrical cord lay haphazardly on the floor, and one was tied to a chair. Papers were strewn everywhere in clusters, held together by matted blood. One rumpled sheet caught Ade's eye. It was bloodstained but also had a note hand-written in ink, evidently by Kohler: "George - Send this NODIS FLASH right away, and do it right." He put the note in a special cellophane cover, and marked the outside for special attention.

Minutes later, Ade found another, longer note in a waste basket. It looked like Kohler's first draft of a cable message, written in apparent haste because it had many abbreviations and scribbles that made it difficult to read. But the words "communist conspiracy" and "plot that will take place at the UN" were clear enough to make out. From what Ade could see, this could be a draft of the warning Kohler broadcast over the radio. If so, something had happened to make him decide to break off sending the message and broadcast in the clear. Did he think someone was trying to break into the Embassy and then had run to the relative safety of the vault? Had Ellerbee refused to send the cable, thereby sealing his fate when Jack interpreted his refusal as being part of the conspiracy? Had Kohler been unraveling for days, and no one noticed, not even Cynthia? Could there have been some basis for Jack's fears? Ade recalled his banal message to Greg: one step at a time. That was the way to proceed, and that way maybe they'd find the answers.

They photographed each room and labeled each item; wrapped them all in plastic cut from garbage bags, and placed them in large canvas diplomatic pouches. When they'd finished they had twelve large duffels of objects.

It was now about five p. m., and Ade was lucky to get through a quick radio call to Yaounde, where he'd left Larry Saviano in charge. He got a good five minutes with Larry before static overwhelmed the conversation. Ade confirmed

Ellerbee's death, briefed Larry on the situation, and left it to him to inform Washington.

Since the Kohlers were safe for the moment with savvy Chris Kanu, Ade went to check on Maria. Carmen and Rogelio Camejo had been able to work her down slowly from her hysteria until she'd collapsed from grief and exhaustion. This morning, though, Maria had awakened with a fresh head of steam. By the time Ade talked to her, she'd calmed down, soothed by the attentive Camejos. But she was still prone to burst into angry tears, which Ade understood even if he felt inadequate in dealing with them. She demanded to know why the Department hadn't known anything was wrong with Jack. She suspected that unknown Americans had plotted to kill her husband. Most of all, she wanted revenge. She listened to Ade's condolences with impatience brimming on her lips, and fury in her eyes. "Why didn't you know something was wrong? How could you have let Jack do this? And to George, who never harmed anyone! I want Jack to pay! And I want to say good-bye to my husband."

"Maria, please don't ask to see George. You saw how he was yesterday. Remember him when he was alive. We've taken good care of his body. He's in a casket in the city morgue, and we've sealed it shut. No one can touch it. All this is important so that we see that justice is done."

"What justice did my husband get?" she cried. "This whole thing stinks! He'll rot here!" Bitter tears rolled down her cheeks.

"The morgue is air conditioned and we're going to get him back to the U. S. just as fast as we can. Please trust us and help us," Ade implored. He felt very sorry for Maria, and sympathized with both her anger and her grief, but she was a land mine in an uncharted field, and any misstep could set her off.

"What about Kohler?" she asked suspiciously.

"We still don't know what happened, or why, but we already have all the physical evidence from the Embassy. Now I'm going to see him. We'll send the Kohlers back right away, and Jack will be taken into custody and charged with murder. But we've got to get him out of here fast. The people here want to execute him."

"It wouldn't be cruel enough for what he did. I want to see him dead!"

Ade asked Carmen and Rogelio to stay with Maria until he could get her to Douala for an onward flight back to the States. As Ade was leaving, Rogelio pulled him aside. "I didn't want to say anything in front of Maria, but you know that Jack and I were good friends. I saw him almost every day.

"So after the Kohlers left the Embassy with Chris Kanu, I rushed over to see if I could help. Jack and Cynthia were in shock, so I didn't stay long. Jack was smoking and drinking *mucho escotch,* but seemed sober. But, Adrian, he had *no* remorse. Even if it was some kind of crazy accident, his own colleague is now dead! Jack showed no concern about Ellerbee and hardly recognized his name when I told him I was so sorry. Jack killed him! Doesn't his behavior seem strange to you?"

Ade admitted that it did. It was another factor to think about, when he had time. But right now he could only thank the Camejos for their help and head for Ambassador Kanu's residence.

When Ade arrived, both entrances to Chris Kanu's residence were blocked by the sedans of the security police and a contingent of perhaps twenty armed guards was lounging nearby. Those who bothered to look at him weren't smiling. He searched out the man in charge, a sun-glassed army captain who told him in Spanish that he couldn't enter. Ade showed his passport, pointed out the diplomatic seal, and explained his position, all to no avail. The captain shrugged his shoulders and stared at Ade, as though daring him to make a move.

The appearance of the Minister of Interior would never be something to gladden Ade's heart, but when his armored sedan rounded the corner it was a welcome sight. Dealing with him was about as much fun as having a tooth pulled, but he was the only person who might resolve the immediate impasse.

Ade walked over to his large tail-finned sedan and said, "Hello, Mr. Minister," as cordially as he could and extended his hand. "Your men are denying me access to Mr. Kohler, and I hope you'll straighten this out."

"They are operating on my instructions," he answered. "Do not obstruct them in their duties." His mood had not improved, and he was still the self-righteous official dealing with a hated imperialist.

"I understand that you want to keep track of Mr. Kohler," Ade said, "but you can't deny me access to a subordinate. I'm acting in the absence of my ambassador, who is accredited to your government."

Sudopo fixed Ade with a look of disdain. "You're dealing with a sovereign country, not an American colony," he said. "An American has committed a crime. Our people will demand that the criminal be punished. I must control access to Mr. Kohler."

Ade said, "There's another factor you should consider. A murder has occurred, and we assume that Mr. Kohler did it. He's now inside the Nigerian Ambassador's residence, with his wife and child, and the Ambassador's wife and children and the rest of their household. They're all in there together and we don't know what state Kohler's in or what's going on in there. One of the reasons I'm here is to stop further violence, and now you're preventing me from doing that. God forbid that there's any more trouble, but if there is it'll surely be on your shoulders. My government would consider that a grave matter. I'm sure the Nigerians wouldn't be very happy, either."

Sudopo hadn't thought of that, and his face lost a touch of its sneer. He would've enjoyed bursting into Chris Kanu's residence and sending him packing, but couldn't risk inflaming the Nigerians. Now Ade had to find a way to persuade him to go along without making him feel he was giving in.

"If you let me talk to Kohler, and if there's no danger, I'll get the family out quickly, along with Mrs. Ellerbee and the body. Believe me, this is the best way. You don't want to be involved, but you'll come out looking good. But we need your help."

Sudopo cared less about Kohler or his family, but he did care about looking good and avoiding anything that might upset his mercurial uncle. And if Tanako and the President looked good, he would benefit.

"You may enter for now," he said. "But the matter of leaving the country must be decided by the President." He then told the captain of the guard force, "Let this man enter, but if any Americans leave, follow and report to me at once."

"We'll be followed, then?" Ade asked.

"Of course."

"I'll see that you are personally recognized for your cooperation." Ade wondered if he caught the irony, as he walked onto the residence grounds. He wasn't home free yet, but his position had improved.

Having the Kohlers in his home must've been a terrible strain on Ambassador Kanu, especially since Kohler's state of mind was a total unknown. Would he still be violent? The Ambassador had his own wife and children to worry about, but his unruffled demeanor showed no sign of concern.

"I wouldn't say that Jack had a restful night," he told Ade, as though he were an innkeeper presiding over a bunch of fussy boarders. "He didn't eat much, and paced about a lot. I mostly left them alone, although once Jack asked me to peek behind the curtains and reassure him that there was no one outside trying to get him. After they went to bed, I stayed up in a chair outside their room, just in case. It was quiet until this morning, when they came out for breakfast. Today, he's much better, but still subdued and wary. But other than that, you wouldn't know that anything had happened. Except that I doubt Jack has scotch every morning for breakfast."

"I'm sure they're still in shock, just taking it one minute at a time. Let me talk to him, and we'll figure out where to go from there," Ade said.

He found Kohler sitting in an easy chair, smoking a cigarette. The window air conditioner was thrumming quietly and the room was cool, a welcome contrast to the blast furnace outside. The blinds were drawn, leaving the room dark except for a reading light on the table between Jack and Cynthia, and a floor lamp by the wall. A pile of cigarette butts nearly overflowed from an ashtray. Ade glanced at the book on the table, Peter Matthiessen's novel about missionaries in the jungles of South America, *At Play in the Fields of the Lord*. A bookmark was inserted at an early chapter. Beside it was a highball glass half-filled with scotch, the ice in it nearly melted. Jack was sitting quietly, apparently lost in thought. His face was vacant.

In the other chair, Cynthia had the baby on her lap, reading him a story. Ade thought this would make a fine American domestic tableau, circa 1945, or maybe a Norman Rockwell cover for the *Saturday Evening Post*. Except that this was Tanako, and the man in the easy chair had just carved up his colleague.

Jack seemed almost relieved to see Ade, looking anxious to learn what would happen but also dreading whatever lay ahead.

"Hello, Jack," Ade said, not shaking hands. Cynthia looked up. "How are you Cynthia, and how's young Robin?"

"Young Robin's just fine," Cynthia said with a brave smile, chucking him under the chin. "As for the rest of us, we could be better." She was cordial but on guard.

Ade said, "Jack, I'd like to speak with you alone for a minute or two." He wanted to see if Jack had anything significant to say, uninfluenced by Cynthia.

Jack looked uncertain, and Cynthia frowned. She clearly didn't want him out of her sight or talking to Ade, but couldn't think of a reason to refuse.

They went into the library. "How're you feeling?" Ade asked.

There was a tug of Kohler's wry smile. "I'm pretty much on a liquid diet," he said. But he turned apprehensive. "I don't want to take a risk in case the food is poisoned."

"Jack, that's absurd," Ade responded. "Chris Kanu is one of your best friends. And by the way, he saved your life."

Kohler looked blank. If what Ade said had registered, he showed no sign of gratitude. He suddenly tugged on Ade's sleeve. "What's going to happen to me?" he asked. "I guess they'll put me on trial for murder."

"I don't know what's been decided. But I'm taking you to the residence to pack a bag for the trip home. We'll get you all out of here on the Douala flight this afternoon."

"Will we be safe? The crowd was ugly when we came out of the Embassy. You can't trust these people. Remember what happened to Nguema!" Recalling the incident, Jack looked shrunken and fearful, a menace to nobody.

"You'll be safe. Now let's tell Cynthia what's happening, pay our respects to Ambassador Kanu for his hospitality and get the hell out of here."

CHAPTER TWENTY-ONE

Getting everyone from Arania, and then to Douala, Paris, and home proved to be a complicated logistical deployment, but Ade knew that Harry Sundel would work it out. The trick was to get the Kohlers on the first Pan Am flight from Douala, followed by Ellerbee's casket, accompanied by Ade and Maria, who insisted on staying with her husband for the long flight home. Harry would remain behind to clear the diplomatic pouches with all the evidence, and secure the Embassy.

Sudopo had not made another appearance, possibly as a result of Secretary Markham's cable to Barreras asking for assistance. Since no one was giving them any trouble at this point, Ade allowed himself a small dollop of relief. What he really wanted to do was to find Nguema, who might be able to shed some light on whether there'd been any altercation between Kohler and Ellerbee. Apparently, no one else was in the Embassy when Jack began his broadcast. Had he sent all the Tanakian employees home early? If so, did that suggest that Jack had planned to kill Ellerbee? But searching for Nguema now would surely earn him another session in the Black Bitch, especially since his American connection had already nearly cost him his life. Any contact with Nguema would have to wait.

Joe Kemper and Ade went with the Kohlers back to their residence so they could pack. Ade glanced around their living room and couldn't help but contrast the quiet order of this place – like rocks in a Zen garden, suggesting calm in a sea of change – with the chaos that Jack had unleashed inside the Embassy.

While Cynthia and Jack were in the kitchen, saying an awkward goodbye to Mba, Ade passed into Jack and Cynthia's bedroom, feeling like an uneasy intruder. The curtains were drawn, so he turned on the lights. The room was spacious but ordinary; two double beds with a night table and reading lamp in between, two large bureaus, a small desk and chair for Cynthia's use: she paid the family bills and ran the residence accounts. There was a large bookcase, with a color portrait of Cynthia, Jack and baby Robin in an ornate sterling silver frame, surrounded by books organized carefully by category: Vietnam, cold war, capitalism and communism. Literature was represented by John Cheever's Wapshot novels, some Updike and Saul Bellow, the usual Faulkner and Hemingway looking a bit faded, perhaps leftovers from college English courses. The Kohlers obviously did a lot of reading, but there were no surprises here. Ade noticed another family picture, of a dignified man in judicial robes; Cynthia's father, he guessed. Beside it, in a much smaller frame, was a full-face snapshot of a pretty, shyly-smiling young lady with straight short hair; probably Cynthia's mother about the time she married. There were no pictures of Jack's family.

Ade opened the drawers of Jack's bureau. His clothes were neatly, meticulously arranged: socks in the top drawer, placed by color; next drawer, underwear in orderly white piles. Jack could've been blind and picked out exactly the item he wanted. His dress shirts were in the third drawer, arranged in two neat columns. Ade tried not to disturb the perfect order of the clothes while he slipped his hand under each pile. In the third drawer, he felt a different shape. He pulled out a lined notebook with an opened letter folded inside. There were only a few pages with entries. At the front, there was a numbered list of things Jack apparently intended to do, such as "find out who prisoners are and where from," "find out names and registries of ships entering port," and the like.

At the back, there was another set of pages, headed "Schreber." Perhaps a contact, a recent visitor he'd met. But the very first entry undermined that hypothesis and left Ade's throat dry with surprise. Kohler had written, "Schreber felt that 'after all it must be nice to be a woman submitting to an act of copulation…" Did Kohler have a secret fantasy? Was he trying his hand at erotic writing?

For the second entry, Kohler had written, "Schreber had feared 'sexual abuse' at the hands of his own doctor." The third and final entry was, "Schreber fears that his doctor tried to commit 'soul-murder' on him."

Taken together, the entries seemed like fragmentary jottings, as though Kohler was working to develop a short story or a screenplay. That was preposterous, but no other explanation came to mind. But the notes were too interesting to risk losing when the Embassy would do a detailed inventory and pack up the Kohlers' effects. Ade took a deep breath and slipped the notebook and letter into his briefcase. Maybe there was a clue here that he could check before turning it over to the investigators. If someone eventually cracked the puzzles surrounding this case, he wanted to be the one to do it.

Ade doused the lights and slipped back to the living room, just as the Kohlers were approaching. While they were packing their suitcases, he called Chris Kanu and the Camejos to ask about Jack's behavior prior to the murder.

They had no useful information. Jack had seemed snappish the past week, but this was not unusual for Tanako. Kohler and Ellerbee were friendly, if not close. No one could recall any incidents between them, or any backbiting; apparently, Kohler never shared his unhappiness over Ellerbee's alleged incompetence with others. Given the closeness of the compact international community, they all said, in effect, "if there'd been any problem, someone would've noticed it."

The commercial flight to Douala was short and uneventful. Jack was distant and glum, but went along passively, almost as though he were in a trance.

When they arrived at Ron's residence in Douala, Pete Kasprzak, the Embassy security officer, had arrived from Yaounde. At least the logistical arrangements were starting to fall into place. Dr. Joe Kemper raced into the consulate to send an *immediate* cable to the Medical Division in the State Department, reporting that "the victim, who apparently died of multiple stab wounds in chest area, has been in unreliable refrigeration. We have placed the body in a sealed coffin. Autopsy or embalming does not appear feasible here."

Ade made a quick call to Ginger. Her voice was warm and she sounded pleased that he'd called, but her tone quickly changed when she began telling him about the aftermath of Greg's school incident. He'd been suspended for a week, and although he hadn't complained he was unusually quiet and Ginger couldn't get through to him. "It'll be better when you get home and we can both talk to him. Will you be home tonight?"

"God, I'm sorry sweetheart, but I've got to go with the casket and Maria to Washington. But I'll do a quick turnaround and be back in a few days."

There was a long pause. Ade could almost feel her reaching out to him and finding thin air. He wanted to tell her what they'd gone through and what the new problems were, but there wasn't time. The brief burst of exhilaration he felt about getting the surviving Americans and George's casket safely out of that awful place gave way to guilt. He knew Ginger understood why he had to go, but he also knew that she felt abandoned and resentful at a time when she needed him.

"Goodbye Ade," she said, her distant voice barely audible through the crackling static. "We'll be all right." Ade started to respond, but she'd hung up.

Within an hour, several messages arrived from Washington, sent by Sally Rogers. The most important was a summary of Tuesday's noon press briefing.

Washington was still in the summer doldrums and many of the top players were away, so news was thin. Frank Maxwell, the spokesman, read from a prepared statement: "Mr. George Ellerbee, an administrative assistant in the United States Embassy in Tanako, was found dead yesterday of multiple stab wounds. His body was found in the Embassy by a consular officer from Douala, who went to investigate indications that Mr. Ellerbee's supervisor, *Charge d'affaires* John Kohler, was experiencing mental difficulties. Mr. Kohler will be returning to the United States, and a full investigation into the incident has begun. The Department expresses its condolences to Mr. Ellerbee's widow, Maria Ellerbee, and to Mr. Ellerbee's family."

Maxwell peered up from his text, and the storm broke. "Is Kohler under arrest?" "What were they up to?" "Where the hell is Tanako?" Maxwell waited for the shouted questions to stop, and said quietly, "I don't have anything more for you right now, but we're trying. The Embassy is on an island, not easily accessible, and we've been on the scene only a short time. The probability of a trial may limit what we can tell you."

Ade finished perusing the cables and called Sally. "How's it playing?"

"It could be big, Ade, and the press is digging. It's a bizarre murder, in a bizarre place. They're asking if there's any tie to the Soviets, Chinese, or Cubans. Even the Africanists know little about the place, except that Barreras is a killer. What was going on between the two guys? Why were they sent there? There's potential for big trouble. Some of the Department-haters on the Hill will surely run with this. Count on them to think conspiracy and coverup. Remember Joe McCarthy? This won't be fun."

Ade knew she was right. Sally had the grace not to say it, but he also realized that a lot of the heat would be directed at him. He took a deep breath and went on to the next item. Sally had sent transfer orders for Kohler and his family, for "medical evacuation." In addition, there was a cable from Lyle Jameson, the Department's lawyer on the Working

Group, saying that "It is extremely important that Kohler arrive at Dulles International Airport. Because it could affect where the case is tried, he should not enter the United States anywhere else."

Sally explained that there could be two tough legal issues even before the trial. One was venue: where should Kohler be tried? The Department wanted Virginia, where there was a no-nonsense federal judge who'd tried a recent case involving a murder on an ice floe in international waters. The Department would try to steer the case his way and hope that he'd rule that the federal court in Virginia was the proper venue. The first step to making that happen was for Kohler to land at Dulles International Airport in Virginia, just outside Washington. The other issue was jurisdiction: who could try an American diplomat committing a crime in an American embassy overseas?

She added that Kohler should not be taken into custody. "You don't have authority to arrest him in any case," she said. Ade replied that Pete Kasprzak would accompany the Kohlers back to the United States, and Sally said, "Make it clear that he's not an arresting officer, but someone who's just going along to help out. And make sure the Kohlers don't get any ideas about escaping."

"What if Kohler breaks and runs?" Ade asked.

"Make sure he doesn't."

It was a typical State Department solution: make someone responsible, but deny him the authority to get the job done. It was Ade's dilemma to solve, so he reassured Sally that the Kohlers wouldn't flee, especially with young Robin with them. "They'll be on the next Pan Am flight," he promised. But to make sure, he decided to keep Kohler under casual surveillance, and that meant separate guest rooms for Jack and Cynthia. At breakfast the next morning, talk was strained. Kohler was in another world, frowning and distant. He picked fitfully at his food while he puffed cigarettes. Cynthia kept busy looking after Robin, who was excited about going on another airplane.

After breakfast, Ade was briefing Cynthia on the travel plans when Jack rushed over, upset. "What're you talking about?" he demanded, standing with his legs apart and breathing heavily.

"While we're waiting, if you'd like to make any kind of statement or answer questions, we can do that," Ade said.

Jack looked suspicious. "Let me talk with my wife." They whispered intensely for a few minutes, and then he went back and told Ade, "There's nothing I want to tell you. And am I under arrest?"

"No, and you're not in custody," Ade said. "You and your family are returning to Washington on medical evacuation, and we're going with you."

Jack went back to brooding in a corner, and Ade made a last attempt to punch through Cynthia's outer shell. "I want to reassure you that your personal effects will be safe. Guards are posted, we'll continue to pay the servants, and there'll be no looting."

She looked relieved. "Thanks, Ade. Most of the things we really care about we had to leave behind. Photo albums, my family silver, Foreign Service mementos. They mean a lot. It's about all we have going for us now."

"I happened to notice that you have an excellent library."

"We brought a lot of books with us. We were able to find more time to read on Tanako than at most Foreign Service posts."

"Does Jack have any interest in writing fiction, anything like that?"

"Not in the slightest. His mind doesn't work that way. He might read a book or two of fiction a year. He's all history, politics and economics."

He decided to roll the dice. "Have you ever heard the term 'soul-murder?'" Cynthia tensed. "No. What an odd term. Why do you ask?"

Ade had gone too far. Cynthia wasn't offering anything, and now he'd made her suspicious. "No reason. I heard the term recently and I don't know what it means."

"In relation to what? Why would I know?"

Ade wished he hadn't started this conversation. "Please don't be offended, Cynthia. A lot of abstract ideas are running around in my head right now. To me, 'soul-murder' sounds vaguely Faulknerian, and I just wondered if you can identify it, seeing as how you've read a lot of Faulkner."

Cynthia shot him a disbelieving look. "The answer's no." She paused, then blurted out, "I can see that everyone's already convicted Jack in their minds, but he's not a murderer. You don't know him. If he killed George, something must have caused him to do it. That's the only explanation."

Cynthia's sincerity left Ade unmoved. He could imagine no inner demon or outside force, or anything that inoffensive George Ellerbee could have done that might have caused Jack to butcher him with heavy shears.

CHAPTER TWENTY-TWO

The Pan Am 707 left for Paris on time. Dr. Joe Kemper sat with Kohler, and Cynthia had two big seats for herself and Robin. Kasprzak sat directly behind them, and carried the tickets and passports. When they landed in Paris, Dave Whitten, a political officer from the Embassy, was at plane-side with urgent instructions from Washington. Pan Am had ordered an unscheduled stop at Boston instead of flying directly to Dulles. This meant that Kemper had to somehow keep the Kohlers on board. Could this happenstance result in a legal challenge on venue, and send the trial to Boston?

On arrival in Boston, technically Kohler was free to go wherever he wanted. After the long flight, Joe worried that he'd want to stretch his legs. So just before landing, Joe said they'd only be on the ground a short time and suggested they all stay on board. Kohler, whose steady intake of scotch had made him sleepy, had been dozing. He nodded, bleary-eyed, and said nothing.

Back in Douala, it was time to focus on Maria Ellerbee and the casket, which had arrived in Douala in Ron's care after having been squeezed onto the chartered Cessna. Ade's plan was to accompany Maria and the casket to Washington on the next flight, and he called the Pan Am rep to confirm. He had bad news: "We can't take a corpse on board unless it's embalmed and we have a valid physicians' certificate."

Ade could see all their hard work coming undone. "There must be a way," he said. "We've got the lid soldered and the casket is steel-banded. I'll assign one of our people to guard it all the way across. Won't that do it?"

"There's nothing I can do."

"You gotta help us. We need to get that body back to the States. One man is already dead and another's fate hinges on whether we do this right."

"I understand," said the Pan Am rep. "If you want to embalm the body, I can help you. Those are the rules. It's out of my hands."

Stymied, Ade called Sally Rogers. "Maybe Hastings or the Secretary can work something with Pan Am in New York. If not, we're sunk."

Ade went to the living room, where Maria was sitting quietly, in tenuous control. He told her, "The Kohlers have gone back to Washington with Dr. Kemper and Pete Kasprzak. When they land, federal officials will take over."

Maria eyed him suspiciously. She wanted to hear 'arrest.' "Won't they put him in jail?" she asked, alarmed. "He killed my husband, and they'll let him go free?"

"I'm sure they'll make sure he's not at liberty. I just don't know the details. Certainly, they'll question him very closely. But remember, under our laws any person suspected of a crime has a lot of rights. A mistake by the prosecution can ruin the case. I know that State and Justice want to handle this one perfectly. There could be some tricky aspects to this case, for example, jurisdiction."

Ade didn't want to alarm her, but she had to realize that there was a lot more involved than just throwing Jack into the slammer until the trial.

"What is justice if a murderer is free to do as he pleases, and an innocent man is not avenged?" she cried, balling her fingers into a fist in frustration.

"Maria, this is just the beginning of a long process. You've got to be patient. For now, we've arranged it so that Jack lands first at Dulles. Where he lands and is first taken into custody is where he has to be tried. So I think that everyone's working hard on having the trial in the right place, and we're all going to testify."

This made sense, and Maria nodded in acquiescence. "*Bien*," she said. "You and Ron have been good to us, but I don't trust anyone else."

Ade had a sudden idea. "Those of us who knew George would like to arrange a memorial service for him here. You know the cathedral in Douala – it's very dignified. If you agree, we could hold it tomorrow morning. Would you like that?"

"Oh, Adrian, that would be special. We should do that." Maria brightened. Part of the problem, he now realized, was that in dealing with the emergency, Maria had been shunted aside. She'd never made any demands, but now that her husband was being paid some respect she began to feel better.

"I never had the chance to get to know George well," Ade said. "But I liked his lack of pretense, and he knew a lot more than he let on."

Maria looked up sharply, and then her eyes softened. "He was not a complicated man. He loved life, and he loved his country. Most of all, he loved people, but maybe he trusted them too much."

Next, Ade called the bishop at the cathedral and arranged a simple prayer and memorial service for the next morning at nine o'clock.

The cathedral in Douala was an oasis amid the city's cacophony, with a central gothic spire and dark wooden pews. Although anti-colonialist rhetoric was common coin in public life, on a personal level the remnants of the French presence, such as the cathedral and the programs of the *Alliance Francaise* were still deeply entrenched, and attended by Cameroonians of all ages.

It wouldn't have been wise to remove George's coffin from cold storage for the service, so Ron, ever-resourceful, found a close facsimile of George's casket in Douala's back alleys and got it to the cathedral, where he draped it with an American flag. Maria didn't notice the difference, and it meant a lot to her to say good-bye to her husband in this peaceful and holy place.

The Department had come through with a graceful condolence message from Secretary Markham drafted by Sally Rogers, commending George for his loyal service, his willingness to serve in difficult posts, and his value as a team player. All cables leaving the Department are signed with the last name of the incumbent secretary of state, but this one had a heading that said, "personal message to Mrs. George Ellerbee from Secretary of State Edward Markham."

Ade read out the Secretary's cable and added a eulogy of his own, praising George as a "conscientious and loyal colleague remembered by those who knew him, as well as by the local community, as a good man. We are confident that his good soul, which we his friends appreciated, will be easily acknowledged elsewhere." He felt awkward at the banality of his little speech, but the words seemed to provide solace to the grieving widow. Ron and Ade then removed the flag from the coffin, folded it neatly, and handed it to Maria. Her eyes were moist and her cheeks were tear-stained, but she looked up and said firmly, "Thank you for doing this for my husband." The little group felt sad, and moved, by her simple dignity.

After the service, they returned to Ron's residence for tea. They weren't there five minutes before the phone rang from Washington.

It was Charlie Stubblefield, Ade's old tennis nemesis who was heading up the Kohler working group. He dispensed with his usual opening banter.

"Pan Am says they can't budge on the coffin. It's international law and there's no wiggle room. But we just may have a plan."

Ade breathed in slowly, wondering what was coming. "OK, Charlie, let's have it."

Charlie's voice was more tense than Ade could ever remember. "The Pentagon says it can divert one of its C-141 Starlifter transports from Ascension Island in the Atlantic to Douala to pick up the casket, provided that we can get all the necessary clearances. Can you do that?"

During the cold war, airplanes from the Strategic Air Command were in the air around the clock, circling the globe lest a missile attack from the Soviet Union catch America with its planes on the ground and its missiles in their silos.

"Sure, we can do that," Ade said, thinking that he'd call a friend at the Ministry of Transportation and that Ron would work the problem with his contacts at the airport, and it could be arranged in a few days if they really pushed.

"Good. You have exactly two hours."

"What?" Ade exploded. "No way, Charlie. You know what it's like out here. Two weeks would be more like it. Tell them we need time."

The State Department is the most senior of the Cabinet departments, but it commands no airplanes. They have to be cajoled from the Defense Department, which has its own missions and imperatives. Apparently, Defense saw no overriding reason why one of its key aircraft should be pulled from its nation-guarding mission to transport a Foreign Service corpse back to the United States. Eventually, with Justice Department help, State prevailed. But the window of opportunity was cruelly brief.

"Two hours," Charlie repeated. "My watch says that it's eleven-fifteen a. m. there. At exactly one-fifteen that plane will touch down at Douala Airport. They can't be on the ground for more than fifteen minutes from touchdown to liftoff. They'll be airborne by one-thirty, casket or no casket. Let me ask you again. Can you do it?"

Ade paused briefly, but his temples were already pounding and mentally he was halfway to the airport. "Let 'er rip!" he shouted.

Ade rounded up Ron and Maria on the run and explained what had to be done. Ron and two Cameroonian admin employees grabbed the consular pick-up and raced for the morgue. Ade told Maria, "You're going home sooner than you thought. We're leaving for the airport NOW!"

They jumped into the Embassy sedan. It was eleven thirty-five. Maria looked relieved to be in motion, leaving behind the horror of her last days in Africa.

Ade was cranked up, reviewing his options, all of them lousy. To go through channels for clearances would take days. And maybe someone in the bureaucracy who didn't like America, some disgruntled francophobe or Soviet acolyte, would sabotage the effort by sitting on the clearances. It happened. If Ade appealed to the airport commander, most likely he'd only be alarmed and go running to his superiors. This was too momentous for a low-ranking airport commander to approve on his own. Ade gulped. There were no good options, but the clock was ticking. He thought again of his favorite general, Kutuzov in *War and Peace* who won by doing...nothing. Well, that was a different time and place and right here in Douala, now, something had to be done.

But that meant the C-141 crew would bring the plane in thinking that clearances had been given. The control tower would have no warning of the plane's arrival. They'd panic, thinking they were being invaded, and scramble the air force, part of which was parked on a military runway adjacent to the airport. There could be a mix-up with other incoming traffic, even a crash. Airport security forces would be called out, troops would be alerted. And whatever happened would be Ade's fault.

Luckily, the dawdling Douala traffic had thinned out for the lunch break, and they made it to the airport in forty minutes without running anyone down. Emeka, the consulate driver, was a real pro, moving the car smoothly around the undulating mass of trucks, cars, bicycles, wagons, and pedestrians with seeming ease.

Security precautions were rudimentary at the airport, so Ade's diplomatic pass got them past the first checkpoint. From that point, Emeka, who knew the airport and the guards well, drove the car through an open side gate right onto the tarmac.

It was now twelve forty-five. Thirty minutes to go. Things had gone well, but this had been the easy part. Ron still had to get through with the casket, and then they had to hope for a miracle when the C-141 arrived.

Maria was OK, but very nervous and apprehensive. Ade paced. He'd concocted a story about a crippled American military plane coming in for an emergency landing, waiting until ten minutes before touchdown to call the control tower. He hoped his alert would be just in time to calm the control tower and too late for them to do anything about it. But the car radio couldn't access the tower frequency, and after three tries he abandoned the effort, slamming the receiver down in frustration.

For now, their only option was to wait for the plane and hope for the best. Small talk was impossible, so they just occupied their respective spaces.

Eight minutes past one. A big Lufthansa 707 lumbered noisily down the runway and was airborne. They kept scanning the sky, straining to see any indication of an incoming. No plane. No Ron.

At 1:10, Ron burst through the employees door of the customs office, pushing an airport dolly with the casket on it. Large beads of sweat dripped from his brow and ran down his cheeks. His shirt was soaked.

At 1:12, they could barely make out a dark speck far in the distance, coming fast and taking shape. At 1:13 it was low over the ocean and starting its approach to the runway. Ade looked up at the control tower but could see no one through the colored glass. It was just as well, because all hell was breaking loose. The pilot had contacted the control tower, but because they knew nothing of the flight they refused permission to land and ordered the plane into a holding pattern. The pilot answered that he was making an emergency landing and the tower better keep everyone out of the way.

The huge C-141 descended steadily and touched down exactly on time, moving fast up the runway toward them. The roaring echoed in their ears as the plane swept past, kicking in the reverse engines to slow forward motion. As it wheeled and turned off the runway, Ron and Ade rushed out on the tarmac, waving frantically.

The officials in the control tower reacted quickly. They notified the airport security police, who sounded the alarm. Within minutes thirty men armed with pistols, rifles and stun grenades rushed out of their barracks on the adjacent air force grounds, jumped into an armed jeep and covered truck and headed for the C-141. An alarm started wailing, and airport workers looked up, startled and concerned.

The C-141 taxied toward the group and swung around in huge jerky motions. The pilot raised the cargo hatch and lowered the ramp. As soon as it touched the tarmac, twelve soldiers in camouflage battle dress ran out, M-16s at the ready, and formed a semi-circle around the rear of the plane. An army captain with the name "Jenkins" stenciled on his uniform hustled out from the cavernous interior of the plane.

"Get the cargo on board and let's get moving!, "he yelled.

Ron and Ade rushed the dolly up the ramp and into the cargo bay, and eight of the soldiers followed. They lifted the casket off the dolly, secured it inside the hold, and ran the dolly back onto the tarmac. Ade gave Ron a strong *abrazo*, grabbed Maria by the hand and hurried back inside the cargo bay, followed by the remaining soldiers.

Ade looked back towards the air base and saw the Cameroonian soldiers gaining on the airplane. This could be right where the whole thing fell apart, and Ade had to leave Ron standing there alone on the tarmac to deal with it. His last sight as the plane swung around and headed for the runway, with the cargo hatch just starting to rise, was of Ron striding towards the oncoming soldiers, frantically waving his massive arms.

The pilot hit full power as the plane lined up with the straightaway and it lunged forward, accelerating fast. Thirty seconds after takeoff it entered a cloud bank and disappeared. Ade looked at Maria and mouthed the words in exaggerated dumb show, "We're going home!" Maria smiled back wanly. The time was one thirty-three.

Just outside the terminal, several baggage handlers had looked up from their chores, gaping at the scene unfolding around the huge plane. They watched in silent fascination, and as the pilot hit the after-burners and the plane barreled down the runway, they burst into applause and whooped it up for a full five minutes.

The situation was less amusing for Ron, stranded on the runway trying to wave down two truckloads of grim-looking soldiers. If they'd arrived seconds earlier, they would've opened fire. The Americans might've responded from the cargo bay, causing a firefight between soldiers of two friendly countries, with the Americans at fault.

Once the soldiers saw that they couldn't catch the C-141, they turned on Ron, whose imposing bulk and diplomatic skills now served him well. His explanation to the airport security chief, larded with apologies, finally prevailed. After a tense hour they let him off, but only after he promised to send an official note taking full responsibility.

The next day, he was summoned to the Foreign Ministry in Yaounde and threatened with expulsion. Ambassador Hellyer, who'd missed all the fun but had stayed in Yaounde to pick up the pieces, was also subjected to some diplomatic scoldings and presented with an official protest.

The Embassy's apology made some sense to the practical Cameroonians, but their dignity had been bruised, to say nothing of their sovereignty. They were embarrassed and outraged that a foreign warplane could land and board cargo and passengers without even a hint of prior consultation. It was lucky that Cameroon wanted America's support on a couple of issues at the UN, and that it could be given without any diplomatic complications. Those chips were called in smartly in the kind of horse-trading that takes place among countries all the time. Eventually, the angry winds subsided, dissipated by the passage of time and the basic soundness of relations with Cameroon. Of course, none of this appeared in the press. It was all behind the scenes.

CHAPTER TWENTY-THREE

The plane carrying the Kohlers and their entourage was the first to reach Washington, landing at Dulles International. Charlie Stubblefield, as head of the Department's working group, was waiting to meet them, along with a U.S. marshal, a doctor from the Medical Division, and a Department security man.

Charlie thought that Jack looked apprehensive, almost haunted. He kept glancing around, as though looking for unseen assailants. Maybe he fears Ellerbee's ghost, or maybe this is what happens to people who serve in Tanako, Charlie thought.

Cynthia, looking calm and self-assured, carried the baby. She could've been any Foreign Service wife coming back for home leave after two years overseas. The contrast between her and Jack was startling.

The U. S. marshal stepped up right away and charged Jack with murder. But the Department wanted to get him straight to the hospital for observation, fearing that he might still be dangerous. Charlie walked up and said merely, "Hello Jack," without shaking hands. Kohler appeared not to recognize him.

"I'm head of the Department's working group. We're going to George Washington Hospital."

"I'm not going to jail, then?" Kohler, still numb, looked only slightly relieved.

"No, but you'll be under observation. I'll give you my number and you can contact me if you wish. Cynthia and the baby will be able to visit, and you can make calls to your family, your lawyer, whoever."

Kohler said only, "Even with all this, it's better to be here."

Family friends had offered Cynthia a place to stay, but she opted to rent an apartment in Arlington Towers in Rosslyn, just across the Potomac from Washington. She and Jack parted simply, but then he gave Robin a long, lingering hug, and turned away with a look of excruciating sadness.

Charlie, Kasprzak and the doctor drove Kohler to the hospital and left him as soon as he was checked into the psychiatric ward.

Several hours later, Ade and Maria landed at Andrews Air Force Base. Maria's sister and her husband were at Andrews to take her in tow, and the Department had made arrangements with the Virginia forensic authorities to take possession of the coffin and proceed with the autopsy.

As soon as Ade reached his hotel, he called Charlie, just finishing out the work day at the Department. They agreed to meet at Clyde's, a popular Georgetown watering hole, which was only a few minutes from the Department.

Charlie's unmistakable saunter and laid-back smile were welcome sights, and they shook hands warmly. "The pay may be lousy and the hours long, but you can't beat the issues," he said. "Who could've imagined this, even if he'd set out to write a lurid thriller?"

Ade felt the tension ease a bit. "I know, Charlie. But I have a feeling it's not over yet. Anyway, it's good to see you, even under these circumstances."

"Yeah, it must have been tough out there. But Ade, couldn't you have handled that airport row in Douala more smoothly? You know the Department regards the brandishing of weaponry and displays of force as unseemly."

"What do you mean? We never fired a shot."

"Well, next time we get the Pentagon to divert one of its planes, we'll have a guy on the ground who can solve problems and observe diplomatic courtesies."

"If you don't choose me, I won't mind. Now, what's been going on?"

"The press is asking why the Department didn't know it had a murderer in its ranks. Conspiracy theorists are grumbling about coverups and God knows what else. Senator Manning is saying that the Department's incompetent and has threatened an investigation. That's the last thing the Secretary wants – there's some high-level stuff going on with China, and it's very closely held. My guess is that restoring diplomatic relations might be in the works. If that were thrown off the tracks there'd be hell to pay."

Senator Hawthorne Manning was the senior senator from Georgia and the Chairman of the Senate Foreign Relations Committee. He regarded the Foreign Service as a refuge for liberal elitists whose luxurious living overseas made them incapable of the hard work of fighting "godless communism." He'd worked hard to prevent any opening to Beijing. His press assistant, Walter Jurgens, bore a simmering hatred for Foreign Service officers stemming from his having failed the oral exam even though he'd easily passed the written. He liked to tell anyone who'd listen that, "Those snotnoses on my oral couldn't take my southern accent and that I was a lot smarter than they were." Ade mulled over what Charlie was saying. "Well, if it'll help, I'll be glad to talk to the Senator, or Jurgens, or brief the press."

"Not a chance. Manning would have you for lunch. He's tough, and if he and Jurgens have an issue they could care less about truth or justice. And don't forget, a Senator as powerful as Manning always has the last word."

"Jesus, Charlie. Right now Ron and I know more about what happened than any other people except Kohler himself. Why shouldn't I talk to them?"

Charlie looked unhappy. "Because the Department doesn't want you to, and don't ask me why, because I don't know."

"Because of what? The airport caper? I thought we pulled that off pretty well." "No, no. You know this building, Ade. There's always more than meets the eye." "Well, if there is, I'm damned well going to stay here until I find out."

"I know how you feel," Charlie said, rubbing his lip. "They want you to stick around for two days to brief the legal and medical people on every detail you can remember, and help us work out a media strategy. Then you'll have to go back. In fact, the Department'll be happy when you're back in far-away Cameroon. Maybe it's just that your being here makes you a magnet for the press and all the speculation. Maybe having Senator Manning on the warpath could undermine the high-level stuff going on. Whatever it is, the Department will protect you, if it can."

"That makes me feel great, Charlie. Something's going on that affects me directly, and I haven't a clue and the Department won't let me find out anything."

"You're not the first guy who's been in that position around here. But relax, pal. Nothing's going to happen to you."

$$* * *$$

Ade was feeling numb with jet lag after the trip and upset that he'd just become expendable to the Kohler case. He went back to his hotel and slumped on the bed, defeated, but suddenly remembered the notebook he'd taken from Jack's drawer. In the rush, he'd had no time to even look at it or the letter folded inside.

The entries under "Schreber" still made no sense to him. He'd make copies, pass the notebook to Charlie to give to the investigators, and see if he could find anyone who might know who Schreber might be. He unfolded the letter and saw that it was addressed to Jack from a Foreign Service friend in Washington who'd served with Ellerbee in Moscow, and dated June 15. After a paragraph of personal news, Ade read: "How're you and George getting along? Ask your little colleague about the visa scam in Moscow, and the charge that he snared the ringleader in a homosexual act."

Ade put down the letter. After the intensity of the last few days, he was now entering a different realm of strange and unconnected elements over which he had no control. His involvement had even become a threat to himself and his family and not at all like the puzzle he once thought he could solve by himself.

He ordered a sandwich from room service and flicked on the TV. His attention was starting to wander as he watched the first routine items, and almost missed the start of what came next: "Senator Hawthorne Manning today charged the State Department with a coverup in a case in which a Foreign Service officer allegedly brutally murdered his subordinate in the tiny African island nation of Tanako. The Senator ridiculed suggestions that the officer had became unhinged by the brutality on the island, and said that a major security lapse might be at the heart of the case."

Senator Manning's face appeared as he read a statement: "I am deeply concerned about the murder of an American employee in our Embassy in Tanako. I have information that one of the American officials was involved in a serious breach of security, that the men were unfit to represent the United States, and engaged in activities offensive to the American people. If necessary, I will use the full investigative powers of the Senate to find out how they passed through the State Department screening process, and those responsible will be punished."

Stunned, Ade called Charlie, who'd missed the newscast. "I'll make some phone calls. Let's meet tomorrow before work, in the State cafeteria. Seven-thirty."

The next morning, Charlie looked somber. "Manning's got information related to a major security leak awhile back. Could be serious."

Ade told Charlie about the notebook and the letter and handed them over. "I can't make it out, but maybe the investigators over at Justice can find something." "The letter looks important, but the notes? They just seem peculiar."

Ade said, "There wasn't a hint of a security breach or improper behavior in either Jack's or George's files. No one I talked to knew anything." *Maybe there was something to Ginger's speculation after all. Now nothing can be ruled out.*

"Manning wouldn't make something up out of the blue," Charlie said. "I was thinking that this case was manageable if we stayed on course. But it's getting scary, and now we're on center stage, or will be shortly."

"But we've done nothing wrong! In fact, I thought I'd done well, including picking those two guys in the first place. There was every reason to think they'd be good." "Right. But now people are twisting things for their own purposes. The Department wants to handle this right, but if keeping a wall around the high-level China stuff means sacrificing low-level folks like us, they won't hesitate even a second."

"We should be able to prevent that."

"I'm not so sure. Despite the risks you took over there, you had the initiative and made the decisions. Here it's different. Powerful people who don't even know us will decide our fate, and we can only react to events."

Ade smiled. "Totally helpless, like Rosencrantz and Guildenstern in *Hamlet*."

"Exactly," Charlie answered, frowning. "Trial preparations are another problem. Kohler's lawyer will do everything to get the case thrown out."

"Sure, he'll claim that the US court has no jurisdiction, but what about venue?" "If Kohler can't be tried in the federal court in Alexandria, the case goes to Boston, where Pan Am made that unscheduled stop. That really screwed things up. But if he can't be tried in either Alexandria or Boston, he walks."

"That's crazy. He's accused of premeditated murder. There's a corpse and no other suspects, and Kohler's admitted that he did it. What more do you need?"

"It seems simple, but there's lots of case law on it. Like anything the lawyers get ahold of, it gets complicated. Also, Kohler has hired himself a first-rate lawyer." "Who's that?"

"Ned Dilbaugh, of Connors and Dilbaugh, one of the city's A-list firms. Cynthia's old man must be paying the tab, because Jack's salary would never cover it. Dilbaugh himself will lead the defense, and if he didn't think he could get a high-profile win, he wouldn't touch it. Oh, and by the way, make sure you see Harlan Hastings before you head back. He wants to have a chat with you."

"Good old laugh-a-minute Harlan. Still, I've always admired his dedication and he's always been decent to me. Wonder what he wants?"

"Me too. Tell me what he says."

CHAPTER TWENTY-FOUR

Harlan Hastings had held two important ambassadorships in Africa and had been Assistant Secretary in Washington for the last two years. Despite his veteran status, very few people knew much about his personal life beyond that he lived in Bethesda with a wife and two children, had a passion for golf that he usually exercised by himself, and vacationed for two weeks every summer on Martha's Vineyard, in a cottage that had been in his wife's family for at least three generations. Ade had known him for seven years and had grown to appreciate his no-frills manner. In all that time, they'd never discussed anything but Africa and the problem of the moment.

Hastings motioned for Ade to sit on the two-seater couch facing his executive desk, while he sat down quickly in a high-backed armchair.

"We're going to pull you out of Yaounde," Hastings said without a hint of introduction. Ade was so astonished he could think of nothing to say.

"You probably heard Senator Manning's broadside. You did nothing wrong, but it's better all-around if you're out of there."

So Charlie was right! "I just got there, Harlan. I went to the murder scene, handled the investigation, got the families out, and all the rest. And we might be on to something with the oil reserves and the non-Africans who might be using that island for terrorism. So now you're pulling me out of it because a Senate windbag makes some wild charges. Good State Department logic, not to mention courage!"

"The Department can't afford to have this case balloon into a scandal. You can have two weeks to go back and say your goodbyes, and tell people you're being considered for an important new post."

"And where would that be? Siberia?"

"Don't know yet. But you can come back here on administrative leave."

"Administrative leave! I won't even have a job, then! Why don't you just say that I'm being fired!"

Hastings didn't appear the slightest bit flustered by Ade's sputtering. "Because you're not. But you need to be out of the way for a while. In fact, if you promise me that you can rein in the impetuous side of your nature, we'll arrange an academic year for you at Georgetown or Johns Hopkins. It could be good for you. Restrain your penchant for excessive activism. Take some courses, give some lectures. Keep a low profile."

"Jesus, I might as well quit. Is that what you want?"

"Ade, this is just a bump in the road. Don't take it too hard. I want you to know that I realize you did a hell of a job out there."

"Thanks, Harlan. It's a funny way of giving recognition."

"I understand. Sooner rather than later, I think you'll come to see that this was necessary and not take it personally. Things like this aren't unusual. It's just that one shouldn't have overblown expectations." Ade had been starting to calm himself down, but this set him off again.

"Overblown expectations! I was just doing the job, as best I could. And now, after I've been curtailed and humili-ated, what should I expect?"

"Around here, whatever it is, don't expect justice."

Ade walked mechanically down the long, so-familiar sixth floor corridor, not noticing anything, numb with hurt and confusion. He was too angry to respond to Harlan's offer of an academic year, and totally uncertain about what to do next, other than go back to Yaounde and pack his bags. That, at least, was a direct order. But what he did know was that, one way or another, he'd find out why Jack Kohler killed George Ellerbee.

✳ ✳ ✳

Ade returned to Yaounde three days later, still bruised, and now seeing both Washington and Tanako as sinister, but in different ways.

Ginger's greeting was warm and welcoming, but Ade sensed a holding back. After his travails, he wanted some outpouring of emotion, short of tears and dependency, but a clear sign that he'd been missed. He didn't get it. But he forced himself to realize that his own problems were only a part of the family mosaic.

Greg had served his suspension, but felt humiliated by the punishment, which he thought was unfair. Ade could well empathize with that. But it was disturbing that Greg had changed from a happy and well-adjusted kid to one who was evasive and brooding, with few friends. "Greg's needed more time with his father," Ginger said, frowning.

"Looks like he'll get it," Ade said. "I've been fired as DCM and we're going back to Washington. I'll be on administrative leave. No more late evenings at work. Weekends free. Somehow, I'm less than elated."

Ginger shared his outrage as he explained Harlan's decision. "They're making you the scapegoat, the bastards!" she said. "They can't do that. You should fight it."

"They've done it. I could resign and blow the whistle, but no one would pay attention for more than half a day. And it could upset the China business, and that really is important. Besides, I just don't feel like attacking the Department."

"You guys, so full of nobility and sense of duty. You do everything they ask, and they walk all over you, not to mention your family! And what does it get you? I'll tell you what you get. You get to lose a part of your humanity."

"Ginger, that's too much. I don't feel that I've lost my humanity by doing the King's business. We agree that I've been screwed, but let's give Harlan the benefit of the doubt. Something good could come out of it. At least the three of us will be back in Washington, with more time for each other." Ade looked at Ginger, waiting for some reaction, but she said nothing.

✳ ✳ ✳

In the few days that Ade was away, Dick Hellyer had reacted testily when so much detailed followup on the Kohler case had dropped on his desk and Ade wasn't there to bulldoze through it. It seemed that suddenly every bureau in the Department had a major interest in the case – medical, legal, congressional relations, admin, consular, and more. All the action cables from those bureaus had to be cleared by Sally Rogers. She did a good job of filtering out items that were less important, but still there was a mountain of demands on the Embassy. So Hellyer fussed, and grumbled that the burden of the Kohler case had fallen on him. There was "important diplomatic business brewing," he said, and this was no time to be distracted by "personality cases."

He was also put out by the decision to recall Ade. Despite their different styles, they had got on well and Hellyer appreciated how much he depended on his deputy. It was that, more than the unfairness of Ade's transfer, that was on his mind.

"Washington wants me to go to Tanako to get Barreras's permission for some FBI investigators to come over and do their thing," he told Ade. "I want you to go with me, so we'll have to do it before you leave. Let's get right on that."

Ade was also anxious to find out if the station chief had obtained the passenger manifests for Tanako flights, and whether they obtained any nuggets. He had, and there were no Japanese passengers on any commercial flights going back a couple of months. That meant that either the Japanese had arrived earlier, or come by non-commercial means. He'd ask Washington to check with Japanese intelligence sources to see if this information matched anything known about the movements and whereabouts of Japanese Red Army members believed to be in Lebanon. So Ade had some urgent new tasks even before he'd checked into his own office. When he did so, his secretary briefed him with a long list of problems, meetings, and appointments to be attended to. "Oh, and a Mr. Corson from Transcon Petroleum wants to see you. He seemed to know all about you and was very insistent, so I gave him a ten o'clock."

"Did he say what he wanted?"

"He said he'd make it clear enough to you. Has to do with Tanako."

Rafael Corson was in his office promptly at ten, a smooth, self-assured man wearing an expensive Italian sport short, three buttons open, with the obligatory gold chain highlighting his hairy chest. Ade resisted the strong temptation to assume that he had close Mafia connections. His card said only, "international business consultant." More interesting was his companion, Madeleine Molnar, a willowy blond who defied place-typing, partly because she spoke flawless, unaccented English. Corson introduced her only as "my assistant." Ade's first impression was that she wasn't the kind of person to be an assistant to anyone. She had on a long wraparound rough cotton African skirt, which parted just enough to afford a glimpse of tantalizingly provocative legs every time she crossed them. Her initial role seemed to be to provide an enticing backdrop to the business at hand, because Corson did the talking.

"We want the drilling rights to the Gulf of Guinea, but we're not the only ones," he explained. "You know what the stakes are – the kind that attracts high players, and sharks. We're an American company, and our friends in Washington want us to succeed. We'd like you to help us."

Because Transcon was a huge international conglomerate, it probably paid very little in taxes to the American treasury, except for those levied on gasoline dispensed at the pump. Nevertheless, embassies often worked hard to make sure that American companies received fair treatment overseas.

"I'd like to help, but there are some problems you may already know about. First, Antonio Barreras is ferocious about keeping foreigners away from his offshore oil. I don't know of anything that's likely to change his mind. Second, we just had a murder on Tanako and our Embassy is closed. Third, I'm being transferred back to Washington around the end of the month."

Corson looked unfazed and Madeleine crossed her legs.

"Yes, your two men there might've been very helpful. A real tragedy," Corson said solemnly. "I'd actually met Ellerbee on a visit there a few months back. One of those unassuming chaps who knew a lot more than he let on. He could've been useful." "For what? Barreras has a tight lid on everything, including oil exploration." "My information is that there may be some changes. If that happens, we want to be ready. Some of the other players, especially the French, are doing the same thing. They're not hesitant to do whatever's necessary, over and under the table, to get what they want. As you know, American companies can't do those things."

"I'll do whatever I can during my remaining time here. I'll probably make one more trip over there before I leave."

"All we'd ask is for you to open some doors for us. I'm located in Paris, so if the time comes I can be here in a day. I hope we meet again soon."

As they were leaving, Madeleine leaned toward him so that her long hair almost brushed his face. "You've been very helpful," she said, in such a way that Ade wasn't sure whether she was being sincere or mocking him.

Ade arrived home that evening to discover several half-filled suitcases upstairs. "You and Greg are really eager to get to Washington," he said.

"We'll get to Washington eventually, but first we're going to Lexington."

"What?" Ade exploded. "What the hell's the sense of that? Everyone's pulling surprises on me these days. All of them awful. At least I thought I could count on you."

Ade's rush put Ginger on the defensive. "It's best if we go to Lexington for this year. You don't know what you'll be doing and you're still absorbed with this case, no matter what Harlan says. I need a full-time husband and Greg needs a father, and this will give us all time to straighten things out so they're right again."

"Good thinking, Ginger. You both need me, so you're going to live 500 miles away. If you really needed me, why didn't you pick California!"

"I've got to do it this way, Ade. Greg's floundering at school. He's very unhappy about a whole lot of things, but maybe it's just growing up. His marks are terrible, the teachers don't see any reason for it and are starting to give up on him. Nothing seems to work. But Lexington has good schools, and Greg has friends there from summer vacations, back in an environment where he's done well. Mom and dad are there so I can spend some time with them before they get too old, and I can pick up my studies." Ade was incredulous. It was quitting. It would destroy the family. He couldn't allow it. "What about you? Do you want to cut out too?"

"I'm not doing this for me. But after we get settled I'll start work again."

"Is that the real reason?" To Ade, this move was all wrong, and Ginger's determination to leave cut deep.

What would have been a long and painful row was cut short by the suddenness of Ginger's travel. She was businesslike, and had already made her reservations. Her cool efficiency left Ade blustery and sulky. He asked, "Is there anything more to this move than what you've said?"

Ginger put her hand on his arm, a gesture more pacifying than reassuring. "I don't think so, Ade. But I'll have a chance to think about some things, us included."

Ade felt always off-balance by her hot and cold ambivalence. One minute an ecstatic affirmation, the next an ambiguous withdrawal. Would he ever really understand his auburn-haired, pony-tailed beauty who wanted to be appreciated for her brains and railed at the lechery of men who leered at her? Ade vowed to find the answer to that puzzle, too.

"I know it's been rough for you," he said, trying to buck up his sagging morale even as he searched for signs of devotion in Ginger. "But we have so much going for us. I never thought you were unhappy."

"Don't be so dramatic," Ginger said, with a smile that failed to give off warmth. "We're still a family, despite everything that's happened. I just need some time."

Driving Ginger and Greg to the airport, Ade kept glancing at her briefly. She ran Ade through a checklist of things she'd done to make his life easier, like special instructions to the cook for food that he liked, as though he'd starve without her preparations. But she was all business, right up to the very end. He wondered if she'd lose interest in the Kohler case when she picked up her new life in Lexington.

He desperately hoped that she'd stay with it. He'd told her about the notebook and the letter. "The letter is surely important," she'd said, "and maybe the notes too. I think I recall a Freudian case about a German government official with a name like that from one of my forensic courses. It's pretty well-known. I'll check it out as soon as I can."

"It would be a lucky hit if that's what it was."

Their surface cordiality didn't alter the bittersweet nature of their parting, outwardly cheerful because they were on the threshold of new experiences and because they wanted to seem upbeat for Greg's benefit. But inside, they both felt ambivalent because their future together was in play. There was a catch in his voice as Ade gave Greg a hug. "I'll miss you kiddo," he said. "Take care of your mother." With repressed emotion, Ginger said, "Look after yourself. We'll be fine, and you will be too."

He stood on the tarmac feeling empty as they climbed the stairs to the plane. In the blink of an eye Ade seemed to have been transformed from an upbeat Foreign Service officer doing his job right to a diplomat on the shelf, struggling to save his career and his marriage, and maybe losing both.

CHAPTER TWENTY-FIVE

Ade had cabled an official request to the Foreign Ministry in Arania for an appointment with Barreras. For such things, the government of Tanako was capriciously unresponsive. Maybe it was Barreras's way of thumbing his nose at Americans, or maybe he just operated on his own voodoo timetable. Three days later, Ade repeated the request, and Tanako finally replied that the President would receive Ambassador Hellyer on September 18 at noon. He and Hellyer decided they'd raise the Transcon request if Barreras approved the FBI visit.

They flew over on September 17, staying at the Embassy residence in Arania. Although the Embassy was still closed, Ade had been able to contact Nguema to round up the driver and meet them at the airport. It was a cheery sight when he spotted Nguema's brave, friendly smile in this place where so much evil had occurred.

Ade greeted him warmly, clasping his left hand to Nguema's shoulder as they shook hands. There had been no new problems since the murder. Barreras probably wanted the Embassy to reopen, as a matter of prestige and to have as a whipping boy. This day, the somber streets of Arania seemed even quieter than usual. No buses, taxis, or public vehicles made their rounds, but a few Tanakians pedaled by ponderously on heavy, black, single-speed Chinese bicycles. The few people in sight moved listlessly, seemingly without direction or purpose. Most shops remained shuttered, their rusted advertising signs the only evidence of their former activity.

They slowed for a traffic light, but it wasn't working. Nguema explained that power was out, with the downtown allotted only three hours of electricity in the morning, and three more in the evening. A young girl ran out towards the car as they braked for the intersection. She was selling cigarettes, not by the pack, but individually. She looked to be about fourteen, but probably was older.

Ade rolled down the window. "How much is one cigarette?" he asked Nguema as the girl approached the car.

"About ninety cents, US," he answered. "People can't afford to buy a whole pack, so they buy them like this."

"Ninety cents!" Hellyer exclaimed. "No wonder they sell them one at a time." Hellyer tended to attribute poverty to human laziness, but that thesis crumbled here, where a young barefoot girl was working hard to sell cigarettes one by one.

Ade crumpled up a five dollar bill and handed it to her, explaining in Spanish that she could keep the cigarette because he didn't smoke. She didn't answer, but her eyes opened wide. As their car pulled away, she allowed herself a little skip of pleasure, but curtailed it quickly lest she be noticed and her new treasure snatched from her.

As they entered the residence, Ade reminded Hellyer how helpful Chris Kanu and the Camejos had been, and suggested a thank-you call. In the Kohlers' pantry, Hellyer came across Kohler's ample liquor supply, and his face brightened at the prospect of doing something gracious at no cost to himself. "Ade, send over a case of Jack's scotch to Ambassador Kanu with my card, and tell him thanks for all his help. Same for the Camejos."

The next morning, Hellyer and Ade drove to the Presidential Palace to meet Barreras. The building was spacious but garish, as though the architect had been told to include every pretentious and non-functional Western architectural idea that he could, while excluding anything reflecting African culture. On nearly every wall, there were large color photographs and oil paintings of the President striking heroic poses.

After thirty minutes, an aide ushered them into the President's sitting room, where he received visitors. Only his inner circle made it into his actual office, the one where the former Foreign Minister had been "defenestrated."

Finally, a door covered with gold leaf opened, and the President entered. He was wearing a suit with a white shirt and conservatively-patterned tie. It was hard to imagine that he'd pushed his Foreign Minister through the window and ordered the torture and executions of thousands of his countrymen. He was about five feet nine, with strong, wide shoulders, but his brown, double-breasted suit concealed a well-developed paunch. Few people beyond Tanako would recognize his picture, but he had the air of a man who's used to being recognized and feared. His gray hair was short and frizzled, and he wore gold-rim glasses, looking incongruously like a prosperous African businessman, not at all like a man who had turned his country into an *abattoir*. "Welcome, Mr. Ambassador," he said in Spanish, his voice guttural.

"Good morning, Mr. President," Hellyer replied. "Thank you for your time. I know that your schedule is very busy."

"Indeed it is. Only this morning I arranged a loan from the International Monetary Fund for a new road to help my people get their goods to market."

Ade had briefed Hellyer on this, so he knew right away that this was nonsense. Barreras had in fact destroyed the markets, and had even said recently that people who produced surpluses for profit were capitalist bloodsuckers. All surpluses would go to the state, he'd said, and violators would be punished. Everyone knew what that meant.

But getting IMF funding was lucrative stuff – construction kickbacks, payoffs, money for Barreras and his cronies. He'd indeed planned a new road, from Arania to his extended family's village, about ten miles away. Other villages on the road would benefit, but no one else. This wasn't economic development, but clan favoritism. Even more blatant than what some American congressmen do for their pals, Ade thought. Hellyer sucked in his breath and responded, "I hope that the road will open up the interior and not just provide access for a few villages."

Barreras eyed him suspiciously. "When you say 'open up,' perhaps what you really mean is opening up our country to foreign exploitation. I won't permit it. With foreign money comes foreign control. We'd rather be poor and free than rich and in chains," said Barreras, repeating an anti-colonial *cliché* resonant throughout Africa.

But your people are poor _and_ in chains, Ade thought. Hellyer pressed on: "What about the Gulf of Guinea?" he asked. "We understand that there are substantial oil reserves there. They could help to develop your country."

"Imperialists are very anxious to exploit our reserves, but I promise you that foreigners will not touch our oil."

"I predict that someday you will find it in your interest to change your mind," Hellyer said. "But the purpose of our visit today concerns the incident in our Embassy a few weeks ago. Mr. Kohler will be tried for murder. We'd like to have three FBI investigators come to Tanako, to make sure we have all possible evidence."

The slight, pinched smile that Barreras had employed to mask his distaste dissolved. He pursed his lips, and his eyes narrowed. "I remember the incident well. Your people trampled on our sovereignty. One of them was not even accredited, and behaved like the Queen's viceroy. Worse, the hasty escape of the murderer, arranged by your government, thwarted the exercise of justice. Here we deal with criminals harshly. Murderers receive summary punishment. We don't condone their crimes." Hellyer argued back. "Sir, this case was unusual. Mr. Zimmerman, who discovered the crime, and Mr. Nadherny here worked directly with your Interior Minister, even permitting an inspection of the Embassy, which is American sovereign territory."

Barreras was unmoved. "The fact is that they had no authority, and my Minister allowed them excessive liberties. I was most unhappy with his performance and was obliged to reprimand him sternly."

Ade worked hard to stifle a smile at the image of Barreras taking his nephew to the woodshed. Hellyer continued his brief. "Never before has a Foreign Service employee been murdered in an American embassy. Only Americans were involved, but we need your help to learn the facts. We've proved to you that there's no plot."

"My Minister discovered some hand grenades," answered Barreras triumphantly, ignoring Hellyer's point. "Evidence of your support for plotters."

Hellyer pulled in his breath again, a mannerism he'd come to use when dealing with frustration. "Those were for self-defense only. There weren't enough of them to attack a candy store, much less assist some plot."

Barreras was growing irritated at Hellyer for continuing to argue when it was clear he'd already made up his mind. "We should put this unhappy incident behind us," he said with a frown. "We're willing to put our grievances aside and consider the case closed. Allowing your FBI to come here would attract unwelcome attention and revive memories that are best forgotten. No FBI investigators will come. My decision is final." Hellyer flushed with irritation, but quickly suppressed it. "Mr. President, I'd like you to reconsider. This case is extremely important to us."

Barreras seemed to be enjoying delivering an unequivocal "no" to the Americans. "There'll be no foreign agents on Tanakian soil," he said. "If you send investigators here, I'll have no choice but to detain them." The room was suddenly chilly.

Hellyer stared at the floor for a moment. "I'm sorry you feel that way, Mr. President. I thank you for your time," Hellyer said with a weary tone, and rose to leave.

He'd done his best, but didn't take defeats easily, which was why he avoided controversies he wasn't sure of winning. He held his own negotiating skills in high regard, and tended to take turndowns personally. But he also worried that he'd be scorned when the Department heard that he'd failed with Barreras. The Department assumed that you'd get your way with such people. That's what ambassadors and embassies were for. So when Hellyer headed right for the airport to avoid spending another night in Arania he'd again turned testy, and had Ade call Washington to relay the bad news, rather than report it himself.

The next morning, Ade went to the Embassy to meet with Nguema and the other Tanakian employees, to reassure them that the Embassy would stay closed for a while but would reopen in a few months. He also wanted to have another look around. Ellerbee's office records were a mess, so at least Kohler was right on that score. More important, they yielded no relevant clues. There was a desk calendar opened to August 30, the day of the murder. Ade thumbed through it and noted that Ellerbee had met with Rafael Corson on May 22. There were no other references to Corson, but Ade made a mental note to do a background check on Corson and his tawny assistant.

It took Ade the rest of the day to touch base with potential witnesses, including Chris Kanu and Rogelio Camejo. They welcomed him as an old friend, but on instructions from their home offices refused to discuss anything connected with the murder. Rogelio at least volunteered, "We had no idea that there was animosity between them." Chris Kanu said simply, "You came the day after the murder and talked to Jack. You saw for yourself how he was, so you know everything I know." Ade wondered how this wall of silence would affect the defense. Testimony on Kohler's state of mind would be crucial if he was going to plead insanity.

It looked like this trip wouldn't yield a single nugget. He'd justified staying on after Hellyer left by insisting that he'd pick up something useful. Now he'd have to go back to Yaounde empty-handed. After a solitary supper at the residence he turned out the light, lonely and frustrated by failure.

He was startled awake by the unmistakable sound of gunfire, the rat-tat of several machine guns, then some answering bursts in the distance. This was followed by an explosion, and more gunfire. Ade quickly slipped into his clothes and crawled to the window so that he could peer out without being seen. The early morning light was rapidly filling the sky in the east, and Ade could make out some black smoke billowing upwards, about a half mile away.

He left his room and found Mba, who lived in a small detached shack just behind the kitchen. She'd come into the main house the minute she'd heard the gunfire, and she was scared.

"Do you know what that could be?" Ade asked.

"No sir. Don't know nothin' about it, but they's fightin' goin' on," she said. Ade looked out onto the grounds of the residence. The Tanakian guards were nowhere to be seen. Sporadic gunfire continued, but it wasn't coming any closer.

Ade switched on the radio. There was only one station on all of Tanako, run by the government, and it came on at six every morning. It was now almost 6:10. Ade got nothing but static as he fine-tuned the dial.

If the government radio station was off the air, that could mean either that there was something wrong with the transmitter, or this was a coup attempt.

At seven o'clock the static was broken by a tape of recorded martial music. At 7:15, a shrill and excited voice read what sounded like a prepared statement: "This morning, patriotic forces of the Committee for Revolutionary Justice attacked the Presidential Palace and captured the tyrant, Antonio Barreras. He and his running dogs have been taken into custody and soon will be judged by the people. The government is now under the control of the Committee. Until order is completely restored, citizens should stay off the streets. The *Juventud* has full authority to maintain order and will carry out the directives of the Committee."

Those guys again, Ade thought. And who controlled the *Juventud*? Alejandro Sudopo, the Interior Minister. *I'll bet he's carried out a coup against his own uncle!*

By 9:30, with the humid morning clouds giving away to the searing equatorial sun, the gunfire had stopped. The radio announcements became more detailed, in Spanish and two local dialects, and it looked like the coup was complete. If so, Barreras's iron rule had been toppled with astonishing speed and efficiency. Ade reasoned that with Barreras so suspicious, only a tiny core of people were really trusted. In that case, the coup plotters would need only a few key officers from Tanako's ragtag army to capture the Palace, kill the President's guards, and seize the radio station, transmitter intact. If they'd moved swiftly, they might've been able to take over the entire government with no more than 100 men. Still, a slip anywhere along the way could've brought disaster.

By noon, two Land Rovers with rooftop loudspeakers were circulating through the city streets, proclaiming the downfall of Barreras and the installation of a new government. One of the residence guards showed up and told Mba that people were appearing in the streets in defiance of the ban, but that the *Juventud* was keeping order and the crowds were peaceful. The people looked happy, he said, and there was cheering and singing. One of the radio broadcasts Ade monitored reported that Alejandro Sudopo, former Minister of the Interior, had been named interim President.

Ade had to see for himself what was going on, so he took the Embassy Plymouth and drove to the square in front of the old cathedral, taking care to park on a side street.

The sudden lifting of years of repression had transformed the garbage-littered square and its crumbling colonial buildings. The people who'd been bottled up in their squalid shop houses for so long exploded into the open, their energies joyously released. The square, usually deserted, was filled with celebrants, clapping, chanting and dancing to a hundred pulsating drums. They had started a bonfire with plywood crates, old cardboard and tires, and posters of Barreras in heroic poses. The flames blackened the stiff paper and peeled away Barreras's face as the people cheered.

Ade positioned himself by a large pillared archway near the cathedral, where he could observe from a central position and duck for cover if necessary. As he watched, fascinated by the crowd's spontaneity, he noted that the square was effectively cut off by small squads of *Juventud* and security police at the key intersections. There would be no triumphal marching through the streets or sacking of the Palace by this crowd.

Suddenly, from a side street only 100 yards away, a group of twenty armed men emerged. They turned and started moving in Ade's direction, clearing the way through the crowd. He eased back against the pillar. As the group approached, Ade recognized the man in the center. It was Alejandro Sudopo, now the Interim President of Tanako, walking on foot and showing his face in the wake of his successful coup.

Ade had to admit that he looked impressive in the flush of victory, a confident smile on his face and a swagger in his step. He was now barely ten yards away, waving to the cheering crowd, when he turned his head and spotted Ade against the pillar. He didn't pause, but his surprise was evident as he approached until he was just five paces from Ade. "You again!" he shouted, not smiling. "Why are you here?"

Ade felt good about the surprise Sudopo was registering. "I'm here to look into reopening our Embassy. I even have an entry visa this time. Now that you're President, I hope you'll want to have better relations with the United States."

Sudopo was trying hard to figure out how Ade knew to be in Arania on this particular day, and not coming up with any answers. Only a few of his own trusted men were in the loop, so how did this meddlesome *gringo* know about it?

"You are welcome here, Mr. Nadherny," Sudopo said, resuming his triumphal posture. "I'm sure we'll meet again."

"I look forward to it, Mr. President."

So Ade returned to Yaounde with a sizable nugget after all. Even Hellyer said, "I don't know how you manage to get yourself involved in so much action when you supposedly have a desk job."

CHAPTER TWENTY-SIX

Ade reported his first person account of the coup to Washington, which found it only marginally interesting because there appeared to be no American priorities involved. But even as he was phasing himself out in Yaounde, Ade was drawn to the drama of a new regime taking over in Arania.

Sudopo had himself proclaimed President of Tanako in his first official act. His second was no less decisive: Barreras was dragged before a firing squad and buried quickly at a secret site, a more humane death than his enemies had received. The new regime announced that Barreras had been executed for "crimes against the people."

Sudopo also lightened the heavy hand that Barreras had imposed on the economy. Fishermen were again allowed to fish, and the cocoa plantations were reopened as government cooperatives. The nightly tortures at the Black Bitch ended, as did the public show trials and executions, but freedom didn't blossom. Schools reopened, but under government control and with emphasis on third world and Marxist indoctrination. Political activities were still forbidden, and the Black Bitch still held many people who had committed no crime other than to be considered potential opposition.

Ade also wondered what the real reason was for the coup. Surely Sudopo didn't have love for the people in mind when he overthrew his uncle. The answer wasn't long in coming. Sudopo announced at the end of his first week in power that Tanako had the potential to be the next major oil producing nation, and that bids for deep water exploration would be opened shortly, with international oil companies eligible to participate. Ade passed this news on to Hellyer, saying, "Blood may be thicker than water, but oil is thicker yet. Maybe this'll get Washington's attention."

"That it will," Hellyer said. "And not just Washington's."

Hellyer was right. The next day he received a phone call from Harlan Hastings, advising him of the impending visit to Tanako of a representative from Transcon, a Mr. Rafael Corson. He was going to Tanako as an advance man, and wanted the Embassy to set up an appointment with the new President and his Minister of Petroleum. Ambassador Hellyer was pleased to tell Hastings that Corson was already known to the Embassy, and in fact Nadherny had already met him.

"Good," Hastings said. "Tell him to render all appropriate assistance. If he has to go over to that damn island again, that's OK too. Transcon has an open door at the White House, and a lot of clout on the Hill. If American oil companies get in there, we'll have to reopen the Embassy and add a citizens services unit. We were going to close that place and save some money."

Shortly after that conversation, Ade received a telephone call from Corson from Paris. "We're arriving in Tanako next Tuesday. If you can, get us into the President and some of his top guys. That's the most important step. But we need to take a look around and scope out the support infrastructure if we decide to come in."

Ade booked a return visit to Tanako for Monday, and to his surprise President Sudopo's office quickly granted the requested appointment for Transcon. The fact that everyone still seemed to be relying on him to get the work done helped to assuage his wounded spirit.

Later, with no official receptions to attend for once, Ade spent a rare evening at home, feeling out of place in an almost-empty house meant for a family and official entertaining. He hadn't talked to Ginger for several days, so he almost rushed to pick up the phone and place the call, hoping to catch her at home at lunchtime. He sorely missed her, but he was still smarting that she'd walked out. Like a hurt child, he'd show her that life went on well without her. The lapse of three days was sufficient to establish that point, at least in his mind, and now he cared only that she be home.

His tenseness fled when Ginger picked up after the fourth ring. Her voice had its familiar lilt, filling his mind's eye with the image of her both earnest and smiling, tilting her head back so her pony tail nipped at her shoulders, making a point. The downside was that she sounded entirely too happy and maybe didn't miss him at all.

"Everyone's fine, and Greg started school yesterday," she said. "He was a bit hesitant at first, but this morning he couldn't wait to be off. I think it was the right decision." *Only back a week, and already congratulating herself.*

Ade brought her quickly up to date on the coup and ensuing developments.

"They kicked you in the ass, but they're still using you up to the last minute," she said. "Typical."

"Ginger, I'm still in the Foreign Service, they're still paying me, and this Embassy still needs a DCM. I don't see anything wrong."

"You wouldn't." Ginger must have realized that this sounded harsh, because she quickly changed the subject. "I have some good news for you. I went to the library and checked out my hunch about those notes of Kohler you gave me, and I was right. There's a fascinating account of a Schreber case in Freud's notebooks. Schreber was a high German government official who exhibited strong symptoms of paranoia over a period of years. Freud never met Schreber but his analysis of the case is well-known to any student of Freudian psychology."

"Ginger, you're amazing. But what does it mean?"

"You remember that Kohler had referred to a 'feminine fantasy,' the enjoyment of being 'a woman submitting to an act of copulation'?"

"How could I forget?"

"Well, according to Freud, Schreber's masculine side rejected this fantasy, but it was too strong to be resisted. Freud concludes that 'the patient was in fear of sexual abuse at the hands of his doctor himself. His struggles against the libidinal impulse produced the conflict which gave rise to the symptoms.' What do you think of that?"

"I'm trying to make sense of it. It's very theoretical. But it's very interesting. Kohler must have read that case and identified to some extent with Schreber."

"Sure. That's a good start. Anyway, according to Freud, Schreber developed paranoic fantasies about being the passive sexual partner of another man, but he couldn't admit to desiring another man and repressed his feeling."

"So you're suggesting that Kohler found Ellerbee sexually attractive?"

"Certainly not overtly, but he may have had some repressed desire."

"Sounds murky to me. "And what about that curious term, 'soul-murder?'"

"OK." Ginger's voice was excited. "Freud discusses that too. He says that Schreber, the patient, had a paranoid delusion, believing that his doctor 'attempted to commit 'soul-murder' upon him – an act which, he thought, was comparable with the efforts made by the devil or by demons to gain possession of a soul…As to what constitutes…'soul-murder,' and as to its technique…I am able to say nothing…'"

Ade didn't know what to say. After a pause, Ginger went on, "I don't know about you Ade, but I find this both horrifying and compelling. Freud couldn't define 'soul-murder,' but maybe Jack found a fit."

Ade was thinking hard. 'Soul-murder' was such an arresting term. Had he heard Kohler use it before? He vaguely thought so, but couldn't remember the context.

"Great work, Ginger. You've found something, for sure. Too bad I won't be involved anymore."

"Not a chance you won't be involved. You can't help yourself."

"Well, I didn't join the Foreign Service to be a time-server, talking only to the foreign office and writing arid cables back to Washington. The world's a dangerous place, and you can't find out about it sitting behind a desk."

"And knowing you, when you get back to Washington, anything can happen." Thinking over the last few weeks, Ade said, "I guess you're right about that."

CHAPTER TWENTY-SEVEN

Ade arranged to meet Corson in Arania two hours before their appointment with Sudopo. Transcon had already rented a small villa in the residential district to house its advance men in case Sudopo gave them a green light. Ade compared Transcon's approach to the State Department's, where the buildings management bureaucrats would raise objections and muffle the project in paperwork for months. That said a lot about the Department, Ade thought: good at managing crises, lousy at planning ahead.

Corson was dressed in a formal guayabera, which looked good on him; Madeleine looked restrained, but coiled and ready. Ade said, "Securing the rights, assuming you're successful, is only the beginning. There'll be huge problems dealing with a country like Tanako. Start with Sudopo: I've met him several times, and he dislikes Americans in general and me specifically. I'm actually surprised that he agreed to this meeting so readily. But the Tanakians are also suspicious of American corporations, because they think one of them screwed them on a cocoa export deal."

Madeleine crossed her legs, and her long skirt parted at the knee.

"Maybe we can help them overcome their aversions," she said.

Ade was thinking, *This babe is unbelievable. Does everything she says have a double meaning?* "They'll be looking for something more than good corporate citizenship. I'm sure you know that."

"Transcon has a lot of international experience," Corson said. "Anyway, you're probably the only American official Sudopo knows, and you know Tanako better than any other American official, so you're the guy who can help us."

Ade was flattered, but wary. "If you stay in the game, you'll need representatives on the ground. We can help you to develop some contacts, and urge Sudopo to keep a level playing field."

On the way to the Palace, Ade noticed that the checkpoints were gone, along with the barbed wire barriers. Of course the city was still broken down and peeling, but more shops were open and the streets were no longer deserted. Maybe the biggest change was the existence of at least one hotel, which had quickly reopened after the coup. The new owner had even managed to find a new awning for out front and open a modest outdoor restaurant with a terrace overlooking the port. Ade wondered what had happened to the previous owner, who had been one of the guests at Black Bitch.

The Palace was as atrociously gaudy as before, but Barreras's ubiquitous portraits had been replaced by a mixture of action photos featuring Sudopo, a heroic oil painting of him in profile, and various African artifacts. Overall, it was a slight improvement. Sudopo welcomed them cordially, and didn't mention the murder or his confrontations with Ade, who introduced Corson as "representing the world's fifth largest oil company." He said, "Mr. Corson will describe the kinds of investments that Transcon could make here if it's successful in obtaining drilling rights."

Corson and Madeleine were impressive, putting on a tryptich color slide show with photos of deepwater well construction, drilling operations, port and road development and happy workers smiling in front of their new prefab housing flashing on the screen before dissolving into the next image, all of it reeking of money and progress, while Corson talked development and profits. Sudopo and his aides listened carefully.

At the end, Corson said, "I'd like the opportunity to talk to your ministers and technical people about the specifics of what we could do here." He casually dropped some statistics about Transcon operations in Venezuela, Angola, and the Middle East, and what they had contributed to their countries of operation.

By the end of the day, Corson had spent two hours with Sudopo and had also met with some of his inner circle, including the Minister of Petroleum. No one made any promises, but it certainly looked as though Transcon had put itself in the running.

After the meeting, they went to the outdoor restaurant. Corson was highly pleased and ordered a round of drinks.

"We're in the game," he said, giving Madeleine a big hug.

"How can you be so sure?" Ade asked. "Sudopo's no fool. He'll play you off against the French and other bidders."

"We can deal with that. We're prepared to incur substantial expenses. The potential here is vast. No single company will get it all, anyway. There'll be lots of players. But

Tanako will need some hand-holding and this garden will need regular tending. Nadherny, you should consider working for Transcon. You could do worse."

Ade's mouth dropped open. "I already have a job. Most days I like it."

"You mean you had a job. We heard about your transfer. Why bust your ass for an outfit that treats people like that?"

"How'd you know they're pulling me out?"

"Well, you told us, but let's also say that we have good sources. Not only at the top, but around the corridors, including the State Department when we need it. Lots of people know what happened to you."

Ade was astonished. "I have to admit, I'm impressed. First-rate sleuthing work."

"What do you make, about $30,000, for a pretty senior diplomat?" Corson's tone was so derisive that Ade didn't want to admit he'd hit it almost on the nose, except that it was $2,000 too high. One didn't join the Foreign Service to get rich.

"Ade, I'm talking wealth, not just a good white collar salary. There's a world of difference." He paused to let that sink in. "If the home office approves, you'll never need to concern yourself about money for the rest of your life."

"What if it didn't work out? Where would I be then?"

"You'd get a nice severance, and you'd have to live by your wits for a change."

Despite his expressions of disinterest, Ade kept asking questions. "What would Transcon want me to do?"

"First, steer us through the bidding, jump start the operation, train the resident manager and get the staff started.

Then troubleshoot the project here, and from New York and Paris. I see about a three to five year project."

"What then?"

"You want a lifetime guarantee? You've been with the government too long. The international oil business is dynamic. Success is rewarded. If you do well, you could name your own ticket."

"Why me?" Ade kept looking for downers but he wasn't finding any.

"You know Africa, you can deal, you're fluent in French and Spanish. You know Washington. You have a good reputation. For this project, that's a good combination."

"What's your position in all this?"

"I fix things. If people want to pay me, I can get things done."

"How about you, Madeleine? What's your role?"

Madeleine unfolded her legs sinuously. "I help, when I'm needed."

This conversation was opening up a whole new vista that had the potential to bestow on him power and money beyond anything he might achieve in the State Department. And maybe give him a career where he wasn't farmed out to pasture and his wife didn't leave him in frustration.

"Don't miss the brass ring," Corson said. "The carousel might come around only once." With that he rose, threw some bills on the table, and said, "I'm going back to the villa to call Paris and take a shower. Come on back in about an hour and we'll think about dinner."

Ade took a deep breath, and a sip of his beer. Madeleine watched him.

"You seem a bit afraid of all this," she said, moving her chair closer.

"No, I'm not, but diplomats are trained to be cautious."

"Is it me you're afraid of? A lot of men are."

"No, but I'm wondering if you're the *femme fatale* in this scenario. *'La Belle Dame Sans Merci.'* She caught the reference, but didn't respond to it.

"As I said, I can help move things along."

"In what direction?"

"Any direction you like."

"That sounds intriguing, but I think I have enough problems already."

"You don't trust people, do you?"

"I'd like to believe that we're having this conversation because of my natural charm and appeal. But the realist in me says it just ain't so."

"Don't underestimate yourself. We could have some fun," she said, bending her face closer. *Things don't happen this way in real life,* he thought. But Madeleine was very real, and now her face was only inches away in the gathering darkness. There was no time to think about propriety. He could only think fleetingly of his resentment and bruised feelings with Ginger.

He kissed her softly on the lips, and was able to sense her entire body coil like a hot wire. Her hand rested lightly on his thigh.

He took a deep breath. The terrace was now dark, and they were alone. He was struggling. "I don't think I should be playing in this league," he said. "Influence peddling doesn't appeal to me, and I have no agenda." He kissed her again, feeling the warmth envelop him. She started to respond, but went slack.

"You think I do?" Her voice was quiet, but sharp.

"For sure. That doesn't mean that I wouldn't like to be on it." Her eyes narrowed and her body stiffened. "Don't flatter yourself, and don't ever try to make a fool of me." She was glaring.

"I'm sorry. I shouldn't have been flip. You're fascinating, and I'd love to spend time with you. I could wish for different circumstances."

"That's something I'm afraid you'll never be able to control," she said rising, and walked away, leaving him in darkness.

He caught up to her as she was about to ask the Embassy driver to take her to the villa. They got in together, but the moment was broken, and they sat in silence. At the villa, Ade noticed that she and Corson had separate rooms.

The next morning, Corson and Madeleine went for a followup meeting with the Minister of Petroleum. Ade wasn't invited. He welcomed the respite from Madeleine's steamy presence and Corson's putdowns, and went by the Embassy, still closed to the public. The African employees were all there, and after telling them the Embassy would open soon because there was a new government in place and the oil would raise Tanako's profile, he sat down with Nguema in Kohler's old office.

Outwardly, Nguema seemed no different: stalwart and serious, responsive to questions, but not initiating any new observations. Ade asked, "Do you recall a Mr. Rafael Corson visiting the Embassy, and talking to Mr. Kohler or Mr. Ellerbee?"

Nguema pulled out an old visitors log kept by the receptionist. He flipped a few pages, and found an entry for May

22, 1971. "I remember him. Not many foreign visitors came here. He talked to Mr. Ellerbee with the door closed."

Ade, Corson, and Madeleine took the afternoon plane back to Douala. Corson was busy making notes, Madeleine was distant. Just as well, Ade thought. They left it that Ade would have a telephone interview with Transcon's Paris chief early the next week, and if that went well he'd go to New York for a final decision. Ade didn't want Corson to think he was easily available, like some Japanese *Ronin* looking for a new patron, and stressed that he was interested but still drawn to the world of foreign policy. Corson ignored the comment, but when they parted at the airport he said, "If you turn out to be the right guy, financial security for you and your family will be set, forever. What do you have now that even comes close?" Ade had no answer.

Madeleine gave him a peck on both cheeks, and whispered in his ear, "We've already established that you're not one to take advantage of an appealing opportunity. *Bonne chance,* Ade." Her soft breath and sultry voice left him tingling.

* * *

Back in Yaounde, Ade called Dave Whitten from the political section in the Paris Embassy, the same friend who'd met the plane carrying the Kohlers back to America to tell them of the unscheduled Boston stopover. That seemed a century ago. Neither the names "Corson" nor "Molnar" yielded any recognition, but he promised to check further.

Two days later, Whitten called back. "This was easier than I thought. There's a lot of background in *Le Monde* and

L'Express. There was a ripe scandal last year involving Elf Aquitaine, the huge French oil conglomerate, and its operations in Gabon. It reached the highest levels of the government. Six cabinet members were fired and twelve senior executives of Elf went to jail. Amazingly, some of them are still there.

"The crux of it was that Elf was using Gabon as a conduit for huge sums of money for bribes, money laundering, even French military and clandestine operations in Africa. The President of Gabon was on the take big time. He had more than $50 million in bank accounts in Switzerland, the British Virgin Islands, and the US. Elf gave him a new airplane, and a string of 'models' he'd have flown out from Paris. He also received regular payments of about $10 million per year, just like a salary. In return, the French got free use of his country, which is France's single largest source of oil, and no questions asked."

"Where does Corson come in?"

"There are only a couple of references to him. He's apparently a behind-the-scenes bagman type, the guy who gets things done. They couldn't pin anything on him, and he never went to jail."

"Well, he admitted himself that he's a fixer. But why would he be working now for Transcon, an American company?"

"He was never part of the Elf executive structure – more of a hired gun, so to speak, a useful and highly paid cutout. Now he's probably hired himself out to Transcon to help them put their deal together."

"What about Madeleine Molnar?"

"She's a world class bimbo. Just from the photo in the newspaper, not one you'd easily forget." Ade nodded and closed his eyes, and her conjured image, powerful and smoldering, floated into his consciousness.

"World class, but definitely no bimbo," Ade found himself saying. "Courtesan, maybe. A woman like that can do anything she wants."

"Well, whatever she wanted, she was a regular Elf employee, but on the take too. That is, she got lavish bonuses for some special work. They used her to get to the Foreign Minister, with the help of a luxury apartment near the *Quai d'Orsay,* plus a monthly salary of $20,000 and a big shopping allowance. She explained that a certain level of dignity was required to develop satisfactory customer relations. I guess! The investigators pulled her in for questioning for three months, and this all spilled out. In return for her information, they let her go."

Ade smiled. It was impossible to picture someone as elegant and formidable as Madeleine Molnar behind bars, and he was glad that she'd been able to save herself.

"Dave, one final question: any mention of US banks involved?"

"Only that some of the money went to the US."

So once again, there was tantalizing evidence that Ellerbee might have been on to something, but had been cut short. But if there was more, and Ade was going to look for it, he'd have to pick up the trail in Washington. The string had run out in Africa.

CHAPTER TWENTY-EIGHT

When Charlie Stubblefield handed Kohler over to the Psychiatric Unit at George Washington University Hospital on September 6, he'd expected to follow the situation closely. Instead, it was as though a velvet curtain had silently enveloped Jack, with the strings controlled by Dr. Milton Wallach, the university's senior psychiatrist. He'd taken over and nobody in the Department heard a thing for nearly three weeks. It seemed that everyone had his own set of proprietary interests, and now Kohler was university property, a subject ripe for study.

Charlie had called Dr. Wallach several times; the response was always a polite but frosty stonewall: Kohler was progressing well, calm and lucid, under close observation and treatment. Dr. Wallach struck Charlie as officious and self-important, and he made it clear that Jack was *his* patient, not the Department's. The only people allowed access were Cynthia and his lawyer, Ned Dilbaugh, both of whom visited him for extended periods every day.

State's initial terse announcement about Ellerbee's death had been duly reported by the *New York Times* and *Washington Post* – "Foreign Service officer murdered in US Embassy in Africa," and "US diplomat held in slaying of colleague," but the story seemed to be fading until Senator Manning came out with his bombshell. The Department, ever cautious, responded that there was "no evidence of previous improprieties" in Kohler's file, but would welcome any information the Senator might want to share.

On September 24 Kohler went to the United States District Court in Alexandria, where he was placed under arrest for the first time and served with a new complaint, charging him with murdering Ellerbee "with premeditation and malice aforethought."

Premeditation? Had something new developed? Charlie checked with Lyle Jameson, who told him, "They just want to make sure they have the most serious offense covered, in case something new turns up. They can still convict him under a lesser charge, or drop the premeditation later on."

With nothing more to detain him in Yaounde, Ade packed out quickly, arranging to take a long weekend in Lexington on his way to Washington. Ginger had rented an apartment not far from her parents, and Ade's joy at being reunited with his family was hedged with chagrin that she and Greg had made an apparently effortless transition, not requiring his steadying presence in the slightest. If Ginger had any regrets about bolting from Cameroon, she'd never admit them; as for Greg, he was excited about a fresh start in a familiar place. Ade thought again how circumstances intervened to poison whatever chance they'd had to enjoy their lives there.

The night before Ade left for Washington, Greg kept the banter lively with details of his activities and new friends, and he seemed to have recaptured some of his old zest. If he could get back on track, their sudden move and impending separation would be worth it, much as Ade would miss their daily presence in his life.

As Greg described his tryout for a school play, Ade kept glancing at Ginger, trying to guess what she was thinking. It was hard to penetrate her surface aloofness, which often masked something she cared about deeply. He also wondered if she was feeling any of the desire he was feeling as the last of his dinner wine eased down his throat. Sneaking swift glances at her face, alternately wreathed in smiles at some comment from Greg, or looking impenetrably pensive, Ade just couldn't tell what was behind her striking blue eyes, almost the color of turquoise.

He had to wait until bedtime for his answer. Ginger was making notes on a case history, but as he got into bed she put her notebook aside and turned to him.

He put his arm around her and drew her close. "You know," he said, "We've had a mostly great life so far but maybe it's time for us to try something else. Your coming here with Greg – was it a warning shot? I still don't like it, but it could turn out for the best. Anyway, with everything that's happened I'm thinking of leaving the Foreign Service. I've even received an offer already."

He told her about Transcon and Corson, leaving out any reference to the supple Madeleine, whose memory was still fresh. "The way I feel today, I just might go to Washington and tell the Department I'm bagging it. I'm tired of being pushed around." As he talked he felt bolder by the second, so by the time he was finished he had almost convinced himself. He looked over at Ginger, but she was frowning disapproval.

"Ade, you love the Service! The involvement, the issues, the excitement – when you have that, you never think of the frustrations. But when things aren't going well, like right now, it's easy to let resentments build up. But you'd be miserable if you left."

Ade was astonished. "If I recall, you said in our last conversation that I was getting screwed. You even packed Greg and yourself out of Yaounde because you were fed up. Now you've totally reversed course. Is this some form of feminine perversity that I just can't understand?"

"All I'm saying is don't jump just because you're frustrated. They've offered you an academic year – take it, make some contacts, think about it. If you want to leave after a year and you have a good offer, then I'd say OK."

"What about you?"

"We need this year to find ourselves, and it'll be much easier with you in Washington than in Cameroon. Let's see how it works."

"Absence doesn't make the heart grow fonder," Abe said, thinking of his near-miss with Madeleine. "It's more 'out of sight, out of mind.' Relationships need nurturing."

Ginger drew Ade's hand close and gently kissed the tips of his fingers. Madeleine's lingering image faded quickly. "Ade, when we met, you were already an FSO. So when I married you, I bought the whole package – not just the great experiences, but the disappointments, dislocations, and family separations. Sure, I was beginning to do some rethinking, but now I'm concerned mostly about Greg. Of course I worry about my career being on hold for years at a time. And more and more, being a Foreign Service wife just isn't enough, so maybe I'm changing. But I'm dealing with it, and not holding anything back. Especially not now."

Ade thought then that Ginger was the most desirable woman in the whole world, and he kissed her hungrily full on the mouth. This time her response was spontaneous, yet already focused and intense – not relaxed or playful, as she sometimes was, when she was having fun but wasn't fully engaged. Her lips were half-parted, and she had a faraway look that was dreamy and erotic. It made him wonder whether she was feeling desire for him or had plugged into some ethereal fantasy. But her power was real enough and propelled him forward, its force becoming his own. Ginger stayed with him the whole way, lush and intense, until they finally lay back, wet and trembling. Whatever lay ahead for them, at this moment they were true partners, united by their shared longing and foreboding. Ade briefly felt that their bonding might even last, just as an inner voice told him that this too would change with the dawn.

The next morning, there were quick hugs all around as Ade departed. "Bye, sweetheart," Ginger said. "We'll miss you." Such a commonplace exchange was hardly adequate to cover all of the unstated emotions that were at play, not to mention the afterglow that still lingered from the night before.

"See you in a few weeks," Ade said with a quick smile, hopped into the waiting taxi and was gone, as though he'd been launched from a cannon into outer space.

CHAPTER TWENTY-NINE

Ade reported to the Department feeling totally cut off from any further involvement with the Kohler case until the trial, when he would have to testify. Sally Rogers told him that his year of study and teaching at Georgetown's School of Foreign Service was on track, and all he had to do was show up and start work. If the Department needed him for anything, they'd call. "Oh by the way," Sally said as Ade was rising to leave, "this brief story about Tanako was in this morning's *Times*. Amnesty International says it welcomes the new government's pledge to end tortures and public executions of political prisoners, but there's still no real political freedom. But there's been progress, and I believe you had something to do with that."

Ade skimmed the story and handed it back to Sally. "Nice going, Ade," she said.

It was nice to be appreciated, even in passing, Ade thought. "Thanks, Sally. Now what about my cables on those Japanese on Tanako and the possibility of a terrorist connection? Did anyone read them?"

"Of course, Ade," she said in a gently admonishing tone. "You've been around this place too long to have your feelings bruised so easily. Before your foray into the bush, they were thinking Baader-Meinhof or one of the Palestinian groups. You've opened up a new range of possibilities."

"Any one of those groups could be dangerous. Everyone around here is so focused on big cold war issues that terrorism in Africa, the Middle East or Europe is like a fire across the river."

"No, Ade, you're wrong. They're trying to follow these groups. In fact, my guess is that they're onto something, and we here in the trenches just aren't in the loop."

Feeling shut out and expendable at the Department, Ade was unable to resist the urge to call Charlie Stubblefield. "I was hoping you'd surface soon," Charlie said. "Guess who just showed up here?"

"I haven't a clue."

"None other than Jack Kohler."

"What? I thought he was in custody at GW Hospital."

"He was, but maybe they're into miracle cures. Whatever, they let him go, and he's free on his own recognizance. Dr. Wallach told us they'd completed their observations and had no basis for detaining him."

"That's ridiculous! What did they say about his sanity?"

"Not much. Wallach wouldn't give details, but said that Jack no longer showed signs of mental illness and was behaving normally. They decided he wasn't a threat to himself or anyone else and there was no reason to keep him."

"Amazing. Does this mean that Jack didn't really go crazy in the vault?"

"I asked Wallach that, and all he'd say was that Jack was under 'severe mental and emotional strain' when he came in. A few weeks with Dr. Wallach and a violent murderer turns into a pussy cat. If cures are that easy, that man has a future."

In Charlie's view, either Jack didn't really lose his mind, in which case the broadcast from the vault and everything that followed was an elaborate charade, or else Dr. Wallach was playing with fire by freeing a man only a few weeks after he'd sliced up his colleague for no known reason. Couldn't he be capable of doing it again? It was barely a month since the murder.

Charlie added that when Jack was released, "he did what any dedicated Foreign Service officer would do: he walked down Twenty-third Street four blocks to the State Department and reported for duty."

Ade tried to picture the open-mouthed amazement at the Department when Kohler walked in. Foreign Service officers are supposed to be unflappable and expect the unexpected, but this was way over the limit.

"Ade, it may sound absurd, but think about it and there's a certain bizarre logic to it. Jack acts normal, so they let him go. That's not a judgment on his mental state at the time of the murder. As for Jack, what's he to do? The only place he can go is where he's still employed as an FSO, and which he still cares deeply about. If he is in fact OK, he wants most of all to put his life back together. Of course he has to face the trial, but between now and then he wants to show the Department that he's like everyone else."

"Charlie, we're dealing with murder! Kohler can't just walk in and say, 'Sorry folks, I lost it back there on that island, but now I'm OK, so let's all go back to work.' What did the personnel folks say when Kohler walked in?"

"They kept their cool. Jack told them that he was free until the trial, and that he and Cynthia had rented an apartment in Foggy Bottom. I checked this out with Justice, and it's all true. The judge agreed that Jack was unlikely to flee, given his family situation. So Cynthia's family put up the bond money and Kohler's on the street.

"Anyway, he gave our colleagues the distinct impression that he regarded the murder as a freak occurrence, tragic to be sure, but one he'd had no control over. Now he wanted to put it behind him and get on with his life."

"Get on with his life!" Ade shouted. "Charlie, this is crazy! Is everyone treating this as a stroll in the park? Maybe some of you should have been with us when we cleaned pieces of Ellerbee off the floor of the vault. Maybe you should all talk to Maria!"

"Calm down, Ade. I know it sounds awful, but if the judge, the shrinks, and Justice are OK with this, who are we to challenge it? It's their call, not ours, and it lets the Department off the hook."

"I thought the Department cared about its image," Ade said, still fuming. "How can a man murder someone and then calmly go back to work? How do you think that'll play? We already have that broadside from Manning, and now this. It's a farce."

Charlie finished his story. "People who talked to him said he really did seem normal. He said he was still 'devastated,' and that his life would never be the same, but that he wanted to prove he still could be a useful human being. He came across as someone who desperately hoped he could be accepted again."

"So he's delusional as well! What'll the Department do with him?"

"This is the good part. You know how the Department seems to think that treating people right is beneath its dignity? You know, delaying promotions, cutting hardship allowances, missing paydays when we transfer? Well, this time it's different. The minute they heard that Jack was in the building, the Seventh Floor – the Under Secretary for Management, the Director General, even the Secretary himself – decided on an immediate, hundred percent disability pension for Jack. He's not eligible for even partial retirement for ten years! They act fast when they want to."

"Marvelous!" Ade exclaimed. "Next they'll name him 'employee of the year' for slashing his personnel complement!" But he couldn't help admire how nimbly the Seventh Floor had circled the wagons to deflect an unsavory distraction and defend the Department's interests.

"What's been the reaction?"

"None, of course. Only a few people know, and nothing will be said publicly. When word filters through the corridors, there certainly will be some outrage, but it will be muted and civilized. That's the norm for this building anyway. Muted outrage."

"What happens next?"

"Well, as far as the Department and Kohler are concerned, it's a done deal. They'd never take him back on active duty, and the quickest way to get rid of him was to give him a full pension. I have to admit, it was pretty slick."

"Now I know how to get an instant pension. But if the word gets out, half the people in the Department won't make it home from work tonight."

"I can see you're not letting go of this case," Charlie said, laughing. "Even after the Department gave you a cushy year at Georgetown."

"Yeah, I'm out of the way, but let's not forget Senator Manning. Will the Department keep him at bay? I'm not counting on it, and neither should you. Now, what about the trial developments. Anything new?"

"The indictment charges Kohler with premeditated murder, and –"

"Premeditated murder and they're giving him a full pension ten years early? Charlie, this is unreal!"

"Let me finish, Ade. If Jack's found guilty, he could get the chair. You and Ron will be key witnesses for the prosecution. As the first two on the crime scene, you'll lay the basis for the evidence you gathered."

"What about Kohler's defense?"

"Their only choice is to plead temporary insanity. As you know, it's not an easy sell, even with all the things pointing to it here."

"Any hints from the hospital about his behavior there?"

"Wallach was really tight-assed with me, but I did talk to one of the psychiatric nurses. She said that Kohler was in bad shape when he checked in. He insisted that his food be sampled before he'd touch it, and pressed his ear to the wall to listen for eavesdropping. He kept looking under the bed, and became edgy if a new floor nurse walked into his room. Most of the nurses thought he was out of his mind."

"If he was that bad, how come they let him go so soon?"

"Good question. Apparently, he made extremely rapid progress. You know, he always seemed thoughtful and articulate. That impressed everyone, and as he got used to his surroundings, his behavior improved by the day."

"Charlie, there's so much evidence against him that the insanity claim looks very shaky to me. I think the prosecution has a lock, don't you?"

Up to now, Charlie hadn't once given his opinion. He said, "Ade, no jury's going to convict that guy. He's damaged goods. There's something wrong with his gourd."

Ade thought, if Charlie's right, there'll be hell to pay from the public and the politicians. He asked, "OK, one more thing. What about Senator Manning?"

Charlie's sprightly tone darkened. "I'm going to the Hill tomorrow to meet Walter Jurgens. Hastings wants me to find out what Manning has in mind."

"I'm sure you'll eat him up."

"I doubt it. The worst thing I could do is underestimate this guy. Beneath that good old boy exterior is a very clever and calculating person. He's smart, he works hard, and he'd do anything to make us look bad."

All these Washington aspects were about politics, and had nothing to do with why Kohler did it, or seeing justice done. Ade wondered, did anyone in Washington really care about that?

CHAPTER THIRTY

Charlie walked into Senator Manning's spacious suite of offices and asked for Walter Jurgens. Jurgens came out, shook hands quickly, and led Charlie to a tiny alcove barely large enough for a paper-cluttered desk and chair, telephone, Rolodex, and bookcase overflowing with everything but books — newspapers, congressional committee documents, magazines like *The New Republic* and *National Review.* There was a small door with direct access to the Senator's office. Few would have guessed that so much power, intimidation, and political bile emanated from this cramped cubicle.

Jurgens pulled over a straightback chair and motioned for Charlie to sit. He was about five-ten, wiry, with wavy dark hair and eyes that darted around nervously. Charlie had trouble making eye contact with him; Jurgens reminded him of a ferret.

"I'd like to address the Senator's concerns about the Kohler case," Charlie said.

"The Department's fucked up again," Jurgens said. "Totally botched from start to finish. The Senator wants some heads to roll."

Charlie swallowed. This was more than he'd expected, by a long shot. "If you know anything we're not aware of, we need to know about it."

"We have solid information. There was something sordid going on between those two guys. They had a relationship. It's all going to come out."

"What's going to come out? I've never been to Tanako, but from what I know of that place, if there was something bad going on, we'd have known about it. You have evidence? Hell, Walter, both men were married."

Jurgen was scornful. "Look at Ellerbee's background. He served in Moscow."

"Yeah. So what?"

"There was a major security breach there at the time. Some crucial documents, including data on nuclear deployments and some Top Secret encryption codes turned up missing. Ellerbee was the duty officer the week it happened. For that week, he had keys to the rooms where the stuff was kept, and combinations to all the safes. In other words, access to all the documents." For the first time, he looked at Charlie straight in the eye. "I'll bet you had no idea about all this. It's all news to you."

Charlie didn't like being on the defensive. "I'd not heard that, I'll admit. But if you don't have a 'need to know,' you don't find out. There was nothing in Ellerbee's file."

Jurgens looked contemptuous. "Of course there wouldn't have been. They couldn't prove anything after the investigation, so nothing happened. It looks to us like the Department covering its ass again."

"But what's the missing information got to do with what you said about Kohler and Ellerbee?"

"Ellerbee was a homosexual. The Soviets found out about it and blackmailed him into passing documents."

Charlie sucked in his breath. "Heavy stuff, Walter. But it sounds dubious. How do you know all this? Where's the evidence?"

"We demanded a briefing on the investigation y'all carried out. Your security boys said that the documents and encryption codes had been compromised, but they couldn't figure out who did it. Hell, only a couple of people below the Ambassador and DCM had access to that stuff. They couldn't even tell whether the Soviets had in fact received the information. It was a wishy-washy report, and pretty typical."

"Not every mystery gets solved," Charlie said. "The Soviets would hardly have jumped up and told us, "Look what we've got!"

"What they almost certainly got was access to our Top Secret cable traffic for two weeks. And the nuclear documents that were missing had to be presumed to have fallen into their hands. It was priceless information."

"That still doesn't prove your allegation. And it says nothing about the relationship between Kohler and Ellerbee."

Jurgens smiled. "You're going to have to wait for the trial for that. But I promised you that it would all come out."

Charlie heard a voice outside the room and Senator Manning suddenly appeared in the doorway.

He was tall, with thinning gray hair, carefully groomed, and his portliness was well-concealed by a blue double-breasted suit. Charlie jumped up and shook hands.

"Pleasure to meet you, Stubblefield," Manning said. "I understand you did a great job in South Africa."

Charlie noted that Jurgens had taken the trouble to check his background and brief the Senator. "Yes, Senator, it was quite an experience."

"I can imagine. Not easy for you, although I've always felt that Americans don't understand much about the situation over there."

There was enough ambiguity in his words to leave doubt about his intended meaning, but it made Charlie uncomfortable, and he didn't respond.

Manning moved on quickly. "Well, nice to meet you, Stubblefield. I'm glad to see more minorities finally showing up in the Foreign Service, and I wish you well. Now you go back to the Department and tell your bosses that *all* the questions raised by the actions of your two colleagues will be answered to *everyone's* satisfaction."

Manning departed, and Charlie moved toward the door. "The Department wants to see justice done. We'll work with you to make sure nothing jeopardizes a fair trial."

Jurgens' scornful look returned. "If you think justice decides anything up here, think again. Up here, it's horse-trading. If you talk about the national interest and look like you're serious, people will think you're either stupid, naïve, or putting them on." He moved towards the door, half closed it, and lowered his voice. "The Senator wants the Department to admit that it hired misfits and deviants and sent them out to do important jobs. Those responsible have to be punished, maybe dismissed. Mind, he understands that this will be embarrassing, so he might agree to say merely that the Department made a gross error in judgment, and forego cranking up a Senate hearing. But if we do that, there's a price."

"Go on," Charlie said, turning to face Jurgens.

"The Senator wants the President to restrict imports of cotton and finished textiles. They're swamping the country, ruining Georgia farmers and textile producers, taking jobs. That's got to stop, and we get it done through you.

"Textile imports are governed by yearly quotas, and there's a lot at stake. They protect our domestic producers and provide vital income to countries that are important to us. Southeast Asia especially needs them now, with the communists winning in Vietnam. If we have an opening with China, textiles will be a key bargaining chip in getting them to cut support for regional insurgencies. For the Japanese, textile exports are basic to the relationship. So limiting exports from Asia isn't as easy as you think.

"That's why we want you involved. Telling foreigners what we want them to do is why we have a State Department, if you only had the balls. I'm sure you can work something out. Take this message back to your pals."

CHAPTER THIRTY-ONE

It took Ade only a few hours at Georgetown to check on his courses and meet with some of his new academic colleagues. This wouldn't match being on the diplomatic frontlines, but it was a new challenge and it wouldn't be boring.

When he returned to his hotel, the Lombardy on Pennsylvania Avenue, he was surprised to find a message from Cynthia Kohler waiting for him. When he returned her call, her voice was businesslike, but not unfriendly. She said she wanted to discuss "things," away from the Department. They agreed to meet the next day at a small café in Georgetown, not far from State. *I'm not able to extricate myself from this case even if I wanted to,* he thought.

Cynthia still projected the image of cool competence that she'd developed at her former law firm. She was dressed in a way that highlighted her still-young figure, with a designer sweater, small gold choker and a knee-level, faux leather skirt tight enough to attract attention without violating the Foreign Service's unstated but conservative ideas about what constituted appropriate dress for spouses. She wore stockings and plain leather pumps, and Ade couldn't help noticing that she had nice legs, shapely stems like two exclamation points. As she slipped her outer jacket onto the back of her chair, the calf muscles in her legs flexed gently. The overall effect was understated but erotic just the same, projecting a person who was in control of herself, but knew she could have an impact on others when she chose.

They exchanged awkward pleasantries. Ade was on guard, Cynthia unsure how to get to the point. Jack, she stressed, was keeping busy: meeting regularly with Dilbaugh's team and taking an active part in the preparation of his defense. He had resumed his voracious reading on international politics and economics. He was also spending a lot of time with Robin, taking him to the zoo, to the playground, even to museums, showing him paintings that told a story that might pique a three-year-old's imagination, like Winslow Homer's dramatic oil painting, "The Gulf Stream."

Cynthia's reference to Robin brought Ade up short. He wondered what all this family trauma would do to him. Such a handsome kid, and a natural charmer. You'd expect an inner-directed couple like Cynthia and Jack to produce an offspring in their own image, but Robin was bright and outgoing. It seemed incongruous to see the restrained Kohler come out of his shell with enthusiasm over his young son. Whenever Ade saw them, Jack always seemed to be holding Robin in his arms, or carrying him on his shoulders. One time he blurted out, "My young son is eminently huggable," combining spontaneous delight with his usual stiff language. He immediately flushed with embarrassment, as though he'd said something inappropriate. Ade thought it touching that Kohler took such unrestrained joy in the boy.

But what Cynthia was putting to Ade not so subtly was that what Kohler had done in Tanako was a one-time aberration.

"I hear Jack's making good progress," he said. Cynthia leaned forward and fixed her eyes on him. "The reason I wanted to meet with you is that I need your help."

"I'm not sure what I can do, but I'm listening."

Cynthia leaned closer. "A good man went berserk because of things in his life that he couldn't control, and now he's condemned as a monster even before his trial. Ade, I'm not demeaning George's death, but that wasn't the real Jack Kohler in that vault. I know him better than anyone else, and the real Jack could never have done something like that." She paused for a second, and added, "Unless he was fighting some inner devil that finally overwhelmed him."

"Cynthia, you know that I respected Jack, and chose him for Tanako. But you're telling me that his inner demons made him crazy and therefore he wasn't responsible for what he did. I know you plan to plead insanity, but frankly almost no one I know accepts it." He didn't tell her that the one exception was Charlie Stubblefield.

Cynthia was unfazed. "You know, Jack agreed to Tanako as a one-time experience, even though he was over-qualified. He loves the Service so much, he forgets that no one will look out for his interests or recognize his achievements unless he does a little pushing. Or I do the pushing for him." Ade was struck by Cynthia's use of the present tense, as though Jack were still an FSO in good standing. Maybe she'd given in to illusions too. He waited for her to continue.

"You probably don't know anything about Jack's background, and what he had to deal with as a child," she said.

"Only what's in his file – education, work experience, things like that. And what you started to tell me that day in Tanako. It seems like years ago."

"You're the only one outside the family who knows this, but Jack suffered terribly from a demanding and abusive father when he was a boy."

Cynthia paused and looked at Ade for a reaction. He said, "Go on, Cynthia. I'm listening."

"His father had a rigid Teutonic personality, and brought the children up according to his own strict formula. Children had to love, honor, and obey their parents, with emphasis on obedience. Even when Jack's father was old and the children grown, he still believed that children were evil creatures at birth, and the evil had to be fought from the start. Any flaws had to be pulled out like weeds, or children's basically sinful natures would take over."

"You mean God and the Devil stuff?"

"Something like that. From the time he was a baby, Jack was always washed in cold water to toughen him. He had to sleep without any heat in his bedroom from the time he was seven. When he was sitting at the table, or studying, he had to sit ramrod straight. If he ever slouched, his father punished him with sharp slaps from a ruler. What do you think you'd be like today if you'd had this kind of upbringing?" Ade couldn't imagine. But he did remember that Kohler once told him he had a chronically sore back. Could it have been a psychological holdover from this childhood persecution?

"In effect, Jack's father programmed him to obey his code of rules, so that even though he had the will and the temptation to act differently – he was only human after all – his father had trained him so rigidly that doing something improper became a moral impossibility. Jack told me that his father used to interrogate him, question after question, trying to root out 'impure thoughts' and crush them. This happened so regularly that the only way he could think of to get his father to leave him alone was to deliberately try to stop thinking!"

Ade was impatient. "That's hard to believe. Jack grew up in America in the 40's, not in some police state. And this is 1971. We know a lot about insanity defenses."

"But not many people talk about the lasting impact of child abuse. Maybe we're not as progressive as we think. There must be thousands – maybe millions – of people who've committed crimes because of horrible things they suffered in childhood."

"If that's so in Jack's case, he must be very resentful to this day."

"This is what's surprising. Even now, he speaks of his father with great respect. He refuses to criticize him, or hear anything critical about him. Jack's always so rational, so this is all pretty amazing. I couldn't understand it, but then it became clear: Jack's father was the ultimate authority figure. Jack couldn't condemn him – it would be like condemning God."

While Cynthia was talking, Ade was thinking about the Schreber case, and what Ginger had said over the telephone. He remembered having asked Cynthia about 'soul-murder' in Douala, and she'd exhibited a blank. He decided to try again. "Have you ever heard of the Schreber case? It's described in one of Freud's notebooks, and apparently it's pretty famous."

"I know a little bit about it. Douala wasn't the place to talk about it, but Jack read about that case and was fascinated by it."

"There was a curious term – 'soul murder. Does that mean anything to you?"

"Not much. My mind works more like a lawyer's than a psychiatrist's. But I've thought about it and wondered if it might throw some light on what happened to Jack."

"What's your conclusion?"

"In the Schreber case, it meant that it was somehow possible to take possession of another person's soul. Only God could do that, or in Schreber's case, his father, who had become the embodiment of God in his mind. But thinking of his father as a 'soul murderer' was impossible for Schreber, because it was an impure thought. Reading about that case, I think I can understand the enormous pressure that built up on that poor, tormented man. Ade, I feel so sorry for him."

"So you think this has a parallel to Jack's situation?"

"Oh yes, it's clear, although I obviously don't know all the psychiatric nuances. We've discussed it with Dr. Wallach, but I don't know if he and Dilbaugh will use it."

"This complicates my vision of Jack. But even if this is all true, it doesn't change his basic guilt. It wasn't Jack's father who killed George, it was Jack."

"I'm only saying that Jack had enormous problems, caused by his father's abuse, which he tried all his life to control. Maybe being on Tanako was more than he could cope with, and his problems just overwhelmed him."

Cynthia's argument was eating into Ade's skepticism. But he caught himself. This was the 1970's, not the world of Kurtz in "*Heart of Darkness.*" Kohler was an ordinary guy, not someone looking into his soul and finding horror. "If your strategy is that dealing with Tanako drove Jack temporarily insane, it's going to be a tough sell. Anyway, why are you telling me all this? Am I a trial balloon?"

"No, I just wanted to talk to you because it's very hard to deal with the picture of my husband, and Robin's father, as some sadistic monster. That's what the papers are suggesting, and even some former friends. I need someone who knows Jack to tell me that he hasn't completely made up his mind, and still regards him as a human being."

"I do see Jack as a complex human being – but I can't forget scraping up pieces of George Ellerbee from the Embassy floor and putting them in a plastic bag. I also have sympathy for Maria Ellerbee, who everyone seems to overlook." The tough words were out of Ade's mouth before he could soften them, but Cynthia didn't blink.

"Ade, you and the others are still Jack's colleagues. Whatever you think of what he did, don't forget that until this happened none of you would've said you were a better man than Jack Kohler."

"And no man could have a more supportive wife, Cynthia. Whatever happens, I wish you and Robin well, and justice for Jack."

Cynthia rose to leave, but Ade had one more question. "If I recall correctly, Schreber had strong homoerotic fantasies. If his case is relevant here, do you think Jack and George could've had a homosexual relationship?"

Cynthia looked hard at Ade, eyes flashing briefly, then gradually calmed. She took a deep breath. "No. It's not plausible. Why would you suggest it?"

"A Senator with an interest in the case says there was a major security breach in Moscow when George was there.

He thinks George was homosexual, the Soviets found about it, and blackmailed him into passing secrets."

"Good God, that's all we need."

"His press aide says he has reliable information." Cynthia sized up Ade one more time. "This much I know, Ade," she said. "George Ellerbee was a homosexual. Jack found out about it from a friend in Moscow and tried to have him fired."

CHAPTER THIRTY-TWO

Two weeks later, Ned Dilbaugh filed pre-trial motions and a hearing was set for November 15. Ade and Ron Zimmerman would have to testify. Lyle Jameson, the Department's lawyer on the case, whom Ade had known slightly during his last Washington tour, asked him to come by to review what would take place.

Lyle's office was in the legal advisers suite on the seventh floor, where the Department's most senior officials were located. Lyle was just under six feet, mid-forties, with dark brown hair and sideburns that stopped just below his ears. He'd put on about ten pounds since they'd last met, but still looked reasonably trim. Like all lawyers who worked in the Department, he dressed more like a lawyer than an FSO, which meant that he wore more expensive clothes and left his jacket on while working. His office, like most in the Department, was austere, but this one had a window with a view of the Potomac and a veneer of dark wood paneling, giving it a faux law office aspect, which Lyle heightened with a sprinkling of legal reference books and two antique duck hunting decoys.

They shook hands, and Lyle beckoned Ade to an easy chair opposite his desk. Lyle sat in the one next to it, separated from Ade by a coffee table. In the Department, if you wanted to offer coffee or tea to a visitor, you had to make it yourself from the office coffee pot. Although most people didn't bother, this was the seventh floor and perhaps Lyle wanted to preserve at least the appearance of amenity. But Ade declined his offer to pour him a cup.

Lyle started the conversation. "You guys did a great job investigating the murder and preserving so much of the evidence. Given the circumstances, I'm hoping what you sent us will stand up in court. You'll have to testify how you gathered it and protected it from taint. It must've been a wild experience." "I'll say that," Ade answered. "We were lucky it wasn't worse. Kohler could've been seized and summarily executed. The Tanakians could've arrested Ron Zimmerman and tainted all the evidence. Kohler could've gone berserk again. And Maria Ellerbee could've totally collapsed. If it hadn't been for Chris Kanu and the Camejos, it would've been much worse."

"And now we're into the next phase. How much do you know about the case since Kohler came back?"

"I don't know much about the legal issues. I'm also worried about Senator Manning's charges and how much of that is true."

"I can't tell you much about that because I'm just working the legal side. The jurisdiction issue could be tricky in the hands of a cagey lawyer like Ned Dilbaugh. That's why we were anxious to bring the case before Judge Wallace Tiernan. He recently tried a similar landmark case, where a sailor killed a shipmate on an ice floe on the high seas, up near the North Pole, raising questions about jurisdiction. If you know any law students, ask them if they've heard of the 'ice floe case,' and I'll bet they have. Anyway, we're hoping Judge Tiernan will make a similar ruling on this case. That's the issue we'll be dealing with at the hearing."

"Kohler killed Ellerbee in the American Embassy, U. S. Government property. That makes jurisdiction clear-cut, doesn't it?"

"I wish it were so. Dilbaugh will challenge whether the Embassy was really American territory and will move to dismiss on the grounds that the court lacks jurisdiction to try a crime that occurred in a foreign country. If they lose, they'll challenge the venue and push for the trial to be moved to Boston."

"So that's why Kohler wasn't taken into custody until he was in Virginia."

"Exactly. And if Tiernan's court has no jurisdiction, there's no case, and Kohler can't be tried."

And if Kohler walks, there's a public outcry, Manning and Jurgens ride the issues all day and two faceless bureaucrats whose names are Nadherny and Stubblefield will be on center stage all by themselves to explain why they didn't know something was wrong with those guys and why they sent them to a place like Tanako. Ade pushed that grim scenario aside. "What's Judge Tiernan like?"

"He's an institution here. Tough, irascible, enjoys baiting the lawyers. He'll often interrupt to put in a barb. He won't put up with any nonsense, and his rulings usually stand up on appeal. If he baits you, don't get rattled. It's often good-natured, and there's usually a valid point behind it. But he'll leave no doubt that he's in control. It's his courtroom, and he enjoys the spotlight.

"As for your testimony, I'll ask you about what you saw and what you know. Like, for instance, whether the Embassy was leased or owned, and whether access to the public was limited."

"What's that got to do with jurisdiction?"

"The defense will argue that since the Embassy was leased and not owned, and because the transaction was with a private Tanakian landlord and not the government of Tanako, it wasn't American territory, and therefore the court lacks jurisdiction."

"If the United States lacks jurisdiction, where should Kohler be tried?"

"If Tiernan rules that the United States has no jurisdiction, Kohler walks. Just picture the news headline: 'Diplomat-murderer immune from prosecution.' Not only would justice be denied, but the Department would be ridiculed. The fallout from a dismissal would take years to clean up."

"But surely the defense can't argue that an American diplomat overseas who commits a crime is immune from prosecution."

"Not exactly, but they have an argument with a number of legal precedents. I think we'll win, but it won't be easy."

"How about Ned Dilbaugh?"

"The best. He's also ambitious and hates to lose even more than most lawyers. He's had some big cases and this is another one. He'll certainly do his best for Jack Kohler, be assured of that. I've gotten to know him a bit, and I like him. He's polite, even courtly, but underneath it you sense a very determined man who expects to win."

Ade was worried. "If Dilbaugh makes me and the Department look incompetent, Senator Manning has a new bombshell for the evening news, and I end up dead meat. I hope the prosecution's good."

"The guy who's doing all the work is Tony Fonseca. Bright, only in his 30's, but he's had a lot of trial experience already. He went to George Washington University, and worked a day job to pay his tuition. Both Fonseca and Dilbaugh are top lawyers and very professional, but underneath that lawyerly reserve, they're ferocious competitors. Anyway, you could do much worse than having Tony Fonseca on your side. You and Zimmerman are two of his key witnesses, so he's not going to let you get chewed up. Overall, I think the prosecution has a strong case. Of course, you can never predict which way a jury is going to swing, but Dilbaugh's got a tough road."

Ade had one final question. "As a lawyer, what do you think about Kohler's insanity defense?"

"Well, like you, I haven't seen the reports from the psychiatrists. Not only Milton Wallach, who will testify for the defense, but at least one shrink hired by the Department had a go at Kohler. My view is that at the time of the murder Kohler was certainly deeply psychologically disturbed, and probably still is, although everyone says that it's safe for him to be walking about. But there are lots of disturbed personalities out there, and most of them know the difference between right and wrong. Being disturbed is not a crime, but it is a crime to act on the basis of your delusions and kill an innocent man."

"That's a good insight, and it should make conviction likely." Ade got up to leave.

"Sure, but there are lots of intangibles. Right now, all bets are off."

* * *

Monday morning, November 15, was gray and chilly, the temperature in the high 20's. It felt much colder to Ade because he was used to the sub-tropical climate of Yaounde, and had only a light topcoat.

He took a bus to Duke Street in Alexandria, and then a cab to the U. S. District Court House in Old Town. It amused him to think that if this was Cameroon, he'd be riding in the back seat of a limo, a professional driver at the wheel, and people would stop to look as he whooshed down the street. But here he was happy to be without ceremonial baggage and able to blend into his surroundings, no different from other Americans going to the office.

The U. S. Court House in Alexandria is a modern brick office building of no distinction, but at least it doesn't jar the colonial and Georgian ambiance of Old Town, the toney part of the city and an historical and architectural gem. The inside is strictly government issue, nothing like the posh K Street suites of the top Washington law firms just across the Potomac River, where the Ned Dilbaughs ply their trade in offices with thick carpeting, dignified art work, and attractive but cold-as-ice gatekeepers.

Tony Fonseca greeted Ade with a smile as he extended his hand. "You've come a long way," he said warmly. His manner was businesslike but friendly. He ushered Ade into his office, which was austere except for the obligatory family photographs on the one table in the room, and a few framed professional awards on the walls.

"Good to meet you," Ade said. "I'm looking forward to testifying, but I'm worried about the commotion over choosing Kohler and Ellerbee for Tanako. They were the pick of the litter, so to speak, and I thought they'd make a good match!"

"You can't beat yourself up about that," Tony said briskly. "A hundred other guys would've made the same decision."

"Maybe, but now Senator Manning is using this to blackmail the Department and I'm in the middle of it. Frankly, I'm worried."

Ade detected a trace of impatience in Fonseca. After all, he had a big case to try, and maybe he thought Ade was putting himself first.

"Look, Mr. Nadherny," he said, "I'm going to give you every chance to tell your story. My opinion is that you and your colleagues should get medals for the way you handled things out there, but I know how things work in this town. But you follow my lead and I don't think Manning will lay a hand on you."

Fonseca's optimism was reassuring, after the worst case scenario mentality that dominated the Department. Ade asked, "Do you know anything about the charge that Ellerbee was a homosexual and that he and Kohler may have had a homosexual relationship? And that in the Soviet Union Ellerbee was blackmailed into giving documents to the Soviets?"

"Yes, Lyle told me about it. What I can tell you for now is that some very important new information will come out at the trial that will prove Kohler's guilt beyond doubt. And it should help to get you off the hook."

"I could use that. Can you tell me what it is?"

"Not for now. Maybe not until the trial. Just trust me."

"I think I have a 'need to know,' as they say in the State Department." Ade had immediately liked Tony, but didn't like being in the dark about aspects of a case that he once had known more about than anyone else.

Tony was evasive. "When I call you, you'll testify about the status of the Embassy and the relationship between Kohler and Ellerbee. Remember, most of us don't know a lot about embassies and how they operate, so don't assume that it's all clear. Try to avoid bureaucratic jargon. After all the stuff you had to contend with, this'll be a piece of cake. Just give factual answers unless you're asked for an opinion."

When they went down to the courtroom a few minutes later, there were only a few people there, maybe thirty in all. It was open to the public, but pre-trial motions didn't excite many people except those few who realized that Jack Kohler could walk out a free man without ever coming to trial. Kohler, with the now-familiar impassive expression on his face, was at the defense table with Ned Dilbaugh. Ade had come to regard his stolid gaze as a mask that concealed not a dull man, but a conflicted soul with many emotions bubbling up inside him. Cynthia sat behind him in the spectator seats, within whispering distance. Ned Dilbaugh was wearing a charcoal gray suit, with a blue shirt and white collar, and a blue and red striped repp tie. Tony Fonseca was huddled with two assistants, and Lyle Jameson had also joined the huddle. Ade spotted Ron's massive form in the spectator seats, and went to sit with him.

As he was picking his way through small knots of spectators, he saw Maria Ellerbee, standing quietly with another woman and a man. He headed over to her and greeted her warmly. "Maria, I'm so glad to see you. You're looking well in spite of all you've been through. How are you?"

"I'm doing all right, Ade," she replied with a wan smile. She was too decent to be rude, and had no reason to be put out with Ade, but it was clear from the determined and sorrowful look on her face that her ordeal was far from over. Seeing stern justice meted out to Jack Kohler would be essential for her rehabilitation process. The couple with her turned out to be her sister, Luisa, and her husband, who was American and worked for Metropolitan Life Insurance over in College Park, Maryland. Maria wouldn't be a witness during the pre-trial motions, but her presence in the courtroom was a visible reminder that Jack Kohler, sane or insane, had killed a man in cold blood. Ade was certain that Maria would be present for every minute of the proceedings.

Ade took leave of Maria and her companions, and joined Ron in the seats behind the prosecution. They'd been seated only a few minutes when the clerk announced, "All rise," and Judge Wallace Tiernan swept into the courtroom. He was about five ten, with thick, wavy gray hair parted in the middle, and bushy dark eyebrows. He didn't bother to look at the spectators who'd nearly filled the benches behind the attorneys' tables. Judge Tiernan exuded the self-confidence of a man who enjoyed the authority vested in him and would tolerate no challenge to it. Ade guessed him to be in his middle to late sixties. He walked briskly to his chair and sat down.

The defense had previously submitted briefs on both jurisdiction and venue. Dilbaugh's briefs also included the contention that Kohler couldn't get a fair trial because material witnesses from Tanako were unavailable.

Judge Tiernan swept the courtroom with a quick gaze, and said, "All right, gentlemen. You can decide which one of these motions to take up first."

Fonseca spoke up. "Your Honor, the government would like to introduce to the court Mr. Lyle Jameson, who is an attorney and is Assistant Legal Adviser for the Department of State. I would like him sitting at counsel's table and would like to move his admission this morning."

Tiernan looked down benignly. "The motion is granted," he said. Looking right at Lyle, he added, "We're happy to have a representative from the Department of State with us and we'll extend to you every courtesy of the court during our proceedings. We know that diplomats are trained to argue any side of a controversy, whenever it suits them. So whatever you do, don't get Mr. Fonseca confused."

There was an amused stir in the courtroom. Those familiar with Judge Tiernan's courtroom barbs smiled knowingly. "It's the defense's motion, isn't it?" he said.

Dilbaugh stepped forward and said, "Your Honor, the accused was clearly in custody from the time he was taken out of the Embassy until he landed in Boston, and that clearly establishes venue in Boston. So obviously he can't be tried in this court."

Tiernan looked at him sharply. "Just because he might be walking around with an American official doesn't, *per se,* put him in custody."

"But because he was in the custody of, and accompanied by, American officials and then landed in Boston puts an end to the matter."

"Because you say so doesn't make it so," responded Tiernan. "Let's have some facts, and then you gentlemen can argue the law."

Fonseca then successively called Ron Zimmerman and Ade to the stand to outline the circumstances and explain the status of diplomatic missions abroad. Ade recounted the ordeal of getting Kohler out safely and Ellerbee's body back to America, which would help if Jurgens charged him with incompetence. Tony also brought out that nobody had authority to arrest Kohler and that no one ever took him into custody. Then Dilbaugh took over and introduced the Department's cable containing instructions to bring Kohler to Dulles Airport in Virginia. He intoned the line, "Because of legal implications, he should not, repeat not, be brought into the U. S. anywhere else even if this entails layover enroute."

Dilbaugh looked up triumphantly. "Your Honor, this exactly proves my point. They recognized that it was crucial for Mr. Kohler to be brought to Dulles, but in fact he landed at Boston. Therefore there's no venue in Virginia and the case shouldn't be tried here. Case closed."

Tiernan's expression didn't change. "Whether an accidental layover may have occurred doesn't strike me as very important. Proceed."

Dilbaugh looked deflated, but rallied quickly. "Let us take up the question of Mr. Kohler's diplomatic immunity," he began. "You mean from prosecution?" Tiernan asked.

"From prosecution."

"Around the world?"

"Around the world."

Tiernan smiled and rolled his eyes. "That's a rather comprehensive assertion. I'll need some authority for that."

"That he in fact enjoys diplomatic immunity?"

"No, that he enjoys immunity from being questioned for the commission of any crime, anywhere." Judge Tiernan fixed Dilbaugh with a stern gaze. "Just so I understand it," he said, "you're saying that any place where the United States has an embassy, an American diplomat can commit a major crime on embassy grounds with impunity, since neither the United States nor the other side has jurisdiction. If that's your contention I'll be glad to hear from you."

"That's our contention." At least it's bold, Ade thought.

Tiernan continued. "I'll need some authority from you, Mr. Dilbaugh, because I don't know any place in the world where you can violate laws just because you're a diplomat. They have rights, but I didn't know about that one."

Dilbaugh waited for the snickering to subside. "It's not a question of rights, your Honor. It's whether this court has jurisdiction over this defendant."

"I think I understand that," Tiernan replied.

"For this court to have jurisdiction over an offense committed in an American embassy there must be specific statutory authority. Only Congress can confer such authority and Congress has manifestly failed to do so."

"Mr. Dilbaugh, is this the first time that a crime of this type has ever before occurred at an American embassy abroad?"

"Prior to this, there has been no murder inside any American embassy."

Tiernan looked up, a smile creasing his lips. "Well, I find that really remarkable. We all know diplomats are nice people, but I never realized they are that nice. It hardly seems possible, all these years and not even one little murder. But if you say it's a fact, I believe it."

"It is a fact, your Honor. And unless Congress has expressly enacted legislation to cover incidents that do not occur on American soil, then the court cannot assume jurisdiction. And without jurisdiction, quite obviously this court cannot try the case. And with that, your Honor, I will rest." Dilbaugh nodded his head for emphasis at Judge Tiernan, and returned to his seat.

Tiernan looked at Fonseca. "Mr. Fonseca?"

Fonseca rose and said, "For purposes of jurisdiction, we say that the Embassy is United States territory, even if it was under lease to a foreigner. The physical control of the premises is the key here. The fact that no one could enter the Embassy without permission of the American officials, and that this was recognized by everyone, even the Tanakian authorities, proves the point."

Tiernan responded, "Well, that may be your opinion, and you're entitled to it, but the burden is on you to show that you have a right to prosecute the accused here. What do you have to say about that?"

"Under international law, even where there's diplomatic immunity, the diplomat can be prosecuted in what's known as the sending state."

Tiernan said, "What I need is some authority on what international law is in this kind of situation, and whether it's binding on the United States."

"I'd like to call on Mr. Jameson of the State Department," said Fonseca.

Lyle flushed slightly and shifted forward in his seat as people in the courtroom looked at him, but he was ready. "If I may, your Honor, the international law in question is the Vienna Convention, an international treaty, which the Senate approved on December 14, 1965, but which has not yet been signed by the President."

"Is it binding then?" asked Tiernan.

"Many of the rules laid out in the convention are binding under international law, even though we haven't ratified the convention itself."

Judge Tiernan added, "So you're saying that international law can be binding on the United States even when a specific treaty hasn't been ratified?"

"That's correct, although it would depend on the circumstances. But as a rule, it's true that diplomats do not escape the jurisdiction of their home state."

As if the matter was settled, Judge Tiernan announced, "We'll take a short break for lunch. It'll be hard to convince me that the accused was technically in custody when no one has presented any facts supporting that contention." He looked at Dilbaugh and said, "At every stop on his trip home, Mr. Kohler was free to go wherever he wanted. In Ghana, he even used the bathroom unaccompanied. He could've walked off and said, 'Well, here I am, in Ghana. You've got nothing to do with me. Goodbye.'

"Neither he nor his wife has said anything to the contrary. And the State Department only made travel arrangements. If that's an arrest I'll hear you on it, but my view is that there was no arrest, and there's no evidence that Mr. Kohler was forcibly brought anywhere. If he was not forcibly brought, is there anything else to hear? There must be some restraint of liberty to constitute an arrest under venue, isn't that so?"

Dilbaugh tried again. "If he wasn't brought back to the United States for the purpose of being prosecuted, why was he brought back?"

"As I recall, and I don't miss much, Mr. Dilbaugh, the defendant was served with a summons and a complaint, but he wasn't formally arrested until he came to this court on September 24. You've already conceded this."

Dilbaugh looked unhappy. "Your Honor, may I please – "

"Now, if you were fooling the court, it'll be much harder to do it again. It happens once in a while. I know you didn't do it intentionally."

Dilbaugh looked exasperated. "We didn't do it at all," he said.

"Mr. Dilbaugh, I don't have to tell you that if a U.S. Marshal has you in custody, he doesn't let you see George Washington Hospital. In other words, Mr. Kohler couldn't go to a private hospital in the District of Columbia if he were under arrest."

"No, your Honor. Mr. Kohler was under arrest and you appointed Dr. Wallach and George Washington Hospital as third party custodian."

Fonseca stood up. "Your Honor, I remember the sequence of events. The problem was to get Mr. Kohler to the hospital as quickly as possible for observation. We frankly didn't know what the effect would be of giving him a summons instead of an arrest warrant. So we took a chance, and he was given a summons but wasn't arrested when he got off the plane."

"I believe you told me that," Tiernan said. "But the point is, was he still free to go where he wanted after he received the summons, like getting a parking ticket to appear at a given place and time?"

"Technically, I suppose that's so," responded Dilbaugh wearily.

"All right," said Tiernan with finality. "Let's recess until 1:30."

The high drama of the courtroom portrayed in the movies or crime novels masks a reality that requires prolonged attention to minutiae for justice to be done. To some, this is tedious – the minute dissection of what seem to be minor points of law, or some detail in the evidence – but to Ade, the early skirmishing over the defense motions only heightened his sense of anticipation. It may have been a preliminary before the main bout, but if the prosecution didn't nail down the issues of venue and jurisdiction, it could mean that a man who had committed murder might not be brought to trial.

Ade kept looking at Kohler for clues to his state of mind. Jack was attentive, but showed no emotion, his unblinking eyes gazing straight ahead. Cynthia often reached over and grasped his hand, but they rarely spoke.

Maria was a total contrast, her black eyes seeming to bore laser-like into the back of Kohler's head, as though by penetrating his skull she would find a clue to the behavior that had taken her husband. So far, the details of the murder had not come up, and maybe this explained why she seemed pretty well in check. Ade wondered how she would do if the case went to trial and Kohler testified in his own defense.

At 1:45, Judge Tiernan resumed his seat and looked down at the two lawyers. "If there's anything more on venue and jurisdiction, now's the time to raise it. The question is whether this court has jurisdiction. If I don't have jurisdiction, I'm wasting my time."

"That's correct, your Honor," Dilbaugh said. "Congress hasn't enacted the necessary legislation."

"Well, let's look at diplomatic immunity," said Tiernan. "For centuries, countries have been granting diplomats more immunity than I get when I go to a foreign country, so under most circumstances they are immune from criminal prosecution – "

Dilbaugh interrupted quickly with a confident smile. "I have no quarrel with that, your Honor. That's exactly what we've been saying – "

" – in the country of their assignment," Tiernan finished his sentence. "Now," he continued, "you argue that the United States has no power to try and punish its representatives who allegedly violate American law in American territory, to wit, an American chancery? Do you take that position?"

"I take the position that the Congress has the right to enact legislation to cover this, but has not done so."

"So, you say that even though this offense is a crime since the days of Moses – I can go a long way back to 'Thou shalt not kill' – we can't even go to trial because Congress didn't expressly fashion a law to cover an offense in an embassy building outside the United States. That's your position, isn't it?"

"That's correct, your Honor," answered Dilbaugh.

"So therefore the accused goes free just because there is no law."

"Presumably this a country of laws, your Honor. I think I've stated our position as well as I can possibly state it."

Tiernan half-smiled. "You haven't done well enough. 'Nobody has any authority to try the case,' and that's your position."

Dilbaugh responded, "And the law your Honor. We have the law."

"You are stronger on enthusiasm than you are on the law," Tiernan said.

Dilbaugh stifled a sigh. "There's another problem, your Honor. The State Department says we can't visit the island to get crucial testimony from material witnesses. This denies the defendant due process."

Fonseca, sensing a win, said, "That's one place I don't particularly care to go, your Honor. We couldn't get in there either."

Tiernan looked down at Fonseca and said, "I'd be happy to send you over there and leave you." Dilbaugh looked pleased. He said, "Your Honor, we contend that if the witnesses are unavailable, putting Mr. Kohler on trial would violate due process."

"If these witnesses won't come, I have no power to make them appear. Much as I might want to, I can't order the Spanish Government to have their ambassador to Tanako testify. If anybody here doesn't understand this, I'll be happy to have our diplomat in residence here, Mr. Jameson, explain it to them."

"We'll plead temporary insanity, and the people we wanted to interview could testify that Mr. Kohler's behavior was extremely unusual prior to the tragedy. Without these witnesses he'll be denied essential elements in pleading his case."

"You seem to want to bring everybody in Tanako over here to show evidence of insanity," Tiernan answered. "Now, if you're testing Mr. Fonseca's sanity, you can't call everybody in Alexandria who's seen him walk down the street in the last six years. We're not going to have that kind of case."

"We understand that, but we need at least some of those witnesses."

Tiernan responded, "Even if none of them are available, that doesn't impress me much because you already have witnesses like Mr. Nadherny and Mr. Zimmerman who were in touch with the accused before the crime, saw the crime scene and came back with the family. I'll also tell you that I haven't decided the motions yet, but I suggest that you should all get ready for trial. Now, anything else?"

For once, the lawyers were speechless.

"Thank you, counselors," said Judge Tiernan, rising, and strode rapidly out of the courtroom. There was no doubt in Ade's mind that he'd already decided, but he wanted some time to make sure there were no slip-ups. Judge Tiernan wasn't going to lose this case on a technicality.

CHAPTER THIRTY-THREE

As they left the Courthouse, Charlie suggested to Ade, "Let's go over to Old Town and have a beer."

They headed for Murphy's, an upscale bar popular with the wine and brie set and the upwardly mobile young career-ists who'd started swarming to Washington with the advent of the Kennedy administration in the 1960s.

"Did you notice Walter Jurgens in the courtroom?" Charlie asked. Ade hadn't, because he'd been nervous about testifying and totally absorbed afterwards. According to Charlie, the little ferret slipped into the back of the court-room as Ron was called to the stand, and stayed just long enough to hear the beginnings of the arguments on the motions. That meant he'd heard Ade's testimony on the sta-tus of the Embassy and Kohler's place in it, and Ade was glad of that. He thought he'd done well enough to give Tony a good basis for arguing that the U. S. had jurisdiction.

"Frank Maxwell has been getting queries on Ellerbee's Moscow assignment," Charlie said. "They're asking if he was ever under suspicion of espionage, and if there was an inves-tigation. So far, nothing about homosexuality, but that can't be far off."

"Our friend Jurgens has been busy," Ade said, frowning. "He feeds the media just enough to keep them on the hook and build interest. He's clever."

"And he just whispers in some reporter's ear, and he's got a headline."

The next day, the *Washington Post* had a short item on the pre-trial motions, focusing on the testimony that Kohler was never in custody, "despite the fact that American officials were with him from the time he emerged from the Embassy after the murder until he landed at Dulles Airport."

Ade scanned the rest of the paper quickly, and received a sudden jolt from this headline in the Business section: "Senator Attacks Rise in Textile Imports; Threatens Reprisals." The article said that Senator Hawthorne Manning had pronounced himself "fed up" with the administration for its "do-nothing" attitude on Asian textiles. According to the Senator, these were flooding the country, costing jobs and bankruptcies nationwide, but especially in Georgia. He charged that Asian countries were violating quota agreements by shipping nearly finished goods to subsidiaries in Latin America that had unused quotas, where they'd add a button, or lapel or something and then send them into the US as non-Asian merchandise.

"I think some of those countries need a little wake-up call," the Senator was quoted as saying. "We should remind them who's sending all that aid and military equipment to fight the communists. But most of all, we need people in the State Department who will stand up for American interests."

That message was sure to resonate, and Manning would ride it even if it upset the Southeast Asians. If South Vietnam fell, it was crucial that the other countries stayed healthy.

Textile exports to the US were crucial to their economies. Some of them cheated on their quotas, but you handled that not by threatening them in public, but through some deft, quiet diplomacy. That could get the job done without causing the Asians to lose face and dig in their heels.

That afternoon, Ade received a yellow telephone message marked "urgent" instructing him to call Harlan Hastings right away. Hastings, so anxious to get rid of him, apparently now wanted him back for something. *This can only mean trouble. It's amazing how quickly they can reach you when there's a problem, and be inaccessible when you need support.* Hastings' secretary didn't waste words. "Mr. Hastings would like to see you tomorrow at eleven-fifteen." Click.

Hastings greeted Ade with a quick smile and a handshake. "I heard your testimony yesterday went well." Charlie and Lyle Jameson undoubtedly had given him a full report. "That's good. You know that this trial is very important to the Department's image, and that there are other issues involved. Big ones."

"Yes, I know that. Or think I do."

"One of them is this brouhaha being stirred up by Senator Manning." Hastings liked to use words like "brouhaha," and "potpourri."

Ade said, "I saw the story in the *Post*. Surely we can handle this without causing the Asians to go on a rampage. There was a big demo in front of the Embassy in Bangkok yesterday. The Asians are playing it as though we're killing their economy by trying to cut textile imports. Burning American flags, throwing rocks – the police finally broke it up with water cannon."

Hastings sighed softly. "Yes, and what a pity our Asian friends don't have the same appreciation for politics in Washington that we here must have."

Ade didn't say anything, because he feared what was coming next.

"Ade, I want you to go to the Hill and see if you can defuse this thing before it gets any worse. Senator Manning says that he'll receive you personally. The only other person in the room will be Walter Jurgens."

"I'm hearing a lot about that guy these days," Ade said sourly.

"Yes, well, uh, he does a very good job for the Senator."

Ade was beginning to see why Hastings had reached the top levels of the Foreign Service. In one short sentence he managed to express his distaste for people like Jurgens, and convey to Ade the necessity of dealing with him regardless, without uttering either sentiment.

"What can I tell Manning? " he asked. "I have exactly zero cards to play."

"I'm about to give you some. What I want you to do is offer him a deal. The same one he offered us, earlier, before we realized he was serious and had some information that could make us look bad. We'll handle the quotas and the Asians, and he stops demagoguing and stirring up the press. And he calls off his bulldog."

"That's no deal!" Ade exclaimed. "You're sending me up there to fold our hand."

"Calm down, Ade. Next spring, we'll be negotiating new agreements and quotas. Until then we don't want that issue muddying the waters. Without Manning baying at the moon, we can handle the Asians, and it's no bad thing if they know we're on to their tactics and they'd better stop. It's always better if you can persuade someone to take corrective action on his own than to humiliate him and force him to his knees."

Ade knew that Hastings was right, but it stuck in his craw that a demagogue Senator and his shifty press aide could force the entire administration to buckle under. If people were really losing their jobs due to foreign imports Manning had a case, but he and his allies in Congress hadn't provided credible evidence. It was easier to blow smoke to the press and special interest groups.

Anyway, Ade really had no choice. Hastings had given him a job and maybe the deal, as bad as it seemed on its merits, served a higher purpose. He said, "OK," in a way that he hoped conveyed his acquiescence to his order but also his unhappiness about the Department's caving in to pressure.

"There's something else. Manning called me personally just before you came in. A Japanese TV crew is going to Georgia to do a special on the textile issue there. They want to visit plants, cotton fields, and workers to gauge just how severe this issue is. They asked the Senator's office to open some doors for them and he hit the roof."

"Why?" Ade asked.

"I think he's afraid they'll go down there and find that this issue is no big deal at the grass roots. Maybe finding a worker who actually lost his job because of Asian imports might be difficult. If that happened, Manning wouldn't have an issue. Anyway, he wants me, which means you, to get in touch with that TV crew and tell them to stay the hell out of Georgia."

"We can't do that," Ade said. "They can go and shoot where they want."

"Well, that's a nice principle, but they can't. Not in this case." Hastings looked at Ade firmly. "You're to tell the Japanese that if they go, we can't guarantee their safety. You can tell them that there's a lot of anti-Asian feeling kicking up down there because of all those textiles coming in."

"But we don't know that that's true at all," Ade responded, trying not to sputter. "You just said yourself that you doubted it."

"Ade, I don't have to tell you how the game is played here. If it will help, use Manning's name. You can say that 'Senator Manning is concerned, and has asked me to call you personally and urge you not to go. If you go, he wants you to understand that he can't guarantee your safety.'"

"Sure, and at the same time he'll be passing the word to his redneck supporters down there that some of the good old boys might like to have some fun with a Japanese TV crew. Do you know what a stink that would cause?"

"I sure do. That's why I'm asking you to try to prevent it."

"Why don't we just let them go, and notify the local police to make sure nothing happens to them? That way, the Japanese would get their footage, and maybe it would show that there's no real issue at all, that it's all stirred up by politicians in Washington."

"We need fast action. Besides, local police don't take orders from the State Department. They might be on the side of the rednecks anyway."

Ade was running out of arguments, and Hastings hadn't moved. "Well, even if we solve this one, we still have the suspicions about Ellerbee, hints of espionage by the Soviets, and cover-up and bumbling by the Department."

"One step at a time. If we manage this one, the others become much easier. Good luck."

If Ade had anything more to say, Hastings didn't want to hear it.

* * *

When Ade arrived at Senator Manning's office, Jurgens was there, undoubtedly having rehearsed the good cop-bad cop routine with his master.

The Senator shook hands warmly. "I've been having some phone conversations with your boss," he said with a smile. "I don't usually have the pleasure of dealing with the working level of the Department."

Ade swallowed. "The Assistant Secretary told me to see whether we can respond to your concerns on textile imports."

"I'm very glad to hear that, Mr. Nadherny. I have great respect for our boys in striped pants. Even though there seems to be an infestation of deviants down there. We may have to look into that real soon. Now, do you have something to tell me?"

Ade related the deal that Hastings had outlined. At each key point, Manning nodded. Jurgens looked furtive, as if expecting to find a double cross.

"That's fine," Manning said. "If you do your part, I'll do mine."

Ade waited to see if they'd mention the TV crew. Jurgens spoke up. "There's also that Jap TV crew. "We want you to keep them out of Georgia."

"I don't have that power," Ade said. "I also think they should be allowed to go there and be given every assistance.

On something so important, they've surely sent their first team, and they'll report all sides. It might even help to have some of your textile people in Georgia explain to a TV audience of millions in Japan why they're upset about so many textiles coming in from Asia."

The twinkle that had been playing in Senator Manning's eyes disappeared. "Those fellows come over here, no tellin' what emotions'd be set loose. I know my people, Mr. Nadherny, and they're fed up with this. There'd be no guaranteeing the safety of those folks. They could wander off and get into all kinds of trouble. I don't think we'd want that to happen, would we?"

"But Japan's a key ally. There's no reason to antagonize them."

Manning smiled indulgently. "I'm in the Senate to protect the interests of my people. I'm not here to protect the interests of Japan. I'll leave that to you boys in the State Department. But I can tell you this, Sir, when American boys are over in Asia fighting the communists" – he called them 'commonists' – "I do wonder why we can't get a little respect from our Asian friends."

"The issues are different, Senator. This has nothing to do with Vietnam."

"Try telling that to my constituents. Anyway, I appreciate your keeping those TV folks out of mah state. It's been a pleasure to talk to you." And with that he rose, shook Ade's hand, and stood until he departed.

Ade called Hastings and relayed the conversation. "They still want me to call the Japanese. It's wrong, and we shouldn't touch it," he said, hoping his conviction would win the point.

"Do it," Hastings said, and hung up.

Feeling sour, Ade called the Japanese. A Mr. Kimura was the producer. As Ade conveyed his message, Kimura, who'd greeted him warmly, seemed to tense audibly as he took in Ade's warning. "Thank you for this information," he said stiffly. "But we came here to do a documentary, and we are going to do it."

"But Senator Manning says that he can't guarantee your safety if you go."

"Mr. Nadherny," Kimura said, "I've always respected the free press in your country. We didn't have that in Japan in World War II, so as a journalist it means so much to me. This is not wartime, and Japan is not your enemy. We'll get footage in Georgia, with or without the help of Senator Manning. And I will reflect on freedom of the press as some people in your government practice it. Good-bye, Mr. Nadherny."

CHAPTER THIRTY-FOUR

For once Murphy's Law didn't apply, and despite Ade's unhappiness about the deals with Senator Manning, he was relieved that they had worked. Manning and Jurgens were keeping quiet about the Kohler case, and Kimura and his crew went to Georgia and emerged unscathed. Manning might be a conniving politician, but he wasn't a thug. As for Hastings, Ade reluctantly admired his skill in crisis management, but wished that the Department would pay more attention to crisis prevention.

Still, Ade wanted to mend fences with the Japanese film crew. He also wondered if Kimura knew anything about Japanese terrorists. He had to learn more about what he and George had seen on their brief foray into the bush outside Arania. He'd been doing some research on the Japanese Red Army at Georgetown, and hoped that Kimura could give him some leads.

What Ade already knew was that the Japanese Red Army was a small group of radicals who got their start in the 60's staging violent demonstrations. Somewhere along the way they'd established relations with their counterparts in Europe, and staged some Mideast hijackings. A couple of them had been killed and some had been caught, but the leader, Keiko Matsumora, was still at large, rumored to be in hiding in a sympathetic country, perhaps Libya or Lebanon.

Ade called Kimura and said he was glad that he and his crew had been able to film in Georgia without mishap. Kimura showed no hostility and replied, "Yes, we got everything we were after and people were almost always friendly towards us. We're leaving for Tokyo next week to edit the footage. It'll be a good program."

"Kimura-san, do you know anything about the Japanese Red Army?"

"Of course. You don't hear much about them anymore, but Keiko Matsumora and a couple of others have never been caught."

"I heard they might be in Libya."

"There was a good update on them in the *Asahi Shimbun* a couple of months back. It said that Japanese intelligence thinks they're in Africa somewhere. Some island country. I don't remember the name."

Ade's mouth suddenly felt dry. "Was it Tanako?"

"That's it. I'm not sure where it is — on the West Coast, I think."

Ade explained that he'd been DCM in Yaounde, had dealt with the aftermath of the Ellerbee murder, and had stumbled on some Japanese living in military austerity out in the bush. "The only plausible explanation for those Japanese being there is that they're terrorists, but I have no evidence. What do you think?"

Kimura sucked in his breath. "Saaa. There could be some connection."

"You might have a great story if you stopped in Tanako on your way back to Japan," Ade suggested. "It's a stretch, but the new government just might let you in."

"If I could break that story, it would be big. Let me work on it. It's worth a try."

A week later, Kimura left for Tokyo via Africa. Sudopo had given him a visa for two days, but turned down his request to bring a cameraman.

On December 12, Judge Tiernan denied the defense motions on both jurisdiction and venue. Tiernan's ruling, picking up a phrase from Fonseca's brief, asserted that "diplomats do not escape the jurisdiction of the courts of their home country."

His ruling on the venue issue was just as terse. He asserted that "the defendant voluntarily returned to the United States prior to the issuance of the indictment, and the complaint was served upon him when he debarked at Dulles International Airport, which is within the territorial confines of the Eastern District of Virginia. This case will proceed to trial as scheduled, beginning at 10:00 a.m. on February 28, 1972."

CHAPTER THIRTY-FIVE

Ron Zimmerman arrived in Washington on Wednesday afternoon, but it was Friday before he and Ade were able to see Tony Fonseca about their upcoming testimony. Fonseca told them, "As I told you, we have evidence we'll introduce early on that'll throw a new light on things."

"Now can you tell us what it is?" Ade asked.

"The crux of it is that the murder was a homosexual lovers' quarrel."

"Aha!" Ron exclaimed, but then began chewing on the revelation. "That could explain some things, but I still don't see how no one knew."

Ade was also calculating what the impact would be on the Department, and Charlie and him. "Well, that will certainly cause a stir," he finally said.

"That it will," Tony answered. He was exuding confidence.

"How will Ned Dilbaugh deal with what you've got?" Ade asked. "I assume it'll be no surprise to him."

"I can hardly wait to find out," said Tony. "Sure, he has the information, but there's nothing he can do about it. I think it'll nail the case for us. It's factual, it's conclusive, and it blows the insanity defense right out of the water."

Maybe Tony could afford to be jaunty, because he now sensed a big win, but Ade figured that any evidence of homosexuality would surely reactivate Manning and Jurgens, rekindling a fire he hoped had been doused.

And what about Kohler and Ellerbee themselves? All this time everyone thought of them as happily married men, but if they were homosexual lovers, obviously there was a lot more going on. What did the wives know? And had Cynthia just been trying to lead Ade away from the trail, to protect her family?

On Monday, when Ade arrived at the courthouse the benches were filling rapidly. The hearing on the defense motions had been only a warm-up; the main event was about to begin, and it had already created a buzz of anticipation. Ade greeted familiar faces, Lyle Jameson, Maria Ellerbee, looking trim and vulnerable, and her sister and brother-in-law. Sally Rogers was there, and Charlie Stubblefield.

By nine forty-five, the courtroom was full. Most of the people there had some connection to the case, either as family, officials of State or Justice, or the press.

Ned Dilbaugh, impeccably dressed in signature navy blue suit, blue shirt with white collar and red patterned tie, entered with his assistants, followed by Jack and Cynthia Kohler. Cynthia looked self-contained, despite whatever inner turmoil she might be experiencing. Did she know what had caused Jack to explode? Had there been some domestic crisis that she was part of?

Jack was dressed in a charcoal gray suit, with a white shirt and striped repp tie. He'd lost some weight, and his face wasn't as puffy as it was during the hearing in November, probably because he was drinking less. With his horn-rim glasses and trim appearance, he looked every bit the career diplomat who could be making a call on the foreign office or heading for a committee meeting at the United Nations.

At 10:05, the clerk of the court announced "All rise!" and Judge Tiernan strode briskly to his chair and took control of the proceedings like a captain taking the helm of a ship. He smiled at the jury, eight men and four women, all looking attentive and resolute, and sat down.

Tony Fonseca called Ron as the first witness, leading him once again through the unimaginable events he'd uncovered on Tanako. He also introduced many exhibits, including the photographs that Ron and Harry Sundel had taken of the murder scene, and the heavy, blood-stained pair of scissors that was the alleged murder weapon. Dilbaugh did his best to have all of this excluded, arguing that it was tainted and too many people could have tampered with it between Tanako and Washington. But the precautions Ade and his colleagues had taken to protect the evidence carried weight with Tiernan, and he allowed almost all of it.

In his unemotional and low-key voice, Ron went on to describe the vault scene, with blood-spattered papers everywhere, and a long length of electrical chord wrapped around a straight-back chair.

The jurors appeared to fix on every word. One woman, mid-forties, with a pretty but deeply-lined face and prematurely grey hair, put her hand to her mouth as though for protection as the gory details poured out.

Ron described in sober and graphic detail how he found the body and had to pry Maria from the still-wet corpse of her husband.

Ade glanced over at her. Maria had her handkerchief wrapped tightly around an index finger, and her eyes were moist, but she showed only intensity as she concentrated on Zimmerman's testimony.

"Now Mr. Zimmerman," Fonseca said, "When you first arrived at the Embassy, did Mr. Kohler strike you as someone who knew what he was doing, or was he upset, distraught, or what?"

"Mr. Kohler knew what he wanted, although his voice was agitated. First, he said he wouldn't talk to me. Then he demanded that I find his wife and son."

"Did you know where they were?"

"No, Mr. Kohler told me where I could probably find them."

"In other words, he may have been agitated, but not so much that he couldn't recall where his wife and son were."

"Objection," Ned Dilbaugh interrupted. "Even a person under extreme mental stress would know where his wife and son were."

"I'm going to allow it. I'll be lenient on anything that might be relevant."

Fonseca said, "And when you returned, and Mrs. Kohler and their son entered the building, did you hear any further conversation from the accused?"

"Yes," answered Ron. "I clearly heard Mr. Kohler say to his wife, 'You've got to help me. They'll never believe me.'"

"And when Mr. Kohler finally came out, did he say anything to you?"

"Yes. When he saw me, he pulled me aside and said, 'Ron, I lost my cool and killed George Ellerbee.'"

A murmur ran through courtroom. Maria Ellerbee nodded grimly. The evidence against Kohler was falling into place.

"Did he say anything else?"

"Yes. He said he'd been under terrible pressure the last few days."

"What was your reaction to this?"

"This was news to me, because I talked to him by radio every day. But I never got a chance to ask him what he meant, because the people outside the embassy surged towards us as soon as he came out."

"Tell us how the accused appeared to you as he told you these things."

"He looked serious, but his tone was businesslike."

"He wasn't emotional or upset?"

"Not at all. He seemed very calm, considering what had happened."

"Did he say or do anything that showed any remorse?"

"Well, no. There was no remorse and no sorrow. It was almost as though he felt a sense of relief."

Another buzz in the courtroom, almost an expression of shock.

Dilbaugh jumped to his feet. "Objection, your Honor! The witness has no way of knowing what the accused was feeling."

"Sustained," said Judge Tiernan. "Counselor, re-phrase your question."

Fonseca said to Ron, "You've told us that the accused made no expression of regret. How did that strike you?"

"I thought it very strange, almost bizarre. Maybe if they never got along, or had some terrible quarrel, Jack's reaction would've been more logical. But if they'd quarreled, Jack would've shown some rage, but he didn't show any."

"Thank you, Mr. Zimmerman," Fonseca said with finality. Looking over at the defense table, he said, "Your witness."

Ned Dilbaugh approached Ron slowly, smiling slightly. He needed him to show doubt about Kohler's mental state, and didn't want him feeling apprehensive or hostile.

"Mr. Zimmerman," he began, "please review for us how you learned that there was a problem at the Embassy in Tanako."

"Mr. Nadherny called me and told me about Mr. Kohler's broadcast and ordered me to get to Tanako and investigate as fast as I could."

Dilbaugh then introduced into evidence the cable with the text of the broadcast, and had Ron verify that that was what he'd heard Kohler say.

He then asked, "When Mr. Kohler said this, what was your reaction?"

"Well, I was flabbergasted. It seemed incredible."

"You mean that you didn't believe it?"

"Not just that. I mean that it seemed totally implausible. I thought Jack must have lost it. The idea that there could be a communist conspiracy that Jack Kohler had uncovered on Tanako was totally off the wall to me."

"What was Mr. Kohler's normal behavior, in your experience?"

"He was articulate and restrained."

"So this was very different."

"Definitely."

"Did you know Mr. Kohler well?"

"Yes. He came over to the Consulate in Douala about every four or five weeks, and we talked on the radio every day."

"Did you have a chance to observe how he got along with Mr. Ellerbee and the other employees of the Embassy?"

"Mr. Kohler could be picky and aloof, but he got along with them all right."

"Are you aware of the situation when one of the Tanakian employees, a Mr. Nguema, was arrested, jailed, and tortured?"

"Yes, I am."

"And what was Mr. Kohler's reaction?"

"I believe that he was genuinely upset that he couldn't get Nguema released."

"So Mr. Kohler showed ample human compassion when a national employee of the Embassy was imprisoned and subjected to physical abuse?"

"Yes, I think so."

"All right. Now, you say that Mr. Kohler showed no remorse when he was leaving the Embassy. Did this strike you as a normal reaction, or inconsistent with what you knew of Mr. Kohler's ability to feel compassion?"

"Well, I certainly thought it strange."

"Thank you, Mr. Zimmerman. No more questions."

Fonseca passed on re-direct examination, and then called Ade to the stand. Ade recounted his encounters with Kohler and the developments on Tanako until all the Americans left. He tried to stress that Kohler was picked for the job because he had a reputation for being "solid as a rock," a phrase Ade vowed never to use again.

On cross-examination, Dilbaugh chipped away at the notion that Kohler was always rational, and elicited from Ade that he'd planned to give Kohler a respite from Tanako. He also established that Kohler had displayed strange behavior just before the killing, and that Ade's first reaction to his broadcast was that he'd suffered a breakdown.

Some of the jury were started to sag with all the details, so Judge Tiernan decided to end the day's proceedings right there.

Tomorrow's first witness was to be Maria Ellerbee.

CHAPTER THIRTY-SIX

The next day, there was a line of spectators stretching down the street about half a block. News of the trial was spreading.

When Judge Tiernan gaveled the courtroom to order and Tony called Maria Ellerbee, the spectators turned in their seats to watch as she slowly made her way to the front. She didn't glance at Jack Kohler as she walked straight to the witness stand, was sworn in, and took her seat. She had on a dark blue suit, with an ivory-colored blouse. Her jewelry was simple and spare: two silver bracelets on her left wrist, and a silver pin in the shape of a small bird with wings outstretched on the lapel of her suit.

Tony Fonseca's voice was soothing as he worked through the first questions. "Now," he said, changing tone slightly, "I'm going to ask you to recall some things that might be painful for you, but I ask you to bear with us."

"I'm ready for your questions," replied Maria, looking resolute.

"First, describe the relationship between your husband and the accused."

"My husband was the administrative officer of the Embassy. The accused was my husband's supervisor and the man in charge of the Embassy."

"Could you describe some of your husband's duties?"

"His day started when he raised the American flag, and it ended when he took it down. In between, he did everything to make the building run. He did it all – fixed the air conditioning when it broke, kept the vehicles running, supervised the Tanakian staff, coded and sent classified telegrams, issued visas, made contacts outside the Embassy, made sure the Embassy had supplies, kept the accounts and petty cash – all that, and much more."

"Did he get along well with the accused?"

"They had a friendly relationship. They were colleagues."

"Did they share common interests, have lunch together, and so forth?"

"Not a lot, but they got on well. My husband liked to joke and be around people. Mr. Kohler was serious, and interested in economics and politics."

"Did you ever have a laugh with him?"

"Oh, sure. He wasn't serious all the time. He often laughed at my husband's jokes, especially if it had to do with someone Mr. Kohler didn't like."

"Did you socialize with Mr. and Mrs. Kohler outside of working hours?"

"Sometimes. On special occasions like July Fourth we'd get together with other expats for a picnic, but we didn't do a lot together."

"Was there any hostility between you?"

"Oh no, not at all. I am Ecuadoran and my husband and I were good friends with the other Latino families in Arania. The Kohlers mixed with people in international organizations like the UN and the World Bank. We just had different interests."

"Did your husband ever talk about his relationship with Mr. Kohler?"

"Oh sure. He thought Mr. Kohler was a fair man, and he trusted him – "

Maria's voice trembled briefly, but she recovered and went on. "Once, he said that Mr. Kohler was a bit strange."

"Can you recall the occasion?" Fonseca asked.

"Well, it was some petty thing, not important. But my husband said that Mr. Kohler could get upset about little things and find small mistakes."

"How would your husband react to this?"

"He never let little things bother him. He had a wonderful sense of humor, and he'd imitate Mr. Kohler acting pompous, and we'd have a laugh."

"When was the last time you talked to your husband?"

"In late morning, he called to say that he and Mr. Kohler were working on a long cable, but that he'd be home for lunch."

"Was there anything that made you suspect there was anything wrong?"

"No. Everything seemed fine. But I began to worry when he didn't come home, and hours went by. I called the Embassy, but no one answered."

"When did you last see the accused prior to your husband's murder?"

"It must've been on Saturday. We stopped by their house briefly. Jack was in the library, reading, so we only said hello. I talked briefly to Cynthia – Mrs. Kohler. She'd been out back playing with Robin."

"So, there was nothing unusual or strange in the Kohlers' household that day, and Mr. Kohler seemed normal?"

"Yes, like always. And two days later he killed my husband for no reason at all."

Judge Tiernan intervened to say, "Strike that from the record. Members of the jury, please disregard that last sentence from the witness."

On cross-examination, Dilbaugh followed up Maria's reference to her husband sometimes finding Kohler "strange," asking her to describe a dinner party at the Kohlers where Jack had ordered Ellerbee to take only one piece of meat when he was served.

Other than that snippet, Maria stuck to her story that Jack seemed normal. She was a good prosecution witness, so Dilbaugh let her go without further questions.

When Maria had been excused and resumed her seat, Fonseca announced, "The prosecution calls Dr. William Thiergard, senior forensic pathologist for the Commonwealth of Virginia."

Dr. Thiergard was a dapper man in his late sixties, with a white moustache. Although he amply filled the rumpled gray suit he was wearing, his step was spry and energetic as he took the stand.

Tony Fonseca moved easily through the preliminaries. He seemed more assured now, almost eager. "How long have you been the senior forensic pathologist for the Commonwealth of Virginia?" he asked.

"Since September of 1956, that is, almost sixteen years."

"Does your specialty include violent and unnatural deaths?"

"Indeed, it does," replied Thiergard. "I've spent many years studying the mind sets that lead to such deaths. Much of my research has been published in medical journals. I've especially concentrated on patterns of violence and the kinds of personalities that might trigger violent behavior. We're making some very promising advances in this field. It's relatively new." The jury and spectators perked up.

"Well, let's start with Mr. Ellerbee's autopsy. Do you recall the details?"

"Yes, certainly. I did it myself."

"Was Mr. Ellerbee's body brought to the hospital in a special container?"

"Yes. It had been handmade in Africa, but was quite sturdy."

"And was it sealed when it came into the hospital?"

"Yes, it still had heavy steel bands around it, and the top and sides had a metal liner that had been nailed shut and soldered."

"So is it reasonable to conclude that the casket as you received it was exactly as it was when it was put on the airplane from Douala, in Cameroon?"

"Objection," shouted Dilbaugh. "The witness knows nothing about the condition of the casket when the deceased was placed in it, and he certainly is in no position to say that it wasn't tampered with enroute."

"You'll have a chance to impeach the credibility of the time line, Mr. Dilbaugh. For now, I'm letting it stand. The witness is only stating his opinion."

Fonseca repeated his question, and Thiergard said, "There was no indication that the casket had been tampered with. And the airway bill of lading and all the other documents appeared to be in order."

"All right. So you opened the casket and proceeded with your autopsy. What did you find? Please tell us in layman's terms."

"First, I found eight or nine stab wounds on the arms, body, and neck of the deceased. There was one stab wound in the neck, that had cut the carotid artery. It was that stab wound that caused the death."

Ade glanced at Maria. Her body had tensed, and she leaned forward, her face ashen. Kohler looked intently at Dr. Thiergard.

Fonseca was speaking very slowly and precisely now, as if for emphasis. "Now Dr. Thiergard, did you examine any other parts of the body?"

"I did. I took smears of the upper respiratory tract."

"The upper respiratory tract. Would that include the mouth and throat?"

"Yes, sir."

"And did you find anything significant?"

"I found a quantity of intact spermatozoa in the victim's mouth, but there were none in the anterior part, and very little in the pharynx and trachea."

There was a collective gasp from the courtroom. Maria's lower jaw had dropped open as far as it could go. Kohler slowly shook his head, his brow heavily furrowed, and lined with perspiration.

"Can you tell us what you concluded from these findings?"

"I concluded that a homosexual act, an act of fellatio, took place between the two men. That is, the deceased performed fellatio on the accused."

With that, a high-pitched, anguished wail issued from Maria as though she were holding the final keening note in a tragic aria – "Ohhhhhh – " and when she had exhausted her breath, she breathed in again and shrieked, "Nooooo!

Never! My husband would never do anything like that!" Her shoulders were shaking with fury.

Judge Tiernan banged his gavel. "Mrs. Ellerbee, you must control yourself. If you need some time to regain your composure, I'll order a recess."

The judge's words soothed her a little, but she was still agitated, looking around the courtroom fiercely. Of course, she'd read the innuendoes about her husband in Moscow, but she knew all about that. But Thiergard's testimony had had the impact of a grenade. She wondered *could there be new and even more hateful information? Was this a plot of the State Department, her husband's employer, but never totally to be trusted?* She took a deep breath and slowly let it out. "I'll be all right," she said, her eyes darting fire at Dr. Thiergard.

Ade wondered how it was possible that neither Fonseca nor Dilbaugh had thought to inform Maria about the autopsy and that the repellent evidence would be presented in court. Hearing in open court that her husband's last living act was to engage in oral sex with his murderer seemed especially cruel. He recalled how Maria was always overlooked at the time of the murder, until they'd thought of holding a memorial service for George. If Cynthia Kohler had been Maria Ellerbee, wouldn't someone have thought of warning her so she wouldn't have been blindsided?

Fonseca pressed on. "Doctor, you said that you found very little sperm in the mouth, pharynx or trachea. What did you conclude from this finding?"

"First, I concluded that the act of fellatio occurred before death. If it had occurred after death, there would've been heavy contamination in the mouth that would not have been dissipated by any normal bodily functions.

"Second, I concluded that the fatal stab wound that cut the carotid artery caused bleeding in the mouth that washed out the sperm already deposited there. Finally, because the sperm that I found in the upper respiratory tract was well-preserved, death occurred right after ejaculation. Generally, if the body is well-preserved the sperm will also be well-preserved, and this was the case."

Ade saw two of the male jurors shake their heads, and shift uncomfortably in their seats.

"Very well. Now, sir, you concluded that the victim performed fellatio on the accused, and that very shortly after that – perhaps just minutes – he was killed by a stab wound to the carotid artery in the neck. You also testified that there were eight or nine stab wounds. From your forensic experience, is there any special significance to these types of wounds – is this a familiar pattern?"

"Yes, it is. I've dealt with many homicides of this type. It's not a matter of opinion but a medical certainty that this was a homosexual murder."

Dilbaugh was on his feet. "Objection, your Honor! The prosecution has presented no evidence that the accused perpetrated this act, and we've had nothing about the custody of the body. There could've been tampering anywhere along the line between Africa and the United States."

"I'm going to allow it. Dr. Thiergard stated that in his opinion the coffin had not been opened or tampered with. Objection overruled."

Jack Kohler had turned ashen, and shook his head slowly but vehemently from side to side. When Dr. Thiergard testified that a homosexual murder had occurred, Jack straightened and whispered harshly to Cynthia, "No! It's not true!"

Cynthia's face was frozen, a fixed glare aimed directly at Dr. Thiergard.

Fonseca followed up. "Doctor, you say that it's a medical certainty that this was a homosexual murder. What led you to this conclusion?"

"Multiple stab wounds don't prove that this was a homosexual murder, but in homosexual violence it's very common, a tell-tale indication, just like a signature."

"Thank you, Dr. Thiergard. No further questions."

Thiergard's testimony settled on the courtroom like a blanket, providing a graphic refutation of Kohler's plea of temporary insanity. The spectators sat back, as though something definitive had just been decided.

Dilbaugh began his cross-examination cautiously. "Doctor, you said that you found no sperm in the anterior part of the dead man's mouth. Correct?"

"Yes."

"But you did find a small quantity of sperm – just traces – in the upper respiratory tract. Is that correct?"

"Yes, it is."

"Why, in your opinion, was there no sperm in the anterior part?"

"As I explained, the sperm went into the trachea prior to the victim's death. When the carotid artery was cut, the victim in effect strangled on his own blood, which washed away most of the sperm."

"But not all of the sperm was washed away."

"No, sir."

"Now, as I understand it, you conducted no tests, or had no real way of knowing whether the sperm you found was from the accused."

"No, sir. I only testified to what I found."

"So it's possible that the sperm you found didn't come from the accused."

"I find that preposterous."

"Well, it could've been placed in the victim after his death. Isn't it physically possible that the sperm could have been deposited after death, by another person?"

"Extremely unlikely. If contamination had come after death, there would've been more sperm, because it wouldn't have been swallowed, or washed away by blood from the fatal wound. So it doesn't make sense that another person could have put it there."

"But it is possible, is it not? Just answer 'yes' or 'no.'"

Thiergard looked resentful that anyone would challenge his testimony. "It doesn't make sense, but it's theoretically possible."

Next, Dilbaugh challenged Dr. Thiergard's assertion that the casket had not been tampered with. After thirty minutes of cross-examination, an exasperated Thiergard finally admitted that it was at least theoretically possible that someone could have tampered with the body and resealed the casket.

Tony Fonseca was almost ready to rest his case, but he wanted to leave the jury with a final impression of Dr. Thiergard's credibility.

"Dr. Thiergard, you stated very clearly that the evidence established that this was a case of homosexual murder. Have you dealt with many such cases?"

"Oh, many. My specialty is forensic pathology, including the study of violent and unnatural deaths. Over the years,

I've come across many instances of homosexual violence, maybe hundreds."

"So if the way the death blows were inflicted conforms to a pattern of homosexual violence, you're talking about hundreds of similar cases?"

"Yes. In such cases, multiple stab wounds have often been inflicted on the victim. It's common enough so that when you see these wounds in a male, homosexual violence immediately comes to mind."

"Thank you very much, Dr. Thiergard." Fonseca looked at Judge Tiernan, the courtroom spectators, and then directly at the jury. He recalled to himself the last two days of relentless effort to get into the record a mountain of evidence that Jack Kohler killed George Ellerbee, and knew what he was doing at the time of the killing. There may not have been premeditation, Fonseca was willing to concede, but he was sure that no jury could find Kohler not guilty after hearing what he had put into evidence.

"The prosecution rests," he said.

CHAPTER THIRTY-SEVEN

When Ade got back to the hotel, there was a message for him at the front desk. He automatically steeled himself for another unpleasant surprise as the desk clerk handed him the note. But the unmistakable hand-writing was Ginger's. She'd arrived from Lexington; Greg was staying with friends, so she'd decided to pay Ade a surprise weekend visit and would be back at six. His world suddenly looked much brighter.

Ginger turned up about thirty minutes later, lithe and beguiling, her dancer's body hardly seeming to touch the ground. One hug, spontaneous and strong, was enough to dissolve his still-hurt feelings, although the underlying problem hadn't even been addressed. But for a brief interlude, the template of Africa which had channeled their perceptions and uncertainties for the past six months seemed very far away.

It was rare for them to have even a few minutes together with no outside problems breaking in. Ginger was feeling relieved about Greg, and Ade was feeling good about his testimony, so their sudden freedom made them as giddy as children in a sandbox. Just being with Ginger when she was relaxed and charming was enough to blot out Ade's worries for a time.

To celebrate, Ade reserved a table at *Chez Francois*, a popular restaurant on Connecticut Avenue a few blocks from the White House. Settled in and sipping on a dry martini, Ade recounted Dr. Thiergard's revelation about what happened in the vault.

Ginger took the news with surprising calm. "Why?" asked Ade. "It hit the rest of us like a thunderbolt."

"It's very telling," she responded, "and certainly it's a big problem for Kohler, but there're still a lot of things that aren't clear. We know *how* Ellerbee was killed, but we still don't know *why*. I've had enough forensic training to know that the obvious explanation isn't always the right one."

They were just finishing their main course, when Ginger looked across the room and said, "Look over there, Ade. Isn't that Stu Loeffler?"

Anyone who has been around Washington long enough and ventures anywhere near the "K Street corridor" where many of the upscale offices, stores, and restaurants are located is almost certain to bump into someone familiar. You wouldn't have to know many people — it's just that many of the people you did know went there too. Ade looked over, and spotted him: tall, tanned, and bald except for white hair on the fringes. Stu was the CIA Station Chief in Nigeria, and an old friend. He and his wife Carol had known Jack for years, and when he married Cynthia they welcomed her as family. Stu had been a player during a lot of the cold war maneuvering in Africa, and always struck Ade as practical and moderate, a brake on the wilder schemes of some of his younger colleagues. And he knew the Continent as well as any American.

Ade caught his eye, and Stu waved in recognition. After he'd settled his bill, he stopped by their table and sat down for coffee.

"Stu, what a surprise!" Ade said. "Are you here for long?"

"Just a few days, and then I'm heading back. I don't have to guess why you're here, but I didn't know that Ginger was involved."

"She's not, at least officially," Ade said, and explained Ginger's presence. "Have you been following the trial?"

"Only what's been in the *Post*, and that's not much," Stu replied.

Ade told him about Dr. Thiergard's testimony, and his relaxed smile disappeared. "You know, we and the Kohlers were friends, from way back. Jack stopped to see us on his way to Tanako, coming ahead of the family."

He paused, and leaned forward confidentially. "I'm going to tell you something that's troubled me ever since his visit. I haven't shared it with anyone, but with what you just told me, I think you should know. It's a bit, uh, repellent, and I hope you won't take offense, Ginger." Ginger shot him a look that said, "Thanks, but I've pretty much heard it all by now."

Stu said, "Anyway, Jack stayed with us for a few days, and we had a really nice visit. I arranged briefings for him at the embassy, and in the evenings we just talked about Africa and old times. He seemed relaxed and ready for his new assignment. He talked about what a fine person Cynthia was and how she'd brought a new focus to his life. But he really glowed when he mentioned Robin. His pride and love for his young son came through very strongly.

"After he left, Carol made a shocking discovery. She went into the guest room to clean up and change the sheets.

She must've dropped something, and when she bent down, she discovered a suitcase under the bed. It was one of Jack's. Carol pulled it out and called to me that Jack had left one of his suitcases. I went into the room, and noticing that the clasps were raised, opened the suitcase.

"We found a quantity of child pornography pictures and magazines. Mostly photographs of young boys in the nude, some in sexual poses."

"Good God," Ade said, looking over at Ginger in astonishment. "How much of this material was there?"

"Lots. It filled half the suitcase. Carol and I were revolted. I took it out back and burned it all."

"Did you tell anyone about this?" Ade asked.

"Who would I tell? It seemed to me that this opened a window into Jack's personal life, and that we'd be better off to forget it. Now, in light of all that's happened, I certainly question that decision."

"Did he ever write or make reference to it? Ginger asked.

"Never. I assumed he was too fearful of drawing attention to it."

Ade said, "It's easy to say in retrospect that you should have reported what you found. I'm in the soup right now because Senator Manning blames me for picking Kohler and Ellerbee for a tough assignment. He thinks the Department is 'infested with deviants' and has threatened to hold hearings."

"I did consider reporting Jack, and discarded the idea. It would've ended his career, full stop. No argument, no appeal. Remember, the Service was his whole professional life. He had no other career interests. And it would've been devastating to Cynthia. What would they have done with no job, and a two year old son? I felt I didn't have the right to do that to him."

"So you kept it to yourself."

"I thought that the next time we met I'd take him aside and urge him to get counseling. I couldn't risk putting anything in writing. I saw it as a flaw in the personality of an otherwise exemplary guy. Obviously, I was wrong. But remember, he was a competent professional, a friend and colleague. As revolted as we were, I couldn't bring myself to destroy his career. But it shows you never know about people. Who would've thought he'd turn out to be totally different?"

Ginger said, "It's not that he was so different, but he had a lot more going on inside than he showed to the world, and he took great pains to conceal it. That's true of most people, but most people aren't murderers."

"So what do you think of our discovery?"

"I think it was a cry for help. Jack was careful and meticulous. How could he have left behind something so compromising?"

Ade looked skeptical. "So you think he wanted Stu and Carol to find a way to help him? Couldn't he have just sought out a shrink on his own?"

"Sure," answered Ginger. "Maybe in a perfect and rational world – "

"Stu," Ade said, "what you've told us is very important. I have to pass it on to Tony Fonseca. You could be called as a witness."

Stu looked unhappy. The CIA would try hard to prevent it, regardless of how important it was. "I don't want to testify, and I don't think I'd be allowed to anyway."

"Well, we'll see. I don't want to put you or the Agency on the spot. But you understand that I have no choice but to pass it on."

They were ready to leave, but Ade had a favor to ask. "Senator Manning and Walter Jurgens have been whispering that Ellerbee was blackmailed by the Soviets when he was in Moscow and there was a big security leak at the time. If there's anything you could find out about that, I'd be very grateful. They also think that Ellerbee was a homosexual. I never saw a thing to support that. And now Cynthia Kohler tells me that Jack found out that Ellerbee was a homosexual and tried to have him fired. It's getting complicated, but the implication for me is that I chose a homosexual and a security risk for a tough assignment in Africa. Manning may want my hide because of it, and still might hold hearings. This being Washington, it could happen."

"I'll see what I can find out," Stu said. He was senior enough in the CIA hierarchy that he might be able to uncover some rocks. He shook hands with Ade, kissed Ginger on the cheek, and walked briskly up Connecticut Avenue.

CHAPTER THIRTY-EIGHT

Early the next morning Ade called Tony and relayed Stu's story. "This reinforces what I thought all along," he said. "The guy's a fruitcake, and he and Ellerbee had something going. We may need your friend to testify, although we already have more than enough to convict."

When Judge Tiernan gaveled the courtroom to order, it was obvious that Jack Kohler, looking dignified at the defense table, would have to give the performance of his life to have a chance before a hostile judge and a shocked and skeptical jury. Maybe he could throw some light on his alleged rapid descent into madness. Maybe he would explain what happened in the vault.

But first, Ned Dilbaugh had to build a case for his insanity defense, and a key element in that edifice was Dr. Milton Wallach, the senior psychiatrist at George Washington University Hospital.

Wallach walked to the witness stand with long, slow strides. He was tall and angular, and had long, bony fingers. His elongated face was topped by a generous crop of salt and pepper hair, parted in the middle. He spoke softly, as one who is used to being listened to and not having his authority questioned.

Dilbaugh began by asking Dr. Wallach how Kohler appeared to him when he was admitted to George Washington Hospital on September 4.

"Mr. Kohler at first was extremely tense and suspicious. He gave guarded answers to even routine questions, and was withdrawn and preoccupied. My first attempts to establish rapport with the patient weren't successful."

Wallach was referring to Kohler as his 'patient,' not as the 'accused.' It was a subtle distinction, but it might make an impression on the jury.

"Did any of your staff have contact with Mr. Kohler that same day?"

"Yes, of course. Two psychiatric nurses were on duty in the ward, and both talked to him and observed his actions."

"And did they report anything noteworthy to you?"

"They said when he entered his room, Mr. Kohler put his ear to the wall as though he were listening for something. Then he got down and looked under the bed. And he wouldn't touch his food until one of the nurses tasted it first."

"And how long did this kind of behavior continue?"

"The very next day, there was marked improvement. He appeared more relaxed, and even made a joke about the hospital food."

"Did this trend continue?"

"Most definitely. I gave Mr. Kohler a range of psychological exams, and he tested in the top five percent for IQ. He's a verbal person and enjoys using words precisely. So, he opened up with me and eventually talked freely."

"About the actual killing?"

"Yes. Mr. Kohler explained how he became suspicious of Mr. Ellerbee, and how this convinced him that Ellerbee was part of a huge communist conspiracy, and that he and his family were in grave danger."

"And did he describe the acts which culminated in Mr. Ellerbee's death?"

"I didn't dwell on them, you understand, because I was more concerned with his state of mind than his physical acts. The latter are more the concern of the law enforcement authorities."

What a pompous ass, Ade thought. Lesser mortals had to deal with such mundane things as blood and murder, while experts such as Wallach handled monumental issues like sanity and insanity.

Dilbaugh continued. "During your examinations of Mr. Kohler, were you able to reach any conclusions about his state of mind?"

"Yes sir," Wallach said confidently. "In addition to the written psychological testing, I also saw him for more than an hour nearly every day."

"And over the course of these very detailed observations, what conclusions did you form about his condition?"

"I concluded that on August 30, the day of the killing, Mr. Kohler was suffering from acute paranoid psychosis. At that time, Mr. Kohler did not have the mental capacity to appreciate the criminality of his act."

Tiernan had to tap for order. Wallach, a renowned psychiatrist who had spent more time with Jack after the killing than anyone other than Cynthia, had spoken without hesitation, as though this was the only explanation possible.

"Dr. Wallach, is there a medical term, or psychological concept, that might help us to understand what happened?"

"Well, there's not much in the medical literature about it, but it's sometimes referred to as a 'catathymic crisis.' An explosive disorder, in which an extremely intense idea temporarily overwhelms a person's internal equilibrium and disrupts his thinking. A catathymic crisis usually involves unprovoked violence, with no outside cause."

"Can you tell us how this crisis might have developed?" asked Dilbaugh.

"Mr. Kohler was under great stress due to the government's wave of repression. He was extremely concerned for an African employee who'd been imprisoned and tortured, and fearful for his own family. Under the weight of these pressures, Mr. Kohler became psychotic. That is, he was mentally disoriented. Every event, every strand of conversation, every gesture, fueled his growing delusion that there was a gigantic plot against the United States."

"You described Mr. Kohler's condition as a 'paranoid psychosis' and said that it was 'acute.' What do you mean by that?"

"It was acute because it developed so rapidly. Mr. Kohler appeared to be a healthy, normally functioning person until just before the events in the vault."

"Isn't it rare for such a complete personality change to occur so rapidly?"

"Not at all, especially with paranoid psychotic disorders."

"And his rapid recovery after he was in your care? Is that normal?"

"It's not uncommon. A sense of relief, almost of calm, often immediately follows the violence that climaxes such a rapid buildup. So, while Mr. Kohler continued to exhibit some nervousness and suspicion for a few days after the act,

his personality overall was taciturn, and well within acceptable parameters for normal behavior."

"Dr. Wallach, let's get back to the term, 'catathymic crisis.' Would you tell us more about what happens to people
who experience this?"

"Certainly," Wallach said, as though lecturing a group
of students. "Simply stated, a person suffering a catathymic
crisis loses his internal controls. An obsession seizes his personality, and *must* be resolved, whatever the cost. Sudden
violence is seen as the only way to relieve the pain."

"So the person who suffers an explosive disorder can't
control himself?"

"Precisely. While he's in its grip his normal restraints
are powerless."

Dilbaugh walked the length of the jury box, looking each
juror in the eye. He then turned to face Dr. Wallach again.
"Please elaborate on this."

Dr. Wallach spoke carefully to avoid jargon and hold his
audience. "A traumatic psychological experience can trigger overwhelming inner turmoil. The subject identifies the
cause with an external situation, and at the climax of the
crisis, a violent act – a human eruption – is the only way to
release the unbearable tension. He has no other choice. The
violence, you see, is his struggle to safeguard his personality.
Afterwards, the tension dissipates quickly, with an apparent
return to normalcy. This is what happened with Mr. Kohler."

"You said, 'to safeguard his personality.' Is it really that dire?"

"Oh yes, to him it's a life-or-death situation."

Dilbaugh's voice rose. "Then, if I understand you correctly, the build-up of emotional tension was so strong that
Mr. Kohler was helpless to deal with it."

"Exactly. Mr. Kohler was in a state of breakdown so violent that he was temporarily unable to understand the consequences of his acts."

"In other words, he was insane?" Dilbaugh asked.

"That is my conclusion."

The jury looked solemn. A case that at first blush seemed so simple now appeared to be much more complicated.

Dilbaugh paused to let this sink in, and asked, "Dr. Wallach, what did your official diagnosis tell you about Mr. Kohler's personality?"

"In laymen's terms, he was extremely vulnerable to the kind of explosive outburst I just described. Life on Tanako made him highly susceptible to forbidden impulses and turbulent emotional upheavals, which he in fact experienced. I also found indications of paranoid personality disorder, marked by suspicion of others and various fantasies, including conspiracy theories."

"Given all this, wasn't it unusual to conclude that Mr. Kohler's return to normalcy was so rapid and complete that you could just let him go?"

"I did keep him under observation for another week. But his recovery was so remarkable that I authorized his release. My sole condition was that he see a therapist every week. The soundness of my diagnosis is borne out by the fact that Mr. Kohler has been living normally up to this moment."

Dilbaugh looked pleased. "Thank you, Doctor. No further questions."

Tony Fonseca came forward slowly, as if pondering a key point.

"Dr. Wallach, we've had expert testimony that intact spermatozoa were found in the victim's upper respiratory tract. What's your explanation for that?"

"That's not really my job," he sniffed. "I don't do autopsies."

Tony looked surprised. "But such a significant event – surely Mr. Kohler must have made some reference to the act that caused this."

"He never did."

Tony looked disbelieving. "He never mentioned a relationship with the deceased, or at least an act they engaged in just before the death of the victim?"

"He made no reference to any such thing."

"And yet we have definitive evidence of the sperm, and expert testimony that it was deposited just prior to the killing. How do you explain it?"

"I can't explain it. It's not my job to explain it."

"Doctor, as an expert on human behavior, surely your curiosity must be picqued just a teeny bit by the fact that the accused totally ignored this central element."

Dilbaugh jumped to his feet. "Objection, your Honor!" he shouted. The prosecution is browbeating the witness!"

"I withdraw my question," said Fonseca quickly. Lowering his voice, he asked, "Is it possible that Mr. Kohler withheld key aspects of what happened in the vault?"

"It's highly unlikely. Once I'd established rapport with Mr. Kohler he was very open with me, and described events in great detail."

"And you believed everything he said?"

"Sir, I have many years of experience with hundreds of psychiatric patients of many kinds. I believe I can judge when a patient is telling the truth."

"All right. Mr. Kohler described what happened in great detail to you, but somehow, perhaps it was just an oversight, he forgot to mention that he'd engaged in oral sex with his victim?"

"Objection!" shouted Dilbaugh. "The prosecution is leading the witness."

"Sustained. Counselor, rephrase your question," Tiernan ordered.

Tony asked, "Given these circumstances, is it just remotely possible that Mr. Kohler may have lied to you?"

Ade looked over at Jack Kohler. He was frowning, and shaking his head.

"I strongly doubt it. I questioned Mr. Kohler closely over several weeks. His answers remained consistent. I believe he was telling me the truth."

"Now, if it turned out that Mr. Kohler was not telling the truth – if he was lying – would that change your diagnosis?"

Dilbaugh shouted, "Objection! That's a hypothetical question."

Tiernan said, "This relates to the state of mind of the accused, which is not a matter of fact but of interpretation. Dr. Wallach is here as an expert witness, so I'm going to allow it. You may answer the question, Doctor."

Dr. Wallach said, "If a patient lies, of course it can affect my diagnosis."

"All right. So if Mr. Kohler was lying to you, is it possible to say that his psychosis developed *after* the killing and not before?"

"I suppose it's theoretically possible," answered Wallach, growing wary.

"Then the psychosis would have developed as a *result* of the killing, and not, as the defendant would have us believe, that it was the *cause* of the killing. Is that so?"

"I suppose so. But I still think he was telling the truth."

Fonseca continued. "I believe you just told us that you'd interviewed hundreds of patients – that's correct, isn't it?"

"Yes," replied Wallach, looking at Tony with hostility.

"And because of the eminence you've achieved, you must've served as an expert witness on psychotic disorders many times. Is that right?"

"Yes. Maybe a hundred times, over the years."

"And you always testified that the subject was insane or mentally incompetent, is that correct?"

"No, not always."

"Well, our research shows that in eighty-four of ninety-three such cases in which you were an expert witness in the last fifteen years, you testified to the subject's mental incapacity. If you want, we have evidence to prove this."

"No, that sounds about right."

"Well, I'm suggesting that your record shows a clear pattern of sympathy with insanity defenses, and they call you because you'll shill for them!"

"Your Honor, I object!" shouted Dilbaugh. "This is totally out of order!"

"Sustained," said Tiernan. "Mr. Fonseca, you know better than to try that here. You may proceed, but your last statement will be stricken from the record."

Tony was unabashed. "As I was saying, can you explain to us why you consistently testify on behalf of insanity defenses?"

Wallach spoke in a low voice, barely containing his outrage. "I am a doctor. I always decide a case on its merits, not on any predisposition."

"But in the case at hand, you totally accepted what the accused told you, even though it was in his interest to lie. And you just told this court that the fact that the accused had oral sex with his victim just before the murder was none of your business! That's not deciding a case on its merits, it's called 'selective judgment!'" And before anyone could object, Tony said to Dilbaugh, "Your witness," turned his back on Wallach and strode back to the prosecution table.

Dilbaugh had underestimated Tony's aggressiveness. He now had to shore up his key witness. He shot a hostile look toward Fonseca and began his re-direct examination. "Dr. Wallach," he asked, "in your experience do people who commit criminal acts have a moral reaction to them?"

"Yes, of course," Dr. Wallach replied. "Not always, but generally they do."

"And in your extensive evaluations of Mr. Kohler you found him, outside of this one violent act, to be a normal person, did you not?"

"Yes, I did."

"A man concerned for the safety and well being of his family and his employees, and his friends and colleagues?

"Yes, all of those."

"And when you talked to Mr. Kohler about what happened inside the vault, he made no mention of any relationship or homosexual act, is that correct?"

"Yes, that's so."

"Can you suggest to us why Mr. Kohler made no mention of this?"

"Well, it certainly would be plausible for a normal and moral person to feel such revulsion at having committed a homosexual act in those circumstances that he totally blocked it from his memory."

"He totally blocked it from his memory," repeated Dilbaugh. "This kind of blockage is not unusual in your experience?"

"No, it's really a form of amnesia. It's common enough in everyday life when we block out things we don't want to hear. In this case the enormity of the act could have caused a massive blockage, amounting to a complete denial."

"So it's entirely possible that Mr. Kohler could recall details of the killing itself, and describe them vividly to you, and yet totally block out any recall of a homosexual act which might have accompanied the murder?"

"Absolutely. He couldn't deny the killing, given the evidence, his presence at the scene, and the absence of other suspects. But the recollection of a homosexual act might be so abhorrent that he erased it from his memory. He also must've been mindful of the shame and embarrassment that would come to his wife and child if this were known. Therefore, he repressed it."

"Thank you," Dilbaugh said. "No further questions."

Tony advanced to the witness stand for his final shot.

"Dr. Wallach," he said, "you described Mr. Kohler as the kind of person whose ordinary behavior appears quite healthy. Would you say – "

"I did," Dr. Wallach interrupted. "But I also said that when Mr. Ellerbee died, Mr. Kohler was experiencing a mental disease so powerful that he formed wild fears of persecution and was unable to comprehend the enormity of his act."

"But if a person wanted to escape punishment for a terrible crime, faking paranoia and pleading temporary insanity would be the way to go, wouldn't it?"

"Objection!" Dilbaugh's indignant voice rang out loud and clear.

"Sustained," said Tiernan.

"I withdraw the question," said Fonseca, knowing that the thought would stay with the jurors despite Tiernan's objection.

"Doctor," he began again, "You said that Mr. Kohler's possible revulsion over a homosexual act with the deceased might have made him block it from his memory. Yet he was able to recall the killing itself in minute detail. Wouldn't he also recall a homosexual act committed just before the killing?"

"It's possible."

"So isn't it more plausible that Mr. Kohler was actually withholding facts, rather than merely failing to remember them?"

"Not necessarily," said Dr. Wallach hesitantly.

"But it becomes clear," insisted Fonseca, homing in. "The fact of the murder can't be denied, but if a homosexual act has occurred, that puts a totally different cast on it." Fonseca's voice was rising, and he looked at Dr. Wallach with heightened intensity. "In that case," he continued, "Mr. Kohler's insanity defense goes out the window. That's why he says he has no recollection of it. And that's why this trial is not about the paranoid delusion of Mr. Kohler but the savage murder of his homosexual lover!"

CHAPTER THIRTY-NINE

Judge Tiernan called a brief recess, and Ade wandered over to where Tony Fonseca was conferring with an assistant. He saw Ade approaching and said, "It looks like your CIA friend will have an opportunity to testify."

"Stu?" Ade said, surprised. "I didn't think he'd agree to do it."

"He didn't. In fact, he refused us outright. His CIA boss did too."

"You don't mean the Director of the CIA?"

"The very one," said Tony with a smile. "They didn't want one of their people testifying, especially a station chief, and invoked all kinds of national security arguments to turn us down."

"So what did the trick?"

"It didn't hurt that we had the Attorney General and the Secretary of State on our side. It finally went to the White House. They just didn't want any political fallout from this case. But we had to agree that there'd be no questions about CIA personnel or operations, past or present. That wasn't really what we wanted anyway, so it was easy to agree to. Of course, Stu Loeffler will have to come out of Nigeria. The government there knows who he is, but not a lot of other people, so they'll bring him out as a matter of policy. I understand he's been there a few years anyway, so maybe he's ready."

Ade thought that Kohler would be pleased to know what titanic, high-level struggles his act had unleashed. It would suit his need to feel important.

Ade's scorecard so far had Tony out in front. The physical evidence they'd gathered in Tanako was compelling, especially the bloody shears. Two of the women jurors looked horrified as they were introduced, almost as though they were visualizing Kohler plunge them into Ellerbee again and again. And Thiergard's solid autopsy report outweighed Wallach's psychological explanation, mainly because Wallach couldn't address the evidence of fellatio.

So it was now crunch time, and it was up to Jack Kohler to save his own skin. Ade thought that he would have to hit one out of the park to do it.

When Jack was called, he rose slowly, squeezed Cynthia's hand, and made his way to the witness stand. Despite the graphic testimony in open court, he looked as though he was once again an FSO carrying out a diplomatic mission. Having heard gruesome details of Ellerbee's last hours, the jurors looked at Kohler with mixed hostility and curiosity, as though wondering what sort of monster was now before them. They were about to be surprised.

Dilbaugh eased Jack through the preliminaries, and he became more confident. His large frame relaxed, and his voice grew authoritative.

"Mr. Kohler," Dilbaugh began in a friendly tone, "tell us a little bit about yourself, where you grew up, and what your family circumstances were."

"I grew up in Toledo, Ohio, in a poor neighborhood. My father had a clerical job with the city government, and my mother worked in a department store. I had an older brother and a younger sister."

Jack described how they always wore secondhand clothes, and never had luxuries like vacations. He admired his mother, who could be charming, but sometimes was cold and distant. His father was a rigid disciplinarian, and punished the children for the slightest transgressions. His mother was intimidated and never intervened.

"My father was the only child of German immigrants," Jack continued. "He was very dogmatic. He came to America as a boy, but he still spoke with a guttural accent. I never understood why he couldn't get rid of it. My mother, whose parents came from Austria at about the same time, spoke English perfectly, with no accent."

As he recalled the events of his childhood, Kohler started to frown and rub his fingers together nervously. "My father had a harsh rule for everything. He thought that children were born sinful, and would become instruments of the devil if the evil in them weren't constantly purged. So he was always disciplining us: cold baths, making us stand in the corner ramrod straight, and whipping us with a strap if we made noise or if he was in a bad mood. He treated me as though I was ugly and sinful, and made me wear short pants until I was twelve. He'd poke me in the genital area and ask me if 'my birdie had feathers on it.'"

Kohler looked stricken as he relived the pain of his childhood, and much of his perennial mask had melted away. His large frame shriveled inward, experiencing again the anguish that a sensitive boy had suffered at the hands of a brutish father. Ade couldn't help feeling sorry for him.

He was trying to read the jurors' reactions and thought he'd detected a softening. Kohler's harrowing childhood had evoked sympathetic nods among the women, and the men no longer looked contemplative.

Tony may have been having similar thoughts. He seemed increasingly impatient, concerned that Kohler might be arousing sympathy. Finally he spoke up from his seat. "Your Honor, I fail to see where this is leading. Counsel for the defense has failed to establish any basis for an insanity plea."

Judge Tiernan peered down at Tony. "I'm allowing the defense the widest possible latitude on anything that might have a bearing on the accused's state of mind while he was in Africa. If it later turns out to be irrelevant, I will so instruct the jury. Proceed, Mr. Dilbaugh."

Ned Dilbaugh suppressed a tight smile. "Despite the abuse and humiliation at home, Mr. Kohler, did you get along well at school?"

"Yes, I got good marks, and eventually won a scholarship to Ohio State."

"When did you become attracted to the Foreign Service?"

"When I was a senior, a State Department recruiter visited the campus. Right then, I wanted to be a diplomat more than anything. I loved the idea of doing important things, and dealing with influential people. I wanted to serve my country, to travel, and have an impact on world events."

"And were these desires realized, after you entered the foreign service?"

"To some extent. I thought being a diplomat was the best thing in the world, especially because I was the first in my family to graduate from college, and I saw that I'd have a bright future."

"Where are some of the places you've been assigned?"

"Bolivia, Egypt, Gabon, and Tanako overseas, and mainly the Economic Bureau in Washington."

Dilbaugh looked sympathetic. "I'm sure that these were all interesting places," he said gently, "but with all due respect, Mr. Kohler, these are not really places from which you could have an impact on world events, were they?"

Kohler's face darkened as he described his disappointment over never getting the recognition due him for his economic expertise. He'd tried for Western Europe, where so many international negotiations took place, but always lost out on the best posts. He wondered if he'd done something wrong, or was unworthy in some way. Or if he was held back because he didn't have the right social connections.

"The Department is still like an Old Boys Club," he said. "Not like it used to be, when you almost had to be Harvard, Yale, or Princeton to get anywhere. But there's still a good bit of that attitude. Having the right connections helps."

"And you didn't have the right connections?"

"Not the son of an immigrant civil servant who went to Ohio State. I didn't fit the mold," Jack said with a resentful tone.

Ade felt a surge of annoyance. Jack had a point – there was still snobbery in the Department, but there were also many top officers whose origins were at least as plebeian as Kohler's. Charlie Stubblefield was a good example. His father worked in a bakery and Charlie graduated from

Hampden-Sydney. And Ade thought of several pedigreed Ivy Leaguers who were still laboring in the vineyards, hoping for a big assignment, just like Jack. Dilbaugh was letting him show how career disappointments could have contributed to his breakdown, and so far his testimony had been effective. But if he fell into his penchant for self-pity and blaming others, he'd blow it.

"After seeing choice posts go to people with better social connections, how did you react to your assignment to Tanako?" Dilbaugh asked.

"We agree to serve anywhere in the world, but going to Tanako bothered me, because I'd be out of the loop and have no chance for promotion."

"So going to Tanako not only put you and your family in a remote, unhealthy, and dangerous country, but actually jeopardized your career?"

"That's true, although of course the Department would never admit that."

"Was the government there friendly to the United States?"

"Hardly. They hated us, and thought we were plotting to overthrow them."

"Tell us something about your life there."

"It was a terrible place, but my family made the best of it. Cynthia spent most of her day taking care of Robin, who was a happy little boy. But this was no ordinary country. The atmosphere of fear hit you the minute you got off the plane, as though you'd crossed a river into a dark and evil place."

Kohler crossed his left leg to his right knee. He'd done with childhood revelations and moved into his role as a diplomat. The sag in his shoulders disappeared as he described the blasted economy, the malaise, the growing terror. This was Jack at his best, a savvy official delivering a lucid analysis.

Dilbaugh offered up a fat pitch: "But you went there knowing it would be tough, and you took your wife and infant son. Surely, if it was dangerous you wouldn't have subjected them to risk."

"The host country is supposed to protect diplomats. But they harassed us instead, and I saw there was no buffer between my family and those thugs."

"Were you or anyone in your family, or anyone in the embassy, ever harmed or placed in direct personal danger?"

Kohler, now speaking softly and factually, described how the police jeered at them at checkpoints, snooped through their garbage, interrogated their household staff, browbeat people they had contact with, and even snatched a toy bow and arrow from Robin while he was playing in his yard.

Some of the spectators shook their heads in sympathy, trying to imagine how they'd cope in a place like that.

Dilbaugh said, "Now, you also had an African staff at the Embassy, and one of them, a Mr. Nguema I believe, was arrested. Can you tell us about that?"

Kohler seemed eager to tell abut Nguema's ordeal. "They threw him into the worst prison in Africa and almost tortured him to death. When they'd finished, he could hardly walk, and was so traumatized that he'd shake whenever he tried to talk about it."

"What had he done to arouse the government's suspicions?"

"He didn't do anything!" Kohler exclaimed. "They got him because he worked for us. They beat him with sticks, opening up wounds all over his body. He almost died. They killed prisoners almost every night. They smashed in their skulls with iron bars. Nguema could hear all that going on. *We* could hear it going on, because we lived right across the street. God, it was awful! I'd never heard human screams like that before."

Some of the jurors were looking queasy.

"When Nguema was arrested, what did you do?"

Jack described his frustration when the Foreign Ministry ignored his protest, and the State Department refused to take it to a higher level.

"So you got no help from the State Department," Dilbaugh summarized.

"No," said Kohler with a trace of his sardonic smile, "and they would've said that's why Jack Kohler's out there, to handle low-level problems like that."

"But when Nguema was finally released alive, you must've felt great relief. Maybe your protest did some good."

"Yes, of course," answered Kohler, as though it was obvious. "When they let him go, he staggered down the street to our house, and we cleaned him up. Aside from the blood, he had vomit and, uh, excreta on him. This wasn't all – the doctor discovered that the jailers had put electric shocks on his genitals!"

Kohler paused and closed his eyes, as if experiencing the pain himself.

Dilbaugh said softly, "Can you continue, Mr. Kohler?"

"Yes...I felt hatred for people who would do this to an innocent man. The injustice, and the cruelty..." Kohler's voice trailed off, but he was now so caught up in his story that he blurted out the next sentence without thinking. "And then it made me think of – of my father!"

The suddenness of his revelation startled the jurors. Jack looked up and flushed crimson, as though he'd committed a deep indiscretion. Ade couldn't believe he'd expected to say that. But what if these grotesque experiences really did break him? Dilbaugh nodded at him to go on.

"We were so relieved that Nguema was alive. I believe that protesting to the Foreign Ministry may have saved his life, and reminded them that they were dealing with the greatest power on earth. As for us, I don't think we ever felt safe after that. We all thought something terrible could happen."

Just a minute! thought Ade, trying to work through the nuances of Jack's testimony. One second Jack was admitting that he was helpless to aid Nguema, and then he boasts that he'd embodied the full majesty of the United States to save him. Maybe the passage of time made him forget that it was actually the Cameroon Ambassador who'd gained Nguema's release.

At this point, Judge Tiernan interrupted. "I'm going to call a fifteen-minute recess. The Court adjourns until two-thirty."

CHAPTER FORTY

Ginger walked over to talk to Maria, and Ade spotted the tanned and bald head of Stu Loeffler at the back of the courtroom. He caught up with him in the corridor outside. "I understand you may be testifying," he said sheepishly.

"Yes, and no thanks to you," Stu replied, frowning. "I realize that you had to pass on that incident about Jack, but it's put the Agency in a hell of a spot."

"I'm sorry, Stu. I couldn't sit on that information. I had to do it."

"We're old friends and I'll try not to hold a grudge," he said, his tone softening. "But Langley's in an uproar. It's a hell of a bad precedent. And it'll blow me out of the water in Nigeria."

"I know, I know," Ade said. "But this is an unusual case. An American diplomat murdered his colleague! Tony thought you might be ready for a change anyway."

"None of his business. Lots of people *like* to serve in Africa. Anyway, it *is* an unusual case. Maybe even more than you realize. Let's step outside for a minute."

It was chilly outside without overcoats, but Stu wanted to talk where they couldn't be overheard.

"It seems I'm always telling you something in confidence, and then regretting it," he said. "But I promised to do some checking for you, and I did."

"What did you find out?"

"You asked me to see if I could find out anything on George Ellerbee and the time he was in Moscow. You said that there was some question that he might have been blackmailed by the Soviets into passing secrets, right?"

"Right." Stu was toying with Ade, building his curiosity.

"And finally you asked me if there was anything to the rumors that he was a homosexual. Is that right?"

"It is."

"OK. I never knew Ellerbee, never heard his name until he went to Tanako. But we did our own investigation of the Moscow leak, and believe me, it was thorough. For starters, we used lie detectors. They're not perfect, but you can learn a lot from them."

"And?"

"There was a leak, and some really valuable stuff was passed. But George didn't do it. It was a Marine guard and he was a victim of sexual entrapment, one of the oldest cons in the world. They whisked him out of there quietly, and it wasn't until now that Walter Jurgens got hold of the story and made something of it."

Ade was elated. "Stu, that's great news. But how do you know?"

"That's one of those questions you shouldn't ask, Ade. But I'm telling you that Ellerbee wasn't involved. Not one bit."

"And the homosexual charge?"

"The same. He was as straight as they come."

"Come on, Stu," Ade said, in a doubting voice. "How do you know?"

Stu looked him right in the eye. "Ellerbee was one of ours, Ade. He was working for us."

CHAPTER FORTY-ONE

Ade's astonishment at Stu's revelation grew even larger as they headed back towards the courthouse. Not only was Ellerbee working under cover for the CIA as a general services officer in the Embassy administrative section, which is not an unusual practice, but his mission was a highly sensitive one: counter espionage. The Ambassador and the CIA were so concerned about constant Soviet attempts to penetrate the embassy that they assigned Ellerbee, an experienced CIA operative, to try to identify vulnerable employees, sniff out sexual entrapment schemes, and foil any Soviet attempts to extract sensitive information. Only the ambassador and the station chief knew that he was under cover, and he reported directly to them at the same time he was doing routine admin work at the embassy. George's sense of humor, non-threatening low-key personality, and ability to get along with people made him welcome in any company, and the Embassy crowd found him a good confidante. Stu also said that his small, almost feminine appearance may have made him attractive to homosexual men. He had in fact uncovered a very lucrative visa fraud operation in the consular section one night when a drunken Russian who was involved in it made a pass at him and talked too much. George also developed the lead that eventually enabled investigators to solve the missing documents case.

The CIA recognized George as a special talent, and gave him a lot of latitude. In Tanako, most of his time was spent on his ostensible assignment, doing the routine chores of a small embassy. But he was to discreetly develop contacts outside the usual embassy orbit, and find out two things: how the Soviets were using their so-called fishing agreement with Tanako, and whether Barreras was turning one of the large expropriated plantations into a training ground for international insurgents. George had no specific timetable, just a mandate to keep his eyes open. Jack wasn't aware of Ellerbee's secret identity, and damn it, Ade realized, neither was he. Hell, probably Maria didn't know, either. Hellyer would've known, but as long as Ade didn't have a "need to know" he saw no reason to tell him. Ade was miffed, but he also had to admit that George's secret had been well kept.

Ellerbee hadn't done much CIA work in Tanako, but in the short period between their foray into the bush and George's murder, he'd started tracking comings and goings from Tanako through an airport contact who passed him copies of passenger manifests, hoping to find some connection to known terrorist organizations. He'd also been trying to recruit replacements for the two sources in Barreras's office who'd been wrapped up when the coup plotters were caught. And, of course, it was Ellerbee who came up with most of the background information on Black Bitch, to supplement Nguema's first-person account and Kohler's analytical writing skills.

As they entered the courthouse, Stu said, "We lost a good agent, so we're determined that no one on the Hill smears a man who died for his country just the same as someone in combat. But you'll have to help me, OK?"

"I owe you one," Ade answered.

He re-entered the courtroom and sat down next to Ginger. There wasn't time to even give her a hint about what Stu had just told him.

The clerk called the courtroom to order, and Judge Tiernan reminded Kohler that he was still under oath.

"OK, you got through the crisis in late June with Nguema," said Ned Dilbaugh, refreshing everyone's memory. "What happened next?"

"Barreras started up another wave of repression, worse than the last."

"And when was this?"

"Just about mid-August. It was like the last one – people were rounded up and harangued. There were tortures, executions, and entire villages were put to the torch and the people chased into the bush. Barreras and his entourage behaved as though they were demi-gods, accountable to no one. It was galling that this man could thumb his nose at us, and no one in Washington cared."

Dilbaugh said, "Was there any occurrence that particularly worried you?" Kohler thought for a moment. "Well, there was a UN employee, a young American lady. She seemed so vulnerable that I was afraid she might come to some harm."

"Was there something that triggered this concern?"

"She was leaving the end of August, and I felt she might be in terrible danger."

"From whom?"

"The government. They were brutal, and had a special hatred for Americans. I feared that they'd soon harm one of us. I thought that Jane – Jane Simmons was her name – would make a perfect victim. She was a single woman, and the UN would never retaliate if anything happened. It has no army, and whenever action is called for, it does nothing but debate! So I felt I had to protect her, and as her departure date got closer, I checked regularly to make sure she was OK.

"When she left, I went to the airport to see her off. She arrived late, and I had a terrible feeling that she'd been taken by the police. I felt a load of tension go when she finally showed up, but I stayed at the airport until she took off. Then I felt better, but a sense of awful foreboding came over me when I headed back to town and was stopped at the first checkpoint. It seemed to me that many things were going on that I couldn't understand, but if I thought about them really hard, there'd be some connection that linked them all together."

This was batty, Ade thought. He'd just described how Barreras had terrorized the population, but what really got to him was a UN friend showing up late at the airport on the way to a vacation. Did the jury notice the disconnect?

Dilbaugh asked, "And what day was all this going on?"

"It was Sunday, August 29, the day before – "

" – the events in question," said Dilbaugh. "The next day, did you feel better?"

"No, but it was the start of the week and I had a lot to do, including an important cable on the new repression, so I went to the Embassy as usual."

"And the situation was normal?"

"Outwardly so, but on the way to the Embassy, I had a sudden insight. All these events – the torture of Nguema, the new wave of repression, the government harassment, the danger to Jane – were part of a pattern, all connected. There was nothing random about them. I began to see things from a completely new angle.

"When I got to the Embassy, I realized that it must be bugged, so I did a quick check of my office and the security vault. I didn't find anything, which made me more suspicious, because now I was dealing with cunning enemies who knew their stuff, and not just the local goons. Maybe the Russians, or the Chinese, or the Cubans were in on it too. Maybe all three!" Jack's voice rose as he recalled his growing alarm.

"Suddenly every conversation, every gesture, seemed to take on new meaning. I couldn't trust any of our African employees, because they'd be in on the plot. It already seemed so vast that I thought it must be about to unfold. I had to warn Washington, and I had to protect my family, and there was no time to lose."

As Kohler described what happened, he seemed to return to the vault. His calm voice became excited and he talked in a stream of consciousness, as though he was describing a motion picture he was watching.

Dilbaugh had to speak in a loud voice to break into Jack's recital. "Mr. Kohler, forgive me for interrupting. Do you recognize these?" He showed Jack a sheaf of smeared papers that had been crumpled up, but were now straightened out. Jack looked at them and said, "That's the message! The one I was dictating to George!"

"I'd like to enter this into evidence," Dilbaugh said.

"Objection!" Fonseca's voice range out, louder than usual.

Judge Tiernan looked over at Dilbaugh. "What's the relevance? We already have a great many items gathered from the vault in evidence."

"Your Honor! This message is the basis of the radio broadcast that the accused made from the vault, warning about a communist conspiracy. It shows that he really believed that there was a conspiracy and didn't make up the broadcast after Mr. Ellerbee was killed! It also proves that Mr. Ellerbee was alive while this document was being prepared, because he was encoding it in his own handwriting. These are facts that are crucial to the defense case, so I'd like to have Mr. Kohler read from it."

Tiernan looked skeptical. "Go ahead, Mr. Dilbaugh, but I'm reserving judgment about admissibility."

Kohler began reading, haltingly, because there were smear marks on the pages. Ade immediately recognized that it was almost identical to Kohler's broadcast from the vault. The pages themselves also looked familiar. He himself had found them stuffed into a burn bag in the vault.

Kohler finished reading the message, and looked up.

Dilbaugh repeated, "I'd like to enter this document into evidence. It clearly shows the complex delusional thinking of the accused at the time."

"Objection!" Tony repeated. "We've already heard ample testimony from Nadherny and Zimmerman on the broadcast, and the various things they found in the vault. Besides, the defense has failed to establish its authenticity."

"Sustained. Proceed with your questioning," Tiernan said to Dilbaugh.

Dilbaugh looked stricken. "Your Honor, I must respectfully protest – "

"If you don't like my ruling, take it to Richmond and the Court of Appeals."

"No doubt about that," Dilbaugh mumbled, scowling. Recovering, he said, "All right, Mr. Kohler, let's pick up where we left off. You were telling us that you were dictating the message to Mr. Ellerbee, and you suddenly perceived him as part of the conspiracy. Please continue."

Kohler started again, but quickly became agitated, and his normally tranquil frame rocked in his chair and his large hands gripped the arms as he described his compulsion to stop George and unmask the conspiracy. "I had to stop him, no matter the cost. This was my duty, the reason I was in this terrible place. And George was trying to trick me out of it. It was as though he was trying to rob me of my very soul!"

Ginger jabbed Ade. "Sound familiar?"

Of course! 'Soul-murder' was the term used by the paranoid Schreber, in describing his fantasy in the Freud case.

Ginger looked totally absorbed, as though a missing piece of a puzzle had suddenly clicked into place.

"I loosened my belt buckle, hoping this would intimidate George and make him realize that I had control. I wanted him to tell me what he'd been up to in Moscow. Maybe then I could understand everything. But he wouldn't talk, and that made me angry. But he kept shuffling his shoes around, as though he were trying to click his heels together. I wondered if he had some kind of James Bond device on them that might cause an explosion. He was still dangerous.

"I knew that I had to stop him, but I couldn't bring myself to do it. A battle was going on inside me. 'Go ahead, you've got to stab him,' I said to myself. But another voice inside me said 'No, don't do it. Don't stab him.'

"Finally, I stabbed him, slowly at first, right about here." Kohler pointed to the tricep on his upper right arm, and rubbed it gently, as though he could feel the point of the scissors breaking his own skin.

"I thought to myself, 'Gee, human skin is much tougher than I thought. If you really want to get the job done, you have to thrust harder. It takes a lot of force to pierce human skin. So I stabbed him again, harder this time. He struggled to get loose and I stabbed him some more. Now, somehow he'd gotten loose. I hadn't tied him up as well as I thought! He was bleeding, but he pushed a chair at me and tripped toward the door, twisted open the big handle and got out into the Embassy reception room. It was happening very fast, but I remember watching him, sort of in slow motion, as he got out the door and lurched from the desk to the cabinet, grasping at the wall, holding himself up as he was trying to escape.

"'I can't let him escape,' I thought, and sprang through the door. I was able to catch him with a couple of strides and hit him again just as he was making a final lunge forward. I thought, 'Dear God, please don't let him make it because I just haven't got the strength to do it again.'

"He staggered a few more steps and slid down, clutching at a file cabinet, and collapsed on the floor. He didn't say anything more, and it must've been about this time that he died. There was a lot of blood, so I covered the body and then dragged it into the adjoining office. I was still afraid to go out."

Dilbaugh interrupted. "Do you recall what you thought, or how you felt, after you determined that Mr. Ellerbee was dead?"

"I had this sudden feeling that an enormous weight had been lifted from my shoulders. Good had triumphed over evil, and I'd won a titanic struggle."

A few of the jurors looked at Kohler in amazement. Dilbaugh paused a few seconds, then asked, "And what happened after that?"

"It was a while before anyone came, and I demanded to see my wife and son, because I was so afraid for them. I was suspicious of everyone, but I finally agreed to go with the Nigerian Ambassador. Everything seemed like a new threat for me. The next few days I felt like I was in a trance, and I don't remember it very well. It wasn't until I got back to the States and to the hospital that I began to feel normal again."

It was as though uttering the word 'normal' propelled Jack out of the vault, away from Tanako, and into the courtroom, where every eye was on him.

Jack heaved a long sigh, and wiped his brow with a handkerchief. He'd been perspiring while he worked through his story, and the sweat showed through his shirt where his jacket was parted. He leaned back in his chair as though he'd just completed a long and arduous journey, and said, "And that's everything I remember from what happened in the vault."

Dilbaugh said quietly, "Thank you, Mr. Kohler. No further questions."

Ade was struck again by Kohler's lack of compassion for Ellerbee. He'd recited in icy detail how he'd stabbed the life out of his colleague, almost as though George was a mere object and not a human being. Even now, Jack described it as something he had to do, not as something he deeply regretted. Yet, his concern for Nguema and the torturing at the Black Bitch seemed genuine. Could Jack have faked that?

Tony Fonseca was on his feet quickly and crowded in close to Jack.

"Mr. Kohler," he began, "you described your career, which encompassed many assignments spanning nearly twenty years, in which living conditions might be described as 'difficult.' Is that an accurate statement?"

"Yes, that's so." Kohler appeared confident, but wary.

"And over the years, you must've dealt with hundreds of different problems almost routinely. Some of these must have been diplomatic crises, maybe even dangerous. Is that true?"

"I dare say it is," replied Kohler, pride in his voice.

"Did you ever worry that you couldn't handle them, or did your supervisors ever avoid giving you a problem because they felt that you couldn't handle it?"

"On the contrary, I have something of a reputation for being unflappable."

"So prior to the events you described, you never had any difficulties with any of the situations you were in, even before you entered the Foreign Service?"

"No, none that I can recall."

"Have you ever been in a mental hospital?"

"Not as a patient. Never."

"Have you ever been treated for any kind of mental illness, or condition, or instability, or anything of that nature?"

"Certainly not," Jack responded, looking offended. Tony paused, to let Jack's assertion of normalcy sink in.

"Now, you've testified about the hardships of daily life on Tanako, and also that things started to get much worse. When did that happen?"

"Oh, probably around the middle of August. Yes, right about then."

Tony walked to the prosecution table and took up a white piece of paper.

"Your Honor, I'd like to introduce this letter into evidence."

Fonseca walked over to the witness stand and handed it to Kohler. "Mr. Kohler, can you identify this document?"

Kohler looked it over warily. "Yes. It's a letter I wrote to a friend of mine, a Foreign Service colleague stationed in Europe."

"And is it in your own handwriting?"

"Yes."

"What's the date?

"August 17, 1971."

"Would you be good enough to read the salutation and first paragraph?"

Kohler took the letter and began to read: 'Dear Frank: Many thanks for your letter of June 4. It may come as a surprise, but Cynthia and I are enjoying Arania very much. Robin, our two year old, is also in top form. My only problem is that I can't lose weight, although my hunger for gourmet meals is largely unrequited here. We hope that you and Nancy will visit us. There are weekly flights from Madrid direct to Arania, at reasonable prices. We can't provide much nightlife, but I promise you lots of peace and quiet. Bring the kids as well."

"OK, that's fine, Mr. Kohler." Jack looked up wanly, and swallowed.

"Surely Mr. Kohler, if things were as bad as you say, you wouldn't have invited a friend for a social visit to enjoy the peace and quiet, and bring his wife and kids."

"I felt that since they'd be staying with us in our residence they'd be safe. I saw it as an exotic trip for them and a good break in the monotony for us."

Tony frowned, deeply skeptical. He stepped back to survey the courtroom, like a matador turning his back on a wounded bull, sharing his disbelief with the jury and spectators. Then he faced Kohler again. "Now let's go to the vault. You tied up Mr. Ellerbee because you feared he was part of a huge conspiracy. Correct?"

"Yes, sir, that's correct."

"And while you were confronting him with so-called evidence of his involvement in this conspiracy, did he say anything in response?"

"Oh, he'd say things like 'I can't believe this is happening,' but he had very little to say about the specific incidents I asked him about."

"Isn't it strange that a man you'd subdued by force, and were brandishing a pair of shears in his face, would have nothing to say?"

"Well, I took this as an indication of guilt. He probably decided to bide his time and try to escape. That's in fact what he tried to do."

"OK, let's move ahead to your appeal over the radio. How long did that take?"

"It must've been about an hour."

"And what did Mr. Ellerbee do during that time?"

"He sat quietly in the chair. I was watching him very closely."

"You're telling us that a man who was in mortal danger just sat quietly in a chair for over an hour while you talked to your superiors about a conspiracy that didn't exist?"

"Well, he didn't have that much freedom of movement. I also think he was afraid, and didn't want to do anything that might provoke me."

"Yet you testified that Mr. Ellerbee got loose after you stabbed him, and even made it to the lobby before you pounced on him again. Is this true?"

"Yes! You must believe me! I'm telling you the truth!"

"I think that Mr. Ellerbee was already dead, and that you've made up these details to support your wild story!"

"Objection, your Honor! The prosecutor is browbeating the witness!" shouted Dilbaugh, leaping to his feet once again.

"Sustained," said Tiernan. "Proceed with your questions, Mr. Fonseca, and please restrain your personal judgments."

Tony had been working the fringes of Kohler's story, probing cracks in the facade. Now it was time to bring down the foundation.

"Mr. Kohler, we have testimony from the senior forensic expert of Virginia that intact spermatozoa were found in the victim's mouth, and that this could only have happened shortly before he was killed. How do you explain this?"

"I have no idea whatsoever."

"You deny that a homosexual act occurred between you and the victim just before he was killed?"

"I deny it. It didn't happen!" said Kohler in an anguished voice. "I have never committed a homosexual act with anyone!"

"And you deny having had a homosexual relationship with the deceased?"

"Yes! Absolutely!"

"So in your view the senior forensic expert in Virginia is lying?"

"I don't know about his testimony. All I know is that I'm not a homosexual!" Kohler's voice had been rising almost to a shout.

Fonseca paused, to allow the impact of Kohler's voice to fade. "Mr. Kohler, you've referred many times to your wife and young son. You've told us of your love for them, and how you especially cherish your son. Is that correct?"

"Yes, it is. Very much so."

"Have you ever felt a physical attraction for young boys?"

Dilbaugh jumped up. "Objection, your Honor! The prosecution is on a fishing expedition. We've had nothing to establish relevance for this question."

Tiernan said, "I've allowed wide latitude to the defense, and I'll accord the same opportunity to the prosecution. If it's irrelevant, it'll be stricken. Proceed, Mr. Fonseca."

"Were you ever stimulated by photos of young boys in the nude?"

"No," said Kohler, now fully on guard.

"Did you ever keep such photos, or magazines that contained them?"

"No," Kohler said, now angry. "I said no!"

"Did you ever have a collection of such items, and carry this collection with you in a suitcase when you went overseas?"

Kohler turned pale. "I didn't," he said, struggling to maintain control.

Ade glanced over at Cynthia, and she looked horrified.

"Very well, Mr. Kohler," Tony said. "No further questions." He turned away and walked slowly back toward the prosecution table. Kohler, ashen-faced, was excused and walked back to his seat. As he sat down, he smiled weakly at Cynthia, who forced a smile and gave him a pat on the hand.

When Fonseca reached his table, he turned and said, "The prosecution calls Mr. Stuart Loeffler."

CHAPTER FORTY-TWO

Stu Loeffler, looking unhappy but very professional, identified himself briskly as the CIA station chief in Lagos, Nigeria,
thereby writing finis to his career in Africa. He told of Jack's
brief visit on his way to Tanako, and when he described what
was in the suitcase, a startled murmur rumbled through
the courtroom. Tiernan rapped for order. A woman juror
gasped, her mouth agape. The men stared hard at Kohler,
who'd turned pale and looked stunned.

Ade glanced over at Cynthia, who closed her eyes slowly,
as though gathering strength for this latest ordeal. Suddenly
Jack was on his feet, shouting, "Don't believe him! It's not
true! Can't you see they're all lying?"

Tiernan started banging his gavel at the first outburst, but
Jack continued to shout, even though the gaveling got louder.
Dilbaugh was also on his feet, his face creased with alarm.
He put his hand on Jack's forearm, and said simply and with
sympathy, "Jack." The gentle gesture worked. Kohler sagged
like a rag doll and fell back into his seat. Dilbaugh said, "I
request a brief recess."

Tiernan announced, "We'll have a fifteen-minute recess.
If there are no further questions, the witness is excused."

When the court reconvened, Kohler had made a rapid recovery, almost back to his usual buttoned-down state. It was now Cynthia's turn at bat and maybe his quick revival was speeded by the hope that he'd at last hear something good about himself.

Throughout the trial, Cynthia had sat quietly in the front row of the spectator seats, just behind the defense table. Although Ade knew that she had close friends, she was always alone, as though determined to bear her burden by herself. At the end of the day she and Jack, hand-in-hand, disappeared quietly with Ned Dilbaugh, whose limousine took them back to their apartment.

Dilbaugh announced, "The defense calls Mrs. Cynthia Kohler."

She looked calm, restrained, and dignified. Stu Loeffler's testimony must have surprised and upset her, but now she was composed.

After she was sworn, Cynthia described her life with Jack up to August 30, 1971 as ordinary but satisfying. She felt that he could be an important figure in the field of international economics, and shared his disappointment that the Department didn't seem to appreciate his abilities. Nevertheless, life was pleasant and the future looked good, especially when little Robin was born.

Dilbaugh asked, "Now, when you arrived in Tanako, how did your husband react to the situation there?"

"We'd been briefed on what to expect, so the hardships and misery of the place didn't surprise us," she answered. "But when our best African employee was arrested and tortured, and we could hear prisoners screaming at night, that changed everything."

"How did your husband react to this?"

"I could see it eating away at him day by day. He became withdrawn, and irritable, which wasn't usual for him. But despite the problems, he found satisfaction in our home life – especially watching Robin grow day by day. He always looked forward to playing with Robin, and they would roll around on the floor and play games. But he even stopped that after a while. When I asked what was bothering him, he would say things like, 'It's getting worse here. I don't know how much farther it can go.' He seemed to have a real sense of foreboding. I'd never seen him so worried."

Dilbaugh asked, "On the week-end before the events in question, did you notice any difference in your husband's behavior?"

"He was nervous and distracted, and started talking to himself, saying things that didn't make sense. He'd mumble something, and his voice would just trail off. It was disconcerting, but I thought he was just tired. Finally, he took some tranquillizers to help him sleep, which he'd never done before."

"Were you concerned about this behavior?"

"Oh, yes. He's so solid, always calm under pressure."

"Now let's move ahead to the events in the vault. When you entered with your son Robin, how did your husband appear to you?"

"He was very distraught, his clothes were disheveled, and he had large blood stains on his shirt and trousers."

"What did he say to you?"

"He said he'd uncovered a communist plot, and that I had to believe him. He said George Ellerbee was involved and he was forced to kill him."

"And your reaction?"

"I was totally shocked, you can imagine. I got him to pull himself together a little, and cleaned him up as best I could." Even Cynthia looked haggard at the recollection. "At the Nigerian Ambassador's, Jack seemed to distrust everyone, even me. Ambassador Kanu brought food, but Jack wouldn't touch it. He said it might be poisoned. But he was drinking a lot of scotch, chain-smoking, and pacing, always pacing. And he was very worried about Robin and me."

"Did this behavior continue until you arrived in Washington?"

"Jack slowly began to relax, especially when we left Douala and headed for home. But he was still suspicious, and was cross if I talked to anyone. He really didn't improve until he'd been in the hospital for a few days."

"Mrs. Kohler, I must now ask some personal questions that I'm sure you'd prefer not to discuss in an open courtroom, but it will help us understand your husband better. Please tell us a little about your marriage with Mr. Kohler."

"It's been a good marriage, based on common interests and mutual respect. We were both mature, already established in our professions, when we met. Although we'd both had relationships before, it was really the first time I'd thought seriously about marriage. As for Jack, he'd been engaged some years earlier, but they'd broken it off and parted friends."

"Was your husband active socially before you met him?"

"Yes, he dated often and enjoyed casual dinners with friends, and good conversation."

"And how did you get on with your husband, when you were together?" "Jack's good company. He's a gentleman.

Even when he might be in a bad mood, he rarely spoke sharply. Before we met, Jack was a catch. Single women often invited him for dinner, or for small parties. He was well-liked."

"Did you and Mr. Kohler have a satisfactory physical relationship?"

"Well, yes, we did," responded Cynthia, averting her eyes. "We were very compatible. We both wanted a child, so shortly after we were married I became pregnant. After Robin was born, he became our focus, and Jack spent every spare minute with him. My husband has always been kind and considerate with me, but he loves that little boy with all his heart."

"Did Jack have any close male friends, or did he ever display affection with any of his male friends?"

"Jack's interests in other men were purely social. He didn't have any really close male friends, especially after we began going together. Jack enjoys company, but he's a reserved person. And dignified. I never saw him display any affection towards another male beyond shaking hands. Except for Robin. He hugged and kissed Robin, and carried him around on his shoulders, and played with him, and read to him with Robin sitting on his lap, whenever he could."

This struck Ade as credible. Jack rarely changed his expression, except when he was with Robin. And then he showed unusual animation.

Dilbaugh continued. "So as far as you knew, your husband never had any physical involvement with another man?"

"Never, from the time we met. When Jack wasn't working, he was with me and Robin, or our friends, and there wasn't the opportunity. Especially on Tanako," Cynthia said, glancing sharply at Tony. "There was no way for my husband to have had any physical relationship with George Ellerbee because we would've known about it."

"OK. Mrs. Kohler, you know your husband better than anyone else. Can you help us understand what might have caused his breakdown?"

"Jack Kohler is a loving husband and a devoted father. What happened was totally out of keeping with his past behavior, and it's very hard to believe some of the things I've heard in this courtroom. But I believe that my husband told you the truth." Her voice wavered, and she suddenly looked much older.

"Thank you, Mrs. Kohler. I have no further questions."

Tony Fonseca approached the witness chair. "Mrs. Kohler, did your husband ever say he felt sorry for George Ellerbee, or Mrs. Ellerbee?"

"For the first few days, I think he was very confused and still struggling with the belief that he'd uncovered a dangerous plot. Remember that he was still suspicious of people even at the hospital, and afraid that his food was poisoned."

"And you were convinced that he really believed this?"

"Oh yes. He was even suspicious of me."

"If he thought you were part of the plot, why did he send for you?"

"I don't know that," said Cynthia, irritated. "He was out of his mind. Maybe I was the only person he could turn to, even if there was a risk."

"Thank you, Mrs. Kohler. No further questions."

Ned Dilbaugh had no other witnesses, so Judge Tiernan called a fifteen-minute recess and the courtroom half-emptied. Ade wandered over to where Maria Ellerbee was standing, and she was quietly seething.

"It's all for show, Ade. Can't you see it?" she asked, not bothering to greet him. "He made up that whole story in the vault to save himself. And those photographs! The man is a beast! The only thing that's true is that he tortured my husband and killed him. He had no reason!"

"I know. George never threatened anyone. He wouldn't have hurt a fly."

Maria wasn't satisfied. "There must be more to it, Ade. Maybe Jack was up to something and George found out. Maybe that's why he was killed."

When in doubt, form a conspiracy theory. Everyone had one – Jack, the Tanakians, and now Maria. But it was at least plausible that George had uncovered something, threatened to expose Jack, and got himself killed for his trouble. Maybe Jack threatened to push for George's firing on grounds of incompetence, and George threatened to expose the relationship to protect himself, whereupon Jack killed him. It was a stretch, but it was possible.

As he was returning to the courtroom, he passed Cynthia, who'd also taken a break. He said to her, "I'm sure your strong support for Jack was comforting to him. His feelings for Robin came through especially clearly."

"Thanks, Ade," replied Cynthia without smiling. "You know, all Jack wanted was to serve his country, and have a happy family life. It was in his grasp, but it all came apart. In the end, his past was too much for him." Cynthia gave Ade a look of infinite sorrow, but she didn't break.

Tony Fonseca had two witnesses in rebuttal, Pete Kasprzak, the Embassy security officer, and Joe Kemper, the doctor. Pete said, "During the entire trip back to Washington, Mr. Kohler seemed to be fully rational." Joe Kemper added, "On the flight home, Mr. Kohler was quiet and cooperative, and an outsider wouldn't have noticed any difference between him and the other passengers." Dilbaugh's cross examination did little damage.

Fonseca's final rebuttal witness was Dr. Stephen Hannabury, a psychiatrist hired by the Department to examine Kohler when he was in the hospital. He had thin, silvery hair brushed back along his temples, giving him a reserved and patrician appearance.

After recounting his background as a consultant for the Department and a psychiatrist with his own practice, Dr. Hannabury explained that he'd examined Jack at length on two occasions, September 10 and 15.

Hannabury had been in the courtroom for the entire trial, and had listened carefully to Jack's account of the events in the vault. Up to now, his face had betrayed no feeling, but now, on the stand, he showed no such reticence.

"Dr. Hannabury," Fonseca began, "please describe the general demeanor of the accused when you met with him on September 10."

"To my surprise, Mr. Kohler wasn't in the least hostile. He seemed to accept me as a State Department colleague. He was almost affable, saying that he was feeling well and hoped to be able to leave soon."

"So you found him to be completely normal, with no signs of stress?"

"Oh, he was nervous, clenching and unclenching his hands, things like that. It wasn't excessive or abnormal."

Tony asked, "Did you discuss the events in the vault?"

"He told me about some plot, which I thought was complete balderdash."

"Dr. Hannabury, I assume you read Dr. Wallach's report of his observations of Mr. Kohler as well as his diagnosis. Do you agree with it?"

"Just a minute," broke in Tiernan sharply. He hadn't said anything for a long while. "We didn't bring you people in here to render opinions on each other's testimony, or to evaluate it. That's strictly up to the jury."

Tony was irritated. "OK. Doctor, do you know the term 'catathymic crisis'?"

"Yes. I believe it refers to insanity that may occur in relation to homosexual violence." This was a definition very different from Dr. Wallach's.

"Could you include the possibility that Mr. Kohler suffered some sort of catathymic crisis at the time of the murder?"

"I saw no evidence that this was a typical paranoid psychotic episode."

"Then can you explain why Mr. Kohler killed his colleague?"

"Objection!" shouted Dilbaugh. "The witness is here as a medical expert, not to render a judgment on the case."

"Sustained," said Tiernan. "The witness doesn't have to explain anything, and only gives the jury his opinion as an expert. You don't call on him to judge this case. Let's get that clear, or no more psychiatrists!"

Tony, momentarily flustered, paused to regroup. "Did you ask Mr. Kohler if he had a homosexual relationship with Mr. Ellerbee, or if a homosexual act had taken place between them at the time of the murder?"

"Yes, and he denied it vociferously. That was the only time that Mr. Kohler became really animated. In fact, I was struck by the contrast between his vehement denial, and his almost detached description of how he killed Mr. Ellerbee."

Tony moved in closer, and spoke very distinctly. "And what was your reaction to his explanation?"

"I didn't believe him. There's nothing to indicate he didn't have the mental capacity to know right from wrong at the time of the murder."

Tony looked out at the courtroom. "So, speaking as a psychiatrist of long experience, would you say that Mr. Kohler, at the time of the killing, knew that it was unlawful to take the life of another human being?"

"Most definitely. And Mr. Kohler had sufficient control over his conduct at the time so that this could not be termed a compulsive murder."

"Are you saying that this act was premeditated?"

"No, it wasn't a planned, purposeful act. Something could have happened in the vault to trigger the violence. Even so, he still had sufficient control of himself to have refrained from the act of murder. There was no solid evidence of psychosis or insanity in anything Mr. Kohler told me."

"Then how do you explain the radio broadcast?"

"In my view, Mr. Kohler feigned mental illness."

"You mean," said Tony Fonseca with mock surprise, "that he made up the story so that anyone hearing the message would think he was crazy?"

"Exactly. There's no doubt in my mind that Mr. Kohler was malingering."

"What led you to this conclusion?"

"Mr. Kohler said in his broadcast that he wasn't losing his mind, and that he wasn't crazy. Now, if he'd just gone crazy he wouldn't be worried about whether people thought he was mentally ill."

"I see," said Fonseca. "Anything else?"

"Yes. The accused testified that he'd suffered a 'paranoid delusion,' and Mr. Zimmerman testified that Mr. Kohler said he'd 'lost his cool' and killed George Ellerbee. Those two statements are inconsistent. A person suffering from a paranoid delusion wouldn't be anything like 'cool.' So that's an excuse he manufactured after the fact, and not a true explanation of what happened."

"Dr. Hannabury, we have iron-clad evidence from Virginia's senior forensic expert that a homosexual act took place in the vault. Does this undermine the accused's claim that he was insane at the time of the murder?"

"It certainly does. According to Mr. Kohler, he was truly convinced that Mr. Ellerbee was so dangerous that he had to be subdued, and then stabbed to death. Now, if Mr. Kohler sincerely believed this, I can't believe that he'd risk the pain and injury involved in putting his penis in Ellerbee's mouth. It's simply not credible."

Hannabury's words dropped on the courtroom like the winning putt on the eighteenth hole. The men in the jury box grimaced in agreement.

"Thank you for explaining why Mr. Kohler's contentions are not credible. Now, one more question: what is your assessment of the accused's behavior?"

"It was quite rational. In the vault, he and Ellerbee engage in oral sex, and for some reason, perhaps a quarrel, Kohler gets angry and kills Ellerbee. To cover up, he concocts a wild story and broadcasts it on the radio so everyone will think he's crazy and there'll be a record of it. But his quick recovery undermines his story. No sir, this is not insanity, but a crafty piece of malingering."

Fonseca looked at the jury, and then out at the courtroom. "No further questions," he said, and walked confidently back to the prosecution table.

Ade doubted whether Ned Dilbaugh, for all his ingenuity, could salvage anything from the stern and unflappable Dr. Hannabury.

"Doctor, you stated that you read Dr. Wallach's report. But did you ever review the actual hospital records regarding Mr. Kohler's treatment?"

"No, I didn't think it was necessary."

"Did you talk to any of the psychiatric nurses who observed Mr.Kohler putting his ear to the walls, looking under his bed, testing his food, and so forth?"

"No."

"Did you ever talk to the attending physician, Dr. Wallach?"

"Well, uh, no. I had an appointment to meet with Dr. Wallach but his secretary called to cancel because he was sick."

"And you never bothered to make another appointment?"

"I thought Dr. Wallach would call me if he thought it was useful."

"In other words, you just didn't think it was important enough."

Tony Fonseca's "Objection!" rang out sharply.

"Objection sustained," responded Judge Tiernan.

"OK," said Dilbaugh, undeterred. "Shouldn't the many signs of Mr. Kohler's suspicious behavior in the hospital be part of your diagnosis?"

"The facts lead me to conclude that the accused wasn't psychotic."

"Dr. Hannabury, in your experience have you ever run across anything that might be termed a 'homosexual crisis?'"

"Yes. Someone who isn't a committed homosexual could commit a homosexual act, and be so traumatized by it as to lash out in an unaccustomed direction."

"Could this have happened in this case?"

"I couldn't rule it out, but Mr. Kohler denied any homosexual experience so totally that it's impossible to use this as an explanation. We know that a homosexual act took place, but we don't know why, or whether it can explain Mr. Kohler's violence."

Dilbaugh was unable to shake Hannabury's certainty that Jack was never insane, and ended the cross-examination, his shoulders sagging.

To Ade, this was close to the end of the game for Dilbaugh and Kohler. Aside from believing that Jack was guilty, Ade wasn't sorry to see a K Street franchise player like Ned Dilbaugh humbled before the workmanlike performance of a Tony Fonseca.

But he'd underestimated Ned Dilbaugh, and the impact of his next witness, a man he'd never heard of.

CHAPTER FORTY-THREE

It was time for rebuttal witnesses for the defense. Dilbaugh had but one, and announced, "The defense calls Mr. Robert Morse."

A tall and wiry man, dressed in a tweed herringbone sports jacket, knitted black tie and gray flannel trousers, came forward slowly. His face was ruddy but deeply lined, and he looked to be in his mid-fifties, maybe older. He had a slight limp, giving a first impression of infirmity, but as he walked up the aisle Ade was struck by his sharp profile and piercing blue eyes, visible from several feet away.

The natural curiosity of the spectators over the identity of this stranger was enhanced by his slow, deliberate manner. His limp may have conveyed infirmity, but the rest of him looked pretty strong, like the understated guy who beats everyone at arm wrestling at the neighborhood bar.

Dilbaugh stepped forward. "State your name and occupation," he said.

"My name is Robert Morse, and I'm a former CIA officer."

"Do you know the accused? If so, please point him out in the courtroom." Morse said, "I know Jack Kohler very well. There he is, over there."

Jack of course knew that Morse was going to testify, but for once he had abandoned his bland unemotional gaze and was looking at Morse intently as though he knew him but didn't quite recognize him.

"Mr. Morse, please tell us where and under what circumstances you met the accused," Dilbaugh said.

"I first met Jack Kohler when we were posted together in Cairo – it must have been about eight years ago. 1964 seems right. Jack was a very promising Foreign Service officer and I was a case officer for the CIA, running a group of agents. It was a big assignment for a person of my age and rank, and both Jack and I were full of optimism that we were headed for great things."

"And so you became friends?"

"Yes, we spent a lot of time together. I liked Jack's intelligence and sense of humor, and we were good social friends as well as colleagues. Jack sometimes affected British mannerisms, and was somewhat fastidious – very neat and tidy, you know. Some people thought his manner was forced, but it was just a pose, for his own amusement. Underneath, he wasn't a bit phony. I was married then, but Jack was still single. He dated a number of women from the Embassy and international community and we often went out together."

"How long did your stay in Egypt coincide with Mr. Kohler's?"

"Almost two years. During that time, we saw each other almost every work day, and usually at least two or three evenings a week socially. Morse hesitated, and lowered his voice. "During this period in my life, I was involved in several extramarital affairs, and was drinking heavily Jack knew about this, and did his best to hold me back from behavior that had become very self-destructive." Morse flushed slightly.

"Wasn't this behavior risky for your career as well as your personal life?"

"Of course it was," said Morse, irritated at having to confirm the obvious. "But the risk was part of the heady attitude I had at the time. I had an exciting job, a lovely wife, and yet I reveled in fast living and chasing every attractive woman I laid my eyes on. There were many in Cairo in those days."

"And what was Mr. Kohler's attitude toward this behavior on your part?"

"Jack liked the chase too, but he was single and never crossed the line."

"What line was that?"

"I'd call it immoral behavior. For example, he never slept with another man's wife, although he had the opportunity. And all the late nights we had I never saw him drunk, although some of the parties were pretty wild. And if his relationship with a woman came to an end, they parted as friends. Women liked him because he treated them with respect."

"And you?"

"Women seemed to like me too, although for different reasons. It was kind of a wild ride with me as long as it lasted, and sometimes they seemed to like the adventure." Morse blushed slightly, as though he wanted to answer truthfully without seeming a braggart.

"And what finally happened?"

"Jack warned me that I was heading for a fall, ruining my marriage and hurting my career. He never moralized. He'd just say, 'Bob, you're going to wreck everything. Pull yourself back.' I didn't listen. My wife finally got fed up and walked out. She left me and went back to the States."

"Mr. Morse, are you aware of the charges that've been made at this trial?"

"I know that the prosecution says that the murder of George Ellerbee resulted from a homosexual lovers quarrel with Jack, if that's what you mean."

"Precisely. On the basis of your friendship with Mr. Kohler, can you tell us anything about his sexual orientation?"

"In Cairo, it was possible to participate in the active homosexual life in the city at that time, but everybody knew everybody else's business, who was sleeping with whom, whose marriage was failing, all kinds of intimate personal details. Someone would have known. *I* would've known."

"Your conclusion, then?"

"Jack Kohler was not a homosexual then, and is not a homosexual now."

Tony was on his feet, and the courtroom was buzzing. "Objection, your Honor! The witness is testifying to matters he has no knowledge of."

"Objection sustained," said Judge Tiernan. "Mr. Morse, confine your answers to things you know personally, from your experience with Mr. Kohler."

"OK, when I knew him what I said was certainly true, and I can't see how it could've changed later."

"All right. Please continue."

Morse shifted in his seat. "When my wife left, I upped my drinking a couple notches. The station chief warned me, but I was on a slippery slope. The CIA pulled me before my tour was over and sent me back to Washington. Jack finished his tour and was transferred to the Department."

"What happened next?"

"The CIA gave me another chance and got me started in rehab, but I never stopped drinking. I was an alcoholic, but always made it to work, even though I'd be hung over and red-eyed. But I finally flamed out of the rehab program, and the CIA had had enough. I was fired."

"What did you do then?"

"I was full of self-pity, blaming everyone except myself. But no one else would hire me, and I drank through my savings and the last of my self-respect. By this time, I was on the skids. I avoided old friends, and hung out only with other boozers. I'd really hit rock bottom, but hadn't realized it. I was evicted from my apartment for not paying rent. I had no place to go, so I used my last few dollars to buy a bottle of cheap booze and proceeded to get falling down drunk, again. I must've passed out in a park, and slept there. If it had been winter, I'm sure I would've died.

"When I awoke, I had no clear idea of where I was or what had happened to me. I was filthy – I had soiled myself – and hadn't washed in days. I don't know what made me think of Jack Kohler – maybe it was a faint memory of our partying days – but maybe it was some kind of survival instinct."

Ade looked around the courtroom. The spectators were following Morse's story closely. The jury was attentive, but seemed unsure where it was leading.

"By some great stroke of luck, I staggered into a drug-store and found Jack's apartment listing in a telephone book. It was two blocks away."

Dilbaugh was standing, motionless, ready to interrupt if Morse strayed.

"Somehow I made my way to his apartment. He must've been astonished when he saw me. I stank; my clothes were in tatters; I'd fallen in the park and had a bloody gash on my forehead.

"Jack took me in. He saved my life that day. I could hardly walk, but he somehow got me into the shower, took off my filthy clothes, washed me, gave me clean clothes to wear, and looked after me the rest of that day. I was too far gone to explain to him what had happened. He never asked, but only saw that I was desperately in need. He just quietly took over.

"The next day he took off from work to take me to the doctor. By then at least I could stand, although I was still wobbly. Jack's doctor gave me a physical and found that I was still OK for a guy my age and had done no permanent damage to myself. Jack and the doctor sat me down and told me that if I wanted to help myself they'd stay with me, but it had to come from me. That started me on the long road back. I stayed with Jack until I rounded the first bend and could stand on my own, about a couple of weeks. He and Cynthia — he'd met her when he came back to Washington and now they were very close - helped me get a job and find an apartment, and often looked in on me. I wouldn't be here today if it hadn't been for Jack. He had nothing to gain from helping me the way he did. He must've been revolted by the filthy derelict I'd become, but he didn't turn away. He could've taken me to a shelter or a hospital and washed his hands, and left with a clear conscience. Instead he cleaned the shit off me - in every way - and gave me a chance to make myself whole again."

Morse looked out at the courtroom. His blue eyes projected from his craggy face like lighthouse beacons on a stormy night. "Everyone in this courtroom should know the real Jack Kohler," he said, almost in a whisper. "He's a very special human being. I know what he's being tried for, but there's only one thing he showed me, and that's Christian love."

Dilbaugh took a long pause. The courtroom was silent. Jack's lips were parted, his eyes blinking. Ade guessed it had been a long time since anyone other than his wife and his hired lawyer had described him as anything other than a depraved monster. A thin smile held his lips for a moment, and Ade saw him mouth the words, "Thank you..." His expression spoke the rest, "for remembering that I'm a human being."

"Thank you, Mr. Morse, for that extraordinary story. I have only one last question. In your experience with Mr. Kohler, do you believe that he might have been engaging in homosexual acts?"

"I'll never let anyone say that," said Morse quietly.

"Thank you, sir. No further questions."

CHAPTER FORTY-FOUR

Judge Tiernan looked over at the jury. "All the evidence is in," he said, but before closing arguments, I want to clarify one or two points.

"First, the original indictment charged premeditated, or first degree murder. After hearing the government's case, the Court ruled that there was insufficient evidence of premeditation. So you can strike that possibility. All other murder is second degree murder, which includes murder with malice aforethought and the lesser offense of voluntary manslaughter. I'll explain these after we've heard closing arguments."

Turning to Tony, he said, "Mr. Fonseca, let's hear what you have to say."

Tony gave his notes a last-second perusal, smiled quickly, rose, and walked toward the jury box.

"Members of the jury," he began, "this is an unusual case, but I hope that this won't lead you down the wrong path. It would be a huge mistake to conclude that because the act itself was shocking and occurred in a very different place, the conduct of the accused was so extraordinary that he must have been insane.

"I hope to convince you that there's nothing here that meets the test of insanity. The government believes that

Kohler killed Ellerbee because they quarreled over some kind of homosexual relationship, and that afterward Kohler faked insanity, because he knew that he'd have to come before a jury sometime. So Mr. Kohler hoped to fool people that he'd gone berserk after experiencing unbearable stress, and that this was not the act of a cold-blooded killer.

"Please don't consider only the homosexual aspect of this case. Yes, it explains the background to the murder, but remember that the Government need not prove a motive in *any* murder case. Of course, it helps to understand motivation, but we don't have to prove it. We only know that a murder occurred and who did it. We don't know who provoked it or why it happened. The only person who really knows is the accused.

"Now, the key to this case is the insistence of the accused that he was temporarily insane. Please look very carefully at the testimony of Mr. and Mrs. Kohler. We contend that Mr. Kohler came in here and lied to you from the witness stand, and that he's lied all along to the psychiatrists and everyone else he talked to. He lied to you about what happened in the vault, and he lied to you about the child pornography. We believe that Mrs. Kohler also lied to you. Since they were both under oath, that would amount to perjury. But we're not trying that issue today, and I'm not angry about it. It's understandable that she might tell her husband, 'I'll stand by you all the way,' and try to save his skin.

"Now, let's look at what's required for a judgment of insanity. The bar is high, and for good reason. All of our law is based on the presumption that a person is responsible for his acts. The defendant is asking you to excuse him. There's absolutely no doubt that he killed Mr. Ellerbee, but he's telling you, 'I did it, but it wasn't my fault.'

"Ladies and gentlemen, there's simply no credible evidence that gives Mr. Kohler an excuse. Oh yes, there's evidence of anxiety, tension, nervousness, suspicion, and panic, but those are personality characteristics we all experience at some point or other. What we don't have is evidence of a defect or disease so deep-rooted that it governs his behavior totally, and just doesn't come and go to fit his mood or circumstances.

"Another key point is that this deep-seated condition must be present at the time of the killing. *At the time of the killing.* So all this testimony about his behavior in the hospital, and what the nurses saw, and all the rest of it, is really irrelevant. We contend that all of this behavior was for show. It was fakery. And remember that even his own psychiatrist – Dr. Wallach – who testified for him, admitted that any paranoia exhibited by the accused could have come *after* the killing, and therefore would be the *result* of the killing, and not the cause.

"So, keep in mind that what's really important is not what came after the killing, but what happened in the vault. To acquit the accused, you would have to decide that his mental disease was so great that in the vault he didn't know what he was doing was wrong, and was unable to stop himself.

"Now, let's look at what the psychiatrists told us. There are two ways that you can arrive at a conclusion about insanity. You can look at the person, his history, his actions, and the facts. If it all adds up to insanity, you have a case.

"The second way is to take a quick look at what happened, call it a mental disease, and then grasp at any straw that might fit the theory. In other words, you start with the premise that a person is insane, and then set out to prove it.

"Consider the testimony of Dr. Wallach. He wasn't much interested in looking into what happened on the day of the murder. His attitude was that he was at the hospital to treat the patient, and the facts of the murder weren't important. In fact, Dr. Wallach's whole diagnosis rests on the presumption that Kohler told him the truth. The murder, the sperm in the throat and all of that, were almost incidental. If Kohler was lying, as we contend, then the conclusion that Kohler was insane and couldn't help himself falls apart.

"Now, let's look at Kohler's story. You don't have to look very hard to see how implausible it is. Let's just take a few examples. First, the accused says he tied up the victim and kept him in the vault for a long time while he confronted him with his suspicions, and then was talking on the radio. During this entire time the victim just sits there quietly, hardly saying a word. Even though the telephone cord was tied loosely, as we heard from Mr. Kohler's own testimony, the victim makes no attempt to escape until it's too late and he's already almost dead from his wounds. Does this make sense?

"What about Kohler's behavior in the hospital? He's calm, almost normal. Maybe he was cured the minute he stepped in there. But it makes more sense that this was all a big act. We know that Mr. Kohler is smart, but he overplayed his hand. You don't need to be a psychiatrist to know that paranoia just doesn't come and go like a whim. But with the defendant, one minute he's gone berserk in the Embassy; then without any treatment at all he's calm at the Nigerian ambassador's; then he's looking under the bed at the hospital; and then he's talking like the Secretary of State to the examining psychologist. Yes, Mr. Kohler is smart all right, but he can't keep up this pretense twenty-four hours a day, and so there're a lot of holes in this picture.

"Now, if he'd really been insane, you would've taken him out of the Embassy in a straight jacket, ranting and raving. Instead, he walked out calmly with his wife and son. Does this make sense?

"Another point. We've heard a lot about the island, its tortures, repression, and danger. But on August 17, the defendant invites a friend to visit and to bring along the wife and kids! And the chief selling point is Tanako's 'peace and quiet!'

"The inconsistencies go on and on. Consider the broadcast from the vault. The defendant says right off the top, 'I'm not crazy.' Not because someone on the other end said, 'Hey, man, you're crazy,' but he volunteered it. Now, if he were really delusional, he wouldn't say 'I'm not crazy!' He would've been totally seized with his delusion.

Tony's voice was scornful. "Look at what he does when Zimmerman arrives. Kohler suspects he's part of the plot. Yet he tells Zimmerman where his wife and son are and tells him to bring them to the Embassy. To the Embassy, which is supposedly surrounded by sinister enemies ready to kill him! He wants Zimmerman to bring his family right into the lion's den! I ask you, what's wrong with this picture?

"Consider Mrs. Kohler. The night before, she sees that her husband is upset and irritable. The next morning, he's irrational, and she's very worried. He's supposed to be home at three o'clock, but by six o'clock he still isn't home. What does she do? Nothing! Her husband's way overdue, she hasn't heard from him, but all she does is go to a friend's house to visit and sip tea!

"Now, what about Mrs. Ellerbee? She knows from experience that Arania is no paradise, that there's political repression, and so forth, but it's nothing special. Any diplomat living abroad is supposed to be able to deal with it, and that's what the Ellerbees did. This is the true picture of life in Tanako and Mrs. Kohler gave you another version because she was trying to help her husband.

"Finally, Mrs. Kohler goes into the Embassy with her son. Her little son, in the middle of all that gore! And she has a rational discussion with her husband! Part of it was overheard by Mr. Zimmerman. He heard Kohler say in a loud whisper, 'You've got to help me. They'll think I'm crazy!' Ladies and gentlemen, he already had his defense worked out and he was enlisting his wife to help him!

"Now if you can accept all these wild contradictions, I'll be very surprised. So I urge you to look at the facts, and go where they lead you. You can discount fanciful theories that sound like they come out of textbooks. What this case comes down to is a willful killing and an attempt to cover it up by faking insanity. I'm confident that you'll not be fooled. Thank you."

Judge Tiernan announced, "The Court will take a thirty-minute recess and then we'll begin the arguments for the defense."

CHAPTER FORTY-FIVE

Ned Dilbaugh slowly paced the length of the jury box and looked at every juror before he began speaking. "Members of the jury, you will soon have to decide the fate of a fellow human being. I know it's a responsibility you are taking very seriously.

"This is a complex and difficult case, because not only are the circumstances unusual – well outside the experience of most Americans – but because you must judge what might cause a man to commit a violent act that's not only shocking to civilized society, but so repugnant to the man himself that the only way he can deal with it is to completely blot it from his memory.

"Now, let's look at what we know. We know that George Ellerbee was killed in the vault. We know that Jack Kohler, who was his colleague and who by all accounts was also his friend, was the person who killed him. You heard Mr. Kohler himself admit it. He described how he was seized by a delusion so strong that he could see Mr. Ellerbee only as part of a gigantic plot. In his mind, this plot was so dangerous and terrifying that Mr. Kohler truly believed that his very life, and the lives of his wife and son were in great and immediate peril. You heard him tell you that the only way he could think of to try and derail this plot was to subdue Mr. Ellerbee and broadcast a warning so that other American embassies in Africa would hear it and spread the alarm.

"Now, this much we know. But Mr. Kohler's delusion was so great that he utterly believed that there was a plot, and that his delusion – an 'acute paranoid psychosis,' as Dr. Wallach described it – so overwhelmed him that he couldn't know right from wrong.

"You've heard evidence from eminent and experienced psychiatrists on their interpretations of Mr. Kohler' state of mind, and you know that their conclusions are not in agreement. Because of that, you might be tempted to think that the experts cancel each other out, and thereby disregard their testimony. That would be a mistake, because the key to what happened, and the much more complex question of why it happened, is in that testimony.

"So let's review what we learned from Dr. Wallach. He is not just your garden-variety psychiatrist. He's a giant in his field, a famous expert on psychiatric disorders. He states that Mr. Kohler was under enormous stress from living in a remote and difficult place ruled by a murderous dictator. Imagine yourselves in Mr. Kohler's place. He's an intelligent and competent diplomat, chosen for this difficult post because he seems able to handle any crisis. When his senior African employee is seized and taken to jail, Mr. Kohler works tirelessly to get him released.

"But there's another factor here. The prison is right across the street from Mr. Kohler's house, so close that the family hears the screams at night from people being tortured. Imagine coming home from a hard day at the office and settling down to dinner with your family, and being subjected to heart-rending screams from victims being tortured within an inch of their lives, and sometimes more than that, from just across the street!

"And those are not random, intermittent screams. Often the screams go on all night, until the dawn finally comes. Would you be able to sleep through something like that? If you knew that the screams were coming from people who were experiencing some of the most hideously gruesome tortures devised by man? Who were in fact being tortured until there was no more life in them? Especially if one of the people being tortured was your most loyal and valuable African employee? Put yourselves in Mr. Kohler's shoes, and ask if that experience, repeated again and again, might cause 'stress,' and affect your behavior?"

Dilbaugh paused and looked at the jurors to let the image sink in. "Of course, this was not all Mr. Kohler had to cope with. Although he did his best to get on with Mr. Ellerbee, we know that the latter was deficient in his work, maybe incompetent, so that Mr. Kohler even tried to have him replaced."

Ade glanced at Maria. She was looking darts at Dilbaugh.

"Now imagine if you were doing your best in a tough job, and the person you relied on most was incompetent. That means that Mr. Kohler has to double check everything. Much of the work has to be done over. Mr. Kohler can't finish his own work because he has to spend so much time supervising his colleague.

"Now, he doesn't blow up, or lose his temper. He plugs away, doing the job like the dedicated Foreign Service officer he is. But he quietly asks that Mr. Ellerbee be transferred. Isn't that reasonable? But what happens? The State Department can't be bothered, and even Ambassador Hellyer, who is not only his superior but his friend, tells him to forget it! If this happened to you, wouldn't you feel aggrieved, perhaps resentful? Couldn't this eat away at you, despite your efforts to keep it under control?

"Now, I'm not suggesting that anyone with a workplace grievance can go out and kill his colleague. If that were true, half the population of the United States would disappear overnight. But things were happening to this man that finally caused him to totally lose control, and for a short time rendered him unable to tell right from wrong."

"Now, let's look at Mr. Kohler's record. It's admirable. In fact, if it were not for this one solitary act, we'd all agree that this is the record of an American to be proud of, someone we could trust to represent our country well.

"Remember, Jack Kohler was the first one of his family to graduate from university. He's bright, so he goes to graduate school and gets into the Foreign Service, fulfilling a childhood ambition. He also overcomes one of the worst experiences that any child can face – being abused by his parents.

"You heard Mr. Kohler describe how his father abused him physically and humiliated him, and subjected him to harsh discipline. And how his mother, whom he loved dearly, withheld her affection from this exemplary little boy. Members of the jury, we heard enough to understand very clearly how the supposedly solid and steady Jack Kohler grew up with terrible scars. But they weren't visible to the outside observer. They were internal scars, and they left him very vulnerable. Even more important, they left a disordered personality, a human being rational and functional on the outside, but inside, scarred and wounded.

"I'm not trying to be a mind reader. I'm a lawyer, not a psychiatrist. But the testimony brings out clearly how such a fine person, with not a blemish on his record more than a traffic ticket, could suddenly kill his colleague.

"What I'm suggesting to you is that there's only one satisfactory explanation for what happened. Consider that prior to August 30, there's not one instance of a temperamental outburst or violence recalled by anyone who's known the accused. Indeed, we've heard that he was good company and treated friends and colleagues with consideration and respect. More, Mr. Morse told you how Jack Kohler took him in, cleaned the excrement from his body and literally saved his life. And how in Cairo Mr. Kohler lived a normal heterosexual life, enjoying the companionship of many women before he himself married.

"Now, ladies and gentleman, the prosecution has based its entire case on the premise that Mr. Kohler and his victim were homosexual lovers, and it was a lovers quarrel that led to the murder. I know, Mr. Fonseca told you that motive doesn't matter, and that the homosexual aspect of the case isn't really important beyond shedding some light on the background to the tragedy. But if it doesn't matter, why did Mr. Fonseca spend so much time constructing a fanciful scenario that makes an honorable but overstressed man into a monstrous deviant, and portrays him and his courageous wife as scheming liars? Even if you give full credit to the forensic evidence in the vault and the accused's possession of unsavory photographs, what emerges is not a portrait of some monster but of a decent man struggling against uncontrollable emotions and finally being overcome by them. In other words, of a man who was driven temporarily insane by forces that finally proved stronger than he was.

"We've heard factual testimony that there was no homo-sexual relationship between the two men. They were both happily married, and they lived in circumstances that made an ongoing relationship of that kind impossible to hide. Yet the prosecution devoted a great deal of time to trying to prove that homosexuality is the key to what happened. Why? Because it's necessary to demonize Jack Kohler in order to undermine the one explanation that truly makes sense. Ladies and gentlemen, homosexuality is not on trial here; a decent and honorable man is. Don't allow the homo-phobia and social biases of our times to sway your judgment of what's right.

"Please consider that the picture of the accused painted by the prosecution is so out of keeping with what we know about his exemplary character that it must be false. And if it doesn't fit, neither does the rest of the scenario. So if what happened in the vault was a one-time occurrence, totally foreign to the character of this good man, the prosecution's explanation loses credibility. And the likelihood that what happened was a unique and tragic incident brought on by temporary madness makes more and more sense. Especially considering that after August 30 Mr. Kohler quickly returns to his accustomed behavior so that he's released in his wife's custody with the only proviso that he see a therapist once a week.

"So here's a man who's established a pattern of positive, consistent, gentle behavior over his lifetime, and who then commits a senseless and violent act so out of keeping with his persona that everyone judges it inexplicable. Doesn't that tell you that something triggered an explosion inside of Jack Kohler? Doesn't it make sense that whatever this thing was, it ignited the unlit fuse that was lying dormant within him, and was a product of his childhood abuse, professional disappointments, the incompetence of his colleague, and certainly, the inhuman behavior of the regime, which battered on his sanity every single day?

"We've heard compelling testimony on all of this. Unfortunately, we've been prevented from obtaining depositions from Tanakians and foreign diplomats who could amply document Mr. Kohler's behavior prior to August 30. They would, I'm sure, testify to his growing nervousness and stress, and to the grim conditions in that dark place. But we were unable to obtain that testimony, and so I can't use it.

"You'll remember that I tried unsuccessfully to have the coded message warning of a plot admitted into evidence. Perhaps because it was never sent, it was deemed unimportant. But its very existence *proves* that Mr. Kohler believed that he was the victim of a communist plot well *before* the slaying occurred. Therefore, he couldn't have made his story up *after* a quarrel with Mr. Ellerbee.

"We've heard from expert psychiatrists that there's a clinical name for what happened to Mr. Kohler. Dr. Wallach described for you a force so strong – a catathymic explosion – that the person who suffers it is powerless to resist it. Utterly powerless. Mr. Kohler is a moral man, a man devoted to his family, but he couldn't resist this mighty force that rose up suddenly and consumed him. For that brief moment, he had no choice.

"As we've heard, paranoia sometimes becomes acute. That is, it can come on so quickly that the only way a person can deal with it is through some act of violence. Afterwards, the victim rapidly returns to a normal state.

Even Dr. Hannabury doesn't disagree, because this condition is well-established in medical literature. But the essence of his testimony is that he simply doesn't believe Mr. Kohler. That's it. He's entitled to his opinion, of course, but it's just the opinion of one man.

"Members of the jury, George Ellerbee's death was indeed tragic, but it was an accident. A decent and loving family man, in a flash of time, was stressed beyond endurance and unleashed a spasm of violence that will burden him and his family the rest of their lives, regardless of what you decide here.

"I ask you to consider the only explanation that makes sense, and that's what I've just outlined for you. A person doesn't suddenly commit a violent act contrary to his entire previous behavior unless there are extreme circumstances. Consider all the things that drove Jack Kohler to madness, and imagine the heroic struggle he waged to contain his inner torment and be a fine person. He succeeded, with the exception of this one explosive act. If you consider all these factors, you'll judge that Jack Kohler not guilty, by reason of temporary madness. Ladies and gentlemen, thank you."

Ned Dilbaugh walked slowly back to his chair and sat down. The courtroom was silent as the spectators mulled over his arguments. Charlie Stubblefield leaned over and whispered, "That was the best possible defense. It could sway some of the jurors temporarily, but in the end they'll find him guilty." Charlie had come a long way from his original idea that a jury would never convict Jack Kohler because he was crazy.

"How about a lesser charge?" Ade asked.

"That's possible," said Charlie.

"But he didn't deal at all with the blow-job in the vault," Ade said. "And the photographs. You can hardly ignore them. Jack committed perjury, plain and simple. Not once, but twice. Dilbaugh tried to make the case that Jack was so shamed by the fellatio and the pictures that he simply blotted them out. Nice try, but I don't buy it."

"And those things will be the key for conviction," responded Charlie.

"There's another factor," said Ginger, joining in. "We all heard that Tiernan was tough, but I didn't expect him to be a hanging judge."

"What do you mean?" asked Charlie.

"The message they were working on. It establishes that Jack was convinced of a plot well before he killed Ellerbee, and didn't make it up after the fact, as the prosecution contends. It's a key piece of evidence for the defense, and Tiernan refused to admit it."

"It'll certainly be the heart of any appeal," Ade said.

After a few seconds, the inevitable cough started a wave of coughs and throat-clearing, and an animated buzz spread through the courtroom.

Judge Tiernan tapped softly for order. He was about to instruct the jury.

CHAPTER FORTY-SIX

Judge Tiernan paused, looked around the courtroom, and began his instructions. "Ladies and gentlemen, you are charged with finding out the truth from all the evidence, and you are the sole judges of the facts." In contrast, he explained, Fonseca and Dilbaugh were "advocates," who emphasized what was most supportive of their cases.

"This is a case involving murder. It includes the lesser offense of manslaughter. Murder is the unlawful killing of a human being with malice aforethought." Malice, he said, was "evil design, a desire to harm or cause suffering to another person." Then, slowing his delivery, he said, "But malice may be *implied* from the *deliberate* use of a deadly weapon, when used to take the life of another human being."

"Voluntary manslaughter is the unlawful killing of a person without malice, upon a sudden quarrel or heat of passion. The test to determine if a killing was in the heat of passion, which reduces a murder to a manslaughter, is whether at the time of the killing the accused was governed by passion to such an extent that he acted irrationally and without judgment. You must determine what degree of murder is involved – murder with malice aforethought, or voluntary manslaughter.

"In federal court, you give no reasons for your verdict. If you have questions, send me a note, but remember that you are the sole judges of the testimony and the credibility of the witnesses. Don't ask the Marshall anything, because he can't answer. When you've reached a verdict, knock on the door, but don't tell the Marshall what the verdict is. Now, let the jury retire." The jury rose and slowly left the courtroom. It was 1:15, Friday afternoon.

At 3:45, the jury sent a note to Judge Tiernan requesting a restatement of second degree murder and manslaughter. The Judge scribbled the definitions on a pad and sent it in.

Just after six, the Marshal announced, "The jury has reached a verdict."

Judge Tiernan told the courtroom spectators, who'd been milling around the room, "The jury is coming in with a verdict. Whatever it is, I won't permit any demonstration or displays of emotion. Understood?" He looked over at Kohler, and said, "Let the defendant stand. The clerk will read the verdict."

As the jurors filed in, expressionless, Kohler rose slowly, the color drained from his face. The clerk read, "We the jury find the defendant, John D. Kohler, guilty of voluntary manslaughter."

Kohler sagged, and Cynthia put her arms around his wide shoulders. Maria nodded slowly, in tight-lipped satisfaction. Judge Tiernan dismissed the jurors, and a clutch of reporters scrambled out to get their reactions.

Tiernan was brisk. "Let the defendant come forward," he said.

Jack walked slowly to the front and stood forlornly before Judge Tiernan. "Mr. Kohler," he said, "you've been judged guilty of voluntary manslaughter. Shall I proceed with sentencing?"

Dilbaugh responded, "Let me confer with my client briefly."

Tiernan tapped his fingers. "OK. Let's wrap it up, one way or the other. You don't need much time to talk it over."

Dilbaugh said, "We'll agree to immediate sentencing. If prison is a possibility, please consider Mr. Kohler's unblemished past. He's also undergoing psychiatric treatment. He has a wife and child, and in light of his chances for rehabilitation –"

"He can continue treatment in an institution, but not outside." Looking at Kohler, Tiernan said, "Mr. Kohler, is there anything you want to tell me prior to my pronouncing sentence? Anything you want."

Kohler, the corners of his mouth turned down, took a deep breath. "I just want to say to everyone in this courtroom that everything I said was the truth." He paused, and his mouth started to twitch. "Sir, I tried so hard!"

Tiernan was unmoved. He said, "I have no doubt you knew what you were doing, and you probably don't either. I think this was a killing without malice, resulting from a sudden quarrel. I just don't believe it happened any other way. Nobody walks up and stabs somebody else without some kind of quarrel. But the victim has paid a heavy price. There've been some sordid inferences directed his way and he's not here to defend himself. Now, you didn't accuse him of being a homosexual. I'll give you credit for that. The government did that. But he's dead and his reputation is tarnished forever. As for you, you accused him of being a communist spy, a betrayer of his country. And now he's paid the maximum penalty. George Ellerbee can't tell his side of the story because you took it away from him."

Dilbaugh said, "Your Honor, we've never minimized the tragedy that resulted from those awful circumstances on that island."

"Well, whatever sentence I impose, he's entitled to be released after serving one-third of it, and the jury has already reduced it from the maximum. Second degree murder has a maximum of a life sentence, but the maximum for voluntary manslaughter is ten years."

Tiernan gazed at the courtroom, drawing his lips back tightly as though he had bit into a lemon. With every eye watching him he pronounced, "It is the judgment of the Court upon the finding of guilty that Mr. Kohler be committed for confinement for a period of ten years. Do you want to appeal, Mr. Kohler?"

"Yes, your Honor," Jack answered.

"Despite what you did, you pose no current threat to society and it's unlikely that you would flee. I'll release you on personal bond. Don't leave the Washington area without the consent of the Court. The Court is adjourned."

CHAPTER FORTY-SEVEN

It was finally over. After all that had happened, the verdict came down to a crime of passion, reducing the strivings and secrets of two men's lives to the equivalent of a fight in a bar-room where someone gets killed. Judge Tiernan had imposed the maximum sentence under the charge, but Kohler would be eligible for release after serving one-third of it. If Dilbaugh could mount a successful appeal, Jack would serve no time at all.

But even though the trial was over, the repercussions were nowhere near finished. The trial had reached a decision but hadn't answered all the questions, and doubts lingered with Ade and Ginger, if not with the public at large. Except for them and Maria Ellerbee, most people and the press seemed satisfied that justice was done. The clincher was the forensic evidence from the vault, and public revulsion at the act that preceded the murder. Ginger said, "If people look back on this case in the future, maybe they'll realize how much the judge and jury were affected by hostility about homosexuality. Just the very suggestion was enough to stigmatize Kohler and Ellerbee and make people accept the worst."

"Not to mention Manning and Jurgens. They agreed to stop the public stuff, but they could still come after me and Charlie."

"They will if it suits them," Ginger agreed.

Ade was hoping that Ginger's interest in the case and being at the trial would make her want to come back to Washington with Greg right away, but her decision to stay in Lexington had hardened into concrete. "You're still married to this case and involved, no matter what the Department tells you," she said. "As for me, I just need some time and some space. And maybe my career again. It'll just be until your year at Georgetown is up. We're not finished, Ade, not by a long shot. You just can't always have things your way."

And so they returned to their separate lives, leaving a dangling marriage connected only by telephone and twice-monthly visits.

Ade vowed to plunge into his new situation, but first he had to fulfill his promise to Stu Loeffler. They arranged to meet for coffee at a small restaurant on H Street.

"I promised you a favor," Ade said. "It's payoff time."

"Ade, this is highly unusual, but I've come to realize that everything about this case is that way. You can help us, and in the process help yourself as well."

"Let's hear it."

"Although I didn't know it until just a few days ago, George Ellerbee was an agent in place, killed in the line of duty by something that was as unexpected as it was bizarre. We can't do anything about the testimony that came out, but we want to stop the trashing of his memory and put an end to all this speculation about him. I just don't believe that he enticed Jack Kohler into some kind of ongoing homosexual relationship, or even that they had one. It doesn't fit with the guy we know. And don't forget that he took at least two or three lie detector tests while he worked for us. There wasn't a blip on any of them. I think if he was homosexual we'd have known, because in that case he couldn't have worked for us. For the same reasons he couldn't have worked for you – vulnerability to blackmail."

"If there was no social stigma to homosexuality, there'd be no vulnerability. Did you ever think of that?"

"Sure. But that's a bit advanced for the 70's. It'll take a long time for attitudes to change. Anyway, all this garbage about him – you know, perversion and depravity – is unfair and devastating to his wife, who didn't know about any of it."

"Poor Maria," Ade said. "She's an innocent victim too."

"There's really only one source for this, and it's Walter Jurgens up on the Hill. He may have stopped talking openly to the press, but the snide innuendo is still spilling from his nasty little mouth. We want you to talk to him."

"He hates Foreign Service officers," Ade said, not anxious to be drawn in again. "Also, he and Senator Manning agreed not to say anything more about the security leak in Moscow, and so far they've kept their word."

Stu looked Ade in the eye. "You may want to take a look at that situation right quick. My information is that they're dropping the security issue but will ride the homosexual angle as far as it will take them. The fallout from the trial will give it a boost. It may be over for Jack Kohler, but you're far from out of it."

Nothing in Washington is ever over. People used to make jokes about how no political issue ever died a natural death, but now it wasn't funny. Charlie and Ade had done nothing wrong, but a Senator and his malicious aide wanted an issue, and if it ruined some faceless bureaucrats that was not their concern. Ade took a deep breath. "Do you have any suggestions?"

"We can't control what's in the newspapers, but we can try to stop Manning and Jurgens from holding hearings and starting a big witch hunt. That would be very harmful to State. Anyway, Manning has always supported the Agency, because he sees it as a much firmer linchpin in the war against 'godless commonism' than the 'spineless' State Department."

"I'd like to help George and I want to keep Charlie Stubblefield and myself out of trouble, but I don't want to talk to Jurgens again. It would have much more impact if you talked to him yourself."

"The Director wants to distance the Agency from this case *now*," Stu said. Ade thought, clever of the Agency to walk away and leave us to clean up the mess. Of course, it *was* our mess to begin with.

"I'm willing," Ade said. "But first, I have to get approval from State, and two, what makes you think Jurgens will believe anything I say? Especially if he's going after me and Charlie as the guys who send out perverts to represent the United States."

"We'll give you a personnel document that shows Ellerbee was an Agency employee, and that our own internal investigation cleared him of any suspicion of passing documents to the Soviets. As for Manning scapegoating you and Charlie, I'd like to help but frankly I don't have a clue. The Department won't do anything more than admit that you and Charlie are Foreign Service officers in good standing, and that you used your best judgment to fill two difficult assignments. If Manning's determined to make an example of you, the Department will sacrifice you to get Manning off its back. It won't take them more than two seconds to decide that one."

Ade admonished Stu for his typical CIA disdain for diplomats, but he feared that Stu might be right. In any case, all he had now was Stu's plan to salvage some respect for George and keep the Agency out of the backwash. Ade was skeptical that it would work, but it beat doing nothing.

He went in to see Harlan Hastings to get his approval for this latest scheme. Hastings too was skeptical but willing to do whatever was necessary to keep Congress from messing around in State's business. "Keep them happy, play to their egos, and never, ever risk a *contretemps* with them," he told Ade once. *'Contretemps'* was another of his favorite words.

"But what if they're wrong?" Ade asked, still hoping to see a decision made on principle rather than expediency.

"Ade, some days mendacity is standing room only on Capitol Hill. Never mind. Go along, and usually it'll work out."

Hastings's attitude was pure pragmatism, devoid of moral considerations. Yet Ade knew him as a good man, loyal to his country, effective in getting things done, and even kind to his wife and children. Was there a total disconnect between his private life and his public persona, where doing the job and protecting the turf of the State Department seemed to be the only priorities? Ade once asked him about this too. "Turf counts," was his total answer.

Ade had one more question. "Harlan, I was as surprised as anyone to learn that Ellerbee worked for the CIA. As DCM in Cameroon, couldn't I have been trusted with that information?" He was still miffed that no one had told him.

"The only one who knew was Hellyer. He could've told you, but George's cover was so perfect that we agreed that the fewer people who knew, the better." Seeing Ade's pained expression he said, "Let me ask you: is there anything you would've done differently if you'd known? Would George Ellerbee still be alive if you'd known? Hell, his own wife didn't know. And Jack Kohler didn't know."

"OK, I'll get over it," Ade said, not willing to concede the point.

"Yes, you will," Hastings said.

Ade had one more stop to make before trudging up to the Hill, and that was to check in with Charlie Stubblefield. He told him what Stu had said about Manning riding the homosexual issue. Charlie frowned. "It fits," he said. "I had a feeling we wouldn't get out of this so easily."

"Joe McCarthy made the same kind of charges, but he failed when people finally stood up to him. Why can't the same thing happen now?"

"Because you know very well that homosexuals are still stigmatized and discriminated against. If Manning gets across the idea that the State Department is riddled with fruits it'll be a disaster."

"Riddled with fruits?' Isn't that a bit much?"

"Sure it's an exaggeration, but even making an issue of one case of homosexuality could be awful. Think of it – homosexuals are depraved, disloyal, child molesters, security risks, and every other bad thing – and now they even commit murder! And please don't talk to me about stereotyping!"

"OK, I get your point. You're talking worst case, and I'm thinking it won't come to that. But regardless, what do you suggest we do? Stu Loeffler didn't have any brilliant suggestions, and neither do I."

Charlie looked at him. "We're trained to be prudent, cover our asses, take only calculated risks," he began. "But, if you're willing to risk everything on one throw of the dice, I have an idea."

Ade paused only a little. "I'm listening," he said.

"Do you know Fred Chaney in 'H,' Congressional Relations? I talked to him the other day, hoping he'd be able to offer some insights on Manning and Jurgens."

"Did he?" Ade asked, impatient.

"Two years ago he was in the political section in Korea when Manning came as the head of a big CODEL." 'Codel' was bureaucratese for congressional delegation.

"Fred was the control officer for the CODEL, which meant that he had to solve all the problems and keep everyone happy. But he also was included in all the after hours stuff. As you know, those occasions that oil the wheels of policy and commerce and create the right mood for making deals.

"Manning's not your standard junketeer. He and Jurgens were demanding, and liked to order the Ambassador and his staff around, but they worked hard and were serious. They understood the tripwire security situation in Korea, and supported our military and economic assistance program. But Manning was also pushing the Koreans hard on the textile issue, and I think his hosts decided to take out a little insurance.

"If you're a high-ranking visitor to one of those ceremonial countries, they know how to treat you right. The Defense Minister threw a dinner for Manning in a private dining room at an exclusive club in Seoul. Jurgens wasn't feeling well and didn't go. The food and booze were great, and the hostesses were beautiful. It wasn't long before they had Manning feeling as though he was the wittiest, smartest, and sexiest man they'd ever met. He's no fool, and has no reputation as a womanizer, but someone was always filling his glass and making an amusing toast, and putting her arm around him, and he was having fun. Fred thought it was time to get him out of there, because the booze was starting to get to him. But the women had him up and learning folk dances, and he wasn't about to leave. At one point he slipped away. Fred thought he'd just gone to the bathroom, but when he didn't come back for about an hour he started to worry. The Defense Minister said with a smile, "I think he's just enjoying himself."

"Well, he surely was because when he finally reappeared he looked very sheepish. He also walked unsteadily and was slurring his words."

"So they trapped him?" Ade asked.

"For sure. They'd probably taken pictures, bugged the room, everything. Anyway, Manning was taking no chances. The next day he cut short his schedule and took the next flight back to Washington. You know, he's always preaching morality and family values, and I think he was genuinely ashamed by his moment of weakness. Fred says he's never returned to Korea, despite continuing invitations. They'd put the welcome mat out for him again."

"That's interesting, Charlie, but what good does it do us?"

"It's going to require some boldness with Jurgens to carry it off."

"That's what I was afraid you were going to say. Charlie, that's blackmail! We can't do that, even in Washington. For one thing, Hastings would have my ass. He's convinced that if you suck up to them you'll get what you want."

"If this works, Hastings'll never find out, and we'll stop this move before it ever gets started. You and I are nothing to Manning, but like any politician he's ferocious about protecting his image. Just tell Jurgens quietly that there're some people who know what happened in Seoul two years ago and wouldn't mind sharing that information with some of Manning's enemies."

"What about you? You've got even more to lose than I do. Think of how far you've come. Of course you're an exemplary fellow, but you're also valuable to the Department as a symbol and they'll protect you. You're foolish to risk it."

Charlie smiled. "Ade, I don't have the exalted opinion of human nature that you do. The Department won't go out on a limb for either of us. No, if I'm going down, I'll go down swinging. Maybe I should go to the Hill with you."

Ade found Charlie's plan repugnant, but also strangely exhilarating. "No, Charlie, thanks for the offer but it's better tactically if I go alone. I know you're willing to go with me. Trust me. I'm going to do it."

CHAPTER FORTY-EIGHT

Walter Jurgens eyed Ade suspiciously as he beckoned to a straightback wooden chair beside his cluttered desk, all pretense of civility dispelled.

Ade said, "We appreciate your restraint on the Moscow leak."

"When Senator Manning gives his word, you don't need a written contract," Jurgens replied. "But we can't just forget this episode, and how you all handled it. What came out at the trial is ugly. It's disgusting. Clearly, Kohler and Ellerbee were having an affair. You were the main guy who hired them, and no one down there seems to give a shit that guys like that were on your rolls for years. God knows what else they did! How'd they get through your screening, assuming you have any? Why weren't they found out long ago?"

Ade started to respond, but Jurgens cut him off. "Just so you understand, Nadherny, we won't tolerate queers in our embassies, living high overseas off the taxpayers. Heads will roll. Nothing personal, but one of them will be yours. The Senator's going to hold hearings. Catch our press conference tomorrow." He got up to go, looking so self-righteous that Ade wanted to punch him.

Ade said, "Before you go ahead, there're a couple of things you should know. I didn't come up here to plead with you. No one really knows what happened in the vault, and despite what the autopsy showed I'm still not convinced they were in the middle of some lovers' tryst. So if you want to go after me, go ahead, but my conscience is clear."

Jurgens was sneering, like a man who knew he held the winning hand against a transparent bluff. "Your conscience isn't the issue. What the country'll want to know is why the State Department is full of perverts and no one ever does anything about it. There's something rotten with you boys down there."

"Would you still say that if I told you that George Ellerbee was a CIA agent under deep cover, that the Agency regarded him as a valuable asset – and totally straight, by the way? And not only was he not involved in the Moscow leaks, he uncovered the evidence that led eventually to the person who was really behind the leaks."

Jurgens's arrogant sneer disappeared and his jaw dropped open.

"How the hell do you know? We have good information."

Ade showed him Stu's document and briefed him on the details. Jurgens' adams apple was bobbing up and down while he read through it quickly. He was doing some heavy swallowing.

After a pause, he said, "OK, so he worked for the CIA. That doesn't let you off the hook. Y'all couldn't even spot a depraved guy like Kohler. He must've been doing that stuff for years. And the pictures! I'll bet you're going to tell me that someone planted them in his suitcase! What do you people do in that building besides cover each other's asses?

I think we'll have to take the doors off the toilet stalls down there."

Ade knew his face was reddening but all he said was, "I hope you'll persuade the Senator to drop the whole thing."

"The hell we will. You're just afraid your ass'll be in a sling. Don't worry, this issue is a lot bigger than you. You're going to have some good company."

Ade struggled to stay calm. "Some people in this town remember vividly what happened in Seoul on your visit there two years ago."

"What're you talking about?"

"Why did the Senator leave so suddenly, before the rest of the CODEL? Why haven't you been back to Korea? They'd welcome you just like last time."

"There's nothing that happened that would do you any good."

It was time to roll the dice. "OK Walter, you leave me no choice. What paper do you want it in?"

CHAPTER FORTY-NINE

It was painful, but Ade came away feeling pleased with himself. Jurgens made no promises, but Ade was pretty sure that he'd scored and this might be the last of it. As he walked back to his newly-rented apartment, he felt that he'd done what he could, and was willing to live by the results.

There was a note in his mailbox from Maria Ellerbee asking him to call her at a number in the Department. He did, and she came on the line. "Thank you for calling back," she said softly. "I didn't think you would."

"Of course I'd call you, Maria. Anytime."

"Could I talk with you for a few minutes? The State cafeteria in an hour?"

"I'll be there. The area nearest the D Street entrance."

Ade made it to the large cafeteria first, just in time to see Maria entering the wide central corridor. She'd had her hair cut short, and it made her look younger. She was still drawn, and all the feistiness had long gone out of her. He could no longer picture her dancing the merengue and tossing her head. They chose a small table well away from the aisle. She said, "Ade, we don't know each other very well, but I always considered you a sympathetic person."

"Thank you, Maria," he said, wondering what was coming.

"I want to ask you, what's a person in my position supposed to do next?"

"Well, I'm not sure what you mean," he answered hesitantly. "Certainly you're not talking about your husband's pension. There should be no problem with that. I understand that it's quite generous, and of course, you'll receive it for life. If you want to stay in Washington, I'm sure the Department will find a good job for you right here."

"That's not what I'm talking about. Yes, the pension gives me a decent income, and everyone has been very helpful. But I can't stay here, not after what happened. I'm going back to Ecuador, to my family. I can also live much cheaper there.

"What I'm talking about is, what am I supposed to do with the rest of my life? My husband, who was a good and faithful man, has been murdered even though he never did anything wrong. He was everything to me. The man who did it, who killed an innocent man in cold blood, gets ten years. You call that punishment? He'll be free in a few years, to do what he wants. He has his wife, his son, he can get a job somewhere.

"But for me, every time anyone thinks of this case, they'll think I was married to a *maricon*, a fruit. That's what the jury believed. That's what the prosecutor believed. He even called it a 'homosexual lovers' quarrel.' *Ay*! I can't live with that! And even worse, my husband is in his grave and everyone who knows him now thinks he got himself into some sex quarrel and got himself murdered. Ade, I *know* that's not what happened."

"I know it's tough, Maria," he said, putting his hand on her arm. "But you can't undo that. There was strong evidence from the autopsy. No one even tried to challenge it."

"Ech, my husband would *never* do something like that. He was forced, by that animal. And then he was murdered. Believe me, I know my husband very, very well. He wasn't perfect, but he was a man, and I know what he would do and what he wouldn't do." She looked straight at Ade, her black eyes strong and unblinking. She was pretty convincing, despite the evidence at the trial.

"Maria, we can't say what happened in the vault. All I can tell you is how it looked to the jury, after considering all the evidence."

"I know that, Ade. Of course I know that." Maria was impatient, and Ade couldn't blame her. But he couldn't give her the assurances that she so desperately wanted.

She tried again. "But is it fair for a good man to lose his life like that? Knifed to death, and thrown into a corner like a piece of road kill?" He started to respond, but she cut him off. "And then, when he's cut to pieces and he can't speak for himself – to lose his reputation and his good name? Ade, not only was George's life taken from him, but his soul as well."

He felt so sorry for her, and started to ask if she knew who George really worked for, even if it would open up a fresh brew of trouble. But she beat him to it. "Ade, I'm going to tell you a secret. Very few people know this. George worked for the CIA. Not all the time, and he rarely talked about it. But he trusted me with *everything*. That's how I know that he and Jack were not lovers."

So Maria knew all the time! Everyone always underestimated her. The irony of it was that Jack always worried about his importance and George not at all, but he was the key guy in that assignment. His seeming lack of importance made him more effective. And Maria knew about it and went along perfectly. No wonder she was bitter. Tears of rage and frustration welled to her eyes, but her voice remained calm. "Ade, is that right? Is that how justice is done in this country? You let a man who has served you well be killed, and then you stand by and let him be smeared? And say nothing to his wife except 'you were married to a *maricon*?' So that his life stood for nothing, and everyone who ever loved him will feel ashamed and humiliated? Is that how things are done here? Ade, that's why I can't stay. That's why I'm going home."

Ade was moved by both her passion and loyalty to George. "Maria, you must keep this to yourself for now, but a couple of us are trying to stop the nasty talk about what happened in the vault that's coming from a certain Senator's office. It's not everything you want, but maybe it will help. All I can do is promise to keep looking for something that'll help us to understand. That's not much, because the case is officially closed. The State Department doesn't want me to have anything more to do with it, and the Senator I mentioned is trying to have me fired. I'm not in a great position to help."

"I have no one else to turn to."

"And don't forget, all of the evidence we're likely to get is already in. There's nothing more to be found in Tanako. None of the witnesses who didn't testify will ever say anything. And Maria, don't forget the evidence. Whatever the circumstances, that's what people are going to remember. But I respect you for wanting to clear George's good name, and removing this stigma from your happy marriage with him. So I'll try, but please, please don't hold me to anything, because I don't think there's much that I or anybody else can do."

Maria took that in without flinching. "I understand that. Listen, I know that all of you think I'm foolish to believe that there was some kind of plot against my husband. But I can only think that he discovered something against Jack so bad that Jack had to kill him. And maybe the State Department is involved, or else why would they ignore that possibility?" Maria was pleading for some encouragement. As for Ade, he'd had enough of plots.

"Maria, we're not going to get far with that. There's just no evidence."

"That doesn't mean it's wrong. What about a cover up?"

Ade could see that she earnestly believed her husband had something on Jack, and that had led to his death. She clung to that shred with all her will.

As they got up, he said, "Maria, if George is looking down at us now, I think he's very proud of you for standing by him and honoring his memory."

"Thank you. I appreciate that. I want to believe there's at least someone who thinks my husband was not what they said. Are you that person, Ade?"

"I've come to believe it, and others too, but there's nothing we can do for now." This wasn't much, but it was a little. Maria rose to leave. He was getting up too when she paused and put her hand on his shoulder.

"I'm going to tell you something else, Ade." She sat down again. "No one else in the whole world knows this. It'll explain why I feel so sure about George.

"When we were in Moscow, he worked for a long time on a huge visa fraud ring operating right out of the embassy." So Maria knew about that too! "The ringleader, a Russian, got drunk one night and made a pass at George. George was humoring him, and he started boasting about all the influence and money he had. He worked full time in the consular section and didn't come from a wealthy family, and his showy life style had already attracted suspicions.

"When they finally confronted him with the evidence, he accused George of trying to entrap him into a homosexual encounter. Because the man was a senior consular employee, they did a quiet investigation. Of course, there was nothing to the charge, and George was totally cleared. The man was fired."

This tracked with what Stu Loeffler had told Ade, but Maria knew more than anyone else. There'd been a Russian involved as well as the American marine guard.

"So that's how you know who George really worked for," I said.

"I already knew. I told you that George told me everything. Anyway, the Russian blabbed his lies around the Embassy to stir up trouble, and it was embarrassing for George for a while. There were lots of rumors and wild stories, but no one really knew the whole story except the Ambassador. So, many people ended up hearing about the incident, but didn't know the facts."

"So in the end, it worked out OK," Ade said.

"But it didn't end. There was more to it. In Moscow, George had to deal with some slimy characters, drinking, hanging out with women, playing his role. Like a lot of mild-mannered people, he had his wild side too. One night he got drunk and ended up in a strange bed, with a man. He was filled with remorse, and begged forgiveness. Of course, I was upset, but I loved him and respected his honesty. After that, he showed me in lots of ways that he was all man."

Maria had a faraway look, and a gentle smile on her face. "He was a man all right," she said, "not the little clerk *sin cajones* that people are making him out to be now. Anyway, with all this, we really weren't surprised when someone wrote Jack in Tanako that George had been involved with homosexuals in Moscow. Jack even showed George the letter. It said, 'Ask your little colleague about the visa scam in Moscow, and the charge that he snared the ringleader in a homosexual act.' George trusted Jack so he explained what happened, including his work for the CIA."

So Jack found out before the murder just who Ellerbee worked for! Ade had the minor satisfaction of thinking that even Harlan Hastings didn't know everything. In Washington, wars are fought with information, not guns. The guy who has the best information and knows when to use it and whom to withhold it from always wins.

He looked closely at Maria. "How did Jack react when George told him?"

"Here's where George was naive. He wasn't defensive at all. He expected Jack to show some kind of approval, or respect, or something. Instead, he just frowned and changed the subject. As though he was jealous."

The revelation was instant. "Maria, of course he was! It helps to explain Jack's savagery in the vault. We know he looked down on George. He suddenly realized that the man he regarded as a little clerk was more important than he was. It must've triggered his final blow-up! He must've been in a frenzy in the vault, and forced himself on poor George with overwhelming savagery For him, it was the ultimate humiliation. I swore I'd stay away from the psychological stuff, but that's got to be one of the keys!"

Maria looked relieved that Ade seemed to be accepting her explanation that Jack and George were not lovers. "Nothing can bring George back, but if you believe the truth maybe others will too," she said.

Maria got up and he watched her walk away, feeling guilty that he couldn't offer the public absolution for George that she was seeking so poignantly.

The next day, Charlie called Ade at Georgetown and told him that Kohler would be in Cynthia's custody while his appeal went forward, and had permission to look for a job. At least for the Kohlers life had the appearance of normalcy, while for Maria everything normal from her previous life had been destroyed. Charlie said it would take six months to decide the appeal. Meanwhile, Kohler was a free man.

"Amazing. He commits a sordid murder and remains free while his lawyer appeals his conviction," Ade said.

"Come on," said Charlie. "It's not that easy. Kohler will have a mark on him for the rest of his life. And consider the effect on Cynthia and the kid. It won't be a picnic for any of them."

"He still has to feel lucky. No one believed him but he got a light sentence. But Maria, whose only crime was loving her husband, ends up worse than the Kohlers."

Charlie said, "I said from the first that he was crazy and that no jury would convict him. But now I think they got it about right. The only puzzle was what caused Jack to blow up in the vault. I still think that he killed George to keep their relationship from being found out. It had to be ongo-ing. Something like that just doesn't happen suddenly in an embassy vault. So malice was clearly involved, but there was no evidence. The sperm in George's throat was taken as evidence of a lover's quarrel, not of any real malice between them. He paused, and added, "But I agree that he came out pretty well, considering what he did. He lost his job, but he's got his money and he'll be a free man in three years. We'll probably see him again."

"I wonder," Ade said. "No one springs back from some-thing like that."

CHAPTER FIFTY

Even with the trial over, Ade still had no sense of finality. He wondered if the outcome would impel the Department's gumshoes to root out anyone remotely suspected of homosexual "tendencies." The McCarthy-era Executive Order was still in force, denying employment to homosexuals. There were ideologues and one-agenda fanatics in any administration, and they could cause immense damage. Ade had no doubt that there were still people around who took it as their solemn duty to rid the government of homosexuals, and had allies in the Congress and media all too ready to help them. They'd be only too happy to snarl the Department in witch hunts and reprisals for years. There was also Ade's promise to Maria, still an unmet challenge.

But he was unsure of his next step, and so plunged into his academic year. He and Ginger talked dutifully three or four nights a week, and he usually made it to Lexington two weekends a month. Ginger was still convinced she'd done the right thing, and Greg's situation gradually improved. Ginger managed two courses per semester in forensic psychology at Boston University, and was progressing rapidly toward her Master's.

In their telephone conversations, Ginger was warm – friendly, rather than loving, full of news and comment, but noncommittal about their future. They had no trouble finding physical pleasure in each other during their conjugal visits, but the spark of emotional affinity was seldom struck. Ade wondered if Ginger was having an affair, but didn't raise the subject because he wasn't ready to deal with the possibility.

Ade was promoted for his work in Cameroon, as was Ron Zimmerman. When he called Ginger to tell her, all she said was "I'm very happy for you, Ade." Meanwhile, Transcon was doing well in Tanako without Ade's help, securing the drilling rights to several choice blocks, including the largest one, a deepwater field with the code name of Palmiro. Mobil, Royal Dutch, Elf, and Chevron also began drilling, and the scramble to exploit the Gulf was on.

Sudopo gave an interview to an American reporter in which he promised that Tanako wouldn't be like Nigeria, Gabon, and other African countries where power-crazed rulers had squandered their countries' resources on luxuries for themselves. Ade ached to know whether he'd really made any changes other than pocketing oil profits, and if Sudopo was really harboring terrorists.

His only hope for direct information was the Japanese TV producer, Kimura. He spent a fruitless morning trying to reach him through the NHK office in Tokyo, finally locating an English-speaking editor who told him that he was heading back to Washington and would arrive in a few days. The month before, he said, Kimura had stopped in several countries in Africa, but he couldn't recall which ones.

Feeling a rush of adrenalin, Ade called NHK's Washington bureau and left an urgent message for Kimura-san to call him as soon as he arrived.

Tuesday of the following week Kimura called. "I'm back. That was a good tip you gave me about Tanako." Ade's heart jumped.

"So you went!"

"Yes, and I was able to find that road into the bush you told me about."

"Anything else?"

"They're gone. The camp is empty, but I found empty cans of Japanese food, and wooden Japanese chopsticks. You were right about that."

"What about the people? Who were they?"

"Of course no one in Tanako would tell me. I interviewed the Minister of Petroleum in his new house. The oil money's starting to flow in. But at least the government's not so hostile to journalists now. I asked about the camp, and he told me that Japanese mining engineers had visited Tanako to do a mineral survey, had stayed in the bush, and their work was done."

"Do you believe that?"

"Of course it's a kind of nonsense."

"Sure, but where does that leave us?"

"I found out in Tokyo from an intelligence contact that the Japanese government suspected for some time there were Red Army people on Tanako. Barreras was hiding them. A senior official confirmed it. Keiko Matsumora was one of them."

"Whew. Kimura-san, you've been busy."

"When Sudopo overthrew Barreras, the Japanese government pressured him to expel the Red Army people. There's no extradition treaty and Japan didn't even have an embassy in Arania, but we dangled the prospect of heavy aid and investment, the establishment of an embassy, and other things that Sudopo wanted. That worked, and Sudopo put Keiko and her friends on a plane for Jordan, but Jordan wouldn't admit them. By then they were hot potatoes and they were put on a plane for Osaka. Keiko Matsumora and three others were arrested yesterday. It hasn't made the papers here yet. Not many people here remember them. The Japanese government thinks she planned several terrorist acts, although maybe she didn't take a direct part. Your tip was a big help."

Ade could hardly believe it. Was this just a stupendous piece of luck, stumbling on a terrorist camp in the jungle? *"Never overlook chance and the interconnectivity of things,"* someone once told him. Who the hell was that? Whoever it was, he was exceedingly wise. Suddenly he remembered who: Harlan Hastings.

CHAPTER FIFTY-ONE

It was September before the Court of Appeals rejected Kohler's appeal on all counts, including the issue on the blood-smeared cable in the vault, which Tiernan had refused to admit into evidence. The Appeals Court said that because it wasn't signed, and hadn't been prepared by Kohler himself, its authenticity couldn't be established. Its existence raised the possibility of "deliberately manufactured self-serving hearsay," and Tiernan's ruling to exclude it was therefore correct. So, Ade thought, Kohler's cable never had a chance with Tiernan and the Appeals Court, despite its crucial importance to the defense. Dilbaugh gamely pushed on to the Supreme Court.

By this time, Dilbaugh's legal fees must have cost Jack a bundle, and Ade had to assume that Cynthia's family, well off but not wealthy, was kicking in with big bucks – maybe part of the *noblesse oblige* of an old southern family. Whatever people thought about Cynthia's aloofness, Ade never heard anyone disparage her, and he admired her for standing by Jack all this time. For now, Jack had found a job in the local public library, and Cynthia had gone back to being a legal secretary.

As soon as the spring semester was over, Ginger and Greg came to Washington, true to Ginger's promise. At first,

Ade felt that their awkward separation hadn't changed much, except that now he'd be less likely to take his exceptional wife for granted. But it gradually began to dawn on him that Ginger's flight from Cameroon was not a selfish cop-out, but a response to growing concerns that life could be passing her by. He realized that in Cameroon she felt powerless to help Greg cope with his floundering, but grasped onto the hope that maybe the dynamism of everyday life in America, even with all its problems and risks, would revitalize them both.

Whether that is what happened was still in question, Ade thought, but Ginger was feeling transformed. With her freshly-minted Master's in hand, she won a part-time internship to the FBI's Behavioral Science Unit at Quantico, Virginia. She was able to reconnect with her former work of counseling battered spouses, so she now had the focus she missed as a Foreign Service wife.

For having served a year in comfortable exile without causing any new problems, Ade was rewarded by becoming deputy assistant secretary to Harlan Hastings. But the Kohler case and Tanako still picked away at him because of his unkept promise to Maria and his nagging doubt about the trial verdict. His brief encounter with Transcon also convinced him that little Tanako would prove again that big problems often start in small places. So his personal Tanako file remained open, beckoning but unattended to, like the "must read" books on his bedside table that he never managed to finish.

Ginger's internship drew her to criminal profiling, just starting to blossom as a tool for crime solvers. Minute examinations of crime scenes and how perpetrators dealt with their victims could lead to important personality clues, since many people leave tell-tale psychological footprints as they might leave a bootprint in the mud.

Ginger learned how to develop a profile of a rapist or child abuser from studying a crime scene. Often these proved uncannily accurate. The same methodology was used by the FBI to track down serial killers, and by the CIA to pursue terrorists.

Maybe because they were getting along better, Ade had almost forgotten his doubts about Ginger's faithfulness, but one evening in a light moment he asked her.

"Ade, that's a question you never want to ask." His heart sank. "There's no answer, true or false, that would satisfy you," she said. "But just this once, I'll tell you anyway, if you promise never to bring it up again."

"Isn't it my business if you sleep with someone?" he asked.

"In theory, maybe. In practice, not if it doesn't help anything."

"OK, so what's the answer?"

"I never had an affair, but I came close."

"What held you back?" he asked, feeling a sharp needle-thrust of jealousy.

"The guy was charming but even more self-centered than you. I discovered I didn't need it and didn't even want it, although it was an exciting idea. And I still loved you, for some strange reason. And that's all I'll ever tell."

It wasn't the answer Ade was looking for, but it was better than he expected, and as a practical matter he could live with it. They'd both had opportunities and temptations, and had pulled back from the brink. Maybe being a diplomat had taught him about the need to compromise, and the emptiness of instant gratification.

"After what we've been through, what does love mean?" he asked.

"Oh Ade, why do you have to define everything? It's like the old saying, 'If you have to ask, you just don't get it.'"

In October, the Supreme Court rejected Jack's appeal and he began serving his sentence at a prison farm in Texas. The Department offered Cynthia a good admin job and she accepted, using her maiden name. She moved to Fairfax, Virginia, which had good schools and no one knew her. Her Foreign Service friends heard from her less and less.

Several months later, she filed for divorce. Her former friends realized the murder and trial had destroyed their marriage and Cynthia was trying to wipe out her past and build a new life for herself and Robin. She didn't want him to have the stigma of a father everyone thought was a psychopathic murderer. When they heard all this, Ade and Ginger understood how Cynthia might feel the need to leave the past behind, but they also wondered if she'd ever really believed Jack's story, or just gone along out of loyalty.

CHAPTER FIFTY-TWO

Ade's new job gave him a large chunk of Africa to look after, so he didn't have time to ferret out the meager bits of information on Tanako that might be coming into the African Bureau. He asked Sally Rogers to flag anything interesting for him, especially regarding oil exploration and revenues. With the Embassy in Arania still closed, all they received regularly was a new government weekly whose sole purpose seemed to be to carry flackery about Sudopo and Tanako's growing importance as an oil supplier.

Leafing quickly through one, Ade noticed this item, in Spanish:

"Major American Bank Seeks Tanako Accounts With Tanako's emergence as a major source of oil, many countries are flocking to Arania to seek expanded drilling rights and to finance economic development schemes. This week, Carl Haberman of the American National Bank visited Arania to meet with President Sudopo and other government officials." There was a picture of Haberman shaking hands with Sudopo, and the article quoted him saying that Tanako should increase its accounts with ANB, since it was the largest bank in the world in deposits from oil revenues.

As it turned out, Haberman was the head of ANB's Washington office, and a week later Ade called him for lunch. Haberman was interested in Ade's account of how Sudopo came to power, and Ade probed Haberman gently for insight on ANB's business interests in Tanako.

"Very quickly, Tanako will move from a dirt-poor barter economy to the world's middle class, in per capita terms. All because of oil revenues. They'll have to invest that money somewhere, and we're going after it aggressively."

"How can you beat out the French? They practically own parts of Africa, especially countries like Gabon."

"The pot's plenty big enough for more than one player. We already have some Gabon accounts, although they're small, from individuals."

"No doubt from the savings-conscious people of Gabon," said Ade.

"If government officials put their money with ANB, that's fine with us."

"Last I heard about Tanako, there was lots of new construction, but it was all in private homes. Big, luxurious ones, belonging to government officials."

"And?"

"The point is that officials who are supposed to be on salaries are siphoning off all the oil revenue for themselves. And then they're putting it in foreign banks like yours. The people stay poor. Doesn't that concern you?"

"Should it? That would seem to be up to the government there."

"But it's the government that's taking the money."

Haberman looked pained, as though this was hugely irrelevant. "We're not a dirty bank, and I'm not sure I welcome your insinuations. Anyway, it's not illegal to accept deposits from leaders of foreign governments."

"Even if it's money laundering, and the amount is hundreds of millions of dollars more than anything they could possibly have made legally? That's what happened in Gabon, and it looks like the pattern is being repeated in Tanako."

"That's just supposition. Where's your proof? Anyway, some president somewhere depositing money from whatever source in an American bank doesn't constitute a crime here. It's out of America's jurisdiction."

"So you have nothing to do with monitoring these huge deposits."

"We're bankers and investors. We create wealth and help people protect it. We make economies grow. This is what the real world is about. You government folks are worried about rules, and making everyone live by your idea of right and wrong. That doesn't put food on the table. That doesn't bring prosperity. Some day you rule-makers will kill the golden goose."

"Without rules, the golden goose will feed only the rich."

"If they bank with us, I wouldn't worry about the rest."

Ade was sufficiently steamed after this conversation to take his worries to Harlan Hastings. "I see you've donned your white cloak and loosed your terrible swift sword again," he said with a smile.

"Harlan, don't we have an interest in breaking up the old pattern where in country after country corrupt rulers steal money that could go to development, kids, and schools, and instead send it overseas to foreign banks? Who benefits? And who pays when the country becomes a basket case and we have to go to the rescue? This isn't crusading, it's self-interest."

"Leave it, Ade. Those things are very, very complicated. It's not our business, and it's not illegal. U. S. law bans money earned from things like drug trafficking, but not corruption. Abnormally large deposits have to be reported to the regulators, and they do get audited. You'd be tangling with the ANB. They have a lot more friends in Washington than you do, and you wouldn't get to first base."

"But it's our taxpayers who pay for aid over the table to help developing countries, and our banks who take it back under the table," Ade said.

Hastings looked pained. "You have a genius for finding powerful people to pick fights with. First it's the President of Tanako. Then the Chairman of the Senate Foreign Relations Committee. Now you want to take on America's largest commercial bank. Nothing small-minded about you, Ade. But you have a job to do, right in this office. It doesn't include reforming the world."

Ade knew when to stop tilting. But he quietly took his case to the senior staff member of the Senate Permanent Committee on Investigations. The staff chief was skeptical, but finally admitted that there was little being done to check illegal sources of huge foreign deposits. "In effect, the regulators accept the banks' assurances that transactions with foreign depositors are just fine," he said.

He agreed to look into the problem further, and in ensuing months Ade fed him anything he could find on Arania's fast-growing oil industry, including classified reports that he sanitized himself before sending. Sudopo's flacks, in portraying their leader's lavish life style as evidence of their country's new importance, were unwittingly establishing that he was amassing personal wealth at a rate that couldn't possibly be legal.

Eventually, the Committee held hearings on money laundering worldwide and the chairman of ANB was called to testify. Regarding charges that Sudopo had accepted bribes from foreign oil companies and had deposited implausibly large amounts in his ANB accounts, the chairman said, "Neither President Sudopo nor ANB have been accused of any wrongdoing. At the bank we've always believed that he is a respected head of government, accepted and supported by the international community."

It took a while, but ANB eventually had to agree to closer screening of large deposits from foreign leaders and their families, and closed out Sudopo's accounts. Congress passed a law making it illegal to launder money in the United States with the proceeds of corruption in foreign countries. And the ANB chairman, looking contrite, said in a TV interview, "Times have changed. Banks now have to worry about how their large depositors might have made their money. Up to now that was never necessary."

One day, Ade asked Hastings if he'd been following the Senate hearings, the new legislation, and the information about Sudopo that came out.

"Sure," he answered. "I was hoping that somehow he'd turn out to be different from the others. But in the end, it was all for the best. The Committee did a fine job, gathering all that information from all over the world. They even managed to get a lot about Tanako. I wonder where it came from."

"Me too," said Ade.

CHAPTER FIFTY-THREE

Jack was released in early 1977, with time off for good behavior. He'd served slightly more than three years, just as Ron Zimmerman had predicted. Ade marveled at the connectivity of life's events as he thought back on how Jack's solitary crime had changed his life. For starters, it had brought him into the world of human rights activism, where he'd made a small contribution. With Charlie's help he'd managed to outmaneuver a powerful Senator who wanted to ruin him and damage the Foreign Service. He'd helped to trigger greater scrutiny of bribery and money laundering by American corporations. His tip accelerated the investigation that resulted in bringing Keiko Matsumore into custody. Finally, his absorption with the Kohler case had almost cost him his marriage, but now provided a vehicle for Ginger's re-involvement with him and the revival of what had seemed lost.

It was an overcast day in February, and Ade was heading for lunch at Jacqueline's, an affordable French restaurant on Pennsylvania Avenue. As he looked up, he saw Jack Kohler walking towards him. He stared, wondering if he was mistaken. But it was Jack, wearing a dark gray overcoat. He'd become jowly and white-haired, and had put on at least twenty pounds. Their eyes met briefly and Ade looked for a sign of recognition, but Kohler's opaque gaze didn't flinch. He looked straight ahead, and passed by without even a nod.

Ade walked on a few steps, thinking if that's what he wanted he should let it be, and then turned back, on impulse. "Jack," he called. "It's Ade Nadherny."

Kohler turned around, unsmiling. "Hello, Ade," he said. He didn't apologize for pretending not to recognize him. They shook hands.

"I'm surprised to see you," Ade said. "I'd heard you were in California."

"Yes, I'm just here for a few days visiting my son. You remember Robin?" His face brightened for a moment. "He's eight years old now. He's a fine boy."

"I'm glad to hear that," Ade said. Their conversation was awkward and perfunctory. "He certainly was cute as a baby."

Jack frowned slightly. "You may've heard that Cynthia and I are divorced, and she's working at the Department. She has custody, so I see Robin once a year here, and once a year he comes to California when school is out."

"I'm sorry to hear about you and Cynthia," Ade said.

"She stayed with me through the long appeals process, but she had to think about what was best for Robin, and for herself." He looked displeased, as though he understood why she split, but disapproved of her doing it.

"And is she well?" Ade still couldn't get away from the stilted response.

"She's OK. Life goes on, doesn't it?" he answered dully.

Ade couldn't help thinking, it does for everyone but George Ellerbee. But now that he'd started the conversation, he had to finish it gracefully.

"And how are things with you?" he asked. "What're you doing?"

"I work in a library in a suburb of San Diego. It's a job. San Diego's pleasant. I sometimes go to a concert or the theatre. That's about it."

"It sounds not too bad, Jack."

"Compared to what we had..." His voice trailed off, and he looked profoundly sad, recalling something precious, now lost forever.

"I can only wish you good luck in the future," Ade said.

Jack looked him straight in the eye, and said matter-of-factly, without a trace of self-pity, "Except for Robin, my life is over."

He looked past Ade's shoulder, a sign that he wanted to end the conversation. Indeed, there was nothing more to say. "Good-bye, Jack," Ade said. Kohler nodded, tightened his lips, and moved on. They didn't shake hands.

CHAPTER FIFTY-FOUR

That evening, Charlie Stubblefield was coming by for a quick-fix supper at the Nadhernys: pasta and a salad, a bottle of chardonnay. Ade got home first, and spent some time bantering with Greg before he settled into a quick stint of homework before dinner. When Ginger came in the door, he put his arms on her shoulders and kissed her, and as she was taking off her coat, he said, "Guess who I ran into today?"

There were so many possibilities in a city like Washington that for once Ginger was stumped. "I haven't a clue," she said.

"Jack Kohler."

Ginger's eyebrows shot up in surprise. "Jack Kohler?" she said. "I thought he was in California."

"He is, but he comes back to visit his son."

A few minutes later, Charlie walked in. Ade poured him a drink.

When Ade told Charlie about running into Jack, his reaction was different from Ginger's. "I knew he'd turn up sooner or later," he said.

"He didn't exactly turn up, Charlie. I ran into him totally by chance on H Street. He wasn't heading for the Department."

"You know what I mean, Ade. This case will always turn up, in one form or another."

"Maybe, but life goes on. A lot of time has passed. Let's see, it'll be six years this summer. Most people have forgotten about it."

But not everyone, as Ade was soon to learn.

"Almost everybody seems satisfied with the trial," said Ginger, "but some, like Ron Zimmerman, still think that Jack got off far too easily. In their view, the system failed, and justice wasn't done."

"We can argue that forever," Ade said. "But if it's any comfort to Ron, Jack was pretty glum. He was never one of life's sunnier creatures anyway. What he said was that his life was as good as finished. Cynthia's divorced him, he sees Robin only twice a year, and he's probably lucky to have a low-level job in the library. He doesn't see much ahead for himself."

"Do you think he'd commit suicide?" Charlie asked.

"I doubt it," said Ginger. "He may be feeling sorry for himself, but it doesn't sound like depression to me. As long as he can blame outside forces or life's unfairness for his troubles, he's not likely to become suicidal."

The evening passed all too quickly. Washington is an early-rising and work-obsessed town, so the guests are usually out the door by eleven. Charlie said good-night at ten forty-five, after setting a time for tennis later in the week.

Ginger and Ade were in bed by eleven, with Ade hoping to read a few pages of V. S. Naipaul's novel about the Congo, "A Bend in the River," which he'd just started. But he could only manage a few pages before starting to nod off. He was straining to keep his eyes open when Ginger said, "You know, the scandal about homosexuality that came out at the trial was never put to rest. Those guys weren't homosexuals at all."

"Huh?" Ade said.

"The murder, Ade – Kohler and Ellerbee," Ginger prodded. "The prosecution and the jury got it wrong. I'm sure of it."

"Umm, I was almost asleep." But he was rapidly returning to full wakefulness. "You really think so? If you're right, wouldn't that be something! I've always wondered what Tony Fonseca really thought about what happened. I'll call him tomorrow."

"I wonder if he's changed his mind after all this time," said Ginger.

CHAPTER FIFTY-FIVE

The next morning, Ade was just about to call Tony Fonseca when Harlan Hastings came into his office and closed the door. This rarely happened, so Ade wondered what was up. Harlan never hesitated to get to the point. "Ade, I've got some unfortunate news. We were planning to nominate you for Kenya, and we had all the clearances within the building. But when we took soundings on the Hill, Jurgens told us Manning would never let you get confirmed. So it's dead. I'm sorry, Ade. You'd have been a good one."

Ade looked dumbstruck. Of course what they say about Washington is true. No issue ever dies, no grievance forgotten. Manning and Jurgens finally had their revenge. Ade couldn't tell Hastings about his Korea end-run, but Harlan surely realized that he'd stirred them up enough about Kohler and Ellerbee so they'd want to checkmate his career.

When Ade didn't answer, Hastings, not the most compassionate of men, tried to console him. "It's not the end of the world, Ade. You know everything's always in motion in this town. You're dogmeat on the Hill today, but nothing's permanent here. You're not finished yet. In the meanwhile, you can continue to advance, as long as we don't put you into anything that requires Senate confirmation and you keep yourself out of trouble."

So that was it, everything he'd worked for. Kenya would've been a great post. At least now he wouldn't have to worry about the family splitting up again.

Ade didn't want to dwell on the thousands of unseen perfidies that take place in Washington every day, so he called Tony Fonseca. Thinking he'd be in court or otherwise tied up, Ade felt lucky when Tony picked up after a short wait.

"Ade, how are you?" he said in his friendly, down-to-earth voice.

"I saw Jack Kohler yesterday…"

"Huh – I'd heard he was free, having served all of three years for killing Ellerbee. And that his wife divorced him. Is there more?"

"That's it as far as I know. But I wanted to ask about some of the things that came out at the trial. I hope you can talk about them now."

"Sure. What do you want to know?"

"Well, first, do you still think that Kohler and Ellerbee were homosexual lovers, and that what happened was a lovers' quarrel?"

"I do. We'll never know for sure, but it's the best explanation, and it's where the evidence took us."

"You know, everyone was astonished when that came out at the trial. Afterwards, people came up with things that fit the stereotype – Jack had a late marriage, the ambassador at an earlier post turned out to be gay, he had close friends who'd never married, all kinds of circumstantial stuff. But nothing solid. I think people bought the idea that he was in the closet, but there's still a sense of bafflement about it."

"There shouldn't be," said Tony. "I don't need to tell you that people are very complex. What they show to the outside world is only a part of what they really are. But we know that a homosexual act took place in the vault shortly before Ellerbee was killed. We know that Kohler did it, both the act and the killing. He denied the first, but admitted the second. Ade, when we presented that evidence we had Kohler dead to rights. When he took the stand, it was obvious he was lying. His wife lied too. Thiergard's testimony made it crystal clear, and they had no answer for it. And the pornography pictures were the icing on the cake. In my view, their argument was very weak, but it was the only thing they could think of, under the circumstances."

"So there was no basis at all to his insanity plea?"

"He certainly was mentally disturbed, and I'm sure that something happened in the vault to make him fly into a rage. But that's not insanity. There was no evidence at all that he didn't know right from wrong. He was lucky to get manslaughter two, a crime of passion. It doesn't seem right that he got out after only three years. Tiernan gave him the maximum sentence for the offense."

"Tony, just between us, is it possible that Kohler was telling the truth? That he was so appalled by what he'd done — I'm talking about the fellatio, not the stabbing – that he blotted it out? In your experience, could that happen?"

Tony paused. "Ade, it's possible, considering the huge spectrum of human behavior and motivations. But I don't believe it happened that way."

Tony's view was unequivocal as ever, and there was nothing that he wanted to add to it. Maybe he was right, but something just didn't fit.

That evening, Ade told Greg he was on his own for a few hours and took Ginger to dinner at Nathan's in Georgetown, a popular watering hole on the corner of M and Wisconsin. Nathan's had recently added some sophistication to the menu and put in some booths in the back, where a couple could have a quiet, candlelight dinner away from the shouted conversations and one-upping that dominated the bar.

"OK, Mama Freud," Ade said teasingly "You've come up with some new wrinkles. You say they weren't homosexuals. Stu Loeffler stoutly maintained that George was straight, but no one ever explained the evidence in the vault. How do you deal with that? Let's have it," he said.

Ginger looked him right in the eye. "The explanation has been staring us in the face, but all of us were blinded by prejudice, and revulsion at what happened."

"How come you suddenly think you've solved a mystery that's had us puzzled for years?" he asked.

"We never managed to pick up all the pieces and fit them into the puzzle correctly. That, plus the fact that we now know more about violent crimes and the personality disorders that trigger them than we did before."

"Are you suggesting that Kohler was really insane, or maybe not guilty at all?" he asked, unbelieving.

"Nothing so dramatic," Ginger answered soberly. "But it does show how easily we can draw faulty conclusions from objective facts, like the sperm in Ellerbee's throat."

"I really want to see how you deal with that," he said. "I call."

"OK. We all know that there's a lot more going on inside a person than we have any idea about. Despite what we've learned about human behavior, there'll always be a sense of mystery about the secrets of the human heart. With me so far?" she asked.

"Sure, but if you can't reveal the secrets of the human heart, I'll be unsatisfied."

"Stay with me, and maybe you won't be," she replied. "Ok, let's start with what we know about Jack's personality," she began, putting her hand firmly on his forearm.

"Would you say he was pre-occupied with his own self-importance?

"Well, there were some things: his putdowns of George, his pompous talk, his feeling that he always deserved better than he'd earned. It was like he felt entitled."

"Good," responded Ginger. "So in a sense he had some unreasonable expectations about himself, almost a feeling of grandiosity. Right?"

"To some extent, that's true."

"Sometimes Jack was arrogant and haughty, and showed no understanding for the feelings of others. He was both petty, and a perfectionist. Remember that incredible time at the dinner party when he told George not to take two pieces of meat? He could be demanding and picky, and it sometimes irritated people. After that incident, George wondered what he'd gotten himself in for."

"And little did he know, poor guy," Ade said.

"No one could've known." Ginger replied. "Anyway, we'll get to that soon. Of course, the best example of all was just after the killing, when Jack showed absolutely no remorse at all over what he'd done, but asked repeatedly what would happen to himself. In other words, he thought that he himself deserved special treatment, but had a hard time relating to the feelings of others. Right?"

"Sounds like a lot of guys I know at the State Department."

"Not funny, Ade," said Ginger, giving him a warning look.

He took the hint. "I have to admit, Ginger, that so far this fits. Go on."

"All these characteristics we're talking about point to a narcissistic personality. That's what Jack was."

"Well, OK, but so what? That doesn't take us very far, and it doesn't have much to do with homosexuality, as far as I can see," he said. He was afraid that Ginger was veering into psychobabble.

Ginger was undeterred. "Consider that there's often a connection between narcissistic personalities and paranoid delusions."

"Maybe," Ade replied, intrigued but skeptical. "But as you said, this was only one aspect of Kohler's personality. There were others, including things that people found pretty attractive, even likable. For example, he was reliable and competent. He wasn't a big turn-on sexually, but women liked him and found him good company. He had a sense of humor. He was a good family man. He loved the Foreign Service. And his selfless help to his needy friend, Bob Morse. And so on. Almost like a Boy Scout."

"Good insight. And after the humiliations of his childhood, when he was both abused and humiliated by his father, and made insecure by the hot and cold behavior of his mother, he desperately wanted to be both respected and respectable. And steady as well. So, sure, that was an important part of his personality."

"OK, then what happened in the vault?" Ade asked.

"I'm coming to that. Let's say that, from what we know of Jack's childhood, he was at least sexually ambivalent. This is often the case with a weak or abusive father, and a mother who could be both seductive and distant."

"So you're saying that Jack was confused about his sexual identity."

"Yes. Now let's look at one very telling bit of evidence that didn't come out until we ran into Stu Loeffler at the restaurant."

"You mean the child pornography pictures? How do you explain them?"

"Here's a guy, to the outside world a well-adjusted family man who loves his wife and dotes on his kid, and he turns out to have a thing for young boys. Maybe he's not a true pedophile, but he was certainly attracted, or otherwise he wouldn't have lugged those magazines halfway around the world and risked being discovered. But for a true pedophile, his pictures are his most valued possession – genuine treasures. This wasn't the case with Jack, because he left them behind. There's no way that could have happened out of simple forgetfulness. Leaving them behind was a cry for help."

"I still don't see why he just didn't go to a shrink."

"He was ashamed, but refused to admit that something was wrong."

"That makes sense," Ade admitted. "Another factor, then. His attitude toward Robin, the adorable son. There's no question that he doted on that kid, and still does. You're suggesting that he felt sexually attracted to his own son?"

"I'd bet on it. And the thought horrified and scared him. Here's a guy clinging desperately to a straight world that holds the key to everything he yearns for – status, family, success, all of it – but he's constantly torn by powerful repressed desires, fantasies as well, that propel him in another direction, toward shame and degradation."

"Pretty good, Ginger. But one minute we're talking about homosexuality, and the next about pedophilia. As far as I know there're not the same. Homosexuals aren't necessarily pedophiles, and vice-versa."

"That's right," said Ginger. "But the two became confused at the trial. Ned Dilbaugh let Tony get away with making the connection. I think he dropped the ball on that one."

"So what does that say about Jack Kohler?"

"He wasn't a true pedophile, but had repressed sexual desires for young boys. He had homosexual fantasies, like a lot of people, but there was no evidence that he was a practicing homosexual. But because of what happened in the vault, everyone assumed that he was and condemned him for it. It tells more about us than it does about him."

Ade was getting impatient. "Such a strait-laced guy on the surface. But underneath, a veritable seething cauldron of repellent longings! Come on, Ginger, that's murky old Freudian stuff. It's all discredited now. Chemicals in the brain control us, not some web of repressed desires and fantasies. They already have mood-altering drugs. Soon there'll be a pill for everything and therapies will all be drug-based."

"Maybe a pill can make you feel better, but it can never make you understand," Ginger answered, shooting Ade another cautionary look. "Ade, I think we're very close to knowing what happened between Jack and George and why. Talk about chemicals all you want, but Jack Kohler was a tormented soul who to all outward appearances was a stable and normal guy. What he did can't be explained by writing it off as a chemical imbalance, but his behavior over time just might provide us the answers."

Ade had provoked Ginger to see how deeply she was involved in resolving the puzzle, and now he had his answer: she cared as much as he did. He squeezed her arm and backed up a bit. "OK, I want to hear the rest of your analysis. If you're right, some pretty smug people will be uncomfortable."

"Don't be so sure. If people are comfortable with something, knowing what really happened might not change their minds. They'd rather not be challenged by the truth."

"We'll see. But how do you explain the letter inviting a friend to visit? Jack wrote it shortly before the murder, and Tony used it to show that Jack exaggerated conditions on the island to help his insanity defense. It was pretty effective."

"Yes it was, but in the final analysis it was misleading. That letter was a part of Jack's normal self, the part that was trying desperately to hold on. The professional diplomat, the sophisticated observer of world events, the man in control. If I'm right, that's not where Jack was at all, and underneath that facade he was ready to come apart. Think about it. We've become so lulled by the expectation of instant cures and self-improvement that we think every human problem can be fixed," Ginger said.

"Freud's view was that we can never stop inner turmoil, or end the turbulence within us. The face we show to the outside world is what we want people to see. But the inner self, that's something else. There, anything goes – fantasies, black desires, unspeakable cruelties, repulsive thoughts — they're all there, to one degree or another, in all of us. Freud said these things are both painful and unavoidable. But we can sometimes come to understand them, and thereby learn to deal with them."

Ade realized that he wanted Ginger to persuade him, to resolve his unease that something was basically wrong with the accepted version of what happened to Kohler. He found himself nodding in agreement.

"There's so much more to people than what we see on the surface, or even what they themselves know about what's in their hearts. Someone once said a face was but 'the lighted side of a shadow.' A mask, sometimes revealing, but more often hiding what really lies inside. We all have it to some extent, but when someone has a severe personality break-down, the mask fails and the shadow emerges."

"All right," Ade said, refilling their glasses with Chardonnay. "Jack has based his entire external life on being 'normal,' so his realization that he has desires that society considers abnormal and repulsive is devastating to the pic-ture he has of himself. "

Ginger continued his thought. "And given the extent of homophobia in this country, and Jack's realization that his inner compulsions could wreck his life, this was another source of severe tension for him."

"Let's take this one step further," Ade said, who with-out missing a beat was now advancing Ginger's thesis. "He's doubly appalled to find that he even has sexual desire towards Ellerbee, his subordinate and someone he considers beneath him professionally and socially. It's too much for him to admit to his desire, so he kills the person who triggers it. Phew! Heavy stuff!"

"That's right," said Ginger, pleased that they were on the same wave length. "Kohler's sudden spasm of violence was really the result of an enormous struggle on his part to safeguard his personality. Remember the reference to the Schreber case? I did more reading on it today. In that case, Schreber couldn't admit his homosexual fantasies toward another man, and therefore repressed them. In Freud's view, Schreber's homosexual fantasy came from a desire to be reunited with his father. Schreber was uncertain of his own masculinity and hoped to tap into his father's."

This seemed plausible to Ade, but he wanted something more solid than theory. "OK," he said impatiently, "cut to the vault."

"Here's where I believe Kohler was essentially telling the truth, and the jury, not having been presented with all these psychological factors, chose the simplest explanation, and got a good bit of it wrong," Ginger explained. "What we know about explosive disorders is that they don't always have a single direct cause. The trigger can be important or trivial. It can be caused by an accident, a misunderstanding, a sense of injustice, accumulated frustrations, or something else."

Ade recalled from Jack's testimony that he had seen George giving the cuckoo signal and rolling his eyes when Jack was trying to dictate the conspiracy cable, and that had suddenly made him believe that George was part of the conspiracy too. "Do you think that could've been the trigger?" he asked.

"Maybe," she said, reflecting on it. "In cases of sexual homicide, fantasy is extremely important to the killer. Sometimes he acts out an entire fantasy play, and can become enraged if his victim interrupts his plan. George's cuckoo gesture could've been the trigger. We also know that sexual killers are extremely sensitive to being considered crazy, because the idea of being considered foolish disrupts their fantasy and fosters the notion that they're not in control, which is an idea they can't tolerate. Anyway, it could've been George's gesture, or a number of things, and not necessarily something that happened right there in the vault. I think that the atmosphere on the island, Jack's career frustrations and inability to have George transferred, and the pressures of his own fantasies and insecurities were all factors."

"So the big puzzle remains. Were they homosexuals and in a relationship? I'm not just curious – but I made a promise to Maria Ellerbee a long time ago."

"No. Jack was ambivalent and had repressed desires, very certainly. We have solid evidence for that. But there's no evidence about George beyond that drunken encounter in Moscow years ago. Maria and Stu Loeffler confirmed that as well."

"So what happened in the vault?"

"There was no sexual gratification involved, and they weren't lovers at all," Ginger said evenly. "What happened was an oral rape."

Ade looked hard at Ginger. Her words were so blunt, the image so graphic and repulsive. "Oral rape!" he exclaimed, letting out his breath. Suddenly another thought hit him. "But the guy who tries something like that is letting himself in for major pain."

"Ade, don't you know what goes on in prisons? It happens a lot, and the victim is often hetero. If you're in fear of your life, which alternative would you choose?"

"But why would Kohler do it?"

"The purpose was to dominate, control, and humiliate his victim. That urge was momentarily stronger than any moral strictures he had against killing, love for his family, horror at the act itself. What happened had nothing at all to do with sex, or some kind of lovers' quarrel."

"It's hard to believe that this urge was so strong that he couldn't control it, unless he was completely crazy."

"The pain overwhelmed him," Ginger replied. "It broke him. For this short time, all his repressed aggressions were projected onto George as though he were the cause of them. The repeated stab wounds both fit a pattern of homosexual violence and the intense desire to totally dominate. And in the end when George tried to escape, that sealed his fate completely, because it aroused Jack to an even greater frenzy."

"What about the communist conspiracy?"

"I doubt if Jack ever logically believed it. But with the unbearable stress that he was enduring, it's easy to see how he imagined that people were undermining him, and he magnified this into a communist conspiracy."

"So, for all of us who've tried to work out this puzzle, no one really got it right."

"And no one got it all wrong, either. Truth often comes in bits and pieces."

"Ron, Maria and some others are outraged that Jack's free after only three years on a prison farm. Robin needs a father, assuming Jack's all right, and the shrinks say he no longer poses a threat, but how can anyone be sure?"

"There's always a risk, although most murderers kill only once. If someone has killed, it doesn't mean he'll do it again. But to some, Jack's punishment seems a tap on the wrist compared to the suffering he caused."

"But it's ironic that the judge and jury drew the wrong conclusions, but they were right to reject the insanity defense, even though Jack clearly ran amok."

"I agree," said Ginger. "And that word, 'amok' — is actually a recognized psychic disturbance. It's a Malaysian word. I looked up the psychiatric meaning: 'Amok is an episode of acute, unrestrained violent behavior for which the person claims amnesia. It typically occurs as a single episode rather than as a pattern of aggressive behavior.' So what happened in the vault is a classic instance of amok."

"Ginger, that's it!" Ade exclaimed. "You've got it! The pieces finally fit!"

"I think so," said Ginger, smiling. For once, she looked content.

But what could come of this resolution? Ellerbee was dead, and Maria had returned in sorrow and bitterness to her home country. Kohler was alone, without family, friends, or career. Perhaps only Cynthia could make something of this, as she rebuilt her life and tried to shield Robin from the shame of his father's crime as he grew to manhood. The tragedy had cut too deeply for any kind of restitution to be made, after all this time. Perhaps all that was left for those who remembered was to understand.

CHAPTER FIFTY-SIX

The following year, Jack Kohler, while walking home from the library where he worked, suddenly jerked forward, clutching at his shirt collar, and fell onto the sidewalk, gasping for breath in huge gulps. While still writhing on the ground, and before anyone could rush to his assistance, his body shook with a second great seizure. The paramedics reached him within minutes, but he was gone. The police eased the gathering crowd back, and an ambulance took him to the morgue.

When he heard the news, Ade was convinced that justice, however imperfect, had been done, although less cleanly than anyone would be comfortable in admitting.

When he told Ginger of Jack's death, her reaction, predictably, was different. "Jack lived his life without knowing who he really was," she said. "He never established his own identity."

"And he never enjoyed his secret lusts, but was tormented by them."

Both the New York Times and the Washington Post carried brief obituaries, with only a passing reference to Kohler's manslaughter conviction. Ade suspected that this was the deft work of Cynthia Kohler. A few weeks later, the monthly

State Department Newsletter had a three-paragraph notice reviewing the skeleton of Kohler's life: education, military service, positions held. The last paragraph read, "Before his retirement in 1972, Mr. Kohler served in Tanako, where he was Principal Officer and *Chargé*. Survivors include his former wife and a son. Mr. Kohler was 56." There was no mention of the murder.

Ade had one final task, and that was to keep his promise to Maria Ellerbee. In the main lobby of the State Department, there is a marble wall with a list of names, carved in gold letters, of Department employees killed in the line of duty. Although old hands still remembered the Kohler murder case, many of the former players had moved on to other things. Ade resolved to have George's name added to the wall and hoped it could be done quietly and without controversy.

This proved more complicated than it first seemed. The case was now almost forgotten, but those who remembered it did so with a distaste amounting to revulsion. Worse, the latest names on the wall were mostly from Vietnam, and Ade's colleagues thought that adding one of the participants in a sordid and dishonorable affair to that list of fallen heroes amounted almost to sacrilege.

But he persisted, and finally persuaded the president of the American Foreign Service Association, the white collar union for the Foreign Service, that he had a case. He had Ade write up his argument and sent it to Secretary of State Edward Markham. Luckily, Markham's executive secretary, Dan Rivers, was a senior FSO and a sometime friend. One of those guys who gets to the top by being a key staff guy to the really powerful, rather than by taking his lumps overseas like most officers. Ade kept after him and finally he agreed to push the memo with the Secretary. Markham could care less about any personnel matter or even the plaque on the wall, but he also didn't want a fight with the employees' union while he attended to managing the globe.

Two weeks later, Ade had his answer. He could have fifteen minutes with the Secretary, who would then make his final decision. Ade couldn't have asked for more than that – the odds were against him, but he had a chance.

Since it was Ginger who'd developed their thesis, and she was by now a licensed forensic psychologist, Ade told Rivers that she'd take the lead in answering any questions. It turned out to be an inspired choice.

Ade had met Secretary Markham briefly on two occasions, but knew he wouldn't be remembered. He also guessed that he wouldn't have read the memo, nor paid much attention to Dan's hurried briefing. But he was known to revel in the company of attractive women, and if they also turned out to be intelligent, he would occasionally permit himself to be dazzled.

When Dan ushered them into the presence, the Secretary rose from his ornate desk and came forward to greet them. Ade was first in line, so he could introduce Ginger and explain in a quick sentence that she was the one who'd solved the enduring mystery, and that she was also his wife.

Markham greeted Ade with a perfunctory handshake, saying only "Nice to see you," and not even making eye contact. It was Ginger who'd caught his eye, and he quickly brushed by Ade and took Ginger's outstretched hand in both of his, a warm smile on his face. "I'm delighted to meet you, Mrs. Nadherny," he said graciously, ushering them to a sitting area with large antique easy chairs.

The effusiveness coming Ginger's way convinced Ade that the faster he turned the meeting over to her, the better it would go.

He said, "Mr. Secretary, we just want to urge the Department to give recognition, however belated, to a man who through no fault of his own was caught up in a bizarre situation and was killed in the line of duty. Ginger was privy to everything that happened from the beginning, and as a forensic psychologist she was the one who unraveled the mystery after everyone else had accepted the conventional wisdom."

This proved to be the right thing to say. Markham was noted as a brilliant analyst who often challenged conventional thinking, and he'd been critical of FSOs who merely did their jobs without pondering the complex nuances of policy.

"I'd like to hear your thesis, Mrs. Nadherny," Markham said attentively.

Without wasting a word, Ginger summarized the essential arguments in about four minutes. Markham listened carefully, interrupting with two brief questions. But much as he liked Ginger, his smile gave way to a frown and Ade didn't think he was convinced. She finished by saying, "Of course, we can't do anything about Ellerbee's murder, but we can restore his good name and give public recognition to the fact that he died in the line of duty."

"This is quite a story," Markham responded, "and you've presented your case exceedingly well. It may even be persuasive, as to the merits. But unfortunately, those who recall this affair remember it as sordid and damaging to the Department. Doing what you ask will stir up those unhelpful memories anew. I don't think I can permit that image to be revived, or leave this administration open to the charge that it condones homosexual violence in its ranks."

Ginger protested. "But that's the point – we'd be honoring one of our own who was killed in the line of duty, and finally clearing up what really happened."

"If I recall correctly," Markham answered, "the victim was a CIA employee. Let them honor him out at Langley. We're not going to put up any plaques honoring homosexuals in *my* State Department. I've got heavy artillery coming at me every day, and taking on something like this is more than I'm prepared to do."

Seeing their disappointment, his face softened. "I'm sorry," he said, "but I don't see how I can support this project."

After such a promising start, it was disheartening to see their initiative slipping down the drain. Despite the 'merits' of the case, as Markham himself admitted. Once again, power and image triumphed over justice.

Ade made one last attempt. "Mr. Secretary, this is important to the Foreign Service. It's true that Ellerbee worked for the CIA, but he died while on assignment with the State Department." Although he had no authority to speak for the Association, he asserted boldly, "We're prepared to proceed on our own, even without your approval, and we can find plenty of people in Washington who'll take up the cause, if that's what it becomes. It was the Association that established the memorial in the first place, and we're the ones who pay for it. If you give your OK, I promise that we'll take any flak and make sure that you're given full credit for making a just and compassionate decision."

The Secretary was not only a brilliant analyst, but also astute in weighing the pluses and minuses of any decision made in the meatgrinder of Washington politics. He paused a second or two while the options snapped around inside his brain.

"I'll give you my decision in a few days," he said, rising and stretching out his hand. "Whatever I decide," he said, looking at Ginger with a smile and ignoring Ade, "Mrs. Nadherny, I wish you well in your forensic endeavors."

There was no doubt who'd impressed him at this meeting, and Ade thought that Ginger's persuasiveness at least gave them a chance, despite what Markham said. But even though he liked Ginger, he'd make his decision only after carefully calculating the likely reaction. If it looked like there'd be any negative fallout, their cause was lost.

Three days later, Dan Rivers called Ade. "Congratulations," he said. "The Secretary will be pleased to add George Ellerbee's name to the wall, along with two others killed in the line of duty this past year. The ceremony is tentatively set for next month. You and Ginger did very well."

"I'm very grateful to you, Dan," Ade stammered, nearly overcome with astonishment. "Who persuaded the Secretary that it would be OK?" he asked.

Dan replied, "Let's just say that he knows Washington very well, and he decided the case on its merits."

It now only remained to contact Maria, and to invite her to the ceremony. The Department was sending her survivor's checks to an address in Quito, and Ade had notified her of Jack's death, to which she didn't respond.

Several weeks went by, and Ade was afraid that she'd disappeared, when a short handwritten letter from her arrived.

She wrote, "I'm glad that after all these years George's good name will be restored to him. You're kind to invite me to the ceremony, but I'm sure you'll understand why I'll not attend. I remarried three years ago, to a local businessman, and we live quietly in the outskirts of Quito. You and Ginger were always good friends, and I'm grateful for what you've done. Sincerely, Maria Estevez."

And so they all moved on. George Ellerbee's name was duly added to the wall in the lobby, under an inscription that says, "Erected by members of the American Foreign Service Association in honor of diplomatic and consular officers of the United States who while on active duty lost their lives under heroic or tragic circumstances."

The removal of George's stigma had other consequences, equally astonishing. A few weeks after the ceremony, Ade received a call from Markham's office. Dan Rivers told him, "The Department's sending your name to the White House to be Ambassador to South Africa. Don't worry about the Hill."

Ade had a number of people to thank for that, but the most important was Ginger. "By solving the case, you made that possible," he said, hugging her happily. "And you had nothing to gain. Will you come with me?"

"Of course I will. It'll be fascinating for both of us. I'm ready."

"But you're doing so well here. How can you give it up?"

"It's only for a while. I'll get back to my career."

So they went to South Africa. And today, in the diplomatic lobby of the State Department, George Ellerbee's name is chiseled in gold letters on the marble wall. Of course, there was no way to memorialize the tormented soul of Jack

Kohler. But those who were there will carry the somber memories of those events, and remain wary of the unspoken forces that lurk within everyone, and of the sudden explosions that can result when a human heart is overwhelmed.

* * *

ACKNOWLEDGMENTS

The basic circumstances of this novel were suggested by an actual event in which a Foreign Service officer killed his subordinate in an American embassy in Africa in 1971 – the only such occurrence in history. It began as a chronicle of the incident and the events surrounding it. But in order to explore more fully some aspects of human behavior that were, to my mind, unleashed by the incident and the setting, and by the consequences that followed, fiction offered a more fertile prospect than strict adherence to the available facts. So, this is a work of fiction, the characters are products of my imagination, and any real people, places, or events are used for purposes of the narrative.

I was fortunate to have been able to interview many people who remembered the incident, were involved in some way, knew one or more of the protagonists, or had contacts who opened up additional insights on the case. They were generous in sharing with me their recollections and insights on what happened and why, and other relevant details. These interviews were held for the most part during the period 1995-96. In this regard, I am especially grateful to Lannon Walker, Leonard Shurtleff, Christine Shurtleff, John Graves, Jack Mower, Raecarol Morgan, Thomas Gallagher, Herman J. Cohen, Donald Norland, Marianne Cook, Brady

Barr, Leona Nieman, R. T. Curran, Everett E. Briggs, Richard Springer, George Aneiro, Edward Fugit, David Rowe, Jonathan Sperling, Dorothy Flores, Ruth Stewart, Vance Pace, Ray Burson, and Sue Romano.

For information on the trial I am indebted to the late Justin Williams, Chief of the Criminal Division and Assistant US Attorney for the Eastern District, especially since the transcript for most of the trial was lost to researchers, and many of the key protagonists of that proceeding are deceased. Williams was the lead prosecutor in the case. Years after the trial, a chance conversation with William McDaniel, the lead defense counsel, refreshed my memory of some of the salient aspects of the trial and outcome.

In addition, an array of forensic experts, scholars, lawyers and psychological counselors offered useful insights and observations, especially Clint Van Zandt, Brian B. Palmer, Reid Maloy, Marc Taylor, Mario Dennis, Dr. Ron Costell, and Marsha Swiss.

Although any deficiencies of this novel are solely my responsibility, I am especially indebted to family, friends and mentors who offered invaluable suggestions and criticisms, especially my wife, Susan, my sister, Joan L. Dorey, and my sons Bill, Eben and Justin. Elizabeth and Tom Wolfson, and Christie Zink read early drafts and offered timely comments. I benefited enormously from participation in the NY Summer Writers Conference at Skidmore College in 1998 and 1999, and from the comments and suggestions of mentors and fellow participants. Among the mentors, Nicholas

Del Banco and Marilynne Robinson, both of whom read several chapters and offered cogent criticisms, and Ann Beattie were especially helpful, as were the comments of my fellow participants. Novelists Douglas Glover and Christopher Noel read completed drafts and offered detailed critiques that were both enormously instructive and encouraging. I am also grateful to Shelby Hearon, whose insights on writing encouraged me to embark on this project. Summer Doucet, book doctor extraordinaire, did two complete line-by-line text analyses and provided many comments that were encouraging, insightful, and practical. Special thanks are also due to Michelle T. Nguyen, gifted graphics designer, who produced the stunning cover design on short notice and also rendered useful advice on such things as print size and paper color. Finally, there are no adequate words to describe my debt to Nick Kotz, my long-time dear friend and mentor, whose patience, support and detailed analyses enabled me to write a better book than I would have otherwise, and whose encouragement and practical assistance helped me at every step.

Works Consulted

American Psychiatric Association: *Diagnostic and Statistical Manual of Mental Disorders,* Fourth Edition, Washington DC, American Psychiatric Association, 1994.

Sigmund Freud, "Psycho-Analytic Notes on an Autobiographical Account of a Case of Paranoia (Dementia Paranoides), *The Standard Edition of the Complete Psychological Works of Sigmund Freud,* volume 12.

J. Reid Meloy, "Violent Attachments," Jason Aronson Inc., Northvale, N. J., 1942.

Ruotolo, A., "Dynamics of Sudden Murder," American Journal of Psychoanalysis, 28: 162-176, 1968.

Eugene Revitch and Louis B. Schlesinger, "Catathymic Homicide," Journal of Offender Counselling, Services and Rehabilitation, 1990, Vol 15 (1), 163-178.

John D'Emilio, "Making Trouble: Essays on Gay History, Politics, and the University," Routledge, New York and London, 1992.

J. Reid Meloy, Ph. D., personal communication, December, 1996.

Craig B. Palmer, Ph. D., personal communication, January 17, 1996.

Robert K. Ressler, Ann W. Burgess, John E. Douglas, "Sexual Homicide, Patterns and Motives," The Free Press, New York 1988.

John E. Douglas, Ann W. Burgess, Allen G. Burgess, Robert K. Ressler, "Crime Classification Manual." A Standard System for Investigating and Classifying Violent Crimes, Lexington Books, New York, 1995.

Robert Klitgaard, "Tropical Gangsters." Basic Books, 1990.

John Douglas and Mark Olshaker, "Mindhunter," Pocket Star Books, New York 1995.

Frederick Forsyth, "The Dogs of War," Viking Press, New York 1974.

US Court of Appeals for the Fourth Circuit, No. 72-1328, United States of America, Appellee v. Alfred Erdos, Appellant, Tennessee Law Printers, PO Box 277, Knoxville, Te.

Robert a. f. Klinteberg, "Equatorial Guinea – Macias Country, the Forgotten Refugees," an International University Exchange Fund (IUEF) field study on the Equatorial Guinea refugee situation, Geneva, 1978.

Wilson, "Diplomatic Privileges and Immunities, 32 (University of Arizona Press, 1967).

Jonathan Fenby, "France on the Brink," Arcade Publishing, New York, 1998.

Lewis, Hoffacker, "A Look Back at the Erdos Case," Foreign Affairs Oral History Project, The Association for Diplomatic Studies and Training, 1998. Hoffacker was Ambassador to Cameroon and Equatorial Guinea in 1971, and offers a detailed personal recollection of the incident and various related aspects.

Len Shurtleff, "A Foreign Service Murder," Foreign Service Journal, October 2007.

Chris Erdos, "Heart of Darkness," Foreign Service Journal, May 2008, VOl. 85, Issue 5, p. 43.

I was also able to obtain numerous documents from the Departments of State and Justice under the Freedom of Information Act, and from the US Federal Court in Alexandria, Virginia, pertaining to trial motions, appeals, and official cables sent at the time of the murder, which were useful for background and reference. Although most of the transcript of the original trial has been lost, I was able to obtain portions of one day's proceedings, which I relied on heavily in describing the forensic evidence. Evaluations done at the time and many significant cables containing information relevant to the case are either lost or still classified.

www.ingramcontent.com/pod-product-compliance
Lightning Source LLC
Chambersburg PA
CBHW020249030726
47499CB00001B/121